DARK
MIRROR

Other STAR TREK Novels by Diane Duane

DARK MIRROR

Diane Duane

SIMON & SCHUSTER

LONDON·SYDNEY·NEW YORK·TOKYO·SINGAPORE·TORONTO

This book is a work of fiction. Names, characters, places and incidents
are either the product of the authors' imagination or are used fictitiously.
Any resemblance to actual events or locales or persons, living or dead,
is entirely coincidental.

First published in Great Britain by Simon & Schuster Ltd, 1993
A Paramount Communications Company

 STAR TREK is a Registered Trademark of Paramount Pictures.

This book is published under exclusive license from Paramount
Pictures.

 Simon & Schuster Ltd
West Garden Place
Kendal Street
London W2 2AQ

Simon & Schuster of Australia Pty Ltd
Sydney

A CIP catalogue record for this book is
available from the British Library.
ISBN 0-671-71853-3

Printed in the U.S.A.

For Rick Sternbach and Mike Okuda,
the men behind the curtain

—but especially for Rick, friend of many years

Acknowledgments

Thanks to the staff of Independent Pizza in South Anne Street, Dublin, where this novel was conceived in October 1991 over a large with extra cheese, extra sauce, pepperoni, and hot chilies, and a medium with extra cheese, double garlic, hot chilies, and onions, along with two bottles of Orvieto Secco and a whole lot of Ballygowan water.

Thanks also to Dave Stern, who returns unexpected phone calls from overexcited people standing in phone booths outside pizzerias.

HISTORIAN'S NOTE

This novel takes place sometime during the fourth season of STAR TREK: THE NEXT GENERATION.

Evil is easy, and has infinite forms.

—Pascal

DARK
MIRROR

CHAPTER 1

There are some parts of space where even the human heart, eternally optimistic, finds it hard to feel itself welcome. At those outer fringes of the Galaxy that the humanities have just begun to reach, the starfield, which elsewhere lies in such rich streams and billows of brightness between the inhabited worlds, thins away and goes chill and pale. Here the starlight is only indefinite, faintly glowing—the million points of light near the heartworlds now dimmed by terrible distance and the clouds of dark matter between the stars to a vague cool fog, hardly to be seen except when one looks away from it. Usually the onlooker finds it hard to look away, forced by the sight to think how small even a galaxy is in the vastness, how tiny even the Local Group is compared to the darkness holding it, and all the other galactic clumps and supergalaxies; and which, beyond the bounds of mere spatial integrity, probably holds other whole universes as well, numberless, all of them subsumed into the greatest dark—that of entropy— which broods and bides its time.

In these, the deserts of space, the oases are few and far between. Once in a half a million cubic parsecs you might find a star that had struggled to bring forth planets in the barrenness and managed it—but for daunting distances around it, there will still be nothing but emptiness, and as background, only the shimmer of light that indicates the hearths of the crowded worlds. In the face of such contrasts that light becomes almost somber, speaking of its impermanence and newness in a universe where for unknown time unnameable darkness gestated, holding the light in it unborn, until the first great laugh, the outburst of newborn power and matter into the old thoughtful void.

Far up here, above the great Galactic Rift, that light seems most tenuous—the darkness not of dust or distance but of simple nothingness. Few sentient beings pass this way; observers are rarer than stars. But every now and then, something breaks the aridity of the dark desert. A distant gleam, a silver flicker, swelling, growing closer; like a memory sought for in a dark mind and suddenly recalled. If the observer had senses not dependent on something besides sluggish light to reflect and carry messages— tachyons, perhaps—they would see it grow and flash past them, touched with a spark of red on the port side, green on the starboard, and the letters NCC 1701-D dark on its hull. Then the memory is off again in the dark, with a trail of rainbow behind it, quickly fading, the legacy of its warpfield. Lone ambassador of the multifariousness of known worlds, here and gone again, out of the darkness, into the darkness: *Enterprise* goes about her business.

In his quarters, Jean-Luc Picard stood away from the canvas and glanced sideways for a moment at the darkness pouring past. He could almost feel it, the thickness of the dark: that strange, empty, but somehow heavy and oppressive quality that it had, this far out from the light and life of the more populated parts of the Federation. They were far out on the fringes, and the relative emptiness of things was chilling. It was at times like this that his thoughts turned elsewhere, to other imageries: warmer, slightly more reassuring—however subjective it was to feel that one needed reassurance in this dark. Picard knew himself well enough not to ignore such feelings, however ill-founded he might suspect them to be. At such times he gladly turned his mind toward home: the hearth of the mind.

He turned back to the canvas. Landscape was not usually something he attempted, and certainly not usually from memory. Which, when he realized it, had driven him immediately to try it.

It was a wood in the Luberon, not far from the vineyards of home. A sunny morning, in the earliest part of autumn: you could tell it from the trees—the green of the birches and oaks in that wood was not the fresh color of spring, but the tireder, resigned, mellowing green of trees whose leaves are thinking of turning. Here and there, in the dapple of the birches against the hard blue sky, you could see a leaf gone yellow, quietly treacherous to summer, starting the change. Typical of the way such things shift, subtly, leaf by leaf: their beginnings "small and hardly to be seen," as the poet says, but seeming so great when we suddenly look up and notice.

Under them, beneath the marginally treacherous birches and oaks, pools of shadow, pools of light; and just there, in the shadow of an oak, but bright with a scrap of sunlight let down past a negligent branch, a little patch of brilliance caught hanging in the air: a butterfly. One of the brown woods butterflies with a broad white stripe, soaring down the glade between the trees. Nothing else stirring, no sense of wind in those trees, no movement, just the perfect still-mellowing heat of the very beginning of the time when the grapes would be ready: the perfect first moment of autumn, earth just beginning to calm to its rest for the year.

Picard stepped back and looked. The harsh blue of the summer south of France showed through the upper branches. Here and there, in the dim background, the feather of one of the windbreak pines showed through. Everything but the touch of light in the middle air, and the blue above the trees, was soft, indefinite: the ground, all littered with the brown of many years. He had been spending a lot of time on that ground, working to get it right. The wrong light, too much detail or too little, would make it all look false. He changed brushes, dabbed at the palette, scrubbed the brush drier, and touched a bit more light onto the butterfly's wings, making it more golden, less white than it had been.

He stood away again and let his eyes go a little unfocused, the better to let his eyes evaluate the canvas. Light, warmth, a feeling of peace: the antithesis to everything out there at the moment.

His glance slid sideways. He thought of the great philosopher, there in his old home, all bounded by noisy streets, who looked out at the tram clanging by, and the bustle of the city in those days, and wrote, "The silence of these infinite spaces frightens me to death." It took a man attuned to hear that silence, *this* silence, in such a place, through all the noise and clatter of civilization. Out here, it required no ear nearly so subtly attuned. Turn away from your work or play for a moment, and those clouds of stars reminded you just how small you were, and how far away from the things that you might love. Picard knew that the philosopher would equally have held that you're no farther from those things than the vein of your neck: since you carry them within you, you and they are coterminous. Some might balk at the seeming contradiction. Picard merely smiled, knowing the ways of philosophers, and reached for another brush.

The door chimed. "Come," he said.

Lieutenant Commander Data stepped in, paused. "I am not interrupting anything, am I, Captain?"

"Nothing of any weight." Picard put the first brush he had selected down, chose another: narrowed, with the

4

fanned edge. Data stepped around to look at the canvas, raising his eyebrows for permission. Picard nodded.

Data looked at it and said, "Ah. *Ladoga camilla.* Or *Limenitis camilla,* in the older Linnaean classification."

Picard's eyebrows went up, too, in surprise. "It's that obvious?" There was barely a square centimeter of paint there, after all, and some only indifferent brushwork.

"The broken white stripe is a clear indicator, Captain."

"Mr. Data," Picard said, shaking his head, "I understand the delight of acquiring information. But you are in a unique position to agree with the detective that the mind is a closed room, with only so much space in which to store information. Whatever moved you to acquire information on Earth's butterflies, when there might be information more important that required the same room?"

"'Man does not live by bread alone,'" Data said. "Or so Keiko O'Brien says. She recommends the butterfly as an excellent example of 'the sound of one hand clapping.'"

Picard smiled slightly. "She's probably right. At least, that's one of the few responses to the koan which makes any sense to *me* . . . though some would tell you, I must admit, that in a koan, sense is the wrong thing to be looking for. Meanwhile, I assume you had something specific to tell me when you came."

"Yes, sir. Within the past hour the Lalairu main group hailed us. They estimate they will be within transporter range within another hour."

"That's excellent. Are the mission specialist's quarters ready for him?"

"Geordi is overseeing the final stages of the installation now, Captain. He said he wanted to add some 'bells and whistles' to it." Data looked slightly quizzical as he examined Picard's canvas. "While I know that the specialist's people are sonically oriented, I did not know that bells and whistles were of any specific value—"

Picard smiled. "I think Mr. La Forge means he wants to

make sure that Commander . . . that the commander's quarters have a little more than the usual fittings. Ask him to notify me when he's done, if you will."

"Certainly, sir." Data spent a moment more gazing at the canvas. "Autumn?"

Picard nodded. "How did you judge that?"

"The white admiral does not achieve such growth until the late summer. Also, the lighting is suggestive of the increased declination of the sun in autumn, as is the leaf color. But the latter judgments are subjective and liable to confusion through individual differences in color perception. The butterfly, however, is diagnostic."

Picard smiled to himself. "Butterflies have been called many things, but, I think, rarely that. Very well, Mr. Data. I'll be along shortly. When you start the usual information exchanges with the Lalairu, my compliments to the Laihe, and I should enjoy speech with her before they pass on."

Data nodded and left. Picard turned back to the canvas, surveying it, letting his mind drift for a moment as the butterfly seemed to drift down the glade between the trees. The warmth, the slanting light, and the silence, the sweetness in the still air among the trees where the late honeysuckle climbed: the Lalairu would visit such a place readily enough. But otherwise they would value it little.

The Lalairu was what they called themselves, though they were not one species, but an association of hundreds. Their language was a farrago of borrowings from the languages of many planets, grammatically bewildering, semantically a nightmare, and difficult to translate accurately, no matter how long you or the universal translator worked at it. They could perhaps be truly described, and uniquely so among Federation peoples, as a "race" in the older sense of the word—a group who shared a way of life by choice.

They were travelers. No one knew how long their huge cobbled-together ships, in families or smaller groups, had been roving the far fringes of known space. Indeed they seemed to know, and frequent, parts of it that no one else did, but good navigational information about those places was difficult to obtain from them because of the equivocal nature of the Lalairsa language as regarded spatial location. Coordinate systems the Lalairu understood, but they had one of their own that seemed to change without warning, so that directions given in it didn't always work for outsiders. In any case, they were rarely interested in giving *tizhne* directions. That was their word for people who lived on planets. It was faintly scornful, but affectionate regardless—a term the Lalairu used with the air of someone talking about a relative's baby who was unwilling to come out of its playpen. Other space travelers they would deal with, trade with, meet with cordially enough, but there was always a feeling of a barrier between them and you, a sense of some choice that in their opinion they had made more wisely than you had, so that they felt faintly sorry for you.

True, they were free: rarely had a people known such freedom. The Lalairu's total lack of connection to the planetbound cultures left them free to go anywhere they pleased, trade with everyone. They made no alliances, no treaties, suffered no entanglements: they would take the Ferengii's goods as readily as the Federation's or the Romulans' or anyone else's. In return they traded rare plants, animals, minerals, manufactured commodities, things elsewhere unseen and unknown—and afterward they vanished into the unknown again, to appear later in known space when and where they pleased. The only thing to be counted on with them was that the Lalairu did not miss appointments they had made, whether to trade or just to meet with you. They were not missing this one, either.

Picard spent a few minutes cleaning his brushes and getting the pigment off himself—he had never been able to break himself of the habit of smudging the canvas with his thumb when he wanted the shading exactly right. He was in the middle of pulling out a uniform tunic when the communicator chirped: *"Captain?"*

It was Data again. "Yes?"

"Mr. La Forge has completed his work on the mission specialist's quarters, and the commander will be beaming over shortly."

"Excellent. I'll go down and greet him. Picard out."

He found Chief O'Brien working thoughtfully over the transporter panel when he got down to transporter room six. "A problem?" Picard said.

O'Brien shook his head. "Just some fine-tuning. The commander wears a field generator for protection in our environment. While the transporter's field analysis routines are pretty thorough, I don't want to take the chance of disrupting his suit."

Picard put his eyebrows up and waited. After a few more moments, O'Brien was satisfied. "Transporting now," he said, and touched the controls.

Out of the glitter and the whine of the transporter effect formed a shape hovering about four feet above the floor, horizontal. The shimmer faded away. Resting on a flexible levitation platform was what looked like a dolphin in an inch-thick coating of glass. At least, it looked that way until the dolphin swung his tail in greeting, and the "glass" moved and rippled slightly, revealing itself as a skin of water being held in place around the dolphin's body by a small envirofield generator strapped around that tail. The dolphin whistled, and his universal translator output said, *"Bonjour, M'sieur Capitaine; permettez bord?"*

Picard smiled. *"Oui, et bienvenue, M'sieur Commandant!* Did you have any luggage?"

"It went to cargo transporter five," Mr. O'Brien said. "It'll go to the commander's quarters from there."

"Very well. Commander, would you like a look at them?"

"Very much, thank you." The dolphin downstroked with his tail, arching his back a bit, and the negative-feedback mechanisms in the levitator pads matched the gesture, flexing the pad so that the dolphin seemed to swim through the air down off the transporter platform and toward the doors. "Before you ask, Captain," the commander said, "it's 'Wheee,' or at least that's close enough. The rest is just a family nickname—part of the official name, but not particularly necessary."

"Thank you," Picard said, slightly relieved: the issue of how to pronounce the commander's names had been causing him concern since he first looked at his Starfleet record. Hwiii ih'iie-uUlak!ha' was one of the cetacean members of the Starfleet navigations research team, a delphine native of Omicron Five's oceanic satellite, nick-named Triton Two by an early Starfleet researcher who, after a prestigious university career at Harvard and the Sorbonne, had signed on with Starfleet to continue "clean-hyperstring" studies in deep space—preferably as deep as possible. After several years spent posted to starbases on the fringes of Federation space, Hwiii had requested a sabbatical to get even farther out and, on its granting, had arranged to hitch a ride with a passing Lalairu vessel on its way to the empty space above the Great Rift. Such a spot was perfect for his chosen work, investigation into the nature of subspace hyperstring structure: space uncontaminated by stars, planets, even dark matter—all of which could render equivocal readings that, for greatest useful-ness, needed to be absolutely certain.

So much Picard knew about the officer from his records, but he had had enough experience with mission specialists to know quite well that the records often left out the most interesting details, or the ones that later turned out to be most necessary to get the job done, whatever it might be.

9

Picard hoped, as always, that he would be able to elicit that information from Hwiii before reassignment took him elsewhere. "Did you have a pleasant stay with the Lalairu?" Picard said as they went into the turbolift. "Deck five."

Hwiii laughed. "As pleasant as possible when your hosts don't see any point in what you're doing. I'm afraid I was more of a curiosity to them than anything else." He looked as if he was smiling: not so much because of his mouth, which looked that way anyhow, but more because of a glitter that his eyes suddenly got. "Not that I'm not used to that anyway. But the feeling was more pronounced with the Lalairu. They behaved toward me the way we might behave toward someone who had come to us to study the art of breathing. We take it so for granted: anyone who spent all their time wanting to talk to us about respiration would probably be considered a little odd. But location and navigational issues are so ingrained in them and their language that they have trouble understanding how navigation can be studied apart from all the rest of life. Like studying cooking without also studying food."

Picard shook his head. "I was looking over the last communication from the Laihe, and I must tell you I had difficulty making head or tail of it. There was a general sense of concern over something being wrong with *someone's* coordinate system . . . but the computer was no more certain of the translation than I was. I wasn't sure whether the Lalairu were claiming that they were lost, or possibly that they thought *we* were. Either way, how lost can either of us be? Using their coordinate system, they found us without any apparent trouble."

Hwiii waved his flippers, a delphine shrug. "Captain, I'll look at the transmission, if you like. But I don't guarantee being able to make any more sense of it than you have. Context-positive translations are thin on the bottom when it comes to Lalairsa."

Coming out of the turbolift, they turned a corner and went a few doors down through guest quarters. Outside one door, Geordi La Forge and Data stood looking in while Geordi scanned the doorway with a tricorder and a critical look.

"Gentlemen," Picard said as they came up. Geordi looked up from the tricorder to grin at the captain. "One of my better efforts, Captain," he said, "if I do say so myself."

"Gentlemen, Commander Hwiii. Commander, Mr. La Forge, Mr. Data."

"Pleased, Commander," Geordi said. Data put his head slightly to one side and uttered a string of sharp clicks and squeaks ending on an up-scaling squeal.

This time there were no two ways about it: Hwiii smiled. "Commander, that's a very good Triton accent, and good fishing to you, too. You've got the Eastern intonation, though: did one of K!eeei's people do the recording?"

"I believe so," Data said. "K!eeei was listed as a source in the Delphine course on cetacean epic poetry."

"Thought so. That accent is unmistakable." Hwiii looked in through the open door of the room. "Are these really my quarters?"

Picard looked in, too, and was impressed. The room had been stripped of the usual furnishings, floored with sand, and flooded. Behind the open door, a force field, like the one Hwiii wore, but more robust, was holding the water inside, flat as a pane of glass. In the pale sand, aquatic plants appeared to be rooted: huge tall ribbons of brown seaweed, interspersed with taller, slenderer fronds of delicately waving translucent green, like hair. Up and down the hairlike seaweed, translucent pods burned with a cool blue light that shimmered, fading and brightening, as the currents in the water moved the weed. Below the apparent ceiling of the quarters, lighting suggested sun above the rippling surface of the water. Across the room, the one feature remaining that seemed slightly out of place was the windows, looking out on space and the stars, for the moment unmoving while the ship ran in impulse. But possibly a spacegoing dolphin would not find this too out of place.

"It's partly constructs, of course," Geordi said, somewhat apologetically. "But the biology department keeps seed in stasis for most of the bigger seaweeds, kelp and so forth, in case an emergency requires bringing up hydroponic support for the oxygen supply. I drew some of those stores, asked bio to clone and force a few specimens for me."

Hwiii chattered softly in Delphine for a moment before saying, "Mr. La Forge, this is palatial! I thank you very much indeed. Too many times I've been stuck swimming around in something that most closely resembled a motel room."

Picard burst out laughing. "I'm sorry, Commander, but when were *you* last in a motel room!"

The eyes mirrored the always-smiling face for a moment. "Don't laugh, Captain. The publicity side of the organization calls me, occasionally, and even Starfleet specialists wind up doing the rubber-chicken circuit. Though in my case it's more usually rubber mackerel."

It occurred to Picard that this particular specialist would probably make more interesting publicity than either the two-legged kind or more alien ones. He suspected Hwiii knew it and took it in good part. "I think you'll find the food to your liking here, though," Picard said. "The synthesizers know what fresh fish should taste like."

Hwiii looked wistful. "I wish they knew what *live* fish tasted like, Captain, but unfortunately, that's something they can't quite manage. The aromatic esters just aren't the same somehow."

Picard looked thoughtful for a moment. "I must admit . . . the caviar does occasionally seem to lack something."

Hwiii chuckled. "It doesn't matter, Captain. I can't fish up here, but I can't do clean-hyperstring research back home, either. Too much interference! No, each thing to its proper place, and the fish can take care of themselves for the moment."

"I would like to discuss your researches with you if you have leisure to do so," Data said. "Especially as regards the relative 'cleanliness' of hyperstring structures in spaces empty of dark matter."

Hwiii snapped his jaws in annoyance. "I wish I had more researches to discuss, but we had just gotten into such space—this area, in fact—when the Laihe decided all of a sudden that she was going to turn back inward toward the settled worlds. We only spent a month and a half in space empty enough to suit the criteria I was investigating, so I haven't much new data to share, or many new conclusions about it. But, at your leisure, let's split a fish or two and discuss what I've got."

"Bridge to Picard," said the captain's communicator. He touched it.

"Picard. Go ahead, Number One."

"A hail from the Laihe, Captain," Riker's voice said. *"She says she'd like to talk to you at your convenience . . . I think."*

Picard smiled ruefully. "I'll be right up . . . Commander Hwiii, will you be all right?"

"Captain," Hwiii said in what sounded like complete satisfaction, "I am going to be as happy as a clam in mud."

"How does one go about quantifying the emotional state of mollusks, Commander?" Data asked innocently as Picard headed back for the turbolift. He almost wished he could stay to see how Hwiii *did* quantify it . . . but he had other fish to fry.

"Ahem," Picard said, amused, as the turbolift doors shut. "Bridge."

* * *

As Picard entered, Commander Riker got up from the center seat. "Captain, if I'm any judge of such things, she sounded downright impatient."

"Not very usual," Picard said. "If anything, the Laihe usually errs in the other direction. How long did it take for her to say 'hello' to you the other day?"

"About ten minutes," Riker said, and grinned slightly, "and nearly that long again for me to understand that that was what she meant."

Picard glanced over at Troi, who was sitting in her seat, arms folded, looking mildly interested. "Counselor?"

Troi shrugged. "A general sense of urgency, but nothing more."

"Very well," Picard said, turning toward the viewer. "Hail the Laihe if you would, Mr. Worf."

"Hailing, Captain." The viewscreen had been looking toward the distant Lalairu fleet, hardly to be seen in this dimness. Now that view changed to an interior, a small private chamber hung about with asymmetric drapes of some kind of dark, rich-looking fabric that held a subdued glitter in its folds.

In front of the subtly glittering curtains or tapestries sat—if that was the word for it—the Laihe. She was a Huraen, one of a species whose homeworld had been destroyed by some natural calamity some centuries before, but since all the Huraen had been traveling as one of the Lalairu peoples since well before that time, none of them particularly cared. By virtue of that ancient association, and because of some unspecified sacrifice that the Huraen had made for the other Lalairu peoples, the Laihe, head of the whole race, was always a Huraen. Huraenti were tall, slender, insectile people, compound-eyed, many-limbed, mostly blue or green in color, their chitin-covered bodies inlaid or figured with complicated patterns in malleable metals or textured plastics: as if someone had taken a praying mantis, given it a slightly mournful, understanding look, and more legs than even a mantis would need. Huraenti were skilled artisans and craftsmen, engineers of extraordinary talent, and had a reputation for being able to understand anything mechanical within seconds. In terms of personality, they tended to be affable, subtle, and fond of the interpersonal arts: chief among them, language. They were loquacious and liked it that way. That was all right in the Huraenti language, which was structured and straight-forward. But the Laihe was much more Lalairu than Huraenti, and her language showed it.

"Graciously greeted is the noblissimus entr'acte Picard chief in command subjective warning," said the Laihe, ratcheting her top set of forelegs together.

That sounds like hello, Picard thought, *and Will was right, she* is *in a hurry.* "I greet you graciously as well, Laihe."

"Urgently spatial coordinate-status misfound illfound illfounded distortion in *nithwaeld* on merest dysfunction hereditary disastrous propulsion!" said the Laihe, or at least, that was all the universal translator could make of it.

Picard nodded and tried to look gravely concerned, which wasn't difficult under the circumstances. "Laihe, forgive us, but our translator lost several words in that last passage. What is *nithwaeld,* please?"

"Ingwe. Or *filamentary."*

"Hyperstrings?"

"Affirmative response."

Picard let out a breath of relief at having gotten that far. "Laihe, you must forgive me when I say that I am as yet only slightly educated in hyperstring studies. Am I to understand that something unexpected, or distressing, is going on in space hereabouts?"

"Affirmative, qualifier variancy-area room-space-lo-cation nonlocating alteration-aversion-shift loss. Loss! Shift!"

Picard found himself wishing that James Joyce had had

some input into the universal translator's programming, or possibly Anthony Burgess. Both of them, by preference. The Lalairsa pleniphrasis, "scatter," and borrowings would have sounded familiar to both of them. Picard glanced over at Troi: she shook her head. Worf said, "The translator is at full function, Captain. This is the best it's able to do."

"Understood. . . . Laihe, we will of course be saving your statement for later analysis and transmission to the Federation, but for the moment, what do you see as the effect of this local 'shift'? And can you describe the nature of it in more detail?"

"Qualified affirmation, technical . . ." And it was, too, as the Laihe went off in a blizzard of verbiage that mixed familiar and relatively familiar physics and astrophysics terminology with words and phrases that Picard had never heard before, and that the translator flatly refused to render. All the while the Laihe sat hunched forward, her forelegs knitting frantically, and her mandibles working hard. "Longterm effect," she said finally, "unknown, dangerous though, emmfozing, ending."

Picard looked over at Troi. *Emmfozing?* he mouthed. Wide-eyed, Troi shook her head, helpless.

"Laihe," Picard said, "our thanks. We will carefully consider your advice." *As soon as we understand it!* "What are your own plans now?"

"Shift unbearable reality nature life, inturn frightened stars inworlds population loss shift lacktime losstime migration *tizhne* mystery major safe haven . . . suggest similar stars inworlds have exit departure lacktime losstime benefit."

"If I understand correctly that you're heading back into more populated areas," Picard said, "then we wish you well on the journey. Our patrol duties lie in this area for a good while yet."

The Laihe's head swiveled from side to side, like that of

someone who's sure you must be speaking to someone else. "Shift unpredictable dataless uncertainties dangerous!"

That Picard thought he understood. "I thank you for your concern. The uncertainties are our business, though: there are few things more important to us, though they can be dangerous, as you say."

The Laihe looked at him mournfully. "Departure imminent, data dump imminent, locations safety, wellwish."

"We would appreciate all the data you have," Picard said. "Please feel free to requisition anything from our data libraries that you may feel would be of help to you. And thank you again for your concern. We'll do our best to look into this problem."

The Laihe nodded—that gesture she knew and understood—and raised a foreleg. The screen winked out, leaving a view of stars, and the dim-lit sparks of the many Lalairu ships lying thousands of miles away, ready to go into warp.

Picard turned away from the viewscreen and sat down thoughtfully in his seat. "Now what did you make of *that?*" he said to Riker and Troi.

Troi shook her head. "Certainly she was distressed, Captain. And she became more so as she got into the technical details . . . as if the more concretely she considered the problem, the worse it became to her. But she obviously seems intent on getting herself and her people out of here as quickly as possible."

"Suggestions?" Picard said, glancing from Troi to Riker.

Riker shrugged. "Hard to make an evaluation without understanding the science involved . . . or, after a statement like that, even which *parts* of science are involved."

"The translation problem, yes . . ." Picard sighed. "As soon as he's settled, I'll ask Commander Hwiii to see if he can make more sense of the Laihe's concerns. There may be idiomatic material in her statement that the computer couldn't correctly analyze. We'll have a briefing when he's

17

made his own assessment. Meanwhile, we continue as scheduled. How is the data acquisition going?"

Riker tried not to make a face, and Picard caught him at it and smiled slightly. Their present mission was a little dry for Riker's tastes, though Picard knew Riker was as much for the acquisition of pure knowledge as anyone else. Starfleet had sent them up into this empty area partly to do research on the energy emissions from their arm of the Galaxy as a whole. In particular, they were to seek corroboration for the presently mooted theory that the Galaxy occasionally threw up from its core and inner arms immense jets or prominences of charged matter, contributing (among other things) to the structure and movement characteristics of the Galactic arms, possibly even to the increased or altered genesis of stars in areas where the "prominences" of matter and energy fell back into the Galactic disk. The *Enterprise*'s usual exploratory duties were, of course, to parallel this research, but up here in the empty dark, there was precious little to explore, and Will was itching for something more interesting to occupy his time.

"Slowly, Captain," Riker said with a wry smile. "And it's not just me saying that. The traces of the 'matterspouts' we're looking for are going to be very slight, even if we should happen to run right into one. You're talking about space so empty that it would make a comet's tail look crowded by comparison. Subatomic particles scattered one to a cubic terameter—not much more closely. And places where the spouts once were are going to look much the same, except for very specific muon and antimuon decays —assuming we can *catch* any of the particles in question decaying." The smile got slightly sour. "A very big haystack . . . some very small needles."

"But patience is the key, as usual," Picard said.

"Oh, yes," Riker said, "there was some excitement yesterday. We caught two antimuons with their pants down, one after the other. The physics lab got so excited, they threw a party."

"I heard," Picard said. "What *did* you say to Lieutenant Hessan that made her put the ice cream down your shirt?"

Riker's casual expression didn't change, but he colored slightly. Troi grinned and turned away.

"Yes," Picard said, "quite." He got up and stretched. "Well, keep at it, Number One. Find enough of those needles and Fleet will let us stop this particular roll in the hay and go somewhere livelier."

Riker leaned back in his chair. "All the same, we may not need to. I really want to know what made the Laihe so nervous."

"Doubtless we'll find out," Picard said.

CHAPTER 2

The briefing happened just after shift change. Riker chuckled a little while setting it up. "A buffet briefing," he said; "this might be setting a dangerous precedent."

Picard smiled. "If civilization is the ability to slide gracefully into customs not our own," he said, "let's get out there and slide."

Food at the briefing was simply courtesy to their guest. While there were species who did not discuss business over food, most of the cetaceans, except under most unusual circumstances, didn't discuss business *without* food. To them, food *was* business—had been, for a long time, the only business they had. Everything else—song, love, birth, death—was counted play—in much the same way, scientists theorized, as Earth's cetaceans had regarded the universe centuries before. When Triton's cetacean species came into the Federation and discovered all the other kinds of business there were, they dove into them gladly, but they insisted on taking a lunch.

The buffet was, in their guest's honor again, mostly a fish dinner. There were turbot, bream, sea trout, salmon fresh and smoked, glinting mackerel, herring in what Picard thought was almost too many kinds—as usual, it reminded him of that Nobel Prize weekend on Earth, at the end of which he thought he would never want to see a herring again. But lobster, crab, fresh mussels, all those were there, too, as perfect as the replicator could make them. Commander Hwiii came gliding in and looked the spread over and squeaked with delight. "Down to business," he said, "please!"

Everyone laughed and started to fill their plates. Hwiii had brought up from his luggage a set of the manipulators he used to manage control panels geared to the ten-fingered. Now Picard watched with interest as Hwiii flicked his watery "sleeves" up and slipped his fins into the manipulators, which promptly sprouted long graceful tendrils of metal, five from each glove. "There's a neural-transfer net installed just under the skin of each flipper," Hwiii said, flexing the tendrils. "It transfers even very small movements of the phalangeal bones to the waldoes."

" 'Cyclic' metal?" Picard said.

"Yes, the only moving part is the long-chain molecule in the metal itself. It's like the Clissman 'self-trimming' struts they use these days in solar-sail craft. Useful on the rubber-chicken circuit." Hwiii dropped his jaw in the genuine delphine grin. "There are people who aren't surprised that a dolphin can talk, but *zut,* are they surprised to see one use a knife and fork!"

"I would imagine. Caviar, Commander?"

"I haven't seen you take any yet," Hwiii said virtuously. "Rude to start before one's host, even among my people."

Picard served out the beluga. *"Bon appétit,"* he said, and for a while there was only small talk, Data querying Riker about the smoking method used on the original salmon, Geordi trying to analyze the wine, as usual, and missing the year by a mile, also as usual. People found seats, got comfortable, while Hwiii floated comfortably on his pad by the captain's chair and talked old neighborhoods and common acquaintances with him, research fellows at the Sorbonne whom they knew in common, gossip about the last year's olive harvest in Provence. But Hwiii could not stay away from his topic for long, and Picard didn't want him to. "It's hardly a specialty for me," he said. "Starship captains can't afford to have too many specialties, by and large. But you've been doing some rather controversial work, if I understand it."

The others had settled back to pay attention, recognizing the sound of their captain calling the meeting to order without seeming to do so. "It has been controversial," Hwiii said, "and to tell you the truth, there are colleagues of mine who are happier to see me out here and out of touch than back home making their lives difficult in the symposia and the journals. I'm seen as a bit of a trouble-maker, I'm afraid."

"Noooo," Riker said, grinning. Picard smiled to himself: that mischievous look in Hwiii's eyes could hardly be mistaken for anything but what it was.

Hwiii glanced at Riker with the mischief very much in place. "Well, thank you for the vote of confidence, Commander. But I have been troublesome, and so far there's not enough evidence to find out whether I'm right or wrong, which would resolve instantly the question of whether the trouble's been worth it."

Hwiii paused for a bite of mackerel. "Starfleet took us on as navigations-research specialists particularly because of our ability to *know* where we were without recourse to maps or charts. They thought that this would be a useful art to incorporate into a starship's repertoire. Now, some of our navigational and orienting ability in water has to do with the perception of local magnetic and gravity fields. But as soon as we went into space, where those fields either fell off to microstrengths or vanished entirely, it turned out that we could *still* navigate. And later investigation showed that we had some ability to perceive and orient ourselves by 'hyperstring' structures in space. . . . What's that, please?"

"Seafood sauce," Riker said, passing the bowl. "Tomato sauce with spices."

"Thank you. Mmmmm. . . . Without oversimplifying, hyperstrings are hyperdimensional, nonphysical structures on which the matter and the energy of the physical universe are more or less 'strung' like beads. They aren't anything to do with the strings you already know about, the strands of dense 'cold' matter that drift about in realspace; but the name was so appropriate that it stuck."

Hwiii put his knife and fork down crosswise on his plate and studied them for a moment. "Now, hyperstrings are, or have been, of no particular use. They're just *there*. Their properties—density and so forth—have been thought to be only marginally affected by objects and occurrences in the physical universe, so there's been some study of them to see whether hyperstrings themselves can be used as the determinants for an 'absolute' coordinate system against which the movements and locations of things in the physical universe, like stars and planets, can be plotted. However . . . my mathematical work is leading me in another direction. I believe that our previous assumptions are wrong, and that hyperstrings are *profoundly* affected by objects in the physical universe . . . even to the point where they might be usable to *predict* changes in it. It's still unproven, but my reading of the theoretical work done so far suggests that when something happens to a physical object, the hyperstring structures it's 'attached' to resonate with the change. But they resonate both forward and backward in time. Like a string, plucked, vibrating both back and forth."

"I bet astrophysicists would find that useful, if it were true," Geordi said. "You could tell if a star was about to go nova—because the hyperstrings it was 'attached' to would be vibrating with the star's explosion before the star itself blew up."

"That's exactly right, Mr. La Forge. And there are endless other possibilities for what comes down, quite simply, to predicting the future, if my conclusions are correct. But there are problems." Hwiii grinned, and Picard smiled wryly at the look of someone so thoroughly enjoying the prospect of "problems." "Especially on the quantum level, the matter of reading hyperstrings and their data becomes more difficult the more hyperstrings, and henceforth matter and energy, there are in an area. Instead of one harpstring vibrating in the stillness, producing a single clear note, imagine many sounding all together, all on different notes."

"Harmonic interferences," Data said. "Dissonances, canceling and partially canceling waves, chaotic sines—"

"Chaotic," Hwiii said, "is the operant term. You hear confusion, a buzz; nothing comes through clearly, especially not the datum you most desire, the one pure note. Interference from matter itself isn't the problem, though hyperstrings and matter are inextricably associated. But the more matter and energy there are in an area, the more hyperstrings there are, and the harder it gets to clearly read any one of them in order to find out what its properties *mean.*"

"Clear-hyperstring studies, then, would involve getting out somewhere where there aren't many hyperstrings because there isn't much matter or energy?" said Troi.

"That's exactly it, Counselor. Our studies of hyperstrings are still in their infancy precisely because no one has spent enough time out this far, taking the kind of measurements that will allow us to understand what hyperstring properties mean. Once obtained, we can take that information and apply it to hyperstrings closer to the populated worlds, eventually using hyperstring detection and analysis to build a navigational system which will exist independent of the moving Galaxy: an absolute coordinate system, utterly dependable."

"Such a thing would be an explorer's dream," Picard said. "Besides the limitations of the speed of today's warpdrive engines, the other main problem hindering exploration out of the Galaxy has been the lack of navigational fix points close enough to a passing ship to be read accurately." Picard reached out to his wineglass, smiling slightly: the prospect was exhilarating, even though it would not be his generation of starship captains who would experience it. "No need to sow thousands of beacons or squint at Cepheid variables that are too distant to be read reliably . . . or to hope the supernova you're steering by in the next galaxy over will keep on behaving itself."

"Yes, indeed," Hwiii said. "Alternatively, we can learn to use hyperstrings to examine matter itself . . . even, perhaps, to predict what matter will do. That will come much later, and the implications for all the humanities are tremendous. But for the moment, the one x2-track of hy-lepton decay in the right place, the one string sounding the one note, will be enough for me."

"The recurrent musical idiom, Commander," Picard said, "is it the poetry of the scientist or the species?"

Hwiii chuckled. "Something specifically delphine? Probably not. All our peoples are musical to one degree or another; but the great singers are the humpbacks and blues—they're the philosophers, music is everything to them. Us, though, we're too practical: we and the orcas. Music is talk, yes, but the talk is more interesting . . . with each other or you or other species." He looked over at the buffet table with an expression of satisfaction. "That salmon, now . . ."

He glided over to help himself. "Lemon," he said,

expertly squeezing a slice over the salmon. "Mmmm.
. . . But anyway, the hyperstring researches. It's early to be
analyzing my data, but I'm seeing signs that the theory I
came out to prove, of retrotemporal hyperstring oscillation, is true. That alone will create some noise when I get
home, for some of my colleagues claim that such oscillations either cannot exist, because of some of the principles
of quantum mechanics, or that they exist but are unread-
able and unidentifiable as such because of the oscillations'
complexity. There'll be trouble in the journals . . . if
there's not more immediate trouble here."

"The Laihe's statement to us," Picard said. "Have you
been able to make more sense of it than we have?"

"Some, I think, though translation is still a problem. I've
been with these people for nearly nine months, and most of
that time was spent trying to solve the linguistic and
semantic difficulties. The rest was spent trying to get a
version that I could use of their data on the general
'stringiness' of this space. About two months ago, I got
what I believed to be a reliable baseline—I think. The
Lalairu's methods of taking readings are as different as
their coordinate system."

Hwiii frowned—this expression looking almost exactly
like a human one. "Anyway, I then started taking my own
readings and barely got a baseline set of my own before the
Lalairu changed course away from the 'empty' spaces—not
bothering to tell *me* why . . . or if they did, I didn't
understand them. However, if I've correctly translated the
statement you copied to me, the Laihe is nervous about
remaining in this space because the Lalairu's *own* baseline
measurements of this area, taken fairly recently hereabouts, are suddenly no longer viable. Hyperstring structures do not match what they 'should be' for this space—
what they were as little as a year ago. For space so empty,
the hyperstrings are becoming very tightly packed together.

Something has been happening to derange the normal structure."

"What does it mean?" Picard said.

"I don't know."

Picard breathed out softly. "If *you* don't know, who do we ask?"

Hwiii laughed somewhat helplessly. "Me . . . later. Sorry, Captain, Starfleet would probably tell you that I'm the best expert they've got. And I don't have enough data yet to give you a better evaluation, which I know is what you want. I have good hopes that, with a starship's resources to aid me, I can find out . . . at which point I'll tell you everything I can. Meanwhile, Mr. Data's reputation as a researcher is a matter of fame. I would hope that with his help in analysis, and possibly Mr. La Forge's to help me tune and install my detection equipment, we can quickly produce some answers for you."

"Well," Picard said, "clearly there's no point in considering any change in our patrol schedule just now. And at this distance, pausing long enough to notify Starfleet and get a response would be a waste of time. We'll continue as planned. Commander, I will expect some news from you at the earliest possible moment as to how *your* former baseline data match present conditions in these spaces. Meanwhile, please see Commander Riker about any technical assistance you need."

"Yes, sir," Hwiii said. "And thank you much for your welcome."

"Are you sure you don't want some more caviar?" Picard said gently.

The dolphin glanced at him, that mischievous look in his eye again. "Another pound or so would be nice."

They went about their business for the next few days in an unremarkable fashion. Picard noticed with amusement how quickly the crew stopped giving second glances to the dolphin swimming down the corridor. Hwiii seemed to spend most of his time in engineering anyway, surprising amounts of time. Picard sometimes began to wonder when he slept, and Geordi began to complain about it.

Picard caught Geordi in Ten-Forward one evening, looking rather haggard and smelling slightly of fish. "The problem is that he's so concentrated," Geordi said. "He's —don't misunderstand me, Captain, he's absolutely amiable, he's a pleasure to work with, competent, knows his subject inside out—but he's just—" Geordi shook his head. "He's collimated, like a phaser beam. When he's in the middle of his work, you couldn't distract him for a second. He can't *be* distracted—he just *goes* straight for the throat of the problem, whatever it is."

"I should think that would be more of an advantage than anything else," Picard said, sipping his tea.

Geordi smiled wanly. "It might seem that way at first. But if there's one thing human beings do when they're working, it's that they *stop* working. They do something to break the tension or the concentration every now and then: a joke, an aside. Hwiii doesn't do that. It's like he's on rails, running right at the question in hand. Or fin."

"Perseverance," Picard said. "I take it the work you're doing is going well."

"We've got most of his equipment hooked up now. We're getting good readings, he says. I'm still getting an idea of what he means by 'good'—half the time it seems to mean blank files." Geordi chuckled. "But we're in a situation here where lack of data can be as diagnostic as solids full of it. In between times, he's been helping Commander Riker with his subparticle hunting—seems that the technology that the Lalairu are using with hyperstrings is somewhat similar and can be altered to our purposes. He's made some changes in the sensors for us."

"Well, I'm glad he's making himself useful."

"It's getting him to stop, Captain, that's the problem. He's having a sleep cycle now, otherwise I wouldn't be here. I must admit, he *is* a fount of information: it's an education just listening to him while he talks. Or sings— you can't help hearing the notes, they resonate through his waterjacket. The engineering crew like it." Geordi smiled. "I can't say I mind it myself. The funny thing is, some of the song turns out to be some kind of delphine opera. He says he doesn't have a great voice, but the singing runs in the family."

"An opera buff. You'd better keep him away from Worf. But I didn't know there was any opera back on Triton."

"Something like it, apparently. Or I may have misunderstood him: it was hard to tell whether Hwiii was describing theater or a ceremony of some kind—or just live performances of some sort of passion play."

Picard nodded and sipped at his tea again. "I had been wondering—"

He stopped.

Something was happening.

Abruptly, everything seemed peculiarly dim. Was it his eyes? Picard blinked, found nothing changed—but at the same time became suddenly certain that his eyes were not at fault.

The effect persisted, got worse, a darkening and squeezing shut of everything around him, as if he were closing his eyes to sneeze. No, as if everything *around* him were closing its eyes to sneeze.

Then it cleared away. He put his tea down, blinked for a moment, and rubbed his head. "That was odd."

Geordi looked at him. "You felt something?"

"Did you?"

Geordi nodded. "Something like—I don't know: everything dimmed out for a moment."

"Dimmed out for *you?*"

"Not light," Geordi said. "Not a decrease in intensity as such. Not visible light, anyway—just—everything went *attenuated,* somehow."

Picard looked around. Other people, at other tables, were looking slightly confused, too, blinking, glancing around them. "Did you feel that?" he said to the ensign at the next table.

"Something, sir," she said. "Something—I thought I was going to sneeze."

Picard touched his badge. "Picard to Crusher."

"Crusher here," the doctor said. *"Captain, did you just feel something odd?"*

"Yes. How many others?"

"Half the ship, it seems."

"What was it?"

Crusher laughed ruefully. *"I had just stood up, and I thought it was orthostatic hypotension—a fall in blood pressure from standing up too fast. That produces transient dimmings of vision like what I had. But it wasn't that . . . not when so many people felt it at once."*

Picard thought about finishing his tea, then stood up frowning. "Very well, out. . . . Sorry to put you straight back into the traces, Mr. La Forge, but this is too odd. I want level-one diagnostics run on all ship's systems. And I want a department chiefs' meeting in an hour."

"Yes, sir," Geordi said, and headed away. Picard paused to look out the windows. The stars slipped by as usual, seemingly untroubled. Everything seemed perfectly normal. *Am I overreacting?* he thought. *We all seem fine now.*

But the memory of that dimming reasserted itself. Not so much a dimming, but—what was it Geordi had said? An attenuation. Things *themselves* going dark and strange, rather than his perception of them.

Picard made his way out hurriedly, heading for the bridge.

* * *

30

He had just seated himself and was having a look at reports from around the ship. Everyone seemed to have experienced the strange hiatus, but no one had experienced any ill effects.

This left Picard feeling uneasy. "Mr. Data, check Federation records for any incidents of this sort."

"I have already done that, Captain," Data said. "There are no such incidents on record as such. I have scanned using homologues for phrases being used by our own crewmen to describe the experience. There are none."

Picard frowned. "Keep working on it."

"Ensign Wooldridge to Commander Riker," said a voice suddenly.

Riker touched his badge. "Riker here, Ensign."

"Sir," said a young male voice, *"I'm down by the mission specialist's quarters: the dolphin gentleman. I think you'd better have someone come down here. He's awful loud in there, and he's not answering his door. I'm not sure he's well."*

Faintly, in the background, they could all hear a high, eerie wailing.

"How long has this been going on?" said Riker.

"I'm not sure, sir," Wooldridge said, raising his voice slightly over the racket. *"I just got off shift. I had been in my quarters to change, and I was heading to Ten-Forward, when I came by here and heard him. He's been at it at least since I came by—ten minutes or so."*

"On my way," Riker said, glancing at Picard. The captain nodded. "Mr. Data, with me. Dr. Crusher to the mission specialist's quarters immediately, please."

From right down the hall from his quarters, it was very plain that something was the matter. A great flood of untranslated Delphine was ringing out down the corridor; not entirely an unpleasant sound, for there was melody in the fluting whistles, squeaks, and shrills of it, and a kind of rhythm as well. But at the same time, independent of the sound, there was such an edge of distress on the song that it made you twitch to listen to it.

Riker and Data came up outside the doors; Dr. Crusher came along toward them from the other direction. Data tapped the entry chime. There was no response—the piercing song merely went on, uninterrupted, from inside.

"What's the matter with him?" Riker said. "What's happened to his translator?"

"I do not know," Data said, listening.

"What *is* that racket?" Crusher said, getting out her tricorder.

Data put his head to one side. "It is part of the *Song of the Twelve,*" he said, "a cetacean epic sung-poetic work in which an ensemble of—"

"Dolphins singing lieder," Riker said, cutting him off. "Spare me." He gestured at the door. "Override it."

Data touched in a combination on the nearest access panel. The door slid open, and Riker saw, to his relief, that the force field inside was still holding the water in place. They gazed in through it.

Hwiii was there, swimming around and around in circles. Riker was suddenly, horribly reminded of old vids he'd seen from when zoo animals on Earth were still kept in tiny enclosures that literally bored them out of their minds: the dreadfully repeated behaviors, heads swinging back and forth again and again in never-changing patterns, beasts pacing back and forth until they dropped from exhaustion, what minds they had now long gone. But at the same time, the song still pouring forth from Hwiii didn't seem to be the kind of sound a dolphin would make when it had gone mad. Then again—

Riker turned to Crusher. "Vital signs?"

She shook her head as she examined her tricorder's readings. "His blood enzyme levels are indicative of great stress, but other than that, no neurological damage that I can see."

"Then why is he like this?" Riker said softly. "What's going on? What caused this?"

His mind went back to that momentary flicker of darkness. He had been talking to Lieutenant Hessan, laughing back at those laughing eyes of hers, and suddenly—

"Wooldridge noticed this, what—twenty minutes ago?"

"That would be approximately correct," Data said. The song scaled up in urgency, and all at once it became a bit too much for Riker. He turned, touched his badge, said, "Riker to Commander Hwiii!" then put two fingers in his mouth, leaned close to the wall of water for maximum effect, and whistled at the top of his lungs.

The dolphin almost matched his whistle a second later, with a shriek of equal volume, one that made them all wince. But then he slowly stopped circling, coasting to a stop, and just hung in the water for a moment—then rose to the top of his quarters to take a breath.

They waited. After a few seconds he drifted down again to the doorway and hung there, looking at them with a rather stunned expression from behind the wall of water. "Commander," Hwiii said weakly, "that was vile language."

"My apologies," Riker said, "but you weren't behaving in a way that suggested sweet reason was going to do much good right then."

"No," Hwiii said, sounding ashamed, "I suppose not. It's just that it was such a shock—" He stared at Riker. "How can you be so calm?"

"Calm isn't high on my list at the moment, believe me," Riker said. "We've had a very odd occurrence in the last hour or so."

"I'll say we have," Hwiii said. "You felt it too, then. We're lost!"

"What?" Crusher said.

The dolphin looked at her in distress. "Can't you feel it?"

"We all felt something a little while ago," Crusher said, "but what it was, we can't say."

"Ship's systems show no change in status," Data said. "All readings, navigational and otherwise, seem nominal."

"Commander, Mr. Data," Hwiii said with dreadful intensity, "we are *lost*. I can feel it in my tail. We're not—" He fumbled for words, and Riker found it odd to watch a being usually so precise now floundering. *"We're not where we were."*

"Will you get into your suit, Commander," Riker said, "and come up to the bridge with me and explain that— since you're the only one around here who seems to have any kind of explanation for what's happening?"

"Gladly," Hwiii said. But his voice still had an uncertain sound to it, almost the sound of a child, abruptly lost in some immensity, and very much wanting some adult to take his hand and tell him things are going to be all right.

Some minutes later, on the bridge, Hwiii was looking critically over Data's shoulder while he brought up detailed readings of their coordinates. "I'm so embarrassed about that," Hwiii said quietly to Data. "I don't usually come all overreligious in moments of crisis."

"I was going to ask whether there was some specific significance in the passage you were singing," Data said, "but that will have to wait. Here are our present coordinates, with course projection. Here are the twelve Cepheids within scan, with their spectra. As you see, they all match their nominal 'fingerprints,' though RY Antliae is showing about point five percent above its baseline at the moment. Here is the master navigational grid, and as you see, our course is as predicted."

Picard stepped down to look, too. "Our location at the

moment is exactly what it should be, considering our past course and speed," he said. "As you can see, the computer confirms the location as well."

Hwiii laughed at that, an unhappy sound. "Yes, but these instruments don't know any better since they're judging by strictly physical guideposts like Cepheid variables." He looked over at Picard. "Captain, I see the readings, and I can vouch for the validity of the instruments' readings since I've been working so closely with them the last few days. But"—and he swung his tail in one of the delphine gestures of negation, a downward slap—"*we are not where we seem to be.* This is not the way space feels, not the way it felt two hours ago. We are somewhere else that looks like here—if you follow me."

Picard's mind abruptly went back to what the Laihe had been saying, or trying to say. "Some kind of—shift—"

Hwiii had made his way up to one of the science stations and was busy at it with his manipulators, reconfiguring it.

"If I understand you correctly," Picard said slowly, "are you suggesting that we have somehow dislocated ourselves into a congruent universe?"

Hwiii laughed, looking up from the controls for a moment. "Captain, I only wish we had done it ourselves! If we had, we might at least have been prepared for it. I was on my sleep cycle, and everything was fine. Then—can you imagine waking up and suddenly finding yourself in some place that your senses tell you is a strange country, a different planet, even—but one that nonetheless looked exactly the same as where you were before you fell asleep?"

Troi looked over at him. "The effect would be much like that of one kind of psychotic break in a human," she said. "The sudden loss of familiar associations—or the certainty that where you *were* is not where you *are.* A terrible disorientation."

"The only problem," Hwiii said, "is that I have something concrete on which to base the experience." The display he had brought up was presently scrolling by in great blocks of a Delphine-based numerical notation, an adapted binary. "It doesn't mean much this way. Wait a second—"

The silver tentacles of the manipulators danced across the keyboard for a moment, then the display shifted to show something that might have been a very tangled knot or braid.

"This is a very crude representation of the major hyperstring structures in the space where we were about two hours ago," Hwiii said, "before I took my last set of readings for the day and turned in. Now this"—he worked for a moment again—"is the same space—I'm scanning the same cubic now—but look."

The second display fitted itself down over the first one. The curves and twists of the bright lines were a close match, very close indeed, but not quite. Here and there some loop or curve stuck out farther than the original, curved differently, crossed another's path sooner, or later, than its partner in the original scan. "A very close congruence, I would say," Hwiii said, his voice a blend of triumph and alarm. "Not quite exact—out by about three percent, I'd say off the fin. This isn't something you have senses for," he said to Picard, "but I felt it as soon as I woke up—and felt it all over me, a derangement of my people's most basic sense." He sounded ashamed again.

"Commander," Picard said gently, "I think you had reason to be upset. Let it pass; if I woke up suddenly and found myself seeing the world so out of joint as you seem to have, I daresay I might have made some noise myself." He shook his head. "Yet at the same time, this universe seems overtly physically the same as our own."

Hwiii swung his head from side to side, the one gesture humans shared with dolphins. "How far the congruences will stretch, Captain, I wouldn't pretend to know."

Picard sighed and said, "Well. Now that it's established that we're here . . . how do we get back?"

Hwiii looked over at Geordi, who had joined them. "Until we know how we got here," Geordi said, "that's hardly a question we can answer."

"Well, get to work on it," Picard said. "This is beginning to make me twitch."

And then they all jumped as the *whoop! whoop! whoop!* of the intruder alarm shattered the quiet of the bridge. Worf hurried to his station, brought up a display, examined it: "There is a security breach in the computer core! At access station two."

"Get a team down there on the double," Riker said, "and join them."

"Aye, sir." Worf touched his console, spoke a few words, and went out of the bridge at a run.

CHAPTER 3

"**G**ive me a shot of access station two," Riker said to the lieutenant who moved up to take Worf's console.

"I'm going down there," Picard said, and headed for the 'lift. Riker opened his mouth and then shut it again, for the security team would beat the captain there by long enough to get their job done. Still, his mouth quirked in a slight smile at the sight of the man leaving the bridge, a man very much in search of answers and unwilling to take "no" for one.

Worf met his team coming out of the 'lift on deck ten, the best of the shift—little slim Ryder, dark Mirish, and tall blue Detaith—his pick for a situation in which there might be physical trouble, for all of them looked unlikely to be able to stop it, and all of them most spectacularly were. *"Mr. Worf—"*

"Ready, Commander." They were standing outside the door to the access station, a little room off the main corridor leading to the cores proper.

"The captain is on his way."

"Intruder's three meters in on the right as you go in," said Lieutenant Mann from the bridge security console. *"He's using one of the stand-up access padds."*

"Good," Worf said. "Ryder, you and I at point. Mirish, behind, in brace. Detaith, hold the door. Now."

Worf touched the door, and he and Ryder went in fast, with weapons ready. They saw a slightly hunched figure in a lieutenant's uniform, human, dark-haired, tapping at the padd console. He looked up, reacted in angry surprise, fumbled at his side for something.

As his hand came up, Worf kicked it, hard, and the weapon went flying up overhead and across the little room. The man cried out, started to turn back toward Worf, but a second later, Ryder hit him feetfirst in the rib cage, carefully knocking the intruder straight sideways to spare the console and any settings that might remain in it. They went down together, but a second later Ryder had bounced back up to a kneeling position, and the intruder was shouting something pained into the carpet while Ryder, kneeling on the intruder's back, twisted his wrist backward and up into a position for which nature had never prepared it.

Worf was pleased: a security action in which the team did not have to stretch itself unduly was an efficient one, which the captain would approve. "Get him up," he said to Ryder. "Keep him restrained."

Ryder and Mirish hauled the man to his feet. Worf studied the rage-twisted face, but no identification came immediately to mind. He touched his badge. "Mann," he said, "get me an ID on this crewman."

"Working, sir."

They stood and waited, looking at the man. "Let me go," he said, struggling. "I can make it worth your while!"

Ryder and Mirish gave each other dubious looks. "What are you doing in this area?" Worf said, frowning.

He was astonished when the crewman actually spat at his feet. "Slave, I don't have to answer to *you!*"

Worf's eyes narrowed . . . for *slave* was not a word one used on a Klingon and lived.

"Lieutenant," Mann said from the bridge, *"pictorial record identifies this crewman as Ensign Mark Stewart, assigned to botany and hydroponics."*

"Curious that you should have decided to go so suddenly into computers, Ensign," Worf said. "A career change?"

"There's only one problem," said Mann. *"The computer says that Ensign Stewart is on deck nine, in his quarters."*

Worf's eyebrows went up, and Ryder and Mirish looked at each other as Detaith stepped aside to let the captain through.

"Our intruder," Picard said, coming up beside Worf.

"Yes, Captain. But we have a problem. Lieutenant Worf to Ensign Stewart."

There was a brief pause, then a somewhat sleepy voice said out of the air, *"Yes, sir? What can I do for you? I'm off shift right now."*

Worf glanced at Picard. The captain's eyes narrowed, and he looked back at "Stewart" again. The young man was staring at him with an expression of anger and terror, but otherwise not reacting. Slowly Picard reached out to him. The man tried to flinch away from the touch, but the security staff held him fast. Picard touched the man's badge: it made no sound.

Worf looked at Picard. "Take him to sickbay," the captain said. "I want him and everything about him thoroughly examined. After that, he's to be secured in the brig once I've consulted with Doctor Crusher."

Worf nodded. "Nothing is required of you at this moment, Ensign," he said to his communicator. "I am sorry to have disturbed your sleep cycle. But would you remain awake for a little while? You may be needed."

"Of course, sir." Worf gestured with his head at his

people. Ryder and Mirish hustled the man out, with Detaith behind them, his sidearm ready.

"I take it he didn't put up much of a struggle," Picard said.

Worf shook his head. "He had no chance. All the same—" He frowned. "I could wish he had. He was . . . rude."

"So I heard," Picard said softly. "Well. We will have answers soon enough . . . and I suspect he will have leisure to repent his rudeness."

They headed out together.

Beverly Crusher pursed her lips and turned away from the man lying bitterly silent and with closed eyes on the diagnostic bed. Beverly was in a bad mood, for mystery annoyed her except in the abstract. When it turned up in her sickbay, she tended to give it short shrift, preferring revealed fact and clean diagnosis to clinical pictures that remained stubbornly shadowy. Right now, though, the shadows were deep.

She breathed out as she worked over her padd, transferring its readings to the computer, then glanced up at the two security people standing on either side of the bed. "Brendan," she said to Ryder, "that arm giving you any more trouble?"

He shook his head, smiling slightly. "That last regeneration did the trick."

"Good. Stop breaking it, now." She smiled briefly at Mirish and headed for her office, pausing a moment as the sickbay door hissed open. It was Jean-Luc; behind him came Geordi.

"Doctor?" said the captain.

"I'm ready for you, Captain," she said, and together they went into her office. The doors shut behind them. "Or as ready as I'm going to be, since this is not one of my more cooperative clients."

She sat down and turned her deskviewer so that they could both see it. "Well," Picard said. "Obviously, the question becomes, who is he?"

"His DNA fingerprint identifies him as Mark Stewart. There is no mistake about that."

Picard breathed out. "Unfortunately," Beverly said, "his *body* does not confirm that identification."

Picard looked at her thoughtfully. "In what way?"

Beverly touched the console, sat back, and watched the data scroll. "This is Mark Stewart's medical record. He's had some minor troubles." She paused the display and pointed. "Since he's one of the ship's flora specialists, he winds up on a lot of away teams, and he's picked up the occasional bug planetside. The worst was a bad case of chronic paronychia—it's a disorder of the nail beds, usually fungal. He picked up an 'abetter' organism on a survey to 1212 Muscae IV: the alien mycete chummed up with a more normal fungus, something a lot of us carry in us routinely, and the two potentiated one another and infected his fingernails badly. Took me a while to knock it down. Mark also has an old complex fracture of the ulna, from falling out of a tree while taking samples." She chuckled. "Seems the tree spoke to him."

Picard looked surprised. "Delusional?"

"He wasn't. The *tree* was, though. But that's another story. Anyway . . ." Beverly touched a control; another human-body graphic came up. "This is the scan of the man on the bed out there. He shows signs of the paronychia— just as the first Mark Stewart does; his nails have some additional ridges on them because of trauma to the nail beds. But *this* man has no trace of the old ulnar fracture . . . and such things cannot be made to vanish without trace, even with our technology. Properly healed bone always shows some slight sign of the heal, the 'callus,' whether you help it with a protoplaser or a splint. More to

the point . . . this man has no appendix; our own Mark
Stewart does." She sighed and sat back again. "So if you're
going to ask me, 'Is this Mark Stewart?' . . . then I'm afraid
the answer is yes and no."

She watched Jean-Luc digest that. "Has he said anything?"

"He made a rude remark about having heard about what
happens to my guinea pigs, which I took merely clinical
note of. But he's said nothing since: he's become the classic
unresponsive patient, though not withdrawn—I see him
peeking out from under those 'closed' eyes every now and
then. He won't answer questions, though."

Picard sat quiet.

"There's something else I don't like the look of, though I
don't know quite what to make of it. The neural diagnostic
routines turned up some near-systemic damage in our
duplicate out there. It's very low-level stuff—myelin-
sheath damage, some minor mononeuropathies, some in-
volvement of dermatomes . . . and I'm not sure what
would cause such a presentation. If the trauma were more
serious, I would suspect something like Hansen's disease,
or even neurotransmitter-substance abuse. But it's *not* that
serious, and I have no diagnosis."

"Which annoys you," Picard said, and smiled slightly.
She made a wry face. "Doctor, I want some answers out of
him."

Beverly shook her head. "Are you going to ask me for
'truth serum'? I'm fresh out. Better see what Deanna can
do. Ah—"

The door opened; Geordi came in and stood by the desk,
holding a tricorder. "Can I dump to your terminal, Doctor? I didn't want to do it out there . . . our boy's watching,
though he's trying not to look it."

"Feel free."

"Report, Mr. La Forge," Picard said.

Geordi looked both annoyed and intrigued. "Captain, both his communicator, as you discovered, and his uniform are forgeries. The communicator's just a dummy, made of base metals, no silicates or transtator components. And the thread in the uniform, though it's replicated material, has the wrong molecular structure. Or at least, a different one from what's in our uniforms." Geordi raised his eyebrows. "More than that—the *tailoring's* bad."

Beverly had to smile. Picard looked momentarily wry. "I assume you're commenting on something besides the workmanship."

"Yes, sir. Normally the computer adjusts fit to change with the changes in your body, using your last uniform as a template. But this was a one-off, if I'm any judge. The computer that made it wasn't sure how to tailor it: it was using some other set of algorithms, and it made a botch of it. What that guy's got on is definitely not the uniform he usually wears. Whatever *that* might be."

"Well. Someone has gone to a lot of trouble to get an impostor onto my ship. I intend to get to the bottom of this—preferably humanely, but . . ." Picard touched his communicator. "Picard to Counselor Troi."

"Yes, Captain?"

"Please access the information presently in Dr. Crusher's terminal regarding our intruder. Then I would be pleased to see you in sickbay to give us the benefit of your impressions."

"Right away, sir."

"One thing first, Mr. La Forge," Picard said. "The first we knew of this intruder was when we detected his presence in the computer core. Why didn't we get any alert to the fact that someone had transported aboard?"

"I don't know, Captain." Geordi looked embarrassed. "I'm looking into it."

"I'll expect answers at the department heads' meeting

later. Meanwhile"—the captain looked out through the glass—"let's see what the counselor discovers."

Having reviewed the security tape of Stewart's capture, and having finished reading Dr. Crusher's report, Deanna Troi made her way down to sickbay in a state of some unease. She knew Stewart slightly, having met him before in Ten-Forward; he had invited her down with some other crewpeople to see his plant collection, and they had spent a cheerful afternoon in one of the greenhouses. But his medical and psych profiles had always been unremarkable. He was simply a good steady crewman, not an under-achiever or overachiever; interested in research—he had been doing some extremely delicate work on one of the more impenetrable alien DNA-analogues. The image of this crewman trying to break into the computer was ridiculous . . . but she already knew it wasn't him. There was no other way to read the data, no matter how impossible it seemed.

She was uneasy, though, at the appearance of this sudden extra persona wearing a body she had thought she was familiar with. As usual when she was uneasy, Deanna had "managed it away"—had gotten right down into the unease, experienced it sufficiently for it to no longer feel actively uncomfortable, and then had sealed it over tempo-rarily. Unfortunately there had been no time to indulge herself in enough self-work to feel completely at rest. The taut sound of the captain's voice had made it plain that time was of the essence. But she still found herself wonder-ing what she was going to find when she went into sickbay.

She paused for a long moment outside the doors, seeing what she felt. There was a knot of tight concentration that she felt sure was the captain, Geordi, and Beverly, for it came in three different flavors—one quite fierce and concentrated, one cool and thoughtful, the third holding itself in check only with difficulty. As always, she could almost, almost hear thoughts moving on the edges of the emotions, but not quite. She had long since given up being frustrated about such things.

There was another source of emotion in the room besides the two security men—their minds, alert and a bit suspicious, she could clearly distinguish. The other—it was certainly not Stewart. Even if she hadn't had an evaluation of his physical condition to go by, she would have known that immediately. Mark had never had such a core of suppressed fury in him. And overlaid on that was bitterness, a dreadful sense of betrayal, and a boiling desire for revenge—but all balked, all frustrated because the person having the feelings knew that there was nothing he could do about any of these things. He was trapped, he had failed somehow, and he was frightened for himself. She could feel his mind moving restlessly like a caged beast, trying to find a way out, finding nothing, repeating the motions because there was no hope, and nothing else to do.

All right, she said to herself, *there's your baseline. What are you waiting for?* Still, it took Deanna a few seconds before she could make herself go in.

Ryder and Detaith looked at her as she came in, smiled at her, and moved aside to let her have easier access to the diagnostic bed. The man on it didn't move, didn't open his eyes—or at least didn't seem to. At the sound of the door, he jumped internally—then, hearing the footsteps pause by his bed, he kept himself very still, a waiting feeling.

Deanna decided to take the initiative: "Hello, Mr. Stewart. Or is that really who you are?"

Out of the corner of her eye she saw Picard, Crusher, and Geordi watching through the glass doors of the doctor's office, saw them react as the man's eyes flew open. She had little attention to spare them, though. She was too busy bracing herself against the abrupt, desperate wash of fear that came blasting out of the man, directed squarely at her.

He was physically holding himself still, and a feeling came to Deanna that translated into the image of a small creature being very quiet, quiet for its life's sake, under the pitiless eye of a predator. He stared at her, opened his mouth, and closed it again. Inside him, utter dread and anguish fought with each other. If the emotions had words, they would have been something like, *Oh, God, oh, no, they never told me.*

Deanna fought for her own balance. It was poor technique to say something simply in order to alter the other's emotions in favor of your own comfort. She was sorely tempted, but she put the urge resolutely aside. "I think you have some explaining to do," she said, purposely holding her body in a nonthreatening position, arms by her side, so as not to encourage him into any response that he didn't generate himself. The line was "nonguiding," too, a good one for giving whatever free-floating anxiety was about a chance to express itself.

"As if you need explanations," Stewart said. His tone had some bravado about it, but the bravado was frightened and ineffective. He despaired of convincing her; he certainly didn't convince himself.

"Suppose you tell me what you were doing trying to get into the computer core."

Stewart stared at her. He was trembling now. Out of the corner of her eye she saw Picard stand up in the next room, looking uncomprehendingly from her to the man on the diagnostic bed. Stewart began to sit up. Ryder and Detaith moved a little closer. Deanna waved them back. "No, it's all right. I want to hear what he has to say."

"So it was all a trick then," Stewart said. "The whole thing. Maybe this, too. A holodeck simulation?" He stared around him, then looked back at Troi, wincing as if it badly frightened him to look at her directly. "Why me?" he burst out. "What have I done wrong? I've always been loyal."

"Exactly how would you say you've been tricked?"

Deanna was having a hard time keeping herself from trembling now. The man's fear was only partly for this situation, this place; most of it was of *her* specifically. She could get no clear sense of why he was so afraid, but there were shapes moving in the back of his mind, lowering, something worse than just dying, worse than just torture, worse than—Deanna shied away from the inchoate images, they were so frightening. In any case, she couldn't make them out clearly, and clarity was needed here, if nothing else.

Stewart gulped. "They told me, 'We're going to beam you over to another *Enterprise.* It's going to look like our *Enterprise,* but it's not. You're not to speak to any of the people you meet there.'" Stewart looked away, his face crumpling. "I'm dead already."

"Not yet," Troi said consolingly, but the look of stark terror the man turned on her . . .

"Please, no," he cried, "please, Counselor, I'm telling you—"

And again that wash of fear, and fear of *her,* as if she were Death standing by the bed, inescapable. She held her face quite still and nodded to him to continue.

He gulped. "They said, 'Get into the computer core,' and they gave me some codes, and they said, 'These'll get you first-level access, get these files . . .'" He rattled off a long string of file names.

Out of the corner of her eye she caught sight of Geordi bending over the doctor's terminal, making notes. Deanna shook her head when he had finished. "They."

"Commander Riker," Stewart said, "and Mr. La Forge."

"All right. What else?"

He looked at her mistrustfully, and all his emotions roiled in him: a man seeing someone behaving most uncharacteristically, not knowing what to make of it, and still deadly afraid.

"They said, 'Here's a transmitter to get out the data we want. As you access the data, it'll feed to this—when it's finished, just go back out into the ship and just wait. We'll pick you up, beam you back in about six hours.'" He gulped again. "It wasn't supposed to happen like this," he moaned. "I did my best, I tried—I did the transmission! Why am I going to be punished now!"

"No one's going to punish you," Troi said, shaken. The look of pure, hating disbelief that Stewart turned on her was a poor echo of the blast of rage and betrayal that hit her now.

"Oh, come on, Counselor," he said sarcastically, turning the title into an epithet. "Why would you be here otherwise? Everybody knows you can't bear to be left out of a little 'conditioning.' Especially at the moment. One of those Betazed 'weird times,' it's more than usually good for you, I hear—" And then he caught himself. Some fear even worse than the fear of *her* briefly impinged. He looked around the room, saw the captain, Geordi, and Crusher looking at him, and his face sagged into hopelessness again. "Are they real?" he whispered. "It doesn't matter, does it? You'll kill me now, won't you? For *him.*" Among the incoherencies, this one stab of cold dread went through Deanna like a spear as the man's eyes fell on Picard. If the feeling could have been put into words, "Abandon hope, all ye—" might have been a good rendering. *No hope. Failed, seen to have failed, seen by the* captain *to have failed—a death sentence.* "Get it over with," Stewart said, sick with fear, and turned away toward the wall, slumped: a man waiting to be shot.

Troi's head was already aching with the onslaught of such bitterness. At the same time, she was rather annoyed. *The problem here,* she thought, *is that I don't know what questions to ask. Or how to ask them. All I can do is be nondirective and hope for the best.* "The security team,"

Deanna said. "You said you could make it worth their while. How exactly did you mean that?"

Stewart looked at her sidewise, the question distracting him from his terror momentarily, so that more normal reactions asserted themselves for the moment. "You of everybody aboard this ship know *that,*" he said. "A little action on the side, someone taken off the promotion ladder here, a bribe or two there, a word whispered somewhere else to help your career along—if it's good enough for you, it's good enough for us little crewmen, isn't it? Why shouldn't I try the same pitch?" And there was a sudden dawning inside him of a wild hope—but caution, caution. His expression was going almost sly. "I wonder what you mean by asking. No disrespect, Counselor," Stewart said hurriedly. But the sly look got stronger. "Getting tired of Number One then, are you?"

The emotional subtext of his words was so amused, and there was such a background of distaste to it—slightly lascivious distaste—that Deanna almost blushed. Not quite: she had that much control over herself left. "If I am?" she said.

"Then maybe I can make it worth your while as well. I know about Betazeds—it's one of the problems, isn't it? There just sort of isn't—enough—at certain times. There are some of us, though, who might surprise you. A little less easy to wear out than"—the man's eyes darted around nervously—"Number One. He's been so busy lately, anyway, what with—" And now Stewart glanced, ever so briefly, at Picard, who had sat back down again in Crusher's office and was trying very hard indeed not to watch them.

"Commander Riker's duty load can be considerable," Deanna said neutrally.

Stewart burst out in a great laugh of anger and amusement. "If we're going to make a deal, let's make it. Let me

go back to my duties—let me out of this test or drill or whatever it is—I'm a good crewman. I'm a loyal crewman. I back my principals. I've never turned my coat on any of them. I'd be good as one of your men, too. You could buy me off my principal easily enough—or take me." His tone was wheedling, now, but under the wheedling the fear remained, and the confusion. There was also a feeling of growing boldness, though: he seemed to think he had achieved something, possibly just by still being alive. "A word, a favor—you have the power on this ship. Everybody knows that. Even *he.*" And his glance slid to Picard again, and away. "You know," he said more softly, "even the captain can't act without the security officer's approval."

Troi had to swallow at that. "Just one more thing. Tell me again what you were told. They said you were to beam over to a ship like the *Enterprise*—but it's not the *Enterprise.*"

"That's what they said. Did they get the phrasing wrong? Is someone *else* going to be punished?" And under the question rose a terrible glee and relief. There was still great uncertainty in him, but now he thought that someone else was in trouble, not him, and this trap was a trap for another crewman.

"That was all?" Troi desperately wanted to add, *Nothing about another space, a parallel universe?* But she would not lead him; that wouldn't help.

Stewart nodded and breathed out, then looked at her sidewise. "I had to wonder. It's rare enough an officer is more interested in one of us than in our agonizers." His hand crept involuntarily to the spot where his badge would have been. "And as for you . . ." The man's fury and fear were so balanced in him that Stewart might have said anything, and Troi would have welcomed such an outburst, probably more revealing than all this terrified fencing.

Come on, she willed him, *tell me what you think of me, let it go.*

Stewart sealed over again, turned away in a roil of frustration, cupidity, confusion, and fright. Troi sighed. "Keep him here for the moment," she said to Ryder and Detaith. "I may want him again later." Then she simply looked at Stewart—and that wave of fear ran through him so vehemently now that he wouldn't meet her eyes. Hopelessness, the fear again of imminent death, the feeling that he would welcome death rather than what *she* would now do.

The emotions were so intense that they almost sorted themselves into thought. As it was, she heard/felt something that she felt sure would have turned into a cry of *monster, murderer, horrible*—and the image of her face, set into a cold, cold smile.

Deanna stepped away, back into Dr. Crusher's office, where the others watched her, uncomprehending. When the door had closed, she sat down quite suddenly in the nearest chair, as if someone had removed the pins from her knee joints. Certainly they felt about as useless, and she sat and shook with Stewart's emotions, and her own.

"A moment or two," she said to the three who waited, "if you don't mind." It took her longer than that—calming her breathing, getting her heart to slow down, doing the exercises common to her people for the management of one's emotions when another's became too much.

"Counselor," Picard said after a moment, "are you all right?"

She shook her head. "Emphatically not, Captain, though functional enough. Let me tell you what I sensed . . .

"He doesn't know what to make of all this," Deanna said after she had finished a description of Stewart's reactions. "He thinks it's some kind of test of his loyalty—apparently such are common, where he comes from. In fact, I believe

he thinks we're really all part of some elaborate illusion, and that he's actually on his ship's holodeck. But his reactions to his officers are not—anything like what we're used to." She shuddered, glancing at Crusher and La Forge. "You two hardly matter to him. In Commander Riker's case, the imagery that comes up is of brutality, a kind of gluttony—" She broke off, uncomfortable. "The captain— he's afraid of, and hates; but at the same time, you're a symbol of something Stewart wants, I think. I didn't understand it. . . . And he's more afraid of *me* than of anything else that could happen to him."

Picard shook his head. "And that was all you could find out?"

"I don't know, Captain. He says things that would probably be most illuminating—if I knew how to take them, if I understood the context. But this is definitely one of those times I wish my mother hadn't been half of a mixed marriage. Right now I would exchange a lot of diversity for being able to hear what that man was actually thinking."

" 'Security officer,' he called you," Geordi said. "Except in the abstract—what's that supposed to mean?"

Deanna shook her head. "I got the sense it was a command-level title. Other than that—there's no telling."

"Conclusions?" Picard said.

Deanna took a long, shuddering breath—she was still having some trouble with control. "Captain, unlikely as it seems, I at least am left with the conclusion that this man is from another *Enterprise;* and one very like ours, for clearly, he knows us, or some of us—and he knew this ship's structure well enough to move around in it fairly easily before he broached a security area and we were alerted to his presence. He was sent here to spy on us, to report, and possibly to return—though I'm not too sure about that last, for much more care seems to have been taken preparing to get him over here than for preparing him to come back. At least he was forthcoming about what information he was after." She looked at Geordi.

He nodded. "I got them. I should be able to find any others he got at the same time, too, since anytime a file is accessed, there's a tag added to it, a bookkeeping trace. I'll check all the tags changed within that time frame."

Picard sat thoughtful. The pool of organization and sober thought that spread from him was reassuring, and Deanna felt, at that moment, that she could use all the reassurance she could get. That wave of fear was still beating at her back. "Doctor, Mr. La Forge, I'm going to want a department heads' meeting in about two hours. I'll be on the bridge if I'm needed."

Geordi went out, heading back to engineering; Crusher stepped out into the main sickbay area to see about her other patients. Troi sat there, looking at the captain; his unease at the way she looked touched her. She shook her head.

"What kind of people are we there?" she said.

Picard looked briefly off into the distance. "Another *Enterprise . . . ,*" he said softly. "Another Troi . . ."

"Another Picard," Deanna said. "Cold, he saw you. A grim, quiet terror, hard, like iron. And another Riker— cruel, and liking the cruelty." She breathed out, feeling Stewart's fear still clawing at her back.

"And you?" Picard said.

"Death," Deanna said, "in an odd uniform. And worse than either of you."

Picard stood up and looked at her with compunction. "Two hours, Counselor," he said, and went out.

She sat there, wondering, *What would it take to turn me into a murderess? . . . and worse?* For Stewart's emotions had hinted that there were things worse than merely being killed. *You spend your life,* Deanna thought, *being grateful that you're no worse, as a person, than you might be—and then you find out what you might be.*

She got up and went after Picard, heading for the bridge. As she passed the bed, the man on it didn't open his eyes, didn't move, but she felt the regard of his terror follow her out into the hall. She was well up to the bridge before it faded into the background and she felt even remotely human again.

CHAPTER 4

The bridge was running on yellow alert now. Picard had paused by the helm, where the helm officer in rotation, Ensign Redpath, was running a navigations diagnostic in a spare moment. "Anything on sensors?" Picard said to Data.

"Negative at the moment, Captain."

"We may have some while yet of this," Picard said. "If what our . . . guest . . . has just told us is true, his ship is expecting to pick him up shortly. I desire him to miss that pickup—preferably without the other ship knowing why."

Picard fingered his lower lip for a moment. "Mr. Data," he said, and glanced over at the young officer manning the helm, "Ensign Redpath—for the time being, if any vessel whatsoever approaches us, no matter how familiar or unfamiliar, I want you to make us scarce. We need time to consider our options, and at the moment I trust no one, and I don't care to be seen. I want all sensors on extreme sweep, and confine yourselves as much as possible to passive sensing—nothing that would alert another ship which might be looking for our scan. And I want to know where everything is around us for as many light-years around as you can manage—*everything,* be it the size of a starship or a bread box. If anything comes near us, I want you to note its location and get us out of what you judge might be *its* sensor range as quickly as possible—while, at the same time, not losing sight of it entirely ourselves."

Data and Ensign Redpath blinked at each other. Then Ensign Redpath nodded his dark head, smiled slightly, and said, "Bumpercars."

It was Picard's turn to blink now. "I beg your pardon, Mr. Redpath?"

"It's a negative-feedback program, sir. You program the sensors to have the helm take the ship out of range anytime they sense anything: it's an analogue of the system your body uses to protect you from pain—burn your hand, it jerks back. Each succeeding contact pushes the ship out of range again. When contact is on the point of being completely lost, the helm is instructed to recoil a little in a direction roughly parallel to the projected course of the object that caused the recoil, so you find it again . . . just. And then start recoiling again. Even if the target vessel gets anything from us, our close mirroring of its own course changes will make us seem like some kind of sensor ghost."

"The ship's course may become quite irregular," Data said.

Picard nodded. "All the same, that sounds like what I want—and I don't mind if the *Enterprise* jumps around like a flea on a hot griddle, as long as she's not *seen.* See to it, Ensign."

"Aye, sir," Redpath said, and started working at his console.

"I want to be notified the minute anything happens," Picard said to the bridge at large. "I'll be in the ready room."

Heads nodded all around. As Picard was heading up that way, Worf approached him. "Captain, if you have a moment . . ."

"Of course."

"Before it became necessary to restrict our scans to passive ones, I found something that you should see. Look."

Worf showed him the readout at one of the science stations. Far away, at nearly three or four light-years' distance, the display showed them a tiny, fuzzy shape that Picard would normally have suspected of being sensor artifact. The computer's sensing of it showed clearly that it was radiating energy.

Worf pointed at one of several waveforms coming from it. "Look, Captain. This pattern closely matches the parameters for the waveform of our transporter carrier."

Picard stared at it. "Mr. Worf, that is—" He shook his head.

"Barely a meter in length. Yes, sir. As far as I can make out—and Mr. La Forge agrees with my assessment at this point—it is a kind of transporter relay station, with a simple 'recording' function built in. Someone begins transport 'to' this object: the pattern is caught halfway, then stored in this portable form, if you like, and held to be sent off in another direction. Light-years, parsecs—then, when close enough, and within range of its object, the transport process is completed."

"It must take a considerable amount of energy."

"Yes, but such would only be apparent when the 'platform' was actually transporting."

"And recklessness," Picard said softly. "If the power should fail . . ."

"Precisely. It is not what you would call a 'low-risk' form of transportation. Interesting enough in its own way: a sort of stasis, or so it could be used. But in this case, I think not. I think our intruder's transport started somewhere else—a long way somewhere else—was caught halfway by this device, and then the device was sent toward us, as we might send a probe. When it came within optimum distance, it transported."

"Then turned away again," Picard said. By the redshift it was showing, the object was now running away from them at about point five cee, not using warp, which would attract their sensors' attention.

Picard shook his head. What kind of people would transport a man's essence into this kind of limbo, then fire him away on the off chance that he would find the object they intended him to spy upon? And if he never found it . . .

"These are not nice people, Mr. Worf."

Worf shook his head. "No, sir. They seem entirely too fond of stealth for my tastes. Honor is apparently quite foreign to them. One other thing, though." He pointed. "Notice the probe's course. Though much slower than ours, it is roughly following us; while I have been watching it, very slight alterations have been made to keep it more or less pacing us, along our course line. It will not get too far away from us, I think. And at some later date, it is doubtless intended to slip back into range and attempt to make a pickup."

Picard nodded. "Tell Dr. Crusher that I want that man checked again, this time for subcutaneous transponders— we may have missed something. Tell her to leave no bone unturned."

Worf nodded. "At any rate, the import of this device is that someone can transport aboard this ship while their home vessel, if vessel there is, is very far away. And without alerting us—for that waveform is how it was managed without immediately triggering the intruder alert." Worf pointed again at the display. "Our systems recognized the pattern as *their own* and therefore did not raise the alarm."

Picard frowned. "Definitely another Federation ship, then."

"Not just a Federation vessel, but one of our class, and in our present state of repair. Otherwise there would be identifiable variations."

"Definitely another *Enterprise,* then."

"The odds would seem to be in its favor."

Picard breathed out uneasily. It all still needed more consideration. "Have you shared your information with Mr. Data?"

"I am doing so now."

"Good. See to it that Chief O'Brien gets it as well. I want him to have a word with the transporters and see to it that their own waveform is slightly altered—just enough to serve as a 'tag,' if he likes, but in such a way that another of these incoming transports will register properly as an intrusion."

"Aye aye, sir."

Picard took himself off into the ready room and spent the next hour or so working on reports about other business. One of the problems with starship command was that no matter how much you managed to delegate or get the computer to do for you, there always seemed to be more of what Dr. Crusher called "administrivia." After a while, he found his tension level rising. *And why not?* he thought, pushing his padd away. *I don't understand what's happening and I don't know what to do about it. A good enough reason.*

He went over to the shelf, scanned the volumes there for a moment, and finally reached for the *Anabasis,* the "Journey of the Ten Thousand": a good textbook for a man who wasn't sure where to go or what to do next. Those Greeks had not, either. Marooned in Asia after their battle with a huge Persian force, their officers assassinated, trapped between the Persians and unknown country full of savage tribes, they headed home the long way—walked across a fourth of Eastern Europe as it was in those days—until they found the sea. Nothing had stopped them, not fear or famine or anything else. Just the thought of their dogged courage in the face of awful odds, and the cool counsel of the man who made himself their leader, Xenophon, was a tonic. Picard sat down and gladly opened the book at random, or not entirely. It fell open at a favorite spot, as so many of his books did—the place where Xenophon addresses the army. *They think that because they have killed our good old general Cleophas that we are helpless. They don't know that we are a whole army of generals, and we will yet find our home.*

He lost himself for a while in the terrible winter walk, the men marching with rag-wrapped feet through the ice and snow of the mountains, through dreadful hunger, not knowing the way, attacked by savage tribes as they went, until finally, cresting the last mountain, they saw the sea. *Thalassa, thalassa!* they cried, weeping for joy as they shouted, racing down to the beaches, and the breath caught in Picard's throat—

—and the red-alert sirens went, and he was up out of his chair before his communicator even had time to speak.

He hurried out of the ready room into the bridge. Everyone looked startled, and Troi, in her seat, looked actively upset. "What is it?" he said to Data. The main screen was showing empty space.

"Nothing now," Data said. "But we have just had a contact—fleeting. The helm took us immediately back out of range, as programmed."

"What was it?"

"Here, Captain." The view on the screen flicked. Same starfield—but there was something in the center of it, very distant, that hadn't been there before: a small steel-gray speck.

"Enlarge ten times," Picard said. The speck seemed to leap forward.

It was *Enterprise*. But not *his Enterprise*. It was a dark gray, even enlarged, a gunmetal color, cool and unfriendly.

The design was overtly the same—the great sloped disk of the primary hull, the nacelles, the secondary hull, all where they should be. But the secondary hull seemed larger; the nacelles were raked farther forward, and lower. The primary hull's curve was deeper and now had a frowning look about it. If ships had expressions, this one had its eyes narrowed. It was a cruel look, and intimidating. Just visible, because of the rake of the primary hull, were the characters *ICC 1701-D ISS ENT*— The rest was curved away out of sight.

Picard's heart seized at the sight of it. In a way, he had been hoping that everything that had happened so far might have some other answer. But the hope, he now saw, was in vain. The proof of the problem had come hunting them. He looked around, seeing the same unhappy look on everyone's face—and Troi still looked ashen.

"Keep us away from it, Mr. Redpath," Picard said. "No heroic measures without my orders: maintain your 'bumpercar' program for the time being. But I want any radical course changes reported to me immediately. It's time to make some choices. Mr. Data"—Picard turned to him—"I want you to go through all available Federation records for anything that might be even slightly pertinent to our problem. Contacts with parallel universes, real or purported, duplicate ships or personnel—*anything,* no matter how farfetched. I need a choice of action, and to do that we must have all the pertinent information we can lay our hands on. Then the department heads' meeting, as scheduled."

"Aye, sir," Data said, and went up to one of the science consoles to see about it.

"Counselor?" Picard said. She looked at him with the expression of someone who would like to be sick, but has too much to do.

"That ship," she said, "emotionally speaking, is a sinkhole. So much rage and fury and hatred, lust and envy and—" Troi shook her head, plainly finding it hard to find words. "I would say that our extra Mr. Stewart is extremely typical of the people you will find there."

Picard nodded. "Department heads' meeting as scheduled," he said, and left the bridge—possibly, he had to admit to himself, in search of his own composure.

An hour later, in the conference room, it was mostly back in place.

"Reports," Picard said. "But first of all, how is our 'guest'?"

"No change, Captain," Dr. Crusher said. "I might suggest we get him out of my sickbay, as I can use that bed."

"All right," Picard said. "Have him put in secure quarters."

"And by the way," Crusher said, "I find no indication of any subcutaneous transporter link anywhere on or in him. I checked everything—his bones, even the fillings in his teeth."

"Fillings?" Geordi said.

"Don't ask," Crusher said. "Their dentistry is a touch on the invasive side."

"All right," said the captain. He looked at Data. "Report, please."

Data folded his hands and looked thoughtful. "I have accessed all Federation data regarding parallel universes. Most of the information is either apocryphal or sheerly theoretical. However, there is at least one recorded instance of a Starfleet crew having had personal experience with and in a parallel universe."

"Where?" Picard said. "When?"

"Where is not necessarily pertinent in this connection and would actually be rather difficult to define," Data said.

"The when is stardate 4428.9; the personnel involved were members of the command crew of NCC 1701, before any of the additional registry letters were added."

"That *Enterprise,*" Picard said softly. "Kirk's *Enterprise.* But this is a tremendous occurrence. How is it that this brush with another universe doesn't appear in the ship's formal service record?"

"All details regarding it were classified immediately afterward," Data said. "Starfleet was apparently concerned about the effects of dissemination of the information: they thought other species might find it either ethically distressing or militarily exploitable."

Picard found that pair of possibilities an odd one. "Continue."

"Apparently the event began as a transporter accident," Data said. "If *accident* is the correct term."

Chief O'Brien made a slightly pained face. "The transporters in those days didn't have the fail-safes built in that ours do now," he said. "In fact, the incident in question caused some fail-safes to be added. *Enterprise* was orbiting omicron Indi III, a planet called Halka. The ship's mission was to negotiate with the planetary government for permission to start dilithium-crystal mining there. Due to ethical constraints of the Halkans—the fear that the crystals might possibly at some future period, if not immediately, be used for warlike purposes—they had refused permission, and the crew were preparing to beam back to the ship. Space in the area was at that time experiencing an ion storm of severe force nine—"

"I'm amazed they considered using the transporter at all under such circumstances," Picard said.

O'Brien looked pained again. "The transporter was more of a rough-and-ready business in those days. More powerful than ours, even if not as sophisticated. Among other things, there were still disagreements about some of the theory affecting it—the effects of field phenomena like ion storms on the transporter, for example. It still wasn't fully understood how some aspects of it worked, or didn't work, under such circumstances. But the sheer power of the transporters of that period often managed to successfully bring people through, even in the face of very adverse conditions."

"However, the conditions in this case were most unusual," Data said, "as the *Enterprise* crew discovered shortly. It was the first known example of events in another universe directly influencing events in this one."

Geordi nodded. "I went through the debrief logs made by the four officers in question—Captain Kirk, his chief engineer, the ship's chief medical officer, and the communications officer. Their debriefs are just exhaustive— apparently they were all absolutely shocked by what they experienced and wanted to make sure that no details were lost. And the chief engineer made sure that the subroutine logs of the transporter during the event were appended to the debrief, which is going to be a big help. Anyway, the *Enterprise* personnel involved worked out that, while they were transporting up from Halka, their counterparts in a very closely associated parallel universe were doing the same thing. The congruence of field-shift densities in two universes so closely neighboring combined with the field-effect shifts caused by the ion storm and the 'troubled' nature of the star in question to produce what the chief engineer later referred to in his paper on the subject as an 'inverlap,' direct one-to-one matchings of field state, Dirac jumps, even shell frequencies, between the two transporting parties. The people from the *Enterprise* of our universe even arrived *inside the uniforms* of their simultaneously transporting counterparts." Geordi shook his head like a man who has just seen a pig fly and is still dealing with the unexpected reality. "But then, only a parallel-universe transfer could have caused something like that. And theory says that congruences between closely associated universes can run much, much closer—which could have had unfortunate effects for the *Enterprise*'s command crew, especially if the universe then running most congruent had been one that looked and felt *no* different from their own. They might have seen and felt nothing wrong or different and proceeded about their next mission . . . thus marooning themselves there forever. And marooning their counterparts here."

Picard put his eyebrows up. "I wonder," he said. "Korzybski would ask whether a difference that makes no difference is no difference."

"But the differences in that other universe might have been perceptible only later, Captain. Imagine, for example, making such an exchange yourself—but later finding that the 'not different' universe you've beamed into doesn't contain, for example, some member of your family . . . or the place where you grew up."

"It's a frightening thought," Picard said. "However, it would seem that the *Enterprise* crew found differences enough."

"Yes, sir, they did. They report that they all felt the abnormal transport during its duration—and that's unusual, too. When transport was finished, they found themselves in an equivalent transporter room, but in an *ISS* 1701—an Imperial starship." Geordi made a face. "You'll want to review the debriefs yourself, Captain. The descriptions that Captain Kirk left, the details—they're very unpleasant."

"In what way?"

Data looked thoughtful again. "There seemed to have been—it is perhaps imprecise to call it a 'moral inversion,' but what was clear was that this Empire, which still contained a Starfleet, was run along much different ethical guidelines, with different moral values, from those which our group of humanoid species take for granted. The captain describes the crewmen as 'savage, brutal, unprincipled.' The command structure of the ship seemed to be run, not on a rank or merit system, but by a system of the strong preying on the weak—'survival of the fittest,' or at least of the cleverest and least principled. Assassination was considered an acceptable way to move up through the ranks. Uniforms had changed, become barbaric, flamboyant. Numerous higher officers had personal guards. There were other changes. Access to many ship's functions had to be cleared by a security officer, whose main function seemed to be ensuring the crew's loyalty and obedience to the Empire and to the present command—however long it might last. This officer seemed to play somewhat the same role as did the 'political officers' on warships of the larger totalitarian regimes in Earth's late twentieth century. Such a security officer might be required, according to Captain Kirk's report, to kill a senior officer who did not carry out Imperial orders correctly—even to move into that officer's position."

Picard felt like shuddering. "I'll look into those records in full," he said. "Meanwhile . . ."

"Meanwhile," said Data, "the *Enterprise* crew from our universe quickly understood what had happened to them, but also quickly found themselves in an increasingly untenable position. Captain Kirk's counterpart was under orders to destroy the Halkan civilization if they refused to comply with the demand of the Empire that they be allowed to mine dilithium crystals there. Captain Kirk was forced to stall for time—and the stalling tactics nearly cost him his life in more than one assassination attempt—while his chief engineer worked out how to duplicate the effect and get them back home before the local field densities shifted back to normal and made the retransfer impossible. Kirk's science officer, faced with the presence of the crewpeople from the Imperial universe, also worked out what had happened and saw to it that his shipmates' counterparts were in the transporter waiting for the transfer when it happened. It was apparently a very close call, but everyone made it back to their appropriate universes in the end."

Picard shook his head. "And now," he said, "we find ourselves in what seems to be our universe—except it's not, exactly; and nearby, another *Enterprise.* Except it's not . . . exactly. It would seem to rule out coincidence." He looked at Data and Geordi. "Speculation?"

"It would appear that someone in that other universe has worked out how to reproduce the accident," Data said. "But at will, and on a different basis—not a transfer, but something more like genuine transporter function—controlled from one end, rather than induced accidentally at both."

"To what purpose?" Picard said.

"Even speculation about that would be difficult at this point," Data said. "But having read the *Enterprise* crew's reports, their descriptions of the aggressive and acquisitive nature of the Empire and its version of Starfleet—I would suggest that the motives of that other ship are very unlikely to involve either the desire for pure scientific knowledge or any spirit of altruism."

"You got *that* in one," Geordi said softly.

"I would stretch speculation this far," Data said. "That that other *Enterprise* is likely to be the instrument of our transfer—overpoweringly likely, for there are no planets or space-based facilities anywhere near here from which such a transfer, or transport, could be engineered. And at the very least, the transport would require a considerable amount of power."

"A starship's?"

"Probably," Data said. "Though it would be difficult to say for sure until we understand more about the actual method of transport. And that ship is liable to be the most reliable source of information. Additionally, I would estimate that the odds are at least good that a process of this sort can be reversed. Certainly that is how the crew of the earlier *Enterprise* managed to make their way back home. We will, of course, have this additional problem: it is possible that the ship and crew which engineered our coming here may not desire us to leave and will not cooperate. Certainly they do not desire us to know much, if anything, about *them*. That they have sent a crewman here covertly would seem to reinforce such a conclusion: otherwise, why did they not contact us openly?"

Picard thought about that for a moment. "Granted. Still, we must be sure of what we're dealing with. They seem to have managed to get a look at what our ship is like—or some one of our ships. I would like to do the same for them before going any further. Can we manage that?"

Geordi and Worf looked at each other. "We can try," Geordi said. "The one thing we did notice about them from that one quick contact is that their shields leak a lot of energy. That means their sensors have a lot of spurious signal to put up with when they're shielded. I think we can either tap their comms directly or put a listener probe very close to them, with enough countermeasures wrapped around it that they'll mistake it for shield-noise artifact."

"Were we able to obtain any other pertinent data about that other ship before we backed off?"

"The contact was very fleeting," Data said. "It is hard to tell as yet what may prove to be pertinent. But one piece of information, an omission rather than a commission: since the other ship knows we are out here somewhere, but has not yet found us, this suggests, further to Mr. La Forge's observations, that its sensors may not be up to the standard of ours."

Worf nodded. "Just as Klingon shipbuilding technology, for quite some time, concentrated on weapons capacity rather than sensor sensitivity . . . since it was considered that the function of a warship was to pursue and destroy, rather than lie quiet and spy."

"It might just be that they *prefer* to lie quiet and wait for what information their spy sends home," Picard said. "I wonder if it would have been wise to let him go on thinking himself undetected: it might have bought us time."

"It might have been the end of us," Riker said sharply, "depending on what he *did* manage to send. If I put a spy on another ship, it would be to find out about weapons and defense capabilities."

"That seems to have been what he was after, all right," Geordi said, "but he didn't get much, as far as I can tell—mostly information on the phaser and photon torpedo installations."

"That's too much as it is," said Picard, "but I suppose we should be grateful. Meanwhile"—he looked at Data and Geordi—"for our own sakes, we must continue to postulate worst case—that we *won't* be able to get the information we need from that other ship. What can you work out about how this interuniversal 'transport' was produced?"

Data and Geordi looked at each other helplessly. "Captain," Geordi said, "I can describe the possibilities to you in general terms—but generalities aren't theory, let alone the concrete equipment needed to produce the effect. And there are five or six different scholia of thought to consider —and growing out of each of those, literally hundreds of theoretical avenues to explore—any one of which might be right, or wrong: there's no way to tell without direct experiment. We don't dare waste the time trying to figure out which experimental pathways are blind. And even if my fairy godmother came down and handed me the theoretical details on a plate, I don't know that I have the material to build the equipment to make it happen. It may have taken *them* a good while, too—maybe the whole hundred-odd years since these people were last heard of."

"Possibly even longer," Data said. "Ship designs aside, there is no guarantee that time is running at the same speed in that universe as in this one, though odds are for it—the congruencies are otherwise generally very close. But in either case, Geordi and I concur. The information is going to have to be obtained from that other ship, one way or another."

"You think you can get at their communications?" Picard said. "Do you think you can get at their computer remotely?"

"Not a chance, Captain," Geordi said. "Someone is going to have to go over there."

Picard saw the set expression on Geordi's face and was sure he was thinking, *Almost certainly me.*

"Our situations are near-mirrors of each other, too," Geordi said. "They want us for something. We can't say what, now . . . but there's a chance that, when we get at their computers, we can find out what they want as well as finding out how to get ourselves home. It's a risk . . . but one we can't afford not to take."

Picard sat quiet a moment. "I must agree," he said at last. "We will have to devise a way to put an away team aboard that ship."

Riker nodded. "Not a large one. Two, maximum. I would think one of them *would* have to be Mr. La Forge, since the work mostly involves the computer, and that's chiefly his area of expertise."

"I concur," said Picard. "And the other?"

Riker looked reluctant. His eyes slid to Troi. She pursed her lips and nodded.

"We certainly know that I'm there," she said to Picard, "and that apparently I'm someone to be reckoned with. My empathic sense will certainly be useful as a warning device. For both reasons, it makes sense."

"Any further choices should probably wait for our first intelligence run," Data said. "Captain Kirk reported that he ran the crew roster and found differences. Crewmen who were aboard his own *Enterprise* were missing or had physical differences—others were present who did not exist aboard his own ship. And there were some whom he had simply not met, whom he met there for the first time. We will have to do some analysis of visuals, and ship's roster if we can get it, to see who is there first."

Troi looked up. "I could ask our 'guest,'" she said with a slight glitter in her eye.

Picard looked at her. "Counselor, if I didn't know you better, I'd think you had a very carefully concealed mean streak."

She shook her head vigorously. "Captain, you do know me better. And the dreadful fear I sense from that man every time I go near him—" She looked sober. "But I would suggest to you at the moment that we need all the tools, or weapons, that we can get. In this particular situation, this is a tool that I wouldn't be ashamed to use. My range varies, as you know, but I am still trying to shake the effects of our closest brush with that ship. It was a psychic midden. I support us getting out of here for personal reasons as well as the obvious practical ones."

"As long as those personal reasons don't contaminate your performance," Picard said.

She smiled at him ruefully. "I'm in no danger of that as yet. But living a life here, if that ship is typical of the surroundings . . ." She shuddered. "No, thank you. In any case, I think our guest will tell us what we ask."

"I wish you could ask him what his ship wants of us," Picard said.

"I don't think he's privy to that, Captain. I got a general sense from him that people in his echelons were not told any more than they needed to be told . . . and indeed he was rather resentful about that, that he wasn't warned, or warned thoroughly enough, about what he was going to find when he got here."

Picard nodded and said to Geordi, "Now, as to method . . ."

Geordi looked thoughtful. "We could hitch a ride back

with our friend's little device, Captain: the transport platform."

Picard shook his head. "Can you guarantee that the thing is carrying enough power to store your pattern as well? Are you willing to bet your life on it?"

Geordi looked uncomfortable.

"No," Picard said. "We'll do this our way."

Worf looked up then. "Possibly, if the alternate Ensign Stewart's original aboard our ship were willing to be sent there in the alternate's stead . . ."

Picard considered that very briefly, then shook his head again. "I would not send someone into that situation without most complete preparation, and I doubt he could be prepared completely enough, or, more to the point, that such a course of action would be very fair to him."

"The honor he would accrue would be considerable," said Worf.

Picard laughed softly. "Mr. Worf, no doubt it would, but I think we must look in other directions. Mr. La Forge, you and Chief O'Brien are going to have to try to work something out."

"At least we have the advantage of knowing what their transporter waveform looks like," O'Brien said. "We won't trigger *their* systems when we beam in."

"Unless they're suspecting we might try something like this," Geordi said, "and have changed *their* waveform, too."

O'Brien rolled his eyes. "Sure you're a pessimist. We can arrange a negotiable tuned-band match if you're worried."

"See to it," Picard said before the two of them got involved in one of the technology duels they loved. "Are there any other ramifications to be considered?"

"One more, I believe," Data said, folding his hands. "While we do not have the same kind of time limit for our intervention that the original *Enterprise* crew had, we may have another. Some theories of multiuniversal structure hold that the universes in a given 'sheaf' are not held rigidly in place in relationship to one another, like the pages of a book, but that they move with relation to one another, in patterns which may or may not recur, one universe sometimes being 'closer,' or easier of access to another given one, sometimes farther away. There is a possibility that this transfer has happened here and now because that other *Enterprise* was waiting for the congruence to be closer than usual."

Picard blinked in surprise. "Do you mean they were shadowing us?"

"No," Data said, "merely going about their patrol schedule—since we are in the same 'sheaf,' our movements can logically be expected to mirror each other's much of the time. However, in any case, I would not care to linger here too long—for if the universes move too far apart, the transfer might become more difficult, more dangerous—or even impossible until the present pattern moves into place again. And we have no way of knowing when that might be."

Picard considered that. "Your point is taken. Speed now becomes of the essence. The sooner we're out of here, the better—and the better our chances of getting out at all." He looked around the table and saw nothing but agreement in the faces there.

"Dismissed," the captain said.

CHAPTER 5

"It's not going to be easy," Geordi said.

Soft laughter came from behind him. "If it were," Eileen said, "you wouldn't be happy."

He turned around, surprised to see her coming toward him through the trees. "I thought you were off duty."

Lieutenant Hessan laughed. "I am. And so are you."

Geordi shook his head. "Not at the moment, I'm not. The captain has a problem he needs solved."

She looked around the forest in which Geordi had been strolling: big old pines, towering up a hundred feet at least, and growing closely enough together that they almost shut out the sky. Above them was some summer noontime, but down here, where they walked in silence on soft pine needles, the effect was a cool noncommittal twilight, with only here and there a ray of sunlight lancing down. "Bad one, huh?" she said. "Can't see the forest for the trees?"

"Huh," Geordi said, and smiled. "No . . . I just come here when I need to think, and staring at the status table isn't helping."

She fell in beside him. "Tell me about it."

"Well, you saw the routines I was starting to set up. 'Get at their computer,' the captain said. But even in our own ship it wouldn't be so easy. Over there—there's no knowing what kind of locks they're going to have on sensitive material. Or even whether they would be the same areas locked down. So I've got to find a way to get into the system that will also take me around the locks. Systems sabotage . . . it's the only way."

"Nasty."

"More than just that. It's a bizarre feeling. Usually it's all I can do to keep things running *right* around here. Now, to be working out ways to make them go wrong . . ." Geordi shook his head.

"If I were you, I'd try to enjoy it. Think of the times the computers have gone down right in the middle of something crucial, and how much you wanted to kick them." Eileen grinned with relish. "Well, now's your chance. And it won't even be your own computers you're kicking. I'd kick them every way I could and run home laughing."

"It's the running home that concerns me," Geordi said ruefully. But a slow smile spread over his face. "You've got a point, though."

"So. Start from the top."

Geordi nodded, scuffing at a pinecone in front of him and kicking it ahead of them as they walked. "We have three main computer cores," he said. "Two in the main hull, one in the engineering hull. They update one another every forty-two milliseconds, so that each of them carries all the ship's data, and any one of them can run the whole ship by itself."

"The usual protective redundancy," Hessan said. "So you've decided not to get at the computer in an obvious way, by one of the access terminals: you want to get at a core directly. And do what?"

"Fail one of them out of the system, probably by killing the subspace generator in the core, or just making it act up.

The other computers would instantly throw the failed one out of the system and shout for help."

Hessan nodded. "Meaning you. Or the other ship's version of you."

Geordi nodded, kicking the pinecone again as they came to it. "I keep thinking about that," he said softly. "Who am I over there?"

"Don't let it distract you. Let's assume that your counterpart is called for, and you or the team with you take him out of commission and get to work. What then?"

Geordi looked thoughtful for a moment, then nodded as they walked. "When the core is off-line and put into repair mode, almost all the lower-level security routines are automatically disabled to let the diagnostics work. I can then access a large amount of data and store it down to iso chips."

"'A large amount,'" Eileen said, smiling grimly. "How many chips can you carry, Geordi? You've got 256 banks of 144 chips each in that core. And how are you going to know which data to download?"

"That's the main problem. I've got the computer working on an 'expert' scan-for program: looking for loaded contexts and phraseology, certain kinds of mathematical and physics statements. Hwiii has made some suggestions and so has Data. Stuff in the program, squirt it into the core, get a fast reading of how many files have multiple matches of text—then do a hands-on assessment."

"That's where you're going to lose most of your time. How long are you planning to spend at this? How long are you going to be able to keep your counterpart on ice?"

"How long do we dare?" Geordi said, pausing to watch a black admiral butterfly soar by, leisurely and unconcerned. "But I have to get as much as I can—winnow it out, then squirt it out, probably. And as soon as I do that, the game's up. I'll have to get away however I can, meet the rest of the team."

"You don't think you're going to make it," Hessan said softly.

Geordi stopped, kicking gently at the pinecone again, scuffing it away and not going after it. "It's bizarre. I'd be less scared to go aboard a Borg ship than I feel about going aboard this one. Because it's familiar. Because it should be us—and it's *not*. Whatever we are over there—we're not what we ought to be, or so it seems."

Hessan sighed and strolled over to the pinecone. "How many chips, do you think?"

"Two hundred fifty-six terabytes per chip." He raised his eyebrows. "Ten or fifteen."

"You could piggyback them. A little surgery: they can take parallel architecture. Tell the replicator to sandwich on another layer of storage solid, with an intervening layer of nutef, or some other insulator. That would bring the chips up to five hundred twelve ters each, and you could still take fifteen if you felt the need. But you're going to want to transmit everything, you said."

Geordi nodded. "I'm bringing a small sealed-squirt transponder. I can hook it into the subspace generators in the core and lock onto a securable frequency—then narrow the squirt down so it'll pierce even erected shields, encrypt it, and blast the whole business back home in a matter of a few seconds."

Hessan nodded. "Better let someone else do the encryption key."

Geordi looked at her in surprise. "Why?"

She shrugged. "If the you over there is *really* like you, he might be able to figure it out, if *you* devised it. Whereas if I do it . . ."

Geordi smiled at her. "Now I understand why Commander Riker's been following you around."

She blushed, and he saw the bloom of infrared quite clearly and refused to comment.

"Oh, yeah?" she said quite coolly.

"Yeah. Because you like to *manage* . . . but you make it look nurturing." He grinned, and slowly, she did, too.

"What do you mean 'look' nurturing? I nurture just fine."

"Yeah," Geordi said innocently. "I heard you with the warp engines last week. 'Is Mummy's naughty little antimatter generator having a tummyache in its matter inlet conditioner? Now, now, have a nice stream of deuterium and everything will be—' "

Eileen clouted Geordi upside the head, not hard enough to unseat his visor, but hard enough to make him see stars that weren't the usual ones. "When I was finished," Eileen inquired sweetly, "did it work?"

"Absolutely it worked, would it have dared not to?" Geordi said, enthusiastic, and half-choked with laughter.

"Well, then," Eileen said, and leaned against the nearest pine tree with her arms folded and a satisfied expression on her face. "I'll do you a crypt key and store it in the computer for you. Don't peek at it."

Geordi nodded. "Can you do that tonight?"

"Only after you come down to Ten-Forward with me and have a cup of coffee or something before you go back to work. I refuse to leave you out here getting lost in the woods and worrying yourself."

From off in the depths of the forest came a long, low howl, almost an amused sound. Geordi grinned at Eileen's sudden reflexive look of alarm. "Arch," he said. The gateway into the corridor appeared, and he headed over that way. "Come on, Lieutenant . . . you can come back later with a picnic basket if you like. Grandma's house is just down that path."

Eileen hit him again, from behind, though not very hard. Chuckling, Geordi headed out into the hall and out of range.

* * *

Will Riker had long since learned that, most especially when he was nervous, micromanaging his people was no good. In any case, the captain knew they were doing their best and had gone off to get what sleep he could—so that was one worry off Riker's mind, at least temporarily. Meanwhile, the ball was in Mr. La Forge's court now, and hanging over his shoulder wouldn't help . . . no matter how much Riker wished it would. He had therefore taken himself out of the way for at least the next few hours and had made himself busy micromanaging someone else: Worf.

Since bringing the extra Stewart to sickbay, Worf had clearly been looking for something to shoot, damage, or otherwise work out his concern on. Riker knew this mood in him of old and had some practice in dealing with it before it got out of hand. Now, therefore, when the door to Worf's quarters opened at his signal, he put his head in and said, "Come on, I want you to see this."

"What is 'this'?" Worf was sitting behind his desk, looking distressed. Riker strolled around and looked: Worf was rerunning a display of the seizure of Stewart.

"Problems?"

Worf frowned. "I am not sure we acted with maximum efficiency."

Riker laughed out loud. "Worf, are you kidding? You acted exactly correctly. You're just upset about this new threat to the ship. A big threat, and you can't do anything about it."

"It is a considerable danger. I desire to anticipate—"

"You don't have enough data. Leave it be. I want you to come see a riot."

Worf looked up at Riker quizzically. "On board *this* ship?" he said, getting up. "And there have been no reports—"

"Come on," Riker said, and headed for the door. "Deck eleven," he said as they got into the turbolift.

A few moments later they stepped out and made their way down the hallway toward one of the main holodecks.

"What is this about?" Worf said, sounding suspicious.

"Another installment of our opera studies," Riker said mildly. Riker had been so fascinated that Klingons *had* opera at all that Worf had some time ago begun broadening his experience of it, tutoring Riker through the contextual barbed-wire tangles of the Old School classics such as *The Warrior's Revenge* and *Tl-Hahkh's Way,* as well as the more modern, outré, and accessible works such as *X and Y.* In return, Riker had started introducing Worf to some of the older Terran works (though he had been slightly startled to find that Worf considered such works as *Pique Dame* and *Der fliegende Holländer* "easy listening" and had lately been finding profound meaning in the Viennese operettas, which Riker had always found more provocative of high blood sugar than anything else.

Worf frowned. "I am not in the mood for *The Merry Widow* at the moment. I have enough problems."

Riker shook his head. "Nothing like that. Remember I told you there were some aspects of opera that you hadn't yet investigated fully?"

"That is so," Worf said, looking doubtful.

"Program *Traviata* One running," the computer said mildly to them as they approached the door.

"Good," Riker said. "Open."

The door slid open, and a roar came out. It was not applause. It was the sound of many voices crying for someone's blood. Worf looked at Riker with a bemused expression; Riker grinned at him. They stepped in, the doors shut behind them.

It took Riker's eyes a few moments to get used to the dark. He suspected Worf's were adjusting faster, to judge by his glance around him, amused, and his slight grin. Slowly the gilded obscurities of the great old opera house of La Scala came into being around them. They were up in one of the second-tier boxes on the right side of the house, and down below them, faintly illuminated by the light of the stage, people in evening clothes were standing in their seats, even on them, throwing things at the stage and howling imprecations.

"I told you we ought to discuss violence in opera," Riker said. "This seemed like a good time."

"I thought you meant *in* opera," Worf said, looking down in mild astonishment as two men in white tie began a fistfight. Several ladies around them fainted decorously; other ladies, and various gentlemen, began betting on the outcome—at least it looked like it, as money was changing hands.

"We are 'in,'" Riker said with a grin, and sat down, leaning on the railing in front of the box. "Or as 'in' as we need to be. I confess, though, I'm curious: does it ever get like this at the Great House at tl'Gekh?"

Worf shook his head, looking down at the stage with delight. The set and flats, depicting a fashionable nineteenth-century salon, were rapidly becoming splattered with broken eggs, and tomatoes better suited to pasta sauce than to salad. Shattered cabbages lay about, and the occasional, doubtless symbolic, lemon. "There are occasional duels," Worf said, "but they take place outside. These days no one would dream of disturbing the performance so."

"Even when it was terrible? The tenor was, this night. Pietro Dominghi, it was. He won't come out now—listen to them yelling for him!"

They listened. The cries were not so much for Dominghi as a whole performer, but for the man in pieces. "Wait till the carabinieri show up," Riker said. "Then you'll see something."

They watched the police show up and plunge into the crowd. The crowd's reaction seemed to indicate that they considered this a private riot, not one that just anyone

could join. Without hesitation they turned on the carabinieri, and soon policemen were flying in all directions,
crashing among the seats, several of them even being tossed
out of the lower boxes and into the aisles.

Riker watched Worf with satisfaction. The Klingon was
twitching slightly in sympathy as blows went home, looking down at the huge fracas with cheerful approval. "These
people are true warriors, and this is great art."

"You think *this* is art," Riker said, "wait till the performance gets started again."

It took some minutes, of course, but the diva in question
chose her moment perfectly, a period a few breaths long in
which the rioting had paused for its own breath. In crimson
lace and an awesome jet-black mantilla, holding in one
hand an oversize fan depicting the Judgment of Paris and
in the other a Baccarat bell-goblet full of champagne, the
great Irish-Czech soprano Mawrdew Czcgowcz strode out
into the brief lacuna of sound and the vegetable-laden
stage. With the fan she imperiously gestured at the conductor for him and his people to stop crouching in the pit as if
they were about to be shelled. They obeyed, as much to
their own surprise as anyone else's. She whispered a word
or two to them; the conductor hissed the same word to the
orchestra as they put themselves back in order. Toscanini
tapped for the downbeat, and the orchestra plunged into
the heady rhythm of the prelude to the *Sempre libera*.

"Follie," Czcgowcz sang, *"FOLLIE!"*—each cry loud
enough to stun anything with ears. The police and the
rioters together stopped fighting and fell silent, staring at
the consumptive apparition now moving in a graceful
whirling dance among the splattered eggs and the cabbages,
beginning to sing in ecstatic upscaling cadenzas of the
delights of living free, no matter how short the life was.

"Now *there* is crowd control," Riker murmured, but
Worf was whispering the words of the aria along with
Czcgowcz, lost in the moment. Riker smiled. Czcgowcz

plunged along with abandon to the *"giaoure!"* passage, and only then did Worf turn to him, on the high B flat, and say, "She is in great pain!"

"No, no, that's just the way she takes her highs." He remembered his grandfather saying to him, "She sounds like a vacuum cleaner, but that's just the way she is." Riker smiled as Czcgowcz headed for the end of the aria, the optional E natural above high C hanging fire, and she hit it and held it in full chest, possibly in violation of several natural laws. There were involuntary shrieks of pain or disbelief from around the opera house, and here and there tiny chiming noises as a few prisms of the Waterford crystal hanging about the houselights shattered in the onslaught of sound. Wild applause went up, a roar as full of praise as the earlier one had been of bloodthirstiness; and Czcgowcz flung the Baccarat goblet at the nearest flat, where it shattered, and bowed herself down to her skirts, among the wild shrieks of approbation and delight. Even the fistfights that shortly started again had an abstracted air about them. Worf applauded wildly, grinning over at Riker.

"More?" Riker said. They reviewed all the best ones— first that evening at the Paris Opera in 1960 when the fighting started in the middle of a performance of *Parsifal,* something to do with an accusation about the tenor and what was going on out of sight in the bottom of one of the swan boats; then the great Metropolitan Opera Riot of 2002, when the holographic special effects malfunctioned in the middle of the new production of the *Ring,* and the critic from the *Times* was tracked down and spray-painted by enthusiasts unknown shortly after the appearance of the morning edition containing his review; then the cloned-Bernstein revival of *West Side Story* on Alphacent in 2238, at which the composer's clone, gone insane from unnoticed single-bit DNA errors, started firing a phaser into the audience in his outrage at having been revived.

"I think I can do better than that," Worf said, and began instructing the computer to retrieve the hard-video storage of the 28844 production of *X and Y,* in which the soprano had declared her family in a blood feud with the tenor's due to a salary dispute and had killed k'Kharis onstage, *before* his aria was finished (etiquette usually mandated letting the performance end first).

"Sounds like a good one," Riker said.

"There were three days of street fighting, and the government fell," Worf said with some relish. "And *then—*"

"Data to Commander Riker."

Riker looked at Worf with a resigned expression and shrugged. "Riker here, Mr. Data."

"Our probe is within range of the other Enterprise," Data said, *"and we are receiving signal leakage per Mr. La Forge's prediction. I think you will want to see this."*

"We're on our way."

When they came onto the bridge, everyone else on it who could possibly spare an eye from his or her duty was gazing at the main viewscreen with expressions ranging from horror through frightened fascination. Riker swung down to where Data sat at his console, working carefully over the controls. "You're recording all this, of course."

Data nodded, glanced up at the screen again. It had been showing a corridor, empty when Riker came in, looking no different from one of their own corridors. Now the view shifted to show a different hallway, with some crewmen in it, going about their business. Their uniforms were odd— one-piece uniforms, more or less duplicating the look of the familiar two-piecers, but the collars were cut uncomfortably high for Riker's tastes, and the uniforms' colors were extremely somber, the maroon gone a dark blood-russet, the green gone green-brown. Some few crewmen wore sashes of some silver or gold material around their waists, an odd and barbaric splash of brilliance against the darkness. But odder, and more ominous to Riker, he noticed that every one of the passing crewmen was armed. Phasers mostly, particularly large and threatening-looking ones. But there were a few knives, as well, and one crewman, a gray-skinned hominid from some species Riker didn't immediately recognize, went by wearing at his waist, unsheathed, something that most closely resembled a machete.

"Naturally we cannot read directly from ship's optical-fiber communications with the present equipment," Data said to Riker as he worked, "but the comms system RF backups are running concurrently, and even quite marginal leakage from them can be read without too much trouble —though that will change if the ship's shields go up."

"That they're not up now," Riker said with some relief, "would seem to imply that they feel themselves to be safe and undetected . . . so far, anyway."

"I would concur," Data said. "I am currently 'piggy-backing' an active internal scan presently being conducted aboard the other ship. Unfortunately, since this surveillance is passive, we are unable to choose what location in the other ship we view. But I am logging RF-transition frequencies and optical output and input data for each view we get. With random factors operating in our favor, we should be able to return to a given established view later, at least while the eavesdropping probe remains in range and undetected."

I hate it when even Data admits we need luck on our side, Riker thought. "If they show any signs of detecting it," he said, "I want it out of there on the double. I don't want them getting their hands on any of *our* technology. Destroy it if necessary."

"Understood," Data said. For a few seconds, the screen was again empty of crewmen, showing an empty corridor.

Then it changed view again, to a different hallway this time, looking down toward a turbolift.

"I am uncertain whether the scan we are seeing is being directed by someone aboard the ship or is an automatic function," Data said. "But one thing is certain: this *Enterprise* has many more internal visual pickups than our own does. There are the usual video pickups associated with personal viewscreens and data readout locations, as well as the basic security surveillance system in high-security areas like engineering and the computer cores . . . but also many more, spread throughout the ship, even in crew quarters. Moreover, those appear not to be under the control of the occupants. The implications are . . . distressing."

"No kidding," Riker said softly as the view changed again, engineering this time. Crewmen moved about their work with what seemed to him more intensity than necessary. No one he had so far seen on this ship seemed able to move with any kind of ease. *But why should they?* Riker thought then. *When anyone might be looking at you, anytime, to see if you're doing your job—and if you're not . . .* He shook his head, thinking about the fear of punishment that Deanna had reported in "Stewart."

"You're keeping tabs of the names and ranks of anyone who shows up in this scan, of course," Riker said.

"Of course. So far we have seen forty-four crewmen whose presence is duplicated aboard our own ship, and only five who are unknown. This would closely approximate—"

The view changed, and Data broke off in midsentence, staring along with everyone else. It was the bridge. At least, the shape was the same, and the general structure of it. But there were differences.

It was darker. *Their night?* Riker thought, then shook his head, doubting it. Paneling and furnishings were in the same sort of gunmetal gray as the exterior of the ship, with lines of paler gray being used more as highlighting than anything else. The computer installations around the upper tier, too, were different. The engineering station was about as it should have been, but mission Ops and the science stations were much reduced, and combined with engineering. Every other station in the upper tier, from the starboard lifts to the main viewer, was now part of a long sweep of weapons-control consoles, with crewmen standing at them, unnervingly vigilant. Riker stared at those consoles, with tree upon tree of power-level readings and weapons status readouts; he thought of the kind of phaser power and photon torpedo loads this vessel must be carrying . . . and he felt like shuddering.

It was not just the emphasis on weaponry: it was that combined with the general look of the bridge, for though dark, it was also much more luxurious than his own *Enterprise's*. The three center seats, empty at the moment, had a plush, easy-chair look about them, and the centermost of them, the captain's chair, looked more like a throne than anything else. You were plainly meant to enjoy sitting in them, at the heart of all this deadly power. Just as plainly to Riker, you were meant to enjoy using it.

The broad back of one crewman had been turned to them until now, while he studied one of the science consoles. Now he turned toward them, back to the security console—also much enlarged, so that the curve of it ran much higher and farther along the back of the center seats than in Riker's own ship. Now he drew in breath at the sight of the man, for he hadn't recognized him without the characteristic sash. It was Worf. He looked the same as always. *Except,* Riker thought. That face wore even more frown than usual, and it was graven deep, a settled look. *Pain,* Riker thought.

He glanced over at his own Worf, who was looking at his counterpart with an expression of which Riker could make nothing.

"Discommoded?" Riker said softly. Worf shook his head, not answering. "Data, can we get sound?"

"Not without losing vision," Data said. "This mode of surveillance will permit us only one sort of bandwidth at a time—sound is carried on another channel. I would have to switch."

Riker opened his mouth to tell him to try it—then shut it again as the captain's ready room door opened.

The shock that went through him, even though he had been expecting to see this man since Deanna's report, was still horribly unsettling. *I don't walk like that!* was his first thought. Well, possibly he himself didn't—though now he had doubts—but this other Riker plainly did. The man who had come out of the ready room now stood for a moment looking at the main viewer, then turned to one of the crewmen at the weapons-control boards and snapped some question or order.

The crewman turned and answered quickly. Riker looked at the other Riker's face, and now he *did* shudder; he couldn't help it. Their faces were identical: this was the face he saw when he trimmed his beard in the morning. And regardless, he hoped no one ever saw *this* face on him. There was a curl to the lip, another of those worn-in frowns, that made this other Riker look like a thug. He remembered his mother, a long time ago, saying, *Don't make those faces, your face will get stuck that way,* and one of his command-psych instructors at Academy saying, *I don't have to ask you how you are: I can tell just by looking at you. Do you really believe that twenty years or more of your emotions and basic outlook telling your facial muscles how to behave, eighteen hours or so a day, doesn't leave any traces? It takes time . . . but it's just like water on stone, and just as impossible to erase once it's done . . . except by changing the mind inside the face. And sometimes not even then.*

Riker looked at his counterpart's face and tried to

imagine what could make a man's face, *his* face, into something like this . . . then shied away from the prospect. Instead he shifted his attention to the man's uniform. It was different, again, but in a new way: it was sleeveless, the black vee yoke that normally ran over the shoulders cut off to leave the muscular arms bare, and the short tunic was belted at the waist with another of those woven-gold sashes, supporting a big nasty-looking phaser on one side, and a ceremonial-looking dagger on the other. The knife seemed to be a recurring motif: in uniforms, and—Riker noticed with shock—even on the doors to the turbolift, where the Starfleet parabola was etched into the paneling —with a square-handled dagger neatly impaling it.

That other Riker sat down in the center seat and looked thoughtfully at the front viewscreen, said something else to the single form minding the conn console: Wesley Crusher. Riker couldn't clearly see Wes's face from this angle, but the ensign turned slightly and made some answer. Apparently the other Riker was satisfied: he sat back in that thronelike chair, pulling at his lower lip.

"No Data," Worf said from behind Will.

Riker shook his head. "Not aboard, you think? Or just somewhere else?"

"We have no way of telling as yet," Data said. "I am trying to devise a way to get at the other *Enterprise*'s crew roster, but frankly, I doubt I will be able to manage it by this means. I suspect Mr. La Forge will have to help us with that when the away team goes over."

Riker shook his head. "Any way to tell where this particular scan is being run from?"

Data shook his head again. "If I were reading this signal from the optical comms network, it would have the usual packet-header information on origin and so forth. But the RF network is usually used for emergencies only and does not employ the headers."

Data stopped again as the turbolift doors opened, and

someone came in. Riker's jaw dropped, and he stood up in astonishment.

"My God," he whispered.

Deanna Troi stood there, a little behind Worf, coolly looking the bridge over. *It's not just faces that change,* Riker found himself thinking, as much in horror as in wonder. The Deanna Troi he knew, true to her training, tended to be nonthreatening, held her body and her vocal and mental attitudes in neutral ways that invited others to reach out. But *this* woman—she stood there erect and dangerous-looking, not trying in the slightest to minimize the effect. She carried herself like a banner, like a weapon. *Like an unsheathed knife.*

"Not the usual uniform," Worf said, managing to sound both disturbed and impressed.

"You're right about that," Riker said. The only thing this woman's uniform had in common with Deanna's usual uniforms was that it was blue. The harness—there was almost too little of it to call it a top, or even a bodice—seemed to be made of woven gold, like the ornamental sashes. More woven metal, blue this time, bordered it, and the bordering met and gathered up at the left shoulder to support the parabola-and-knife insignia. From the gather, over the shoulder, fell several folds of the blue fabric, the gold interwoven with it, down to about waist height. The right shoulder was bare, as was this Troi's midriff. Then, quite low on the hips, the skirt began—that blue metallic fabric again, gracefully flowing down just past the tops of the above-the-knee boots this Troi wore, but cut right up to the weapons belt at the hip on the right side, leaving a handspan's space bare between its attachment to the belt at front and back. A phaser hung holstered there, and in a neat sleeve down on the outside of the right-hand boot lived the dagger, which Riker was now beginning to think was standard wear for officers.

Ensign Redpath was staring at all this wide-eyed. Riker

could hardly blame him. As they watched, the other Troi made her way down to the command level, looked at the main viewer for a moment, then turned to Riker and simply gazed at him, the kind of look, Riker thought, that a barbarian queen might turn on some jumped-up commoner who dared to sit in her chair.

The other Riker simply leaned back for a moment, looked at her lazily, and smiled slightly. The thought that seemed to live behind that smile actually made Riker go hot with embarrassment: he was irrationally glad that Deanna wasn't on the bridge. After a moment, the other Riker said something, then tilted his head to one side to watch Troi's reaction.

She made none: that lovely face seemed frozen. But Riker's face changed abruptly. He got up out of the center seat in a way that suggested he was trying not to make it look as if he were in a hurry—though he desperately *was*. Troi watched him get up, let him stand for a moment, just watching him. Their eyes locked again, and once again, the other Riker was the first to look away.

Then Troi stepped forward and sat down in that center seat, like a queen enthroning herself, and looked at the viewscreen for a long moment, then up at Riker.

And smiled—an expression of pleased threat and absolute mastery, an expression like poison over ice.

Riker's heart seized inside him. The screen went blank. He wanted to say to Data, "Get that back!"—except that he wasn't really sure he *wanted* it back.

"Scan discontinued at the other end," Data said after a moment. "I will try to lock on to another."

"Who was running that scan, I wonder?" Riker murmured.

Data looked thoughtful. "It is a question I had been considering. Normally surveillance scans are done by personnel superior in rank to those who are being observed. But in this case . . ." Data shook his head.

Riker breathed out. "How much sleep has the captain had?"

"I would estimate some five hours," Data said, "assuming he was able to *get* to sleep."

"Give him another hour," Riker said. "Try to get another scan if you can. Then page him."

"Affirmative."

Beverly Crusher was sitting wearily at her desk, cleaning up some backed-up work—the evaluation of the anomalous members of a group of routine tissue serologies—when a voice said out of the air, *"Ryder to Dr. Crusher."*

She touched her badge absently. "Yes, Brendan, what is it?"

"Doctor, I think we'd better get Stewart back to sickbay."

"Why?" she said, sitting up straighter. "What's the matter with him?"

"Well, he was asleep, and I thought his breathing started to sound kind of funny. So I woke him up—or tried to; he wouldn't wake up, not all the way. He's lying here looking groggy, and he doesn't seem able to speak."

"Bring him straight down!" Beverly said, getting up and heading out of her office. Somehow she found that this occurrence didn't surprise her at all: she had had one of those edgy feelings all this evening, the sense that something was going to go wrong, or more wrong than it had gone to date. "Bob," she said to her late-shift nurse, "is Three available again? Pull up Stewart's readings on it, I want them for a baseline."

"He's coming back?" Lieutenant Rawlings said, and moved to the bed. As if in answer the sickbay doors opened and in came Ryder and Detaith, in their haste not even having bothered to break out a floater, but carrying Stewart between them.

They put him hurriedly but carefully on the diagnostic bed, and Beverly moved in, glancing at the baseline readings, then watching them change. Stewart's temperature was pushing thirty-nine centigrade, he was pale and clammy with perspiration, his breathing was stertorous enough so that the rasp of it going in and out was audible, and though his eyes were partly open and the pupils were reactive, Stewart was plainly stuporous.

She waved the medipheral over him, watching the readout over the bed. *Infection,* she thought, *but where the hell from?* The symptoms looked almost like one of the dreadful old respiratories such as diphtheria or typhus. Even now, such were not wiped out right across known space. Old stocks of one pathogen or another would lie dormant for years or mutate into drug-resistant forms and have to be beaten down all over again.

Beverly swallowed as the diagnostic bed reported the patient's blood to be teeming with viral organisms. *They weren't there four hours ago!* she thought in angry protest, but her anger was doing her patient no good. For the moment, symptomatic treatment was in order, then detailed analysis of the virus or viroid.

Bob had come up beside her with loaded hypos. "Aerosal?"

She nodded, glancing at the hypo he held out. "Double that dosage; I want his temp down fast. Then a broad-spectrum antiviral." Bob held out a second hypo, loaded with Scopalovir this time. "Right," she said, "and beam a blood sample out of him, and have Helen analyze that virus and start tailoring antibodies. Then get the immune stimulator on him, too, and start selective fluid transport out of that right lung—it's congested worse than the other. I'll be right back."

She stepped into her office, waiting for the door to close, and touched her badge. "Sickbay to Riker."

"Riker. What's up, Doctor?"

"Stewart's temperature—and a lot of other things are

wrong, too. The man's halfway to congestive heart failure. He's full of something viral."

"Life-threatening?"

"I believe so."

"Contagious?"

"Unknown, but somehow I doubt it." Her mouth set grim. "Isn't this about the time his *Enterprise* was supposed to 'pick him up'?"

There was a brief silence.

"Damn," Riker said.

"My thought exactly. Is the captain available? He ought to be informed."

"He's just awake now. He was expecting to be on the bridge in about twenty minutes, he said."

"Better ask him to come down here, then, after you've briefed him. This is going to be touch and go."

"Will do. Out."

Beverly went back outside and plunged into the fight for Stewart's life.

Half an hour later, Beverly looked up from her desk viewer to see Picard walk into sickbay. He paused by Stewart's bed. The man lay there with Rawlings working over him, one of the silver "space" blankets pulled up over him. Rawlings glanced at Picard with a subdued expression. Picard nodded to Rawlings and headed for Beverly's office.

As the door closed behind him, she glanced up at Jean-Luc with some concern. "Did you get enough sleep?"

He waved the question away, though not as irritably as he might have, and sat down. "I take it that the prognosis isn't good."

She shook her head, looked out through the office walls. "What treatment we're giving him is essentially palliative at this point. We could keep him on life support indefinitely, of course, but besides the ethical constraints, there would be no point in it: his nervous system is disintegrating."

Picard blinked. "Is this something secondary to that neural damage you mentioned?"

"No, but that's making him a lot easier to kill." She turned her viewer so that he could see the screen. "Look."

Picard looked at the diagram there: the familiar shell-coat and coiled-DNA interior of a virus. "This is what's infesting him?"

"This is what he was inoculated with," Beverly said, once again feeling her insides twist up with loathing at the thought. "This virus is tailored specifically to his genetic structure. Stewart came aboard carrying it. It was hiding inside him, like one of the old 'slow' viruses. This one has been instructed to hide inside white blood cells, encapsulated, so as not to trigger either the immune response or our scans."

"A nasty variation of the 'purloined-letter' technique."

Beverly nodded. "Worse yet, the thing was programmed to go off at a specific time. It's doable enough—you program a secondary protein casing around the virus that defeats the virus's attempts to reproduce, then simply tell the coating when to come apart and turn the little monsters loose. It's actually a variation of a technique that's used for therapy on intractable cancers in quite a few different species. A perversion of it, rather."

"I take it," Picard said, looking over his shoulder for a moment, "Stewart's time ran out."

Beverly nodded again, wearily. "By the time the security people noticed that something was wrong with him, the damage was already mostly done. The virus was keyed to attack the myelin sheaths of his nerves—meaning the white matter of his brain as well as the major myelinized conduits in his spinal cord. Cerebellar malfunction follows, along with respiratory dysfunction, coronary insuffi-

ciency, not to mention brain damage—his corpus callo-
sum is almost fused."

"He will die, then."

"He will." For a moment they were both quiet. "The
worst of it," Beverly said, "is that they never planned to
pick him up. Probably they assumed that, if we didn't find
him first, he would start feeling bad and hide himself
somewhere—then die quietly in a corner."

Picard's face was very still; but he looked up at her
without expressing anything more of what he was feeling.
"If I know you," he said very gently, "that is *not* the worst
of it."

She looked up at him and sighed at her own readability
at times like this. "No," Beverly said finally, "it's not.
What *is* worst is the probability that it was my counterpart
on the other *Enterprise* who is responsible for this."

The look of shock on Jean-Luc's face said that he
understood the problem.

"The work has my fingerprints all over it. The structure
of the outer coat on the virus, even the spiral-structured
flagellum it used to site itself in the lymph nodes—they're
details I've built into cancer cures before." Beverly swallowed. "What kind of universe is it where the usages of
medicine allow a practitioner to do such things? What *is* a
doctor here? Or worse—"

"What kind of doctor does such things if the usages of
medicine *don't* allow them?" Picard said softly.

"Exactly," Beverly said, and couldn't bring herself to say
anything more.

"Doctor?" said Lieutenant Rawlings, putting his head in
the door.

She and Picard both looked up. "Captain," Bob said.
"I'm sorry, Doctor, he's gone. Even the cortical stimulator
couldn't keep him going any longer. There wasn't enough
myelin left on the bronchial nerves or the coronaries to
transmit the stimulus."

"All right," Beverly said. "Put him in stasis for the time being: I'll want to do the autopsy in a while."

"And what about *your* sleep?" Jean-Luc said. Beverly opened her mouth, and the captain raised a finger to stop her as he got up. "I need you functional. Physician, heal thyself *first.*"

She made a wry face at him. "Yes, sir, Captain, sir," she said as insubordinately as she could. She wished greatly that she could smile at him a bit, but there was no smiling in her at the moment.

"I'll want a report when you've had at least four hours' sleep. No sooner. That *is* how long you're always telling me it takes the body to 'do its laundry,' isn't it?"

Beverly got up. "I would report you for parroting professional advice without a license if I could do it without dropping off in the middle of the report."

The captain raised an eyebrow at her, then went out, but not without a long, thoughtful gaze at the shape on the diagnostic bed, now wholly shrouded in silver, and very still.

Geordi and O'Brien were going over the last of the schematics at the master display console in engineering when Picard came in. Both of them looked worn, but also excited, and O'Brien's expression was almost one of triumph.

"Mr. Riker tells me you gentlemen have your options in place," Picard said. "Report, please."

"The logistics first," O'Brien said. "Captain, you wanted some way to get people aboard the other *Enterprise* that didn't involve shoving them into that little probe-platform and hoping their pattern comes out all right at the other end."

"Yes."

"Well, the basic idea was sound," O'Brien said, "so I stole it. The problem with the platform was the danger it exposed the subject to. Transporter pattern is really not meant to be stored in such a poorly powered pattern buffer. Well enough. So how about using a regular one?" He grinned. "We take a shuttlecraft, install a transporter pad and complete buffer structure in it."

Picard blinked. "Is that feasible?" he said to Geordi.

Geordi shrugged. "No reason whatever it can't be done, with fairly minor alterations to the shuttle's power systems. Our shuttles are overpowered anyway, the assumption being that they'll have to serve power and coprocessor needs for mobile research and intervention platforms—planetside installations and so forth."

"So," O'Brien said, "the away team takes the shuttle out to the point from which they want to beam over—and does so."

"What about detection, though?" Picard said, frowning. "No point in this exercise if that other ship notices it happening."

"Well," Geordi said, and got a sort of bad-boy grin. "Captain, I think I may have mentioned to you that I had written a couple of research papers for the *IEEE Journal* on field-phase theory as it affects the Romulan cloaking device."

"You did mention it," Picard said, somewhat surprised, "but I wasn't quite sure that you weren't joking with me—or that the paper itself wasn't a joke. You seemed to be implying that you had worked out the theory."

"I had. But you know how it is, things get busy and I wasn't able to spend much time building the prototype to test the theoretical assumptions. Well, we've had enough encounters with Romulan ships over time, both cloaked and uncloaked, to get a lot of data on the phase shifts inherent in the generated 'cloak' field. I don't say that I've duplicated *the* 'proprietary' Romulan cloaking device, but I've produced a small, low-level 'generic' one. So they won't be after us for copyright infringement." Geordi grinned. "It's mostly a phase-shifted optical redirection field—it looks at the starfield or other background behind you, inverts it, and 'redistributes' it forward, adjusting for parallax effects and so forth in whatever's most likely looking at you. There are also self-cancellative functions built in, so that it seems not to be there, eight milliseconds out of ten, even when you scan specifically for it. It doesn't do what the real Romulan cloak does in terms of energy output—damping down shield and propulsion artifact—but for a shuttlecraft, it won't have to: that shielding can be managed mechanically."

"What about mass sensing?" Picard said.

Geordi smiled. "I did a little tinkering. The field is doubled with a graviton mirroring field on its inside. Gravitons are only half of the way we sense mass, but they're the important half: it's the 'particulate' component of gravity that triggers our mass sensors, and I'm betting theirs are the same. The field can be collapsed for millisecond periods to keep graviton-buildup anomalies from becoming a problem."

Picard sighed. "Well, that would seem to solve the problem. I would congratulate you, gentlemen—if the success weren't going to imminently place one of you in even worse danger." He looked from O'Brien to Geordi again. "But you're quite sure about the feasibility of this work on the shuttlecraft?"

"Yes, sir," Geordi said. "It won't exactly be a stroll down O'Connell Street."

O'Brien said, "Well, *marginally* simpler. But it can certainly be done. It waits only your order."

"Then make it so."

"I'll get the engineering team down there," O'Brien said, and went off to see to it.

"Meanwhile," Picard said, "have you finished preparing your 'raid' on the computer core?"

Geordi nodded. "Yes, sir. It's as complete as I could

make it. Hwiii had a few suggestions, and he's looking the routines over and making additions even as we speak. By the time we have the shuttlecraft ready, the scan-and-download routine will be complete, and I'll be ready to go."

"Good." Picard sighed, then added, "Commander Riker tells me that a short while ago he got a scan of your counterpart in the other ship. He says your uniform will be ready in an hour or so—he wanted to work with the design team to make sure the tailoring was correct. He describes it, though, as 'somewhat drafty.'"

Geordi shook his head, bemused, and grinned. "The man's a perfectionist."

"Lieutenant," Picard said somewhat uncomfortably, and Geordi looked at him. "Understand that you are at liberty, even now, to refuse this mission if you feel it cannot be managed, or if the danger is too great. You'll be needed to implement the information you're going to fetch. There is no use losing you."

Geordi shook his head again, slowly this time. "Captain, it's got to be me. We've still got no evidence that Data is there. The counselor can't handle this . . . and she's going to have her hands full, anyway, watching my back for whatever might sneak up behind it. Don't you worry about me."

"I always worry, as you well know. Be sure that you take great care."

After that, work began in earnest down in the main shuttle bay. Picard went down to see the work once it was well in hand and found that O'Brien had been serious when he said that the alterations he planned wouldn't take long. He had simply had Geordi lend him nearly every engineering crew member on shift at that point, all but those supervising the engine room proper. About sixty people were swarming all over the shuttlecraft *Hawking,* taking out the extra chairs, flooring, and the other usual fittings, and installing the guts of a transporter array. It was still not a small-time installation, even with the considerable man-power working at it. Right now they had actually taken the side of the shuttlecraft off—the paneling first, then every-thing right down to the duranium framework—to fit in the two big round "tubs" that held the main and backup pattern buffer tanks, and the biofilter structures. They could have beamed the buffer tubs in, but there was so much work to be done routing the associated optical and other cabling through the body of the shuttle that it was as simple to partially disassemble it. The transporter's targeting scanners and the energizing and phase-transition coils were already installed against the ceiling of the shuttle. The control console, being modular, had taken the least trouble and had been put in first, slotted into one of the aft auxiliary-control bays. Other crew were busy install-ing Geordi's custom screen generators, and the relays by which O'Brien would be controlling the away team's trans-ports from the *Enterprise.*

"About half an hour till we're finished, sir," O'Brien said, "and then about half an hour for testing. Then Mr. La Forge and the counselor can go whenever they're ready."

"Very well," Picard said. "I wouldn't want to wait much longer than that. I'm having enough trouble understanding our counterparts' state of mind as it is, but I don't believe they'll think it would take us very long to notice"—he frowned—"a dead body. The sooner we get on with this and get our people back, the better I'll like it."

"Yes. I've installed an extra decontam routine in the biofilter circuits," O'Brien said quietly, "after what Dr. Crusher told me about Stewart. There's no telling whether other crew members might be carrying such tailored bugs around inside them—and I wouldn't want Mr. La Forge or the counselor to bring back copies of their own. We'll be taking very careful baseline measurements on their transport out, to make sure we have clean data to compare them against when they come home again."

Picard nodded approval. Across from them, the doors to the corridor opened, and Commander Hwiii came swimming in on his pad, carrying several isolinear chips in one of his manipulators.

"Captain," he said as he came up with them, "Chief—how is it going?"

"We'll be ready shortly," O'Brien said.

Picard reached out, curious at the different look of the chips. "Ah," he said, turning one over in his hands, "these are the new high-density chips."

"That's right," Hwiii said, "five hundred twelve terabytes each. Mr. La Forge should be able to pack a fair amount of what he needs into these, assuming that *this* does what we intend." He held one of them up.

"The search routines," Picard said.

Hwiii swung his tail in agreement. "He asked me to add what I could. The one thing I feel sure of, Captain, is that what's happened to us has something to do with the odd way that the hyperstring structure was behaving in our home space, just before we swapped over into this one. Besides Mr. La Forge's searches on crew information, history, and engineering science, I've added search parameters for everything that would seem to pertain to hyperstring theory in conjunction with engine performance, shield function, warpfield, and transporter theory —you sing it, it's here." Hwiii looked resigned. "The best I can manage. Nothing to do now but sound a few notes in the One's waters and hope for the best."

Picard felt more or less the same way. "Thank you, Commander," he said.

"Don't say it, Eileen!" came Geordi's voice from the doorway, sounding annoyed—though the annoyance still had a cheerful sound to it. Picard turned, saw him coming, and had to school his face to stillness.

" 'Drafty,' " he said to Geordi as the chief engineer of the *Enterprise* came up to them, his expression a study in rueful amusement. "I think Mr. Riker may have been understating somewhat."

Geordi spread his well-muscled arms for a moment in a helpless gesture, then let them drop. There was no doubt about the quality of their musculature, for the top half of the uniform he was wearing was more of that gold-mesh material, cut as an open-fronted vest. The rest of it was a matching sash at the waist, and black breeches that looked to have been sprayed onto him, the ensemble completed by high black boots and another of the officer-level knives.

Geordi was plainly caught between outrage and laughter. "This isn't an engineer's uniform, it's a stoker's jacket! What have they got in that ship, solid-fuel engines? 'Motors'? How hot does it *get* over there?" He waved his arms and laughed again, thoroughly embarrassed.

Picard had to cover his mouth, for the vest was skimpy, and while it showed off Geordi's physique to good advantage, it was no protection against anything whatsoever. The pants were as bad. Picard considered that he would have been nervous of bending over in breeches that looked like those—or even just wearing them, designed as they were to reinforce others' impression of the wearer's muscular, or other, puissance.

"Mr. La Forge," Picard said after a moment, "I'm sure you'll acquit yourself splendidly, regardless of the costume. Or the heat."

"There's more than one kind of heat, Captain," Geordi said, smiling slightly, "but I'll do my best. What's the score, Chief?"

O'Brien grinned a little crookedly. "Skin three, uniform nil, I'd say. . . . Oh, you mean the *shuttle,*" he added innocently as Geordi threw a mock-threatening look at him. "About another ten minutes, then we'll start testing cycles. Come on, have a look."

They went about it, and Picard watched the work crew finish the installation work on the shuttle, seal it up, and then start running diagnostics and beaming test objects in and out. O'Brien, in the right-hand seat of the shuttle, was busying himself with checking the scrambled subspace-radio relays to his own master transport console. "We'll be monitoring them constantly," he said to Picard, without turning around, when the captain drifted quietly up behind him at one point. "The doctor has put subcutaneous transponders in each of them. We won't use the communicator functions unless there's no choice—the signal generation, even though it's scrambled, would almost certainly draw unwanted attention to them. But we can still lock on and pull them out in a hurry if we have to."

"As long as that ship doesn't raise its shields," Picard said. That was one thought that had been haunting him.

O'Brien nodded. "If they can just keep from being noticed, they'll be all right."

"Quite so," Picard said, and got out of the shuttle, aware of his own nerves, not desiring to get on any of his people's. The feeling of helplessness that so often came over him when sending crew into danger was building in him now, much worse than usual. Unknown danger was one thing. *Known* danger was worse, in its way, and this mixture of the two was worse still. *These people are us . . . but somehow changed—and no way to tell how changed but by putting ourselves, or some of ourselves, in their way.* The thought was not even slightly reassuring. Kirk's notes on the old *Enterprise*'s experience had been as exhaustive as Geordi had said, and as upsetting. Ambassador Spock's formal notes regarding the alternate captain and other command crew had been fairly dry, speaking also of an apparent moral inversion and of great emotional lability in the subjects, a tendency toward uncontrolled rages, threats, and attempts at bribery, all of which would normally be distasteful to a Vulcan. But McCoy, then the ship's surgeon, had covertly (and with some apparent relish) made a note of Spock's informal, off-record assessment of the counterparts as "brutal, savage, unprincipled, uncivilized, treacherous . . . in every way, splendid examples of *Homo sapiens;* the very flower of humanity." Picard could not imagine Spock, however young, using those words unless he absolutely meant them and had experienced firsthand evidence of every trait. The thought gave Picard the shudders, for the originals of whom the counterparts were mirrors were all extraordinary people, decorated heroes, professionals of a high caliber, some of the greatest names of the Starfleet of their time. Human beings, yes, and as such inevitably flawed, but still . . .

He looked up and saw the crew beginning to clear away from the shuttle, packing up their equipment and carrying it away, or guiding it out on floaters. Geordi, O'Brien, and Hwiii were standing off to one side with their heads bent over a padd while Geordi checked the chips he was carrying against it.

The corridor doors opened and Troi walked in—or strode in, rather, her head tilted up, her face cool and neutral. The room went somewhat quiet with people taking in the sight of her—the changed walk, the clothes. Picard, who had seen the recording of the counterpart Troi made earlier, looked at the counselor and thought it wisest not to comment on her style of dress. He did note, though, that she had also seen that recording—probably, to judge by her gait, numerous times. She looked taller: it was not just that more of her was showing than usual. Picard began, right then, in a small way, to be afraid for her. A walk, an attitude, was one thing to mimic. But he could not imagine Deanna Troi's face wearing the cold, hard look that the other's had worn. *And she's going to* have *to learn to wear it, quickly, or else.*

Geordi blinked at the sight of her, then grinned widely. "Counselor, I'm *envious.* You've got more on than I have!"

Troi smiled. "Probably just by a few percentage points, I think. I take it we're about ready?"

Geordi nodded. "We're loading in some provisions—we had to strip the replicator out: no room for it. Everything else is aboard."

"I brought a copy of this," Troi said, holding up a chip. "The view we got of the other Troi, and the other La Forge. We'll have about an hour or so on impulse before we reach the beam-in point?" Geordi nodded. "A little more time to spend studying these, then."

"Very well," Picard said. Behind him the corridor doors opened again. Riker came in and stood quietly behind Picard, but Picard knew where Riker's attention was turned and found it completely understandable.

"It seems inadequate to wish you luck," Picard said. "But I do. Complete your mission and come back safely, as quickly as you can."

They nodded and got into the shuttlecraft; its door sealed down, and the whisper of the maneuvering system came up softly as it began to warm toward ready. The engineering crew headed quickly out of the shuttle bay, until only Picard, Riker, O'Brien, and Hwiii remained, watching. Then Picard turned toward the doorway.

"Number One," he said, to spare Will the pain of remaining the extra few seconds, and headed off for the bridge, the others following him, the doors shutting softly behind them.

CHAPTER 6

There was no sound in the shuttlecraft but the soft hum of its impulse engines and a different small sound, one Troi had never noticed before, made by the transporter: a tiny, soft, continuous "shimmer" of sound that mirrored the larger sound made during transport. Deanna sat and listened to it, using the slight, soft phasing she heard in the sound as a focus to help keep herself centered and calm. It needed a fair amount of doing.

Beside her, Geordi was gazing at the screen, watching the brief recording of his counterpart in the other *Enterprise's* engine room. "I don't see much difference, Counselor," he said, glancing up at Deanna.

"There is some, though. Computer, stop. Reverse to"— she eyed the display—"44002.2." The image raced backward, blurred, then froze on the other Geordi, standing over the master engineering console. He swung away from it after a moment, walked into one of the ancillary bays, and leaned over one of his staff working there. "He swaggers a little," Deanna said. "Look at the extra arm movement. Computer, repeat."

Geordi watched the screen thoughtfully. "I'm still not sure I see it."

"Wait for it. It comes up again." They watched together as the other Geordi nudged the crewman whose work he was supervising—not a friendly gesture—and moved on back to the main console.

"Hands-on management," Geordi muttered, not liking the look of it. "It is a swagger, though. Look at that." He shook his head. "I can't do that."

"Don't try to mimic the movement. Just be familiar with it. It's going to be more effective to try to think yourself into the mind-set that causes the motion. Look at his face instead."

"I've been trying to avoid it," Geordi muttered, but he ran the recording back again and did so. There was a curl to the other La Forge's lip that suggested emotions normally alien to Geordi: a nasty enjoyment of someone else's discomfiture, at the very least. Troi viewed the expression on the counterpart La Forge's face with nearly as much unease as she had felt on first seeing her own face set in that very alien mold—the chilly look, the look of luxurious superiority, of pleased domination. Nonetheless, these were the people she and he had to be, at least for a little while, if they were to do the *Enterprise* any good.

"Pretending is going to be your main protection," Deanna said. "Be angry—start being angry now—and stay that way. That at least will steer your body language in the right direction. *His* body language says he spends most of his time thinking angry, contemptuous thoughts; his face says the same. So steer yourself in that direction. It'll do for the moment—and with luck, maybe we won't be seen at all. We're beaming directly into the core control chamber, after all."

Geordi nodded, then glanced away from the playback to have a look at the shuttle's autopilot. At almost the same moment, the communications panel chirped.

"Hawking," Geordi said softly, as if someone might overhear him.

"You're within range," O'Brien's voice said. *"Ready?"*

"Stand by." Geordi glanced at Troi, muted the circuit for a moment. "Did I mention," he said, "that I'm scared out of my ever-lovin' mind?"

She smiled at him as reassuringly as she could, but the smile had a rueful edge, Deanna knew, for she was as frightened as he was. "I got that sense," she said. "Did I mention that I was, too?"

They stood up. He laughed, just a breath. "Come on, Counselor, let's go bell the cat."

They moved to the transporter pads. Geordi was wearing a small belt pouch with the isolinear chips and a few other small pieces of hardware. Troi, first on the pads, watched him touch the relay transporter console into life, then he climbed up beside her. It was a tight fit—what with the low ceiling of the shuttle, the emitter arrays were barely six inches above their heads, and Troi kept feeling as if she wanted to duck a little. But she was sure that the other Troi would never stand anything less than regally straight. She almost laughed at the memory of her mother's voice saying severely, *Stand up, little one, you're one of the daughters of the Fifth House; whoever heard of one of us slouching?*

"Ready, Chief," Geordi said.

"The console reports all the preset routines are answering," O'Brien said. *"All you have to do is hail the shuttle and the transporter's computer will bring you home on demand. Or call us—but you know the routine. Try not to have to. The signal strength required to drive a call out our way may be noticed—and if there's a problem with the transport . . ."*

"Understood," Geordi said.

"Well, then, Godspeed," O'Brien said. *"Energizing . . ."*

And the world dissolved in light—

—and reasserted itself: a tiny room, really, no more than

110

a pie slice carved out of the top of the secondary computer core, with a chair, a sit-down terminal, some wall displays—

—and a crewman leveling a phaser at them, with his face working between astonishment and fear. Astonishment at the sight of Geordi, then fear at the sight of Deanna.

His fear froze him briefly as it also stabbed Troi's fear and made her angry—she having turned herself toward that emotional set already, by way of self-defense. Without a moment's hesitation she kicked the phaser out of his hand. No sooner was her leg out of the way than Geordi jumped him, a blur of speed and fear-turned-rage. A second or so later, the man was down on the floor, nearly unconscious, and Geordi came up with the hypospray from his belt pouch and let the man have it in the leg, one of the fast-absorption sites that Dr. Crusher had shown him. The man sighed and was still.

"He'll be out of it for a few hours," Geordi said, getting hurriedly to his feet. "But I don't like him being here. Either they were expecting us or the security levels around here are too high for *my* liking. Let's get on with it."

He moved to the console, sat down, and started to work. Deanna stood by him, only half watching; the rest of her was trying to cope with the feel of the many minds around her.

Normally this was something she had to endure anew every morning: the pressure of all those minds against her own, the brief disorientation on waking up from sleep to find that there were a thousand people, more or less, in bed with you—not in terms of their thoughts, but the ebb and flow of their emotions, like a low roar of ocean noise, peaking here and there in a whitecap of excitement or annoyance. At times when the ship was nervous—such as the past day or so—the volume of that noise increased greatly, and the variability of it, so that you could sit there naming other people's emotions all day and hardly repeat yourself once, for it was Deanna's experience that negative emotions tended to be endlessly varied, while positive ones tended to feel more or less the same. At such times she had to spend more time than usual working on the inner disciplines that helped a Betazed shut out the noise, and occasionally, during periods of great tension, she found herself relieved that she could hear *only* the emotional noise and not the details of each person's fears, endlessly reiterated.

Now, though, she found herself wishing she were completely mindblind, even though it would have rendered her useless for this mission. Her description of this ship's gestalt to Picard as "a midden," Deanna now found, had been an understatement. The only consolation was that there seemed to be fewer minds—a fact that left her uneasy, for reasons she didn't have time to evaluate just now. No matter: those minds, fewer though they might be, were for the most part horribly vital, and much of that vitality was being spent on a constant flow of malice, wariness, and stifled fury. This, too, was as dreadfully varied as negative emotion was on her own *Enterprise*—hundreds of combinations, each reflecting its home mind's preferences and the stimulus of the moment: sullen dislike and discontent and vengeful passion, animosity and envy, broad-based ill will and focused resentment, jealousy and smothered rage—"Name an emotion," Will would say to her sometimes, teasing. Now Deanna found herself heartily wishing she had just one to name. And this perception was at a distance. Confronted with any one of the people feeling these things, her own perceptions, as always, would narrow down, locking on to the personality at the forefront of her attention, and those presently unfocused feelings would hit her full on, at pressure, like a firehose.

One of them did so now—but it was Geordi's. *"Damn!"* he whispered.

"What's the matter?" Deanna said, glad of the distraction, and ashamed of herself for it.

"I can't get into the core. Security." She looked over his shoulder. "See," Geordi said, pointing at the console. "I can't even get in far enough to fail out the core. It keeps asking me for an access code."

"Voice override?"

"That leaves traces, I'd rather not. But . . ."

He frowned for a moment. "Let's do this first." He pulled out the isolinear chip that was in the slot, substituted another. "Computer, copy of present crew roster and nonprotected personnel files to hard medium reader."

"Chief engineer voiceprint match confirmed," the computer said. Deanna started, as did Geordi: the voice was male. "Security officer's clearance required."

Deanna swallowed. "This is Deanna Troi. Confirm voiceprint and acknowledge clearance."

"Clearance acknowledged," the computer said after a second. "Copy in progress."

It only took a few seconds. "Copy ship's history and condensed nonclassified Starfleet history to hard medium reader," Geordi said.

"Security officer's clearance required," said the computer.

"Cleared," Deanna said. "Comply."

"Voiceprint clearance acknowledged," the computer said. "Working . . ."

"I don't want to do too much more of this," Geordi muttered. "This kind of request leaves trails, too, if anyone thinks to look for them. Take this." He pulled the chip out of the read/write device. "And here." Out of his belt pouch he removed a tiny device that he clipped onto the chip. "Activate that; the transporter in the shuttle'll pick it up and pass it back to the *Enterprise*. I don't like beaming back anything before we're ready to go ourselves, but this operation already isn't going according to plan, and they've got to get this stuff if nothing else."

Deanna touched the tiny stud on the clipped-on device, a small flat disc, then she put the chip down on the floor. It vanished in a small patch of glitter.

"Now then," Geordi said, pulling in a long breath and letting it out as he thought. "I can't think of any other way around this; we're going to have to risk it. Computer, read program file 'Run1' from hard data reader."

It cheeped. "Run program 'Run1.'" It cheeped again. There was a second silence. Geordi looked at Troi, a grin beginning to spread across his face. And then the computer said, "Specified program affects security-sensitive areas. Security officer's or captain's authorization required."

"Authorized," Deanna said.

"Security officer's authorization code required," said the computer.

Troi stared at Geordi. He made a quick cut-his-throat gesture, and Troi said, "Abort run."

"Aborted," said the computer.

The smile was gone as if it had never been there. Geordi looked at her thoughtfully. "Do you have a password that you routinely use on your voice-locked files? Most people do—they tend to repeat two or three of them."

Deanna blinked. "I have four or five. I rotate through them."

Geordi shook his head. "Too many to chance it. If you try giving this thing a wrong password, it'll set off alarms all through the system, from the looks of it. At least it does in ours. What it's going to do in this place—they're too paranoid here for words." He made a face. "I don't see how we can risk it. No. There must be some other way to get into the core."

The console chirped and a voice said, "Security to Kowalski. Hourly check."

Troi and Geordi stared at each other. Then Geordi

leaned over sideways in his chair, reached underneath the control panel, and swiftly removed a facing: the panel went dead.

"What did you do?" Troi said.

"Killed the main power coupling. Now . . ." He looked around the tiny room, then back at Troi. "We have to decide how we want to leave this place."

"You don't mean beam back—"

"No," he said, but he glanced over at the crewman whom they had incapacitated. "It had better look like his board failed, and he went to get help."

Troi swallowed and nodded. "What about us?"

"My guess is that they're going to have somebody up here in about a minute, maybe a minute and a half," Geordi said, getting up and heading toward one of the wall panels. He touched it in a couple of places; it obediently fell away, revealing another panel behind it with much incomprehensible engineerese imprinted on it. This, too, he touched, in what looked to Troi like a coded sequence, and it fell away as well. "In," he said. "Hurry up. Two meters back, the access tunnel bends to the right. A meter and a half past the first bend there's a long drop, a vertical tunnel with ladder rungs set either side of the access. Go down one. There's a big red line drawn right around the vertical tunnel, a meter and a half where it meets the access tunnel. When you go down the ladder, make sure your body is *below* that line, but whatever you do, don't get your head below it."

Troi gulped, feeling his fear, and at the same time an odd exhilaration that she didn't fully understand. She went straight in, headfirst; the access tunnel was small enough that crawling was easier than crouching. Immediately she found the right-hand bend and went on around it; then she came to the drop. There was no more gulping in her when she saw it; her mouth went dry. Heights had never been one of her strong points . . . and this, this was a height and a

115

half. Down below her yawned a cylindrical pit, smooth-walled, dimly lit with engineering telltales in its walls—at least two hundred feet deep, maybe more. She saw the two sets of projecting ladder rungs, set one on each side of the cylindrical tunnel, leading downward. She saw the red line and wondered what it was about, at the same time feeling a faint buzzing hum that lingered on her skin, like an itch that hadn't quite started to be an itch yet.

Behind her she could hear soft scrabbling sounds up in the access tunnel: the click of paneling, another set of clicks, then the soft sound of Geordi making his way down to join her. His head peered over the edge to see which set of rungs she was on, and he quickly scrambled down onto the other.

"Not used to closing those from the inside," Geordi said softly, "but I managed it finally. Remind me to drop a note about an inward-closing utility to the people at Fleet Engineering."

"Absolutely," Deanna said. "But won't this be the first place they look?"

Geordi chuckled as he settled himself in position on the ladder across from hers. "Counselor, do you know there are nineteen computer subprocessors in the bridge?"

"Well, yes, that's common knowledge; they link to the cores in the primary and secondary hulls."

"Right. Where are they?"

Troi opened her mouth and shut it again.

"Within plain sight," Geordi said. "Take a guess."

"I wouldn't know where to start."

Geordi chuckled very softly. "And neither would anybody else but engineering personnel. They're in the wall behind the science stations, aft of Worf's console, between the two turbolifts; but because of its positioning, everybody thinks of that area as just another wall. It's the commonest thing about life on a starship: everybody but engineering assumes, on a day-to-day basis, that everything that looks like a wall really *is* a wall. I promise you that the access panels are the *last* place most people, and even our own security people, would look . . . and truly they have the odds in their favor looking in other places, simply because it's so simple to *go* other places. But the *Enterprise* is a honeycomb, full of interesting opportunities for people who want to get places without using the corridors . . . and *extremely* full of places to hide. There is, of course, one problem: scan for life-signs."

Deanna let out a long breath. "I was going to mention that." And she twitched and blinked a little, for that itching, buzzing feeling was getting stronger. It ran up her body to just above her shoulders. She was neck-height to that red line, and the feeling stopped there; but still the faint sound of buzzing was in her ears as well, as if the sensation were trying to ascend higher.

Geordi shook his head and grinned, but the grin had a slight edge to it. "Not down here. We've got a whole lot of duranium framing around us, and a ton of superconducted current and optical signal . . . and a lot of it's traveling faster than light. We're down in the subspace field."

She stared at him. "Is that safe?"

Geordi looked at her with a slight shrug. "I think it's safer than getting shot with one of those phasers. What do *you* think?"

She could find no quick answer to that. The surge of Geordi's own fear was subsiding for the moment: he was in his element, in his own hidey-hole, feeling much better, though still unnerved by how wrong things were going. "And besides," he said, "I really don't think they'll give the room more than a second glance. Our friend is inside the panel, still sleeping the sleep of the just. As long as he doesn't start snoring, we'll be fine."

"But couldn't they pick *him* up on a scan?"

Geordi shook his head. "I doubt it. I was being extra careful in our case. But the subspace field puts up such a bloom of *bremmstrahlung* and other radiation that I doubt whether they'll get more than the faintest buzz from him, and they'll probably discount it as artifact from being so close to the core. That's one of the reasons we keep sensor equipment so far away: you can't be sure of getting a decent reading if you're even within thirty or forty meters of an FTL-aided core."

They stood there, poised above the polished abyss for a long while, it seemed to Troi. Geordi was much calmer now, and the interference made by the sudden upsurge of his emotion had gone off. Troi cast her sensitivities back up the little access passage and into the core room they had vacated.

"What did you do with the console?" she said.

Geordi raised his eyebrows. "I fused a very minor component in one of the packet shunt boards. When it's checked, it'll look like a routine time-of-life failure . . . that component looked like it was about five years old anyway." He shook his head. "Sloppy maintenance. I'd never leave a part in place that long, at least not one that didn't have four times that long an estimated active life."

Deanna made a small amused expression at Geordi's fastidiousness and went back to what she was doing, listening with all of her. Up above them she felt a faint bloom of concern, confusion, curiosity tinged with suspicion, but not tinged too strongly—well mixed with the sense of someone not particularly caring, the vague satisfaction and relief that there was actually nothing here to respond to. The level of emotion here was consonant with someone who did think that the crewman who had been here really had stepped away briefly because of an equipment failure. "I think it may be all right," Troi said.

"Yeah," Geordi said, "for about five minutes. And when they find out that that crewman *hasn't* gone for help and isn't anywhere to be found . . ."

"What are we going to do with him?"

Geordi shook his head. "I would beam him over to the *Enterprise*, but I don't think the captain would thank me for that—and we can't leave him in the shuttle. And the more beaming around we do, the more likely these people are to notice something, even though the transporter carrier *is* tuned to match their own. I think the guy's better left here. He's got another four or five hours' snoozing left to him, from what the doctor told me about those doses we're carrying. I'm more concerned about us at the moment."

That tingling, buzzing feeling appeared to be trying to wrap itself around Troi's ears. She shook her head. Her eyes were feeling bleary, too, as if she had just awakened early. She said, "Exactly how long is it safe for us to stay down here?"

Geordi shrugged. "I've got two answers for that. The practical one is, 'Twenty seconds after those guys have gone, it's safe for us to come out and go somewhere else.' And as to where, I'll happily entertain your suggestions. If you're asking me about the physiological effects of a faster-than-light field on the body . . ."

"That *was* what I had in mind."

Geordi shook his head with a wry expression. "No one's done double-blind testing, and when there's heavy maintenance to do, we shut the field down first. But no one's ever died of it. Fortunately, the body's software is used to running at one speed—and even when it can run faster, it tends to stay at the old speed, because it tends not to believe that anything faster is possible. Spend too long in the field, and I think possibly your body might start noticing the possibilities, and trying to take advantage of them—with bad effects when the speed drops down to 'normal' again. I've spent more time down here sometimes than was wise, I think: the headache—" He shook his head. "But that's why we usually try to keep our heads up out of the field. More sensitive 'hardware' than just the motor nerves, and more of it. But if we have to stay down here much longer, don't try to make any fast moves—you may surprise yourself."

They waited. After a while Deanna felt the typical "slackening" effect of someone who had decided to give up and try something else; then the attenuation of a mind moving away in space as well as intention. "They're leaving," she said.

"Just as well . . . I was starting to get tired of this."

They went carefully up the ladders again, hoisted themselves up over the edge of the core cylinder, and sat there for a moment, rubbing their legs and getting their composure back. "You feel all right?" Geordi said.

"My head is buzzing a little, but it's already less than it was a few seconds ago."

"Good. I was afraid we might get more of the experience than we wanted."

Deanna smiled at him. "I guess you'll just have to write a paper on this."

"It was that," he said with a grin, "or write a paper on being dead. Now what?"

"I don't much like the thought of trying to make our way out through those corridors at the moment. And the shaft-and-access tunnel method is going to take too much time—of which we have very little. I would think it's going to have to be intraship beaming."

Geordi nodded. "I agree. We'd better send a note home and tell them so—I agree with Chief O'Brien: I don't want to use even scrambled communicators unless we absolutely have to." He picked up an isolinear chip. "This one's configured for voice. They'll beam it in and slap it straight into a reader. I'll flag it to the captain's attention—the computer will transfer the audio straight to him. Go on, Counselor."

"Captain, we have a problem . . ." Succinctly she described their present location and the events of the last twenty minutes. "We need to be beamed away from here, but not off the ship, unless you feel it necessary. Someplace safe from scan, and preferably someplace where we stand some chance of not being disturbed."

"Other problems," Geordi said. Quickly he spelled out their difficulty with getting into the computer core. "The information we need requires voiceprint and authorization codes from the security officer or the captain. The counselor has at best one chance in five of getting the right one without instantly alerting the system, and almost certainly her counterpart as well. But the captain could order the security officer to release those codes . . . I think."

Troi looked at him, opened her mouth, and shut it again at what he was suggesting. That Captain Picard should beam over here as well . . .

"We have *no* other chance of getting the material we need out of the computer," Geordi said. "The thing's security protocols are phenomenal—there are blocks all up and down the line. If you want to pull us out, we'll come home. But my guess is that once they realize for certain that a crewman has gone missing, they'll raise their shields, and after that no one will be able to transport in or out. So you've got about five minutes to make the call or pull us out of here. Awaiting orders. Out."

He touched the control on the isolinear pad, put it down: it vanished in transporter effect.

They stared at the spot where it had lain and waited.

Picard was sitting in his ready room—that being as good a place as any to be nervous and keep the fact more or less private. His tea had gone cold, forgotten in the face of the material that the away team had beamed over a short while ago. The sociological and historical analysis teams were already working on it, but he could hardly afford the luxury of waiting to see what they said: he had pulled the Starfleet historical material and was skimming it. Picard was terrified by it, and fascinated at the same time—fascinated by the strangeness of it, terrified that he didn't know where to set to work on it that would do the most good. The feeling wouldn't go away that there was some vital piece of information buried in it that would make all the difference to his own ship's problem. And all the while, the continuing silence of the away team had brought the hair up on the nape of his neck again and again, even though he had ordered it, even though it meant they were still all right.

He sighed and turned his attention back to the history of the alternate Starfleet. It was already compulsive reading —and horrific. Its roots appeared to be founded in the chaos surrounding the Eugenics Wars. Khan Noonian Singh and his genetically engineered companions had not been overthrown and driven out in this universe, but rose to command several empires spread over several continents before finally turning on one another in territorial and dynastic warfare, and wiping one another out—not to mention large numbers of other people—with nuclear weapons. The delivery systems for the weapons were not missiles, against which all sides had adequate protection, but large, slow ion-drive craft adapted from the DY-100 "sleepers," which were maneuverable enough to dodge any antimissile or particle beam fired at them on their way to target. Numerous improvements were made in the ion propulsion systems by the admittedly brilliant science teams of the various warring factions. When the dust settled over the graves of the victors and the vanquished, the technology remained—a propulsion system good enough to push spacecraft into local space travel—even into relativistic travel, dead end though it might be.

Picard reflexively reached for his tea, found it colder than ever, drank some anyway as he read. The cultures that had pulled themselves together out of the radioactive ashes of the downfall of the Engineered never quite lost the memory of their little empires, of a time when people were ruled for their own good by men and women of power. Their later, slowly assembled governments became empires, too, finally just one Empire, nostalgically harking back to those "good old days," seen as better by far than their present post-Holocaust world, a blasted place where everything must be tightly controlled so that everyone who lived would have enough to eat, a place to live and work. Slowly the earth greened again, starting to heal itself, nature proving, one more time, to be more powerful than those whose thoughtlessness threatened her—at least insofar as she had much more time to work with than they did. But though the world greened again, the hearts of the people who lived in her stayed sere and cold, not trusting the new spring. And the rulers of that world looked out at space, considering that they had had a very close call. They looked into the darkness and saw, not a silent wonder to explore, but a replacement home, a way to make sure that they would never almost be wiped out again.

Serious intrasystem space travel began. Mars was terraformed over the space of forty years—Picard rubbed his forehead at the casual reports of the Martian artifacts, the great ancient buried sculptures in the caves and the writing laid down deep for preservation in the sandstone strata, all gone—blasted away in the casual leveling of mountain ranges, the excavations of new seabeds. Millions of people relocated to the new world when it was ready— many of them being relocated by force. After all, reasoned the government of the Empire of Earth, didn't a planet need enough colonists to make it self-sufficient—then productive enough to send minerals and so forth home to the mother planet? And when Mars was well settled, the government looked out farther yet. After all, *one* extra planet wasn't enough, was it? What if something happened to the sun? Humanity's survival must be assured—and indeed that had become their watchword, the motto of the new Empire, appearing in its arms, while they still bothered with such things: *We Survive.*

Research in long-distance ships that would push toward the edges of the relativistic envelope began in earnest. The late twenty-first century and the beginning of the twenty-second saw the first large sleeper and colony ships built and launched, but they were overtaken—literally—by the development, by Zephram Cochrane and his team, of the first warpfields and warp engines, enabling the colonization of Alphacent and various planets of the other nearer stars.

Picard got up and went over to the replicator, trying to stretch the cramps out of his back, as much a matter of nervous tension as anything else. *No Third World War,* he thought. *Ironic that these people should have become what they seem to have become by avoiding all that bloodshed, the 40 million lives lost. . . . But then—if they had suffered that terrible interregnum—who knows? They might have renounced the terror, the death.*

He took the fresh tea back to his desk, sat down, sipped it carefully, and went back to his reading. They had found alien life on Alphacent, hominid life, colonists from one of the other Centauri worlds. They had wiped them out, apparently uncertain that there were any other habitable planets in this part of space, unwilling to take the chance. When they later deciphered the Centauri language and discovered that gamma Centauri was the homeworld of the aliens they had found, they took their time, reconnoitered it—and then used "clean" atomics on the planet to wipe out its inhabitants and colonize it themselves.

Picard made an unhappy face. Then they had met the Romulans. At first the encounters had been as tragic and fatal for the Imperials as for the Earth-based space forces in Picard's own universe. Finally, as had happened in his own universe, the Battle of Cheron befell, a dreadful defeat for the Romulans. But there was no negotiation afterward, no Treaty of Algeron, no Neutral Zone. The Imperials had gotten their hands on the Romulans' weapons, especially the terrible molecular disassociator, and had improved them a hundredfold. About two weeks after Cheron, the Imperial ships battered their way through the last of their enemies' defenses and appeared above the two Romulan homeworlds. Shortly thereafter, one of them, the smaller of the two, was nothing but dust drifting in its orbit. To the inhabitants of the other, after the predictable tectonic events had died down, the Imperials offered a choice: to suffer the same fate or to become a "subject world" of the Earth Empire, supplying natural resources, workers, and taxes to their conquerors. In return they would be allowed to continue living on their homeworld, with only moderate changes in their laws to enforce their new status.

The Imperials were most surprised when the inhabitants of the remaining world, on the eve of the deadline for their answer, committed suicide en masse. Back on Earth, the government shrugged and started loading up another colony ship. An empty planet *would* probably be less trouble. . . .

Picard sat back in his chair, feeling shaky with the calm and rational way in which the historical material from the other ship laid all this out, as inevitable, the fault of the conquered, of those who tried to stand in the way of progress, of mankind's simple need to have a home that it could count on surviving in. *There are some kinds of security that are below contempt,* he thought. But as they had started, so no doubt they had gone on. There had never been a Federation: he didn't need to read the history to know that, now. No grouping so tolerant would ever have occurred to these people. They became the United Empire of Planets—united by a rule of fear and inevitable destruction of those who opposed them. Picard found himself wondering how the Vulcans had survived meeting them— but as he read on, he got a sense that in this universe, the

Vulcans' history, too, was different. While still a logical people, they were also as piratical and ruthless in their way as the Imperials. *No Surak,* Picard thought sorrowfully, paging down the readout. *Yet the Imperials found them before they had quite warred one another into oblivion— and recognized them as kindred spirits.* They had made common cause and gone out to plunder the Galaxy together.

"O'Brien to Captain Picard."

"Yes, Chief?"

"We've got another chip in from the away team." In the background Picard could hear O'Brien slipping it into the reader slot in his console. *"Voice message, it looks like."*

"Computer," Picard said, "copy incoming voice message to Commander Riker."

The computer chirped. Then Troi's voice said, *"Captain, we have a problem . . ."*

He listened, his mouth going dry as he began to understand the import of it. About halfway through the message, his door signal went off. He smiled slightly through his fear, knowing who it was. "Come," he said while the message continued, and Riker hurried in, standing there with an expression of distress, while Geordi's voice said, *"So you've got about five minutes to make the call or pull us out of here."*

Silence fell. "It has the advantage of boldness," Picard said, almost musing. "Strike at the top."

"You lost me, sir," said Riker in a voice that suggested Picard hadn't lost him at all and desperately wanted to hear an explanation of his captain's thoughts that didn't include what he seemed to be implying.

"Mr. La Forge's suggestion seems fairly plain. He and Counselor Troi are suggesting that they take the other captain out of commission and substitute me for him. I will then be in a position to order the other Troi to release the computer core to Mr. La Forge for"—he smiled gently—

"maintenance. Doubtless we can throw a few spanners into the works at the same time."

"Sir!" It was almost a shout.

Picard looked at Riker; he subsided. "Will, please don't say anything further for at least thirty seconds. No, make it sixty."

Riker sat down slowly, watching him. Picard thought.

Troi sat there, feeling Geordi's tension beginning to rise, and looked over at him thoughtfully. He caught her glance, cocked his head at her, smiled. "It's bad, huh," he said.

"I try to manage it," she said, "but I think you do better than I do. Or than most."

He smiled at her. "Nice to know. It's just that this method of communications . . . raises the old blood pressure a little."

"Like passing notes at school," Troi said wryly. Geordi laughed out loud, though without taking his eyes off the spot on the floor from which the iso chip had vanished. He picked up the small tricorder that he had brought with him and hefted it, then flipped it open and touched a couple of the controls.

"I thought you said you couldn't get a decent scan so close to the FTL field."

"Not what I'm used to, no," Geordi said absently, adjusting another control. "But a passive scan, very low-power, 'blunt' and unfocused, will still work—and the core's proximity will act to confuse any system that might be listening."

Geordi gazed at the display, reading its mysteries. Troi shook her head and waited, trying to stay calm. "A few possibilities," he said. "Down by the field generators for the structural integrity field: there are blind spots there. Back of the deck just above the shuttle bay, the field generators for the irising atmosphere-integrity field would interfere." He paused then, looking slightly astonished.

"What is it?" Troi said, leaning over his shoulder to look. He pointed at the display. A large fuzzy blot showed off to one side of the schematic of the primary hull, which Geordi was studying. Another, smaller blot counterbalanced it to forward. "Deck eleven, right," he said softly.

"The captain's quarters," said Deanna. "It would make sense, here—one of the few spots in the ship that can't be scanned."

"And unoccupied," Geordi said. *"That* one isn't." Deanna looked at the second spot on the schematic to which he was pointing and swallowed. She knew very well the location of her own quarters. "Now," Geordi said, "scan for electromagnetics and life-signs won't work, but see . . ." He made an adjustment: the larger blurs vanished, and in the area to port, a slight small glowing smudge appeared, with a faint trail behind it. "Plain old heat shows just fine. Thirty-seven point six centigrade." And on the starboard side, there were several small blurs outside the captain's quarters, but none inside.

"That's the spot," Geordi said, grinning—the grin had gone wolflike. "Let's make a note and send them one more chip."

Picard looked up finally and said, "I'll go."

"Captain!"

"I'm willing to hear what else you have to suggest," he said to Riker as calmly as he could—and it was hard: it felt to him as if his blood were jangling. "But you have about one minute to convince me. Otherwise that other ship's security is going to come down around our people's ears."

"I'm not sure that the risk to them is as great as the risk would be to you," Riker said. Picard looked at him with veiled admiration. *What must it take for the man to say that when one of the away team is Deanna?* he thought. "If they were caught, even killed, the damage to the *Enterprise* would not be as great as it would be should *you* be lost. And

128

besides—we're reasoning from very old data. There may have been changes."

"Number One," Picard said a touch sharply. "You've read Kirk's report by now. Though our . . . management styles . . . might differ somewhat, he was an excellent commander and never prone to exaggeration. You've read his description of the people among whom he found himself. Are you willing to bet that the crew of that ship, descendants of that earlier culture, have changed *that* much in eighty years? Are you willing to bet the away team's *lives* on the premise that a miracle might have happened?—because their lives are the counters on the table at the moment."

Riker frowned harder than before, if possible. "It's just that—"

"You don't want to let the captain risk himself, yes, yes, we've had this argument how many times?—and will have it again many times more."

"That's what I'm trying to ensure," Riker said angrily. "You know as well as I that in high-threat situations, when the ship itself is threatened, the away teams' lives are considered expendable."

"When the ship itself is threatened, so is mine."

Riker said nothing, only looked at him hard. "That's exactly where we stand," Picard said. "They have uncovered the problem to which there is only one possible answer, and unfortunately for me, it's spelled 'Picard.'" Riker opened his mouth, and Picard said, "No. The ship itself, as you say, is threatened. If we do not obtain the information we need from that other *Enterprise's* computer core, we stand little chance of ever getting home again: we will be stranded here, all of us. Not only the crew, who understand the risks one takes on active mission, but their dependents as well, who do indeed depend on us for their safety and well-being. I am not a great one for children, but I for one do not choose to have any of *our* children grow up in *this* world. If they survive so long, which I begin to have my doubts that they would do." Picard frowned as grimly as Riker had been doing. "And besides—I will not take the chance of my ship falling into these people's hands— which sooner or later she would, for even should we destroy this other *Enterprise,* I will lay you long odds that this universe's Starfleet knows perfectly well by now that we're here. They will come to take us by force. When that happens, I will destroy this ship rather than let her and her crew fall into their hands. So—let us be clear about our options. We have none."

"If we just had more time . . ." Riker said softly.

"We don't. Picard to Crusher."

"Crusher here."

"Doctor, I need two hyposprays and multiple refills for them—the same incapacitant you gave the away team. Have them beamed directly to my ready room."

"Yes, Captain. Out."

He turned to Riker. "You got an image of my counterpart, I take it."

Now Riker shook his head, looking very concerned indeed. "We didn't, Captain. No scan picked him up at all—and believe me, we tried."

"Never mind. The uniform will be provided. Picard to Chief O'Brien."

"Here, Captain."

"We're in a bit of a rush, Chief. You will beam me directly from my ready room to the shuttlecraft, and from there to the—" He paused. "Where *is* the away team at the moment?"

"Still at last reported location, Captain. They're indicating they're ready to move, though, on your orders."

"Where to?"

"Deck eleven, right."

Picard smiled, a quick angry grin. "There's the uniform problem solved. Very well. They'll have to precede me.

Acknowledge their request and beam them there immediately. I'll be following them shortly." From off to one side came a subdued shimmer of sound, the hyposprays and refills, on a small pouch with a strap. Picard picked it up, slung it over his shoulder. "Mr. Worf."

A second later, the door to the ready room opened. In it Worf stood, holding one of the phasers that had been cosmetically modified to resemble the standard-issue, wicked-looking phasers of the other ship. Worf stepped forward and offered it to Picard.

"I took the measurements from your grip template in the armory files," Worf said. Picard took the phaser and, having nowhere to holster it, simply held it. "You anticipated this," he said to Worf with some surprise.

"It seemed an eventuality for which one should be prepared. Captain—be careful."

"I assure you, Lieutenant, I will be as careful as the three-legged mouse at the cat show, because that's what I feel like." Picard looked over at Riker. "Now here are your orders, Number One. Your priorities are to get this ship home by whatever means you find possible. If she cannot be gotten home, you must destroy her cleanly—don't let her fall into those people's hands. Take no chances. Understood?"

"Understood," Riker said, though obviously not at all happy about it. "Captain, you *can't* go without having an intradermal put in! If something goes wrong, we won't be able to find you or pick you up."

"I have one in at the moment," Picard said calmly. "Dr. Crusher installed it this morning." He flicked an amused glance at Worf. "Anticipation is sometimes an art form."

"On that our cultures would agree," Worf said. "Success to you, Captain."

"Thank you, Lieutenant. . . . Mr. O'Brien, have the away team made their transfer?"

"Thirty seconds ago, Captain."

"Very good. I'm ready. Energize."
The ready room dissolved around him.

The interior of the captain's quarters shimmered into being around them. Phasers in hand, they looked around hurriedly. No one was in sight.

Deanna looked around curiously. The room, as far as she could tell, was exactly the same as the captain's rooms aboard their own *Enterprise:* even the bookshelves seemed the same to her.

Geordi glanced around, apparently having the same thought, then nodded briefly to her and went softly over toward the door, stopping just out of the range of its opening sensor and touching the control that would lock it from the inside. He gestured at the door with his head and raised his eyebrows at her.

She cast her sensitivities that way and got nothing but a sense of nearby boredom—the guard outside. That was something else she was still having trouble with. She had had just time enough to read the transcript left by Spock of the alternates' presence aboard her own universe's *Enterprise* and of the angry shout of the other Captain Kirk: "Where's my personal guard?" The implications of those words alone had so shocked her that she was almost unable to take in the rest of the report: his offers to that Spock, of power, money, and command. This was a place where a captain not only did not expect his crew to trust him, but expected them to try to kill him on a fairly regular basis.

Deanna let her perceptions range a little more widely. They were still overwhelmingly negative . . . but it seemed to be troubling her a little less. Possibly, like a bad smell, if you stayed in the midst of it for long enough, it stopped bothering you as much. Deanna shuddered. She wasn't sure she wanted such emotions to stop bothering her.

Geordi nodded and moved off to one side of the room, toward the captain's closet—pulling out his tricorder, now muted, and checking the closet for booby traps. Satisfied, he touched a control. The door slid aside, revealing neatly hung uniforms.

"Uh-oh," he said softly.

Troi looked at him. "Problems?"

"Not really. It's just that all these uniforms"—he went through several on the rack—"are like mine, but more so. The captain's going to love that."

Deanna let out a small breath of amusement, then turned her attention once again toward what she could sense outside the room. She moved about slowly, past the bed, toward the far side of the room and the windows on the stars, letting the motion calm her and help her think. There was a doorway at the far end of the room where as far as she could remember there had been none before, but for the moment she let that pass, stopping short of it while she stood there and cast about her with her mind. That same low, almost snarling background noise, of anger, frustration, low-level hatred. That was the worst of it: the hatred was so ingrained that much of it was more or less taken for granted, habitual—like mental nail-biting. Here and there a bright spot sparked, a place where the emotion flared—anger, here and there pleasure—but too rarely.

She let her mind quest outward—forward, yes, and to port a little ways—

Shock stopped her then, and an odd feeling, so strange, so like— For a fraction of a second she struggled for simile. Like having your leg fall asleep, then touching it and being unable to feel it, but knowing it's yours. That wasn't quite it either. This was a cast of mind so familiar—and no surprise, for it was hers. But it wasn't *her*. It was the other Troi, at rest for the moment, calm enough. But the taste of that mind—Deanna wanted to jerk her whole inner self back as if she had touched something burning hot. But she knew that the vehemence of the movement might attract the other's attention. Slowly she edged away, like a bird avoiding a sunning snake. The comparison was apt. The emotional level in that other mind was consonant with that to be experienced in someone who was in meditation or a centering exercise. But underlying the calm was slow, pleased rage; this, too, had a habitual feel to it, as of someone who was more or less permanently furious with the world, and more or less permanently punishing it for whatever transgression it had committed. It was perfectly strong and steady, a mind unused to being denied anything it wanted. Deanna moved slowly and steadily away from the fringes of that mind, withdrawing her presence, resisting her own near-loathing. It was like looking into a mirror and finding the image warped, or rather, quite clear—but frowning back when you were looking into it without expression. And perniciously the question arose, which is more real? Which side is the mirror?

"Anything?" Geordi said.

Troi shook her head.

"You all right?" Geordi said, seeing what she quite understood must be a most shocked look on her face.

"You were right about my quarters being occupied. Don't fall foul of her, Geordi. Don't."

He nodded. "That's odd—what about that other door?" He lifted the tricorder, scanned the doorway. Then he shook his head, shrugged, turned away. "More living quarters."

"Connecting to the captain's? Maybe—"

Then Troi stopped, interrupted by the soft singing hum of the transporter. Geordi threw Troi a look of shock when he saw the phaser in her hand, leveled on the spot where the materialization was starting. "You sure you're all right?" he said as the captain's shape began to become apparent.

She shook her head, unable to get rid of the memory of that aura of leisurely calculation, amusement: a thinking mind, an anticipating mind, more frightening in its way

134

than the unleashed emotion there was to feel elsewhere aboard this ship.

The captain finished materializing, looked around him somewhat hurriedly. He, too, Deanna was glad to see, was holding a phaser, and the expression on his face on seeing them was relieved. "How long have you been here?" he said.

"About a minute now," Geordi said. "Captain, you'd better get changed."

"First things first," he said, and went directly to the little terminal on the desk. "Computer, this is Capt. Jean-Luc Picard."

"Acknowledged," the computer said. He motioned Geordi over. Geordi produced the isolinear chip with the search program in it, tucked it into the reader. "Computer," Picard said, "read program in hard data reader."

It chirruped softly.

"Execute."

"Program requires coded authorization from security officer," the computer said.

"Authorize run of program," said the captain sternly.

"Program requires coded authorization from security officer."

The captain sighed. "Abort."

"Aborted."

"Merde," Picard said softly. "Well, it had to be tried. But normally I can authorize any function on this ship to be performed by anyone I please. What kind of ship—" He shook his head. "No matter: we'll soon enough get a better idea. I'll get changed."

He went back to the closet, reached into it dubiously. "The problem is working out which one to change into. There doesn't seem much to choose between them." He looked over the uniforms and reached out for one in particular.

"What do you think the odds are that he's wearing that one today, Captain?" said Geordi softly.

Picard made a wry face. "At this point, odds aren't something we can accurately judge. I've simply picked the one I'd be least likely to wear if I had any choice in the matter. Excuse me." He took himself off into the bathroom to change.

"Now this is strange," Geordi was saying. He was still poking around in the closet.

"What?"

He pulled out a uniform top, like the one they had seen the alternate Riker wearing. It was a sort of wraparound vest that left the arms bare, though the shoulders on this one were capped, and from each of them to the neckline ran a band of the glittering gold, as braid. The top itself was a rich dark maroon like congealed blood that glittered the same way the blue material in Troi's skirt did.

She raised her eyebrows at the sight of it. "It will look good on him, but his natural modesty being what it is, I can't say he'll enjoy it."

"No, that's not what I meant." Geordi prodded the communicator badge fastened to the breast of the uniform. It did nothing. "Even ours at least chirp if another living hand touches them. Maybe it's personalized to the captain?"

"Have him try it when he comes out—" That was when she caught it, the quick upsurge of emotion from just outside the door, from the guard standing there. Alertness at the sound of footsteps, and then recognition.

"Quick!" she whispered, and pushed Geordi back out of sight of the door—just as it opened.

Picard strode in. He glanced around and stopped as his eyes fixed on her. The door shut behind him.

She hardly knew what expression she had expected to see on this man. What he turned on her now was a look of mild surprise, almost of pleasure; but there was a curl to the lips that would have betrayed, had she not already been able to feel it, the suspicion and annoyance he felt, tinged with both apprehension and a peculiar kind of anticipatory pleasure.

"Counselor," he said.

She smiled at him: a slight smile such as she had seen on the face of her counterpart on the bridge. It was very much a willed act, and it took everything she had to hold it there. "Captain," she said politely, trying to sound offhand, as if she felt she had every right to be here.

"This is an unexpected pleasure," the captain said, coming slowly toward her. "Normally you don't choose to visit my quarters—and certainly not without your people with you."

"I have my reasons for caution," she said, still smiling.

The apprehension was acquiring an amused edge now, but there was also anger growing around the boundaries of it.

"You seem to have thrown the caution away for the moment," said this Picard, coming closer to her. She forced herself not to back away. "I have ways of knowing when the computer in my quarters is being used without my authorization. Or is this another of your little tests?" He smiled, and she recognized the expression as a parody of her own. "Just checking to see that the captain's security isn't likely to be compromised?"

"That is a duty I undertake occasionally."

"Well, I assure you, Counselor"—and the way he said the word was more a curse than anything else: a slur, and a nasty one—"that if anything goes wrong with this mission, it won't be because of anything *I* have done or failed to do. And you can tell your master at Starfleet, whichever of them is holding the leash this week, as much. The only failure there's been has been one of *your* staff." He smiled. "A little personnel difficulty with Kowalski? Got his last promotion too soon for someone else's tastes, perhaps?"

Troi smiled, too, harder, and, greatly daring, turned her back on him and strolled slowly toward the windows, gazing out on the starry night—trying hard to hang on to her composure. She could feel preparation, eagerness, not too far away; but much closer, riding up behind her, came that feeling of combined suspicion, amusement, and pleasure—the kind of pleasure she had no desire to feel any more of.

"You know how it is in my department," she said, turning to look over her shoulder and flash that smile at him again. "The occasional disagreement. Not all of my people agree with me *all* the time."

The counterpart Picard chuckled softly. " 'Occasional,' " he said, mocking. "Indeed, it seems more than occasional lately. No, I don't think it was a promotion problem. An evening's entertainment that went wrong, perhaps? A crewman less than discreet about your . . . preferences?" That smile got wider; "No, indeed, you couldn't leave someone to run about discussing *that*. Others might get ideas. So . . . someone from your own department, promised a little something extra—of one kind or another—slips in to visit a comrade on a lonely post. Something like that?" He was drawing closer to her now, and there was nowhere to go. "Or maybe not," said this Picard, his voice dropping to a whisper. "Perhaps—"

There was no telling what else he might have thought of, for in that second Geordi, stepping up softly behind the other Picard, hit him in the back with the hypospray. His eyes went wide; he grabbed for Troi. She backed out of his way and he fell, but common sense overcame her revulsion and she caught him halfway down, to prevent what she feared would be the all-too-audible sound of a body hitting the floor.

"How long?" the captain said, slipping out of concealment to join them.

"It should be between three and four hours," Geordi said, "but it's variable. Dr. Crusher said that body weight and differences in body chemistry can make a difference. Probably it's not safe to count on more than three hours."

"I desperately hope we will be out of here by then," Picard said, "and on our way home—or at least working on it." Troi watched him look down at the crumpled form. The unconscious man was wearing the same uniform that their own Picard had changed into.

"Well," Picard said softly. "Ill met by starlight. And worse still, his taste in uniforms is as bad as I thought it was. Never mind. Mr. La Forge, have you got your hiding place picked out?"

"Yes, sir. Deck thirty-six, the aft skinfield generator on the starboard side. There are two small service cubbies convenient to it; we use them for storage mostly. Compartment . . ." He rattled off numbers that marked the place's location in the ship's coordinate system.

"Noted," Picard said. "We'll risk one last intraship beaming—there's no other way to get him out of here and keep this situation alive. Counselor, your counterpart?"

"She's in her quarters, Captain. She's centering. I would imagine it's something she might have to do fairly frequently."

Picard nodded. "Assuming that she has your abilities—how do I 'pass'?"

"If the experience of the last few minutes is anything to judge by," Troi said, looking down at the unconscious alternate Picard as Geordi sat him up against a table leg and began to fold him into a more transportable position, "then suspicion and anger, constantly generated, should be enough to keep her from reading you much more closely than that. But I'm troubled. I got a sense from him that he was expecting something *more* from me, more—" She shook her head. "I don't know. Expectation of something bad—mild surprise when it didn't materialize. Followed by a desire to follow up on that failure. It was news, somehow."

"So your counterpart may have some ability that we don't expect."

"I just can't say," said Deanna, upset that she could throw no more light on the problem at so crucial a time. "But still—Captain, even the most powerful telepaths have trouble reading through intense emotion, or through 'obsessive thought.' Either can be exhausting to maintain, but shifting from one to the other can work. Try to inwardly act great emotion—call up the memory of something that frightened you, enraged you—probably around here, rage would be better. It won't necessarily show as a block, either. But be flamboyant about it. The harder you project, the more effective it'll be. Even full Betazoids, fully trained, often can't sort out the thought they want between the racket of emotion and the usual quarreling of several of the audient's ego states at a given moment. Or else, forcefully occupy your brain with something that you've had trouble getting out of it in the past. If you know some piece of music that persists in your mind once you think of it, a poem, a song—start running it in your mind and keep it there any way you can. It may drive you half-mad, but rest assured it'll be doing the same thing to the telepath who's trying to read you."

"Singing," Picard said ruefully. "Not out loud, I hope."

"If it works, yes, but it may work inwardly just as well."

"I greatly hope it doesn't come to that," Picard said.

Troi smiled at the captain's discomfiture, and it felt good to have something genuine to smile about. "Now then," he said. "You two take yourselves out of here quickly. Mr. La Forge, I am going to find an excuse to get those authorization codes released and get you at that core . . . but it may take a while. While I am working on that, I want you to devise a way to take your counterpart out of circulation without being able to transport him anywhere. That cubby of yours—can you get out of that by means other than walking down some corridor?"

Geordi smiled grimly. "There's a Jeffries tube that feeds right into it, Captain. That's one of the reasons I picked it. It can take a lot of time to get around this ship without being seen, by way of access tubes—but it can be done, and I know how to do it."

"Very well," Picard said. "Think about how you might get at either engineering or this La Forge's quarters without being detected. At least we're all still going to be in the primary hull: that's a mercy. And I will find out whatever I can about exactly what these people want from us."

"Our own communicators are working scrambled at the moment," Geordi said. "I've changed the frequency to a very high one that even we don't normally use. It shouldn't trigger any alarms . . . as far as I know. But one thing you should notice, Captain—these people's badges don't seem to work as communicators. The ones on your counterpart's uniforms appear to be just jewelry." Geordi looked puzzled. "If you can, see if you can find out what those things are for, if they're not for talking to each other, or being found."

"Very well. Here, wait a moment." Picard reached down to his counterpart and worked at his vest for a moment to remove several objects that stuck to the material in the same way the communicators did. They came away with a tug. "Decorations," Picard said, putting the first few in place on his own tunic. "For what, I don't like to think. But—" He finished, straightened up. "There. Get him out of here—and keep yourselves as safe as you can. Counselor, if you feel any major eruption of emotion on this ship that I should know about . . ." He touched his badge. "I've set this on vibrate rather than sound. Understand that there may be a pause between your call and my reply: I may have to get away from people and back to somewhere that I'm not likely to be scanned—probably here."

"Yes, sir," Troi said. "And, Captain—don't forget your personal guard. For whatever reasons, they seem to be loyal to 'you' here. They're help you shouldn't be afraid to use."

He nodded. "The concept of such a group existing bothers me as it is, but the point is well taken. It appears, from what that one said"—he motioned with his head at the other Picard—"that your counterpart has a guard of her own. If you can get any sense of their movements, and let me know as need arises."

"I'll do my best," Troi said. "There's this at least: there are a lot fewer people on this ship to be kept track of. I haven't sensed any children's minds, and very few couples."

Geordi looked up. "Come on, Counselor, Chief O'Brien's got the coordinates."

Reluctantly, Troi moved over to join him. "Energize," Geordi said. And she and he and the alternate Picard were lost in shimmer and vanished away.

CHAPTER 7

Picard stood there in the silence for a moment, watching them go. He looked around the room and found it physically much the same. It was only small details that were changed, such as the uniforms hanging in the closet.

One thing *was* the same: the covered easel off to one side. He stepped over to it softly, tossed the cover back from it. The wood in the Luberon: the beams of sunlight strung on the woodland dimness like harpstrings; the tiny scrap of light, the wavering wings caught, frozen in a golden moment under the trees, among the honeysuckle. Picard shook his head. *How can that man*—he was carefully avoiding using the word *I,* for that would be a fallacy, possibly a fatal one—*how can that man do this and still be what he is? Or be what he is—and do this?* He thought of Data looking over his shoulder. That at least could never happen here. Data's creator had been killed in a purge of scientists on his home planet: a great genius, shot out of hand for injudiciously expressing the wrong political opinions—that was to say, anything that didn't support the Empire. It was not a universe that tended to treat kindly any dissidence, difference, or any novelty that didn't immediately throw itself at the Empire's feet.

He shook his head. There was no time for this now: he had business. He needed, first of all, to set up some situation that would make it natural for the ship's security officer to release the computer core to Geordi's ministrations. There was no way to tell exactly how he could do that as yet. But he would find out soon enough.

He paused by the mirror near the closet to look himself over. The uniform was indecently tight, but fortunately quite comfortable. It turned out he didn't have to worry about bending over after all—he did a couple of experimental deep knee bends, pulled down the tunic to straighten it, and found, rather to his distress, that it didn't need pulling down, that it *was* down as far as it was going to go, despite his movement. It annoyed him that these people had managed a solution to this particular problem that his own universe never had.

Meanwhile, it was time to get out there. His mouth was dry. He got a drink of water from the replicator—at least *that* worked the same here—and headed for the door.

He stepped out into the hall, and the man standing there saluted him—an odd gesture: a thump of the right chest, the hand then extended flat outward. Picard returned the salute as easily as he could while keeping his face as calm as possible, for the man standing guard outside his quarters was Barclay, wearing lieutenant commander's insignia over the more or less normal-looking uniform of the junior officers.

"Any problem, Captain?" Barclay said, falling in with Picard as he walked down the hall. Another man, stationed farther down the hall, dropped into step behind them, maintaining a respectful distance.

Picard studied Barclay briefly from the corner of one eye as they walked. This was not the innocent, sometimes bemused young crewman he knew. That bemusement had an edge to it now; the slightly crazed creativity of the man, his quirkiness, seemed to have been redirected. His face had a calculating look about it, like that of someone who spends his life anticipating trouble and isn't entirely disappointed when it finally arrives.

"No," Picard said, "no, Mr. Barclay, no problems."

"I had wondered," Barclay said thoughtfully. "It's not a time of day when you usually bother with your quarters."

"I wanted to check something, that's all."

They came to the turbolift: it opened for them. Picard started to step into it and was briefly surprised when Barclay brushed past him as if he hadn't been there. At first he was ready to write it off to discourtesy, then Picard saw Barclay alertly looking around the 'lift, checking it for—who knew what?—devices, people, lying in wait. Picard kept his mouth shut and waited. Finally Barclay glanced up at him and said, "Bridge, sir?"

"Bridge," Picard said, and got in. The 'lift started moving. They stood in a silence that, for the lack of tension in it, at the moment felt almost amiable.

"Captain," Barclay said. "Possibly I shouldn't be telling you this . . ."

Picard put his eyebrows up and waited.

"The day before yesterday, Commander Riker made me an offer for my services."

Picard kept his face as still as he could and finally fell back on Counselor Troi's technique. "How did you feel about that?"

Barclay looked uncomfortable. "Captain, it's not as if you haven't always treated me well. A cut of the booty."

Booty! Picard thought. "Jumps in rank, better quarters. It's just that—" It was his turn for his eyes to slide sideways. "It's not always safe to say no to Commander Riker. People have a tendency to, uh—" He took a moment to find the right phrase. "Come to grief." He swallowed. "And even chief bodyguards sometimes have accidents."

Picard nodded slowly. "What were you planning to do about it?"

"Sir—I want to refuse him. But afterwards, I'm going to need your protection. For the moment, though, I can stall."

"You'll need my protection." Picard smiled thinly. "A reversal of roles, is that it? Do you need to be taken off duty for a while?"

"If you think that's the right idea, Captain," Barclay said, sounding doubtful. He sounded very afraid, as well. Picard would have liked to say something to reassure him, but didn't dare: he thought it might be out of character. "I'll do what I can, Mr. Barclay. It's the least return I can make for loyalty." But he wondered what in heaven's name he *could* do. "Meantime . . ." He allowed himself a slight smile. "As far as Commander Riker is concerned, this conversation never happened."

"Yes, sir," Barclay said, sounding grateful. "Thank you, sir."

The doors opened. There were guards on either side of them; as Picard came out, they snapped to attention and saluted. He returned the salute, trying to seem idle about it, and glanced around him, trying to keep the look casual.

The bridge was as he had seen it in the recorded scan. It seemed smaller than his own because of the darker colors, but somehow plusher at the same time. The sense of luxury was more pronounced in the softer carpeting on the floor, the gleam of polished metal here and there, the somber colors. And down there in the center seat—

The other Will Riker stood up and saluted him, smiling a crooked smile. The gesture, which looked too formal, too respectful on everyone else, this Riker somehow made appear sloppy and insulting. The expression in his eyes was chilly, but amused. Picard found himself wishing very much that he had even a smattering of the counselor's ability to directly sense emotion. For the time being, he had to make do with his own aptitude in that area—not inconsiderable. On any other man's face, he would have read the expressions there as meaning insolence, insubordination simmering below the surface, treachery waiting for a chance. The problem was that this was Will Riker's face as well, and Picard had never caught so much as a hint of any of those emotions in Will. This led him toward a tendency of unbelief. But forcefully Picard reminded himself that in this situation particularly, he must not allow that unbelief to affect him by reflex.

"Report," he said as he swung down toward the three center seats. "Ship's status?"

"Unchanged," Riker said. "Still no sensor contact with the target. We're sure they're avoiding us: we're continuing our search pattern."

"Very well," Picard said, and made for his chair. Riker did not immediately move away from it, so that for a moment he and Picard were almost nose to nose, and Riker looked down at him with an expression that bordered on amused pleasure at making Picard wait. Insolence again. What was the man waiting for? Picard remembered quite clearly Kirk's report, and how officers in this universe routinely moved up in rank via assassination. Did they duel as well? Picard found himself wondering. Was this Riker trying to provoke a confrontation? Had he been trying for a while? No way to tell now.

"Mr. Riker," Picard said as pleasantly as he could, "kindly take yourself away from my seat before I am forced to request my chief bodyguard to put his phaser up one of those unlovely nostrils of yours and give your brainpan, such as it is, a much-overdue cleaning."

There were muted snickers around the bridge, just as there had been long ago in the Academy when one of Picard's cadet martial-arts instructors made the same comment to *him*. Riker backed away—but only just, with a smile that suggested he thought Picard's chief bodyguard might not do what he was told. *Or am I reading too much into this?* Picard thought. He doubted it, though. It seemed unwise to take anything for granted at the moment, and in this milieu, it seemed to him that paranoia might be the most logical approach to staying alive and getting his job done.

He sat down in that center seat, astonished to feel the soft give of it under him: a seat that tempted a man to feel comfortable. He disliked the feeling intensely. On his own bridge, Picard wanted to feel alert, not to be tempted to drowse off—especially not around here.

Picard turned his attention to the main viewer. It showed empty space, the stars flowing slowly by, just as on his own ship. For a moment, despite the short time he had been here, he felt a dreadful sense of homesickness. He wanted his own bridge back, and crewmen whom he could trust. But there was no use wishing.

"Anything else to report?" he said to Riker.

"We're still searching for Ensign Kowalski," Riker said, frowning now.

"I should have thought there would be some sign. Does anyone have any new thoughts on why he should have gone missing?"

"Well, there may have been a matter of advancement involved." Riker's eyes flicked briefly up toward the 'lift doors, where Barclay still stood at ease, his eyes on Picard.

"Kowalski's, or someone else's?"

"Difficult to say, Captain. There were crewmen underneath him who didn't like his style—who may have waited for him to get a rotation that would put him out of plain sight and give someone an opportunity to hit him. We're questioning the few who might have had motive."

"Very good," Picard said, as if none of it mattered. But he had his own ideas about what that questioning probably involved. And knowing the cause of Kowalski's disappearance, he felt unhappy about it. Under no circumstance, though, could that be allowed to show. "Carry on, then, and make sure all systems remain in readiness. Otherwise you'll have a little less cause to smile."

He had the satisfaction of seeing some of that smirk fall away from Riker, and to cover his own annoyance at having to treat a fellow officer that way, even in a place like this, he leaned back and said, "Get me Mr. La Forge."

With a sullen look, Riker leaned over toward the center seat, touched one of the controls on its arm. "Engineering," he said. "La Forge."

"La Forge here, Commander," said Geordi's voice. It sounded annoyed. *"Is old Shiny still having his nap?"*

Riker grinned like a schoolboy hearing another one get caught in a wicked act.

"I stopped needing afternoon naps after kindergarten, Mr. La Forge," Picard said softly. "The refulgence of my head is unabated, and as for you, *you* are asking for trouble."

"Uh, just a joke, Captain," said the voice from engineering, rather desperately. *"You and Commander Riker both know I have the highest respect—"*

"Spare me the platitudes," Picard said, resigning himself to the fact that he was going to have to conduct himself like an Academy instructor with a crowd of rude, raw, obstreperous one-week's cadets, all jockeying for position to see who could be the boldest, all continually needing to be slapped down. "Status report!"

"Engines are nominal, Captain."

"When I say 'report,'" Picard said, trying to keep his voice soft, and he much hoped dangerous, "I mean a *full* report, Mr. La Forge, not these sullen half-answers you seem to find so amusing. Must I come down there myself and apply a little encouragement toward more detail?"

"Uh, no sir," La Forge said, somewhat hurriedly, a slightly cringing tone to his voice now. *"But really, there's nothing else to report. The switchback equipment is on standby for the moment. We're checking it over as per*

routine to make sure it took no damage during the inclusion."

"See to it," Picard said, "and make quite sure. I may well be down for a visit myself later on. It would be rather annoying to come all this way and then have a malfunction. Certain people would not be amused."

This was a stab in the dark, but he could guess that this ship would not have been sent out this far, and had the results it had had, and be expected to fail. The interest at Starfleet, *this* Starfleet, must be tremendous—and he suspected the penalties for failure, right up and down the line, would be dreadful.

"Uh, no sir," Geordi said. *Not Geordi,* Picard reminded himself with pain. *This La Forge.*

"Very well. Out." Picard hit the control that Riker had touched and saw a look of faint scorn on Riker's face. "You have something to contribute, Number One? Feel free."

"You're too easy on him. One of these days he's going to get the wrong idea and try something smart."

"For him?" Picard said softly. "Or for you?"

The stroke went home. Riker looked very briefly taken aback, then smoothed his face over with that smile again and said, "Captain, you know I support you completely."

The lie was so total and transparent that Picard couldn't hold his face still, much less keep the look of incredulousness off it. Then again, neither could anyone else on the bridge. He glanced swiftly around at their actions. O'Brien was in the seat that was usually Data's: Picard found himself wondering who was transporter chief here, whether there even was such a function. He rather thought that someone from security probably managed the transporter. Beside him sat Ensign Crusher—*an* Ensign Crusher. For a moment he fought the urge to lean forward and get a look at that young face, to see what changes were in it here. But Wesley looked fixedly ahead, giving all his attention to the screen.

Behind Picard, Worf stood, without his Klingon sash of rank, as he had appeared in the recording earlier. It would have been unwise to spare him more than a glance, but somehow Picard got the odd feeling that this Worf might be more like the one he was familiar with than the rest of these people. His face seemed little changed. *It's not necessarily an indication,* Picard reminded himself. *Judging alien expression, even in a species as humanoid as the Klingons, could be a business full of pitfalls.*

He leaned back in his seat again. "Of *course* you do, Number One," Picard said as smoothly as he could. "And I trust you implicitly." *The two or three meters I can throw you!*

"So there's our ration of humor for today," Picard said mildly. He got up as casually as he could and began to stroll around the bridge, doing his best to master his responses once again. It was a sobering walk, and one that filled him with distress. The ship's bridge was at best a parody of his own. He walked quietly past the bank after bank of weaponry control and status readouts. The controls for photon torpedoes, and the master status boards for the phaser banks, he understood. There were other panels new to him, giving status in numbers of "disassociation packages," "sterilizers," "nova devices." The first he guessed was the derivative from the old Romulan weapon. He shuddered again at the thought of the dust of a dead world traveling companionably in the orbit of another, so that falling stars would seem to rain down constantly through a sky toward which no eye turned anymore in the evening. . . . But these other weapons—he would have to do some quiet research work, and as quickly as he could.

He passed behind Worf, watching the Klingon's eyes shift to follow him. Not a nervous look, but speculative. Casually Picard leaned up against a bulkhead and studied a ship's schematic, trying to look preoccupied. *What on earth,* he thought, *are those great empty bays down in engineering? And what's happened to all the personnel quarters in the primary hull?* There were large spaces showing down there, areas that were formerly subdivided into family quarters, entertainment areas, gyms, libraries: even the arboretum was gone. He leaned in closely enough to pretend to be wiping at a smudge on one of the viewing panels and saw several of those large areas labeled *Primary, Secondary, Tertiary Disassociator Storage; Mass Weapons Transporter One, Two; Razor Field Generation; Terraforming Equipment: Atomics.* Atomics in several different flavors.

Dégueulasse, he thought, thoroughly disgusted. He moved casually away and stopped by the engineering panel, gazed at it, still trying to look lost in thought. His revulsion at the weapons load the ship was carrying was briefly replaced by astonishment at the power readings he saw—especially the graph for available power from the warp engines. He made a mental note not to bother trying to outrun this craft, if it came to that. This one could hold high warp speeds, to judge by the engine ratings here, for three or four times as long as his own *Enterprise.* It could also feed much larger reserves of power to the phasers and the photon torpedoes than his own could. He had already been upset by the photon torpedo complement, six times what his own ship had on board. Now he understood the profligacy: he understood where all that power came from. He touched the panel idly, brought up the schematic of the engineering hull, and gazed at it for a moment, thinking that Geordi might have a better chance of getting his counterpart away undetected than they had previously thought—for this engine room was like a barn. It was at least four times the size of the one on his *Enterprise.*

He touched the panel again, casually bringing up a schematic of the various power conduits and feeds into and out of the engineering section. There appeared to be three major pathways: one for distribution of power to ship's systems; another, bifurcated farther down the line, for the warp nacelles; and a third. This went to some large unlabeled apparatus in the engine room.

Picard swallowed and turned away. *What is that?* he thought. From his memory of their last briefing, he remembered Data's voice saying, *A considerable amount of power would be required, and there is no planet or other fixed facility in this neighborhood to produce such an effect.* From the look of it, that installation, whatever it was, seemed to be absorbing fully a third of the output of these massive engines.

He strolled away from the panel, looking thoughtfully at the forward viewscreen and the slow passage of stars upon it. *Wait here a little while more,* he thought. *Then as soon as it seems natural, I'll go down to engineering and get a look at that—whatever it is.*

Behind him, the 'lift doors slid open, and from around the bridge came the soft sound of people rising to their feet and saluting. For a calculated moment, Picard didn't turn.

"Well, good morning, Captain," said the soft voice from behind him.

Calmly he looked her way, seeing in the background that even Riker had risen. Deanna Troi was standing behind him, arms behind her back, eyeing him with a slight smile.

He felt it, then—the brush across his mind, light but in no way tentative, like a veil blown across the skin of his face. There and gone again. He blinked, surprised, and immediately smothered the surprise under an anger that was not entirely generated on purpose. "Counselor," he said, frowning at her to help the effect.

She raised her eyebrows at him, genially enough, it seemed. "A little nervous this morning, are we?" she said.

He had always hated the medical *we* when it was used on him, and he liked it no better in this form. "You may be able to overhear them, Counselor," he said, "but *my* emotions are not joint property. When I want your help with analyzing them, I'll ask for it. Meanwhile"—*Toujours l'audace,* he thought, *any move not an attack is ground lost!*—"I should think *you* would be the one who should be nervous. One of your staff missing without a trace . . ." He had had only a few minutes to study the original's attitude toward Troi, earlier, but it was better than nothing, and the content might as well be used, too. "This is a poor time for your department to start having trouble, considering how heavy its responsibilities are. But then these things will happen, I suppose. Personality conflicts. Perhaps Kowalski's last promotion came a little too quickly for someone?" He did his best to smile like a man who had a secret. "Or some cause more sensitive . . . more private. Someone who might have been indiscreet—and someone willing to prevent it, for a price."

"And if it was?" Troi smiled and turned away from him, utterly unconcerned. "What's the point of rank if it doesn't have its occasional perquisites?" She looked sideways at him, enjoying the game. "You haven't been entirely be-hindhand in that regard yourself, Captain. Though it has been a matter of comment occasionally that you haven't taken more. Some people would wonder about that. They'd take it as a sign you're getting soft."

"Personal preference," Picard said, sounding aloof, and wondering what the devil she was talking about. "But never mind that. What efforts have you made to find our missing crewman?"

"Routine investigations are being made. I'll let you know when we have results."

It was a dismissal: of him. He didn't care for it. "And what have you to report on the status of"—he waved at the screen—"our quarry?"

She was moving slowly toward his seat. In just as leisurely a manner, Picard slipped past her and sat down, looking up at her in the manner of a superior expecting a report from a standing subordinate. Troi made an expression of amusement and surprise and sat down beside him as if she had intended nothing else.

"Since our last contact," she said, "nothing concrete. A general unfocused sense of low-level anxiety. Not, I must admit, what we would expect from the crew of a ship in the other one's predicament." She frowned slightly. "It might indicate that they didn't understand the predicament they're in."

"Surely they will have worked it out by now," Picard said dryly. "I think you underestimate them, Counselor. Such tendencies are dangerous."

"If they have worked it out," she said confidently, "then their behavior is exactly what we would have hoped from these people, at the very best, and closely conforms to the old reports." The scorn in her voice was considerable. "They're busily running away, doing their best to avoid us. Whether they know we have both the strategic and tactical advantage of them is hard to say. There's some indication that their sensors may be better than ours. It hardly matters if they are. Our agent aboard got us the necessary information about their weaponry before his"—she smiled slightly—"unfortunate demise. We'll be ready for the next phase shortly: within a matter of a couple of hours."

"Very well," Picard said then, getting up. "Until then, there are some matters I wish to attend to. Feel free to call me if I'm needed."

He moved toward the turbolift doors. Barclay, standing there, waved the doors open for him and started to go in ahead of him. Picard let him look the 'lift over, but then shook his head minutely and gestured with his head toward Troi. "Keep an eye on her," he said softly.

Barclay looked alarmed. "Sir—"

"It'll be all right. I want to know what she does."

"Yes, sir." Barclay dropped his voice to a whisper so

slight that Picard could barely hear it and said, "I'll send someone after you. Be careful, sir—she has eyes everywhere."

Picard nodded and stepped into the 'lift. The doors closed.

"Deck thirty-eight," he said. One thing had to be done, and he thought it was safe to do it here, since Barclay hadn't been afraid to speak to him about Riker. Quickly Picard touched his badge, bent his head right over it so that his lip movement couldn't be seen in case someone *was* scanning this area visually, and whispered, "Mr. La Forge—don't answer. Add the terms *switchback* and *inclusion* to your search: it's important. Out."

He leaned against the 'lift wall and breathed out hard, letting it all go just for a second. He still had trouble thinking of it without shuddering, that sensation of something trailing across his mind—not so much the feeling itself, but what it implied. This Troi definitely was differently equipped than his own counselor. Or could Troi do such things? He much doubted it. At any rate, there had been no pressure behind that touch, but he had caught, dimly, the implication that there could have been, if she had wished. That this Troi had wanted him to realize that, or more likely to be reminded of it. There was also something uncomfortably sexual about the touch, like being fondled without permission or desire. This Troi's manner suggested that such minor harassments were a pleasure to her, one she indulged whenever she liked. And from the fear the other crewmen seemed to evince in her presence, no one was safe. *Not even Riker,* Picard thought, remembering the look of reluctant, sullen rage as he moved out of the center seat to let her sit there. Here was a danger as concrete as any of the obscenities down in the holds of this ship, the planet-killing weapons, the atomics. . . .

The 'lift stopped. Picard stepped out slowly, looking carefully around him. In this universe, at least, it seemed safer to stay with the paranoid tendencies in order to keep himself functional. The corridor was empty: there were no salutes to return. He went down it with care, trying not to look hurried, though all his senses were shouting at him that nothing was safe here. He thought of Geordi and his own Troi, cramped into that tiny storage area, waiting for him.

Behind him he heard the soft sound of the turbolift doors opening. He half-turned, feeling ashamed even as he did it that he should so exhibit his jumpiness—

And that was all that saved him from taking the phaser stun in the worst place, the spine and the back of the head, where it would have infallibly incapacitated him completely. Instead he caught it sideways, his turned body minimizing the target, giving the phaser less area to affect. Nonetheless he crashed to the floor with all his nerves on fire, unable even to put his hands out to break his fall, and the shock of the impact all up and down his body was almost as bad as the stun itself. He heard the sound of running footsteps, but couldn't do the least thing about them, lying there, blind, his limbs refusing to answer him. *Folly,* said a severe voice back in his head, *to venture out on your own in a place where captains* need *personal guards.*

The footsteps stopped. Someone thumped down beside him. He couldn't see, but he could hear breathing, hoarse, right above his head. He partly felt someone fumbling at his waist—and then the prick of something sharp between his chin and the soft part of his throat.

"Finally," the voice whispered hoarsely. "Finally. It had to happen: even *you* had to get careless eventually. I've been waiting years for this. Ever since I could understand . . ."

After stun, said the cool voice in the back of his head, *you only get one chance. Rest: conserve yourself. Pick the moment: choose your target correctly. Then give it everything you've got, because what you've got probably isn't*

157

much at that point. In fact, all you've really got is surprise, because no one expects a stunned body to do anything.

The whispering voice, so close to his face that he could actually feel the breath of it now, told him where the throat was. He was on his back: he could tell that much. He could also feel that point, jabbed into his throat, sinking in a bit deeper. "I'll probably make lieutenant now," whispered the voice. "Not that I care. This is for my father—"

Picard rolled and swung, crashing his left forearm as hard as he could sidewise into the neck of the person leaning over him. The sharpness scored away from his throat as he rolled to pin the other's body under him, finding its throat again with the now-free hand, pushing the left forearm down over it. There was a clatter. *My knife,* he thought, and it sounded as if it was out of range and out of reach. He leaned on that forearm, hearing horribly satisfying choking noises.

His eyesight started to clear. He found himself looking down into Wesley Crusher's face, which was turning an interesting shade of puce. Picard let up the pressure—but not by much. "Mr. Crusher," he growled, "you had better explain yourself."

The young man choked and coughed and glared up into Picard's eyes. "Just kill me and be done with it," he sneered. "Don't pretend the idea hasn't crossed your mind before."

Picard refrained from comment, electing to play the innocent for the moment. "Now why should I want to kill you?"

Ensign Crusher laughed bitterly. "For neatness's sake, maybe. Wouldn't it be so much tidier? To make a clean sweep? Two Crushers dead, and one who might as well be."

Picard stared at him in horror. He suddenly felt sick to his stomach and wasn't sure whether it was the stun or the awful suspicion that was rising in him. At least he was starting to feel strong enough to get up.

He did, hauling Wesley to his feet with him. "What are you doing away from your post?" he said, pinning the ensign against the wall by his throat and unholstering his phaser.

Wesley laughed again, that horrible, bitter, lost sound, and actually turned his head and spat on the floor at Picard's feet, glaring defiance. "As if Riker and Troi wouldn't let me go! They knew what I had in mind. It's been everybody's little joke for a long time. But you gave me the opening—and the commander let me leave. After all . . . there was a chance it might have worked. If it had . . ." He shrugged. "Everyone moves up. No one would mind. The counselor isn't very pleased with you, neither is Riker, for a while now. If it didn't work—then their hands are clean. They didn't know what was going to happen, they'll say. I'm the one who gets it in the neck." He spat again. "It was worth the chance just to see you with your own knife at your throat, mister high-and-mighty captain with all those years of experience—sweating it for a moment like anybody else who made a dumb move. It was worth it—even if it's the only thing I'll have left."

The 'lift doors opened again. Two security people came running down toward them. Picard, watching them come, saw them fix their eyes on him, with their phasers in their hands, and had a moment of panic. *My bodyguard?* he thought. And some nasty suspicious thought said to him, *How many of them do you think Commander Riker might have made an offer to? Or possibly Counselor Troi? How many of them are really committed to you—or this you? Will you ever be able to turn your back on anybody while you're here?*

"Are you all right, sir?" one of the men said, coming to him quickly. It was Ryder, or the equivalent of him. His hair was shorter than Picard's own Ryder's, and he was missing the mustache.

Picard nodded, putting a hand to his head for a moment

as he had one of those transient pains you get sometimes after you've been stunned. "I'm well enough. But Mr. Crusher here seems to have a problem."

"I don't doubt it," said the second guard; it was Detaith. He grabbed Ensign Crusher and yanked his arms behind him. "Go on, Brendan, give him a taste. Let him see what happens to people who dare to touch the captain."

Ryder reached out to Wesley's badge, slowly, smiling a little. Crusher's face worked through rage and fear, fear winning as the hand got closer. It touched the badge. There was a soft humming sound.

And Crusher's body bent half-double backward while Detaith held him. His face convulsed with pain, and he began to scream. Picard held himself rigidly still, not daring to react for fear of what it would betray. He remembered, now, in a flash, the look of fear on Stewart's face as he had reached tentatively for the man's badge. This, too, had been in Kirk's report. He had thought, had hoped, that perhaps it had gone away, since he hadn't seen the devices of which Kirk had spoken hanging at people's belts. Now, though, he saw the hope was in vain. These people would never throw away such a useful device. Refine it, make it smaller, more convenient, more effective.

Picard held himself still. Wesley screamed and screamed again and lost breath for screaming, and a kind of broken sobbing came out of him instead of breath. He began going blue: hypoxia, the lung muscles seized up in the terrible spasms of pain. Ryder drew his hand back from the badge. "That'll do for the moment," he said. "Wouldn't want him to die right off like that. He's due a long tour in the Agony Booth, I should think."

That, too, was a name Picard remembered from the report. "Not until I'm ready," he said, and added, as cover, "not until I can enjoy it. Confine him to quarters under guard."

"Yes, sir," Detaith said, and half-carried, half-dragged the sobbing, helpless Crusher away.

Ryder watched them go and said, "Sir, Mr. Barclay sent us as soon as he could, but you shouldn't wander around the ship alone like this. There are all kinds of people who wouldn't mind a shift in the status quo at the moment. Nerves are a little on edge." Ryder shook his head, watching Detaith and Crusher vanish into the turbolift. "What was *that* about?"

Picard rubbed the cut place on his throat. "Something about his father."

Ryder smiled knowingly, then let the look go as he realized Picard was staring at him. "Well, sir, you'd know more about that than I would," he said hurriedly. But was that the slightest sound of satisfaction in his voice? "You're bleeding, sir."

Picard looked at his fingers. "So I am. It's not very serious, I'll stop by sickbay later. In the meantime, you had better accompany me to engineering."

Picard headed off down the hall, with Ryder close behind him, uncomfortable thought running in the back of his mind, like the trickle of blood, hot and persistent. *Toujours l'audace,* he thought, somewhat bitterly, as he went. He longed for his own universe, though it should be infested with Romulans and every kind of unknown danger. Better than this dark mirror of his own, where one's worst fears kept threatening to come true.

CHAPTER 8

Elsewhere, in the darkness, another island of light floated, swept along a wildly varying path; alone in the darkness, trying to stay that way.

Will Riker sat at Picard's desk in his ready room, staring at the reports coming up on his screen. He hardly saw them; he was afraid. Not for himself: paradoxically, that was something he usually felt most acutely after a crisis. Occasionally, more than occasionally, he had had cause to bless that fact. But there had been no communication from the landing party for an hour now. Not that any had been planned—but the silence was as racking as communication might have been. He didn't know which to prefer. The thought of his friend, his commander, and Deanna, enduring who knew what over there, all at once, out of help, out of range, was almost more than he could bear.

"Riker to Chief O'Brien."

"O'Brien here."

"Any change?"

"No change, Commander. Their life-sign telemetry is coming back just fine."

There was that to be grateful for, at least. "Very well, Chief. You'll let me know if there's any change . . ."

"Right away, sir. Count on it." O'Brien's voice was gentle.

"Thank you, Miles. Out." Riker made a grim face at his own uneasiness and turned his attention back to the screen. He had had a bad hour with two sets of data: the first information that Geordi had sent back from the other *Enterprise,* and Geordi's own list of the files that Stewart had managed to transfer to that ship. To Riker's horror, the latter were not only information about the *Enterprise's* weapons array, engine capacity, and power, but also almost all of her threat-response files—the computer-managed programs that helped the helm officer and weapons officer "fight" the ship, taking most of the work off them and leaving them free to orchestrate new and different moves that would specifically address an enemy's weaknesses in the heat of combat. With this information, that other *Enterprise's* computers could predict, preempt, almost all the defensive moves and many of the aggressive moves that his own *Enterprise* might make in a battle situation. To discover that their enemies had this data was, to put it mildly, not good news.

Riker was certain that the only reason they hadn't been attacked so far was that the computer and crew on board the other *Enterprise* were busy analyzing this information, and using their own computer to incorporate and invent responses to it. It was a grim certainty, but as far as Riker was concerned, there was no reason that two couldn't play at that game. For the past hour or so he had had a considerable amount of computer space freed for the business of analyzing and creating threat responses to the weapons array and capabilities of the other ship.

Riker was glad to have the information to work with, but battle with this other vessel was still going to be a nasty prospect. The other *Enterprise* had nearly 80 percent again their engine capacity and was hideously overweaponed— not only in terms of phasers and photon torpedoes, but in terms of other weapons he had never heard of. No matter, he would prepare his ship as well as he could. They would fight the good fight and make the other *Enterprise* sorry it had ever started this business.

He allowed himself a grin that he would not have allowed any of the crew to see at that point. If worse came to worst, and if there was any way to manage it, he would make sure that if his own universe was going to lose an *Enterprise,* so would this one. *Symmetry,* he thought ironically, *must be maintained.*

He rather welcomed the angry feelings, actually: they helped him avoid thinking about other things that would cause him too much pain and distract him from his work. Riker turned his attention back to the files he was presently perusing, the historical records Picard had been reading. It was definitely not a universe to choose to live in. He could fully understand the captain's orders to destroy the ship should they be left with no other choice. All the same, he would not leave them over there—that much Riker would assure, whether they were dead or alive. If this ship was to be destroyed, her captain would be aboard her, whatever happened—he promised himself that.

And Deanna. He turned away in pain from the thought. Her attempts in the old days to teach him the Betazed mind-disciplines had never worked out well. Now he wished with all his heart that he had a bit more ability, that he'd tried harder—anything, so that he could possibly reach out to her perceptions and let her know that he was with her in mind, if no other way. *She knows that anyway,* he told herself. But did she really? At such times, the certainty would have been worth more than gold. But it wasn't available. *And you have more than a thousand other lives to look after as well,* he reminded himself, as severely as he could.

The door chime went off. Visitors were the last thing he wanted at the moment, but there was nothing to be done about it. "Come," he said.

Hwiii glided in. "Am I interrupting something, Commander? If so, I'll come back later."

"No, come in, Hwiii. Sit—" And even in his present mood, he had to laugh a little. "I was going to tell you to sit down."

The dolphin turned that sideways grin on him. "It's a common reflex," Hwiii said, lowering his pad to a height just about a foot above desk height.

"How's your work going?"

"It's going well," Hwiii said. "Mr. Data and I have been able to very closely categorize the overt qualities of this space. This is going to be extremely useful information when we get back home. Up until now, obviously we've never had any direct instrumental measurement of another universe's physical and nonphysical qualities."

Riker raised his eyebrows and smiled slightly at the absolute certainty of the "when," but he was in no mood to argue the point. "I take it there's something you need from me, then."

"There is, Commander. I need to get out."

"Out?"

"Outside the *Enterprise* for a brief period."

Riker was mildly surprised. "Well, there's no problem with that. I'll have a shuttlecraft authorized for your use immediately. As long as you don't go into warp—"

"No, Commander, I'm sorry: I was unclear. I don't need a shuttle. I just need to go out by myself for a little while."

"You mean EVA?"

"Yes, just for a little while. We have a saying, my people"—and the dolphin's jaw dropped in a broader

165

smile—"'you might as well try to sing in air as judge direction out of water.'"

Riker could hardly begrudge a smile at that, either. "Mr. Worf and I possibly should have a talk with you in more detail about that. We have this thing called 'opera.'"

"I should be delighted to find out a little more about it. And it's true that in some matters the saying has become obsolete: even some of our own singing now has parts written for 'airborne voice'—human specialists come to sing with us sometimes, these days. But the saying is still good in this respect: to judge a medium most accurately—the instruments can take one of my people only so far—for best evaluation of hyperstring structure and nature, I really need to get out there and feel it on me. The *Enterprise,* unfortunately, is of such a mass that it creates a certain amount of interference, distortion, in what I'm most desperately needing to sense. All the readings are inevitably colored by the mass in which they rest. I should like to get away—not very far: even a few hundred meters would be fine—and do some 'fine-tuning,' as it were, of perceptions and instrumentation."

"Will it take you long?"

Hwiii swung his tail no. "No more than an hour. Can you spare me that long?"

"Is this in aid of your own research, or is this something that has to do with our present predicament?"

"Both! Sea alone knows, there are times when even the most assiduously pursued research needs to be put aside. I would do so gladly, but fortunately the two problems are swimming in pod at the moment. No, there are definitely differences in this space that seem to have nothing to do with hyperstring structure per se. I'm trying to follow those up. Without going into too much technical detail, hyperstring structure here seems to be both slightly more complex and slightly more . . . *elastic* is the best word I can use . . . than it is in our universe. If what Mr. Data and I suspect about the methods used to bring us here is in fact correct—if this information is in fact corroborated by what Mr. La Forge is able to bring back with him, once the other *Enterprise*'s computer cores have been penetrated—then we may be able to ensure against its happening again. I think that space in a given area of, say, *this* universe can be caused to infect, contaminate, influence, space in a congruent area of a neighboring universe, briefly—to cause the congruent universe's hyperstring structure to become more 'flexible,' in tune with its own. So that a ship like ours might be propelled across the boundary."

"Or sucked in," Riker said thoughtfully.

"Sucked would be an adequate description, since energy tends to flow from areas of higher concentration to those of lesser, and the movement can be perceived as a suction on at least one side of the transaction. And if such a transfer was timed so that the hyperstring structure was more energetic on, say, our home side of the transfer and less energetic here, then everything in that area of space—and it wouldn't have to be very large—would find itself drawn or pulled or sucked into the congruent space." Hwiii shook his fins in a gesture Riker assumed was meant as a shrug. "It's possible, but there are more tests I need to run, and the simplest and most conclusive of them will involve me getting out there in my skin."

"Without a *space suit?*"

"No, Commander, I'm sorry: I was being idiomatic. I have a space suit—it's in my luggage."

"You have a maneuvering pack on that?" Riker said, slightly uneasy.

"Yes, sir, it's quite well equipped. It's the delphine form of the standard spacecraft maintenance and installation suit that they use at the Yards at Utopia Planitia. Manipulators and so forth are all installed."

Riker thought about it. "All right, Commander. Just one thing. Thrusters or not, I would prefer that you be tethered.

That way, if for some reason we have to move quickly, at least you'll still be inside the warpfield and matching our velocity so that we can beam you in without any trouble."

"I was going to suggest as much. Five hundred meters will more than satisfy my needs, if you agree."

"Make it so. And let me know what you find out."

"Absolutely I will." Hwiii boosted himself up on his pad and started to back a little toward the door, then paused. Riker had let his eyes drop to the screen. "Something else?"

"Commander." Hwiii paused. "I would hope not to be intruding . . ."

"In what regard?"

The dolphin looked uncomfortable, but resolute. "You're very troubled. I would intervene on your behalf."

The phrasing struck Riker as odd: *would* not as a conditional but as a statement of intent. "Intervene with who?" he said, somewhat puzzled.

The dolphin let out a little blowhole-snort of laughter. "I wasn't using the word in the personal sense. With the universe, I suppose. You are being greatly tried."

"I wish you could," Riker said somewhat ruefully. The dolphin hung there looking at him quietly. Will had a powerful urge to tell him to go away, and just as powerful an urge to confide in him. *Who do you go to for advice,* he thought, *when the counselor's gone?* He had no time for Ten-Forward just now. The friend to whom he might most readily have turned, the fellow officer and professional whom he might have consulted in that capacity, and the mentor and command figure who was also good for advice —all three were missing. *Worf*—Riker smiled a little at his own thought. Occasionally Worf's viewpoint was a little too alien to be of use in a given matter: this was probably one of them. And Data, full of knowledge as he was, was still a novice in emotional matters. *But what kind of good advice is someone going to be able to give you who spends all his time underwater?* said a snide voice in the back of Riker's mind.

He knew the sound of his own hopelessness and ignored it. "I am troubled," he said to Hwiii. "My commanding officer and two of my shipmates are absent in circumstances of extreme danger. And I'm particularly close to all those people."

"But especially to one of them."

"Gossip gets around, doesn't it?" Riker said softly.

Hwiii swung his tail. "Observation is enough, Commander. Circumstances like these can be extremely painful. I honor your commitment."

"You mean my bloody-mindedness," Riker said softly, "to suggest that she—that I send my shipmates into a situation like this."

Hwiii settled a little toward the desk, put a forefin out, and studied it thoughtfully for a moment.

"Intervene," Riker said. "It's an odd word."

Hwiii blew a bubble of laughter. "Many of the aquatic peoples' viewpoints tend to be . . . a little on the passive side, by human reckoning. Thought and discussion are usually considered superior to action, in our cultures. To do almost anything but eat, sleep, and sing is considered in some quarters to be 'intervention in the business of the universe.'"

"Which is expected to manage it by itself, I take it."

"Through our lives, yes. . . . The evening you came and shouted that dreadful word at me, I was singing. Mr. Data correctly identified the source."

"The *Song of the Twelve.*"

"Yes. It's hard to explain to someone not aquatically acculturated. We aren't a great people for ceremonial, but some ceremonies we do enact at more or less regular intervals, or when circumstances seem to require it. The *Song* is one of those. It's not so much a reenactment— though it does describe something that happened a long time ago—but a pro-enactment, you might call it. You can never tell quite how it's going to end, even though there are general guidelines."

"Is it a religious ceremony?" Riker said cautiously.

Hwiii looked thoughtful. "Well, it would be hard for me to say: I'm no expert in human religions, but—don't they usually involve belief, and belief systems?"

"Often."

Hwiii glanced at the chair on his side of the desk. "Well. Do you believe in that chair?"

Riker blinked. "I don't know if it would make a difference if I did or not. The chair's there."

"That's right," Hwiii said very cheerfully. "It's like that. Anyway, there are twelve parts to the *Song*—well, thirteen, actually, one part is more or less virtual. Some of them are potentially fatal."

"There must not be a lot of demand for them, then," Riker said, wondering what this was leading to.

"Oh, no, on the contrary, people fight for the right to sing them. Fatality isn't always certain. There are always people who like to take that kind of risk, for the glory of it or the honor, or other personal reasons." Hwiii shrugged. "Anyway, I had a partner who thought she might sing one of those parts."

"One of the fatal ones."

"Oh, yes. And she came to me for advice about it finally. I wasn't quite sure what to say. It's worse because I'm considered something of an adviser—because I do all this work with Starfleet, and a lot of work with humans." Hwiii blew a small sound of bemusement. "Bear in mind, there are quite a lot of our people who don't feel that we *should* have more to do with humans than we can help. Because of what you did to your cetaceans. To *our* cousins, as it were. Other alien races are another story, but some of us prefer to dwell on that old bad history. Now, my feeling personally is that you can't live in the past forever, or you don't get much living done—except dead people's lives, and even *they're* done with theirs. But all the same, here I was being asked because I was such an expert"—and the irony was now unmistakable—"whether I thought my best friend, as she was, should possibly go off and get killed. At the same time, I understood the ethical questions. You don't sing the *Song of the Twelve* for entertainment; you sing it because it needs doing, because people need to be reminded who they are and where they came from. The *Song* does that. And if people forget who they are, they lose the nature of it. So I told her, absolutely, she should go away and do it."

Hwiii was quiet for a long time.

"So what happened?" Riker said finally, intrigued.

"Oh, she lived," Hwiii said, looking thoughtfully into some distance, probably one filled with water rather than air. "In fact, she got podded because of it, she and a couple of the other singers. They've settled up off the Carolinas somewhere." His eyes came back to the here and now. "The point is, I know how you feel. Necessity is hard on love. But love is tough. It survives it . . . if you don't assume it's going to die."

Riker looked at the smiling face and detected the somberness behind it. "Hwiii, I much appreciate it."

The dolphin swung his tail sideways and headed for the door. "Keep your tail up," he said.

Riker breathed out, smiled a small smile, and went back to his reading.

In that other ship, Picard strolled into engineering, with Barclay, who had come running after Ryder reported the incident with Wesley, right behind him. All around him, crewmen saluted. He returned the salute and sauntered on in, carefully keeping his astonishment out of view. He found he had erred in thinking of engineering as merely "as big as a barn": it was more like a cathedral.

The main axis of it appeared to run at least halfway

down the primary hull, lined on both sides, on several levels, by rows and rows of paneling, instrumentation, engine-status and shield-status readouts, all the paraphernalia of an engine room. In the middle of it, the "nave" as it were, where the power conduits would branch off to either side and service the warp nacelles, stood the huge tower of the main matter/antimatter exchanger, four times the height of the one on his own ship, piercing upward through several decks and downward through several more. With the ship running on impulse, the throb of the engines was much muted: only the occasional soft, shuddering *boom* ran through the great space. Everything was dimly lit except for various pools of light at workstations, and the light byproduct of the matter/antimatter exchanger. It was a cathedral indeed, a cathedral to Force, on a sheer brutal level that Picard had not thought possible.

"Now where do you think Mr. La Forge will be in all this?" he said to Barclay casually as they walked along.

"Probably down at the main status readouts, Captain," Barclay said, "or in his office. We'll look down there first."

Picard nodded and walked along with him, looking around casually. It was still very odd to be in a version of his ship where you couldn't tell immediately where someone was—but these people apparently felt that communication was a lesser priority, not a necessity. That by itself was so diagnostic of them. . . . Talking was not in their style. Bullying, yes; commanding, and then destroying if the orders weren't obeyed. No discussion, no give-and-take: just take. *Though it's true, too,* Picard thought ruefully, *that among these people, communications like ours would be dreadfully abused. You could immediately find out where that person was that you wanted to assassinate, track his movements.*

Barclay gestured with his chin toward the matter/antimatter exchanger. "There he is, sir."

They walked down the great open space through the soft

murmur of machinery and crewmen attending their stations. The main status readout board was an overblown version of Geordi's main board in engineering, this one positioned just in front of the matter/antimatter exchanger column, and looking uncomfortably like an altar to the great god Power. La Forge was leaning over the board, studying readings. He looked up, saw them coming, and hurried to come to attention and salute.

Picard simply stood and let him hold it for a long second or two before returning the salute, then moved around the board toward him, slowly.

"Well, Mr. La Forge, about that report . . ."

La Forge stood his ground as Picard drew near and lifted one hand near La Forge's badge. La Forge actually set his teeth. Picard wagged a finger of the raised hand at him and said, "Be more careful next time. I should dislike losing my chief engineer just as I've gotten him broken in."

La Forge sagged a little. Picard said, "Now. You seem to be studying something here with some interest?"

La Forge looked concerned for a moment, turning his attention back to the panel. "Yes, Captain. I was noticing some odd energy readings over the last couple of hours—fluctuations I'm not sure how to explain." He added hurriedly, "We'll find out what they are, no problem."

"I wouldn't expect anything less of you, Mr. La Forge," Picard said as mildly as he could, and wandered around the status board, thinking, *They've noticed our transports, small as they are. I'll have to tell Troi and Geordi not to risk any further ones.* He brushed a hand idly over the board as he passed, changing some of the displays until he found one that showed, as the bridge display had, the main power couplings to the nacelles, to ship's systems and shielding, and to that third source. Here it had a label: *Inclusion Apparatus.*

Greatly daring, he tapped that spot on the schematic and said, "How's this behaving itself?"

"Come and see." La Forge led him off down the great right-hand corridor leading away from the exchange column, down one of the "transepts." Picard followed him, not too quickly, with Barclay in tow.

They turned left into a huge bay some twenty meters wide and thirty deep. In the midst of this, connected by optical, computer, and power conduits that vanished under the floor, was an apparatus that seemed to be housed in several great cabinets. It made no sound. Several status boards were erected around it, one at each corner of the installation. The whole thing had a balanced and symmetrical look, and Picard found himself wondering whether that symmetry had something to do with the basic theory of it.

He paused by one of the boards, tapped it a few times to cycle through its available display configurations, and tried desperately to memorize what he was seeing—for Geordi would need this information. He wished Geordi himself were here to make some kind of sense of it. *Just have to do the best I can by myself.* There were references to "chord ingress" and "egress," "oscillation." He remembered abruptly that Hwiii had been discussing oscillation in relation to hyperstrings. "Negative sines," "positive sines." He shook his head. "It's a masterwork," he said, "that much I understand."

He started to walk around the installation slowly with Geordi beside him and Barclay bringing up the rear.

"Everything continues to test out normal," Geordi said. "The local structure of space is continuing to show some slight irregularities, but that's understandable under the circumstances."

"You're sure it won't produce a problem?" Picard said sharply.

"Oh, no, Captain, not for the time that ship will be here. If it were here too long, there would be growing field disturbances. After all, this universe would have just gotten heavier by one point five million metric tons. On the macro scale, the universe can absorb that kind of change of mass. On the local scale, though, in median time, say within a few hundred thousand parsecs, things could get pretty shaken up—the space of our universe being closed, after all, and balanced for a certain amount of matter, the amount present at its inception. It's a good thing there aren't any stars or planets in this area: they would have reacted adversely by now."

Picard nodded at all this. His brain was resounding now with the phrase *for the time that ship will be here.* "And when it's gone?" he said, trailing off.

"Then everything snaps back to normal."

"Even after—energy discharges, photon torpedoes, and so forth?" He purposely kept his phrasing vague.

"Oh, yes, Captain," La Forge said. "As long as no matter more than ten to the sixteenth grams is left here, there won't be any ill effects to our universe."

That clinched it, then. Picard suddenly knew what was going to happen. *As long as that threshold amount of mass is left here. They're not, then, merely planning to capture the ship and destroy it.* "When it's gone . . ." *They're going to send it back. Not with one of our crews. With* theirs . . . ! That at least seemed perfectly clear. "Mass less than ten to the sixteenth grams. . . ." He thought briefly. *If you took all the weight of all the bodies on the* Enterprise . . . *let's see now . . . average weight per person, say a hundred kilos . . .* He did the sum in his head. All the human beings and other creatures aboard the *Enterprise* lumped together would be *much* less than ten to the sixteenth grams. And in his mind, Picard saw the sudden image of many, many bodies, floating frozen in space or phasered out of existence. . . . Matter could neither be created nor destroyed, of course: their component mass would still exist, in other forms. But this universe wouldn't be harmed. And it wouldn't matter to these people how his crew died, so long as they did and left room on the *Enterprise* for their own people, their counterparts.

He nodded and walked on around the great apparatus in its cabinets. At a stroke, he had been deprived of one option he had been considering, in which he had instructed Riker: the option of destroying the *Enterprise* while still in this universe, if they couldn't get back. *They would have reacted adversely,* La Forge had said. Was he understating? How much? Could hundreds of thousands of parsecs of space *really* be affected by the permanent presence of this extra mass? And if it could—could the destruction of his *Enterprise* here destroy life in *this* universe? He couldn't imagine the exact mode of the destruction, but somehow he was sure it would happen. So far he had not found a single bright spot about any of this situation: *this* unpalatable prospect wasn't very likely to be the exception.

Even in this universe—skewed and warped as it seemed —on some of these planets, around some of these stars, there had to be innocent lives, millions of them, people not responsible for this situation, not contributing to it. He would not be their murderer. Yet, at the same time, a cold voice far back in his brain said, *Are you sure this universe wouldn't profit from being killed? Are you* very *sure?* Look *at it! Is this life?*

He thrust that thought resolutely away. *Transporter or no transporter, I must find a way to warn the* Enterprise *about this. At least, I have to get this information to Geordi and Troi. They might be able to devise something.* And he himself would have to devise quickly a way to get Geordi into the core, and some way to incapacitate this ship as thoroughly as possible. Two birds with one stone would be best, if it could be managed.

There was a sound of footsteps, and he and Geordi and Barclay all turned to see Lieutenant Worf approaching them. "Commander Riker sent me to ask whether eighteen hundred hours will be all right for that briefing you wanted."

What briefing? Picard almost said, and caught himself in a hurry. He wondered whether this was some sort of trick, or simply something his counterpart had asked for before going to his quarters. "Briefing," he said, trying to sound neither too vague nor too certain. "Eighteen hundred will be fine. Though—" He paused for a moment. "Never mind. Was there anything else?"

"No, Captain," said Worf.

"Good," La Forge said. "Then get out of here, slave."

Picard, looking at La Forge, was not entirely surprised to see the flare of jealousy and protectiveness. But this was not just an exaggerated case of what command-level personnel sometimes called "engineer's disease," the tendency for engineering personnel to consider their department, and by extension the whole ship, as their personal property, and to treat any intrusion into engineering by anyone, even the captain, as just that—an intrusion. In this La Forge it had a nasty edge to it, and he used it, apparently, as an excuse to express his personal contempt for Worf.

It abruptly became too much for Picard. "Mr. La Forge," he said, being careful to keep his phrasing neutral, keeping the anger out of his voice, "I will have my senior officers treat my junior officers with due respect."

La Forge laughed, a single harsh, disbelieving bark. "Him? His people have lost any respect *they* might have ever had."

Picard glanced sideways toward Worf. He merely looked at La Forge, his eyes surprisingly calm, and said nothing.

"Whatever the case may be regarding that," Picard said, "he is an officer aboard my ship." And he looked La Forge thoughtfully in the visor, then down at his badge, and up at his visor again.

"Yes, Captain," La Forge said, actually through gritted

teeth. "Well, if there's anything else you need, please call me. *I* have work to do." And, undismissed, he stalked away.

He is very certain of his position, Picard thought, *and of his necessity to what's going on here. He bears watching.*

"I'm sorry about that," Picard said to Worf. "It seems uncalled for."

"On the contrary, he's quite right." The calm way that Worf put it had some unspoken tragedy at the bottom of it.

"Walk with me, Lieutenant," Picard said. Together they began to make their way out of engineering, with Barclay behind at a respectful distance. They said little until they were well past the matter/antimatter exchange column and heading down the great main hall toward the exit.

"I do not condone his rudeness," Picard said. "If discipline and effectiveness are to be maintained . . ."

Worf shook his head. "Captain, you have not often spoken to me in this mode."

Picard glanced from left to right and back to Worf again. "Possibly, because the walls seem to have ears around here. I doubt many people on this ship speak what they're thinking."

"Indeed not," Worf said. "To reveal your thoughts to a superior could be suicidal; to reveal them to an equal might alert them too soon to some trap you were laying for them. And as for inferiors, like myself . . ." He shrugged, and there was no tone of bitterness about the way he said it. "That would betray weakness. No one here betrays weakness and lives long to tell about it."

Picard recalled an early writer's description of hell as a bureaucracy run along much the same lines and repressed a shudder. "I should dislike to think that any of my crewmen actually considered themselves to be inferior, Mr. Worf."

Beside him Worf shook his head slightly as they went out into the corridor. "Captain, when one comes from a race that has submitted, there is no other way to be perceived by most of the population of Starfleet, or any Starfleet ship. If you are not Earth human, or from one of the Earth-colonized worlds; or if you are not Vulcan, or from one of the Vulcan provincial planets—then you are a second-class citizen. A species that cannot at least fight the Empire to a standstill cannot be considered fit to stand with it in command, in rule. A species that submits or is warred down is good only to 'hew wood and draw water.' Slaves at worst—a sort of tame curiosity at best."

Worf was silent for a moment as they came around a curve in the hallway, and both he and Barclay looked ahead to see who was there. Then Worf said, "After their long war with the Empire, outweaponed and outnumbered as they were, the survivors of my people decided that life was sweeter than honor. By surrender, they thought, they could at least purchase the lives of the noncombatants on the Klingon homeworld. Perhaps they deluded themselves by thinking that at some later date, resistance could begin again and honor could be regained: their descendants would live to fight another day. But a delusion it was. Their descendants have known nothing but the Empire for three generations now. At this point in time, I doubt whether the fighting will happen on any 'other day' at all." He looked at Picard. "They have grown used to their position . . . perhaps wisely. For who can resist the Empire? Not that there is much of anyone left to try. Otherwise, why would we be here?"

Picard's mind had begun to run in small circles. *The Klingons here . . . not allies, but a conquered race?* He could barely imagine such a thing. *What kind of power did the Empire have to reduce them to this?* And then, more dreadful still, the words *No one left to try. Why else would we be here?*

There were a hundred questions Picard wanted to ask

about that phrase, and none that he dared utter just now. "Mr. Worf, all this is very old history. How does it affect your honor here and now?"

"Captain, it hardly matters. My whole planet was 'discommended' nearly a century ago now, when the Earth fleets first beat our own spaceforce back into our own space, cutting us off from our ally worlds and then destroying them. It was the last time our fate was in our hands, and we threw it away." Worf looked dreadfully resigned: it was the face of a man discussing a cause lost before he was born, and unlikely ever to be found. "It hardly matters now."

"It matters very much," Picard said. "Especially insofar as it affects your . . . efficiency."

Worf looked at him rather oddly. "I serve and am content to do that. And mostly I am left alone, and that contents me as well." The resignation and the pain again . . . it was almost more than Picard could bear. "But I thank you for your show of concern, Captain. It is very—" He actually stumbled over the word, as if it was one he had never considered saying to the man he spoke with. "Very kind of you."

"A matter of efficiency only, Mr. Worf," Picard said as briskly as he could. But he was lying, and he knew from the look on Worf's face that Worf knew he was—and that something was going on in the captain's mind that had never been suspected there before. "You're dismissed."

"Thank you, Captain," Worf said, and plainly meant it.

He strode ahead, making for the turbolift.

Picard watched him go and swallowed hard. The determination in him was growing to do something, *something* about all this . . . something to put it right.

But what?

CHAPTER 9

"**M**r. Barclay," Picard said as they came to the turbolift, "I don't know about you, but assassination attempts make me sweat. I wouldn't mind a shower and a change."

"Yes, sir," Barclay said as they stepped into the 'lift. "Deck eleven."

The 'lift took off. Barclay eyed the scratch on Picard's chin. "You were lucky to get away with so little, sir. *Please* be more careful."

Picard's mood was not entirely sanguine. "Is that strictly professional concern? Is there anybody on this ship who would really care dreadfully if I died?"

"We wouldn't like to lose you, Captain."

"Ah, but you get perks for taking care of me. Isn't that so?"

"Captain, you've never been less than generous. Some people say you've been more generous than you had to be."

A virtue at last? Picard thought sourly. *Or just my counterpart making sure he gets value for his money?*

"And then there's Dr. Crusher, of course," said Barclay as they stepped out of the 'lift.

Picard nodded. Here as in his own *Enterprise,* old family connections, old tragedies, got talked about just as everything else. If there was anything he was certain these two ships would have in common, gossip was it. "Yes, of course. Well, never mind. At the moment, I guess we should be grateful there aren't more attempts—eh, Mr. Barclay?"

"Yes, sir," Barclay said ruefully. "But that's what we're here for . . . we're as much of a deterrent as anything else."

"Point taken," Picard said as they came to his quarters. "Keep guard, will you, Mr. Barclay? I don't care to be disturbed just now."

"Yes, sir." Barclay stationed himself by the doorway. Picard walked in, paused, touched the control to lock the door as it shut. *Interesting,* he thought, *that he didn't check this space out before he let me in. Apparently the captain's quarters are expected to be secure. Or else someone has them under scan.* The thought made his hair rise again. Could everything that had happened so far be an act, masking the fact that someone had seen the snatch of this ship's Picard happen and was just biding time, waiting for the right moment to take *him* out of circulation? Could it mean— But no. He shook his head. There was such a thing as being *too* paranoid, even here.

He headed into the shower, turned it on, then bent briefly over his communicator. "Mr. La Forge," he whispered, "this is urgent. The 'inclusion' apparatus responsible for our being here is in the engine room. *Enterprise*"—he assumed Geordi would know which one he meant—"must *not* remain in this locality. Equally urgent: intent is that *Enterprise* will be restaffed with others, then returned. Also, transport has been noticed. End message. One acknowledgment if you two are all right, two if there's a problem."

The badge buzzed once under his fingertips and did nothing else.

There's a relief, Picard thought, and started stripping out of the uniform, carefully removing the badge and medals. Geordi had been confident enough that this area couldn't be scanned, but Picard still preferred paranoia: if the sound hadn't blocked out his words, they themselves might still be fairly confusing to any local listener. He could only hope for the best.

In the shower, he thought hard. He needed a quick way to incapacitate at least one of the ship's major systems. There was no way to get away with it quietly in engineering: there were simply too many people down there, and he wouldn't know where to begin. The smartest way would be the back way, the way Geordi had tried. Some different back way, though—not so carefully watched. The trouble was telling which ones were watched, here. Almost everything seemed to be. How any undertaking as colossal as a starship, or a Starfleet, could be sustained in such an atmosphere of profound mistrust . . . Picard found it difficult to understand.

A couple of hours, Troi had said, *until the next phase begins.* Not very long. *And what next phase?* One possibility presented itself: that they were ready to move against the *Enterprise,* that they intended to batter her into submission, take her, and put their own crew aboard. *For the time that ship will be here . . . until she's gone,* Geordi had said. Picard could find no other way to interpret that. They would take her back to her home universe, with their own crew . . . and do what? *There's no way they could take on all of Starfleet . . .*

. . . could they? Perhaps this had been a test to see whether a Starfleet ship could be sucked out of her own universe—"included" into theirs—restaffed with matching crew and sent back . . . to pass as herself. The pretense couldn't be kept up forever. But did they mean it to? And did they need it to? On one of these missions such as his *Enterprise* was running now, far out in the middle of

183

nowhere, how often did a starship actually contact another ship, or planet? They might be out of touch with anything but Starfleet Command for weeks at a time, sometimes, depending on the distance, even months. Eventually the pretense would come apart—they would be ordered back into space where details about the crew were known, back to a starbase or back to Earth, even, for maintenance, for some other mission. Sooner or later someone would detect that crew members weren't acting the way they should. And indeed that acting would be the worst part of it, for a crew from this universe. Spock's note to his debriefing document was pertinent: that the only reason his captain and shipmates had survived their experience was because it was easier for a civilized man to pretend to be a barbarian than for a barbarian to pretend to be civilized. But even so, the pretense could be kept up for a good while. And during that time, someone willing to put his mind to it could find out all kinds of things about the Federation from the *Enterprise's* computers, and from the regular data downloads from Starfleet Command. What could be done to one ship . . .

. . . could be done to more. There had to be more to what they were planning. Just that realization was enough to convince Picard that they had to be stopped, even if it meant destroying this ship with him on it.

But that might not be enough. If the *Enterprise* didn't manage to get a warning home to its own universe, it would all happen again, at some other time, with some other ship, and heaven only knew what the end would be.

He got out of the shower, put on another uniform matching the one he had been wearing, reapplied the badge and medals, then went back into the room and just stood there a moment, trying to calm himself. An idea would come, if he could just keep calm. Something always came.

He looked around, trying briefly to identify any small differences between his own quarters and these. But everything seemed unnervingly as it ought to be. Bed made, furnishings just as in his own quarters, nothing out of place.

His eye fell on the bookshelf. It was exactly as his old friends at home had warned him: there was no such thing as keeping "just a few books," not even here on a starship, the most space-conscious and weight-conscious of environments. Still the books bred, no matter how carefully he tried to choose them: people gave him books as presents, or books leapt into his hands when he was on leave on strange worlds, as if they knew a sympathetic reader. Now he looked at the books suspiciously—but they were the same, just the same.

Or so he thought. He wandered over to gaze at them. Some of them were very much what you might expect in a limited collection of someone native to Earth: the complete Shakespeare, and the ancient King James Bible, there, he cheerfully admitted, more for the antique beauty of its language than for most of the contents: a pairing that Admiral Parry-Smyth had laughed at, when she had last visited, making an obscure reference to something called "Desert Island Discs." The rest of the collection was suitably—possibly, the admiral had claimed, pathologically—eclectic: the three original-edition Dixon Hill books, of course: *Murder in Camera, The Knowing Look,* and *Under the Sun.* Then two of the venerable old hardcover Everyman editions of Kipling, *Barrack Room Ballads* and *Kim.* One of the first Centauri Press editions, a reprint of Glocken's *The Stars out of Joint;* various others—a book of Restoration poets, Sun Tzu's *The Art of War* in the long-lost Cordwainer Smith translation, along with Rouse's prose *Iliad* and *Odyssey,* and Hamilton's peerless translations of Aristotle and the great comedies of Aristophanes. The Oxford University Press hardcover of Eddison's *Eriks Saga,* next to a weary, broken-spined trade paperback of *Little, Big;* and so many others. . . . There was even a very late addition to the collection, a present from Will Riker just a month ago on his return from a leave trip to Hay-on-Wye—the Eyre and Spottiswoode edition of Colin Watson's droll and acute *Snobbery with Violence,* the best (and, appropriately, the least snobbish) analysis ever done of the early Terran detective novelists. Everything here, all accounted for.

He found that this shook him as badly as everything else, the whole barbaric world outside the doors of his quarters. *Who am I here,* he thought, *that what I see here can so completely match what exists back on the—back home?*

"Computer," he said softly. It chirped. "Read out record of present command," he said, his mouth dry.

"Picard, Jean-Luc," the computer said. "Assumed command ICC 1701-D *Enterprise* on stardate 41124, after destruction of previous command, ICC 2055 *Stargazer,* subsequent to victory at Battle of Maxia, stardate 33070. First action: destruction of Farpoint Station due to attack on ship by alien spacegoing life-form. Second action: enforcement action on planet Ligon II. Third action—"

"Stop. Nature of enforcement action on Ligon II."

"South continent of Ligon II rendered uninhabitable by high-gamma fission-producing devices to induce planetary government to provide vaccine necessary to control plague on planet Stryris IV."

They irradiated—we irradiated a whole continent? "How many casualties?" he whispered.

"Neutralizations estimated in excess of thirty million," the computer said calmly.

The choice of words said everything. "Continue," Picard said, and not because he wanted to.

"Third action: neutralization of Tarellian plague ship attempting to make landfall on Haven. Fourth action: recovery of stolen T-9 energy converter from Ferengii Alliance ship. Fifth action: prejudicial terraforming and

186

orbital reconfiguration of Ferengii home planet. Sixth action—"

What did we do to them? Picard thought, shocked. While not exactly fond of the Ferengii, he felt that they had as much right to live untroubled as anyone else. He swallowed. "Computer—clarify intervention at Ferengii home planet."

"Planet surface was cleansed of alien life-forms; later relocated to orbit around gamma Cephei prior to resettlement by approved species."

He swallowed again. "Go on."

"Sixth action: excision of hostile alien life-form on Rubicon III and incorporation of native species into Empire. Seventh action . . ."

It went on and on that way, and he made himself sit still and listen to it: the destruction of the Jaradan species, the murder of the intelligent inorganic life-form on Velara III so that the terraforming of that planet could continue, the punitive decimation of the Aldeans after their attempt to abduct *Enterprise* crew. . . . It was a long recitation, and when the computer finally fell silent, Picard was shaking with horror and rage.

He got up and started to pace, unable to keep himself still. *At least,* he thought, trying to force himself to calm, *we should be thankful for small favors: they've never met Q. Or the Borg.* Though he found himself wondering whether a meeting with the Borg might not have been good for these people—for this Empire as a whole—if the catalog of *Enterprise*'s pillagings, slaughters, planetary destructions, and other horrific actions was typical of this universe's Starfleet. *The Borg might even be beneficent by comparison,* he thought bitterly. *They might be cold and inhuman, but they aren't sadistic or purposefully cruel.*

That thought, that he would wish the Borg on anybody, no matter how they acted, so shocked Picard that he stopped himself in his tracks and just breathed in and out a few times, which his own Troi would doubtless have told him to do if she were there. Picard turned to the bookshelves, desperate for something dependable, some breath of plain clean air in this miasma of destructiveness and cruelty, and reached out to the Shakespeare.

It fell open, typically, at a favorite spot near the end of *The Merchant of Venice.* Despite his distress, he smiled at the sight of the page: Portia's speech. *The quality of mercy is not strained; / it falleth as the gentle rain from heaven / upon the place beneath; it is twice blest; / it blesseth him that gives and him that . . .*

He blinked. Expectation and familiarity had deceived him, for the words weren't there. Or, no, some of them were, but— He scanned down the page.

POR. And hath this Shylock not such right to justice
    as much as any other man in Venice?
    Did not Antonio the merchant there
    know well enough the rigor of the bond
    when first its terms were named? Yea, though he did,
    did he not laugh, and bind himself therewith,
    no matter that he did not love the Jew?
    Though justice be his plea, consider this:
    that even so the Jew lent on his gold,
    trusting the just completion of his bond.
    And now Antonio comes, and mercy asks,
    in lieu of justice in this noble court.
    What, shall the weight of our old dreadful law
    be bent by mere fond pity and soft loves,
    the oak bowed while the reed stands by and mocks?
    The quality of mercy must be earned,
    and not strewn gratis on the common ground
    as pearls for rooting swine, to any fool
    who staggers eyeblind into his own folly

and cries, "Oh pity me!" Else mercy's self
grows cheap and tawdry from her overuse.

SHY. O wise young judge, how do I honor thee!
    Now, forfeiture: now justice, and my bond!

POR. Nor shall men trifle with our law's sense,
    seeking their own escape. Saith not the bond
    'a pound of flesh'? And who beyond child's years
    is such a fool to think that flesh is cut
    without blood shed? Such wry and cogging thought
    does but betray itself as treachery,
    deception in the egg, addled ere hatched.

SHY. 'Tis very true: most wise and upright judge!
    We trifle time: I pray thee, pursue sentence!

POR. A pound of that Antonio's flesh is thine:
    the law allows it and the court awards it.
    And let what blood may in this surgery run
    be interest on three thousand ducats lost.

SHY. Most learned judge! A sentence! Come, prepare!
            Antonio being held, he cuts out his
            heart and weighs it.

ANT. Oh, I die! A curse on all your heads!

SHY. Fie, such felons' mouthings shall miss merely.
    Nay, 'tis too much. Prithee, give it him back.
            He throweth the excess back.

Horrified, Picard scanned back up the text of the play
and found nothing but long humorous passages about the
folly of people who entered into agreements and then

189

depended on the putative kindness of the other parties. The whole play was seen as an example of the triumph of the state over the pettifogging of special interests and sentiment, and everything in it was as blatantly and sensationally done as anything in *The Revenger's Tragedy,* with stage directions to match—in Jessica's case, where Lorenzo betrays her and then laughs in her face, *She runs on his sword and kills herself.*

Picard swallowed, his throat gone dry, more betrayed by the black ink on the yellowed page than by anything that had happened to him so far. He turned the pages and found what frightened him more second by second: a Shakespeare horribly changed in all but the parts that were already horrible. *Titus Andronicus* was much as it had been. So was *Macbeth,* and oddly, *Lear;* but Picard paged through the latter and breathed out unhappily, almost a moan, to find one small part missing: that of Cornwall's "first servant," who tries to protect old Gloucester from having his eyes plucked out and is immediately killed—a matter of a few lines in the original, now gone completely. And the other two servants gone dumb, and not even a single voice raised, now, to protest the old man's fate at the hands of Lear's hateful daughter and her husband.

Slowly Picard shut the book, put it back, and looked mistrustfully at the Bible—and, beautiful language or not, decided not to pick it up.

Other books he did look at, briefly—just long enough to see that plots and other details were changed in some cases, not in others. The *Iliad* looked about as it should have. After its time, though, something seemed to have started—a slow, relentless moral inversion. Kindness, compassion, charity, seemed to have been declared a waste of time; greed, violence, the survival of the fittest—in this case, the most ruthless—seemed to have been deemed more useful to a species "getting ahead in the world." The perfect government, in Plato, was now one in which "fear is meted out to the populace in proper proportion by the wise ruler." Civic virtue soon only mattered insofar as it served self-advancement. Acquisition, especially of power, but also of material goods and wealth—having, and *keeping,* at whatever expense to others—seemed to have become of paramount importance. It was a ruthless world, enthusiastically embodying the worst of many traits that humanity had been trying to shake for millennia. Some that *had* been shaken, in Picard's own world, remained in full and evil flower here. In one spot and another, a little light of virtue, a kind deed or moment of pity, still shone through the prose. Shakespeare was not wholly lost; Kipling, idiosyncratic as always, was still himself; so was Aristotle. But the closer the books came to modern times, the more corrupt their philosophies seemed—and even the oldest ones betrayed him abruptly, for at the end of this universe's *Iliad,* Achilles killed old King Priam while the pitiable old man was on his knees before him, begging in tears for the release of Hector's body for the burial rites. *The one time in the poem when that terrible man showed mercy,* Picard thought, closing the *Iliad* and putting it down; *that one moment of awful pain and humanity . . . But not here, it seems. Not here.* There was no question, now, why the horrible events of this Earth's twentieth and twenty-first centuries had produced the result they did. They were, perhaps, the final flowering of all this history: not a turning point, as he had thought, or a watershed, but rather the final roar of an avalanche that had started slowly, thousands of years before, in the slow settling of layer upon layer of coldheartedness and cruelty onto the high ground of the nature of Man.

He was filled with pity and horror for all the innocent lives in this universe that suffered from the result of the difference; and pitied, too, the "conquerors," the Empire and its allies, who imagined that they rode this whirlwind and were its masters. *There must be something that can be done,* he thought. *Something to stop all this, the suffering, the wanton destruction.*

But what . . . ? He would have to try to find a way. Meantime, there was other business more desperate still. Picard went back to the desk and sat down at the computer again. "Computer, read mission instructions."

"Retinal scan required," said the computer voice. He leaned close, hoping against hope that his counterpart hadn't had any injuries or surgery that he hadn't also had. The light flashed red in his eye.

"Retinal scan confirmed," said the computer, and the first screenful of data came up—

—and then the door opened, and Beverly Crusher walked in.

I thought I locked that, was the first thought that went through his head, closely followed by, *Do I want anyone to see me looking at this?* He brought his hand down on the console and cleared the screen. "Stop run," he said to the computer.

He was annoyed enough to be about to ask the doctor when knocking had gone out of style, but something about her look restrained him. She came slowly over to his desk, wearing the expression of a tired woman, and looked at him. "You *did* get a good one there, didn't you?" Beverly said, sounding slightly annoyed.

He shrugged. "I cleaned it up."

"Yes, you saved me that much trouble. Well, come on down to sickbay and we'll get you put right."

They went out together. As they passed Barclay, Picard threw him a later-for-*you* look; in return, Barclay made an expression that seemed to say, "Nothing to do with *me.*"

"You'll have heard how I got this, then," Picard said to Dr. Crusher as they came to the turbolift.

"I heard, all right. Not that he hadn't been thinking of it for a good while, under the circumstances. I suppose he had to try it eventually."

They got into the 'lift and it closed and took off. Picard

looked at Beverly in slight disbelief, while Barclay carefully examined the 'lift's ceiling. "You mean you're not—concerned?"

"He knew the risks," Crusher said, looking resigned. "If he's going to try stunts like that . . . there's nothing much I can do about it. And I'm not fool enough to try to save him from the consequences."

You're his mother! Picard was tempted to shout. He restrained himself. This place tended to bring out the desire to shout more strongly than usual. Instead, he said, "I've told Troi not to do anything further without my authorization."

Beverly breathed out, a little laugh. "You think that'll work this time? Well, you can never tell. I admit, I had a feeling you might not simply let her go ahead and kill him. He is of some value as an officer: he has a gift with the helm, and math, that's true enough." She breathed out and looked over at him. "But I think you're just storing up trouble by letting him off. Eventually, he *will* come after you again."

"Doesn't the thought that he might succeed concern you?"

She shook her head slightly. "Well, granted, my own position would be affected. But I have a fair amount of goodwill stored up, and the ship can't do without a chief surgeon. . . . Anyway, he won't get another chance. It's a surprise he got even one. What got into you? What on earth were you thinking of? Especially with Riker hot at your heels all through this to get his hands on your position, to get the credit and the glory for this mission? Did you think he was going to try to stop *any* attempt to assassinate you at this point?"

"I suppose it was foolish," Picard muttered as the 'lift stopped. Barclay put his head out, checked the area, then waved them out.

They headed for sickbay. Picard had already heard so many baffling things in one conversation that he decided to just let it drop. When they came into sickbay, Picard found it slightly different from the one aboard his own ship. The color scheme was different, darker, as most things were, so that the feeling of space and airiness in the sickbay on his own *Enterprise* was missing: this one felt smaller. The diagnostic beds were a bit closer together, the ceiling a bit lower. "Where do you want me?" he said.

"Right where I've got you," Beverly said, flashing him a small smile with more sheer wickedness about it than he had seen in anyone else's face since he got here. "All I need is a protoplaser. Just sit down where you like." She went to fetch the instrument.

Picard wandered around for a few moments, looking at the place, the diagnostic panels, the cabinets—and then he froze as his eye fell on one in particular. Everything fell into place.

He remembered looking at that cabinet back on his own *Enterprise,* and saying to Beverly, "This needs much better security—I want multiple authorizations required before . . ."

But that had plainly not happened here. It was open: it was unlocked. He slid one clear facing aside, reached in, and took the small container and the wafer that lay beside it, slipped them down into his tunic, and shut the cabinet again smoothly. He was wandering around again in the middle of sickbay before Beverly came back.

"Come on, sit down," she said. "I have other things to do today."

He sat. She ran the protoplaser along his jawline, and he felt the usual tingle as the severed nerves were reknit and complained about it, as skin sealed over and the derma rewove itself. She turned away, and he sat there rubbing his skin in the usual futile attempts to deal with the itch, which wouldn't go away for another day or so.

"You're very lucky it wasn't any deeper than that," she said. "You would have had a very amateur tracheotomy:

that knife grazed right past the cricoid cartilage. Now how are you feeling otherwise?"

"The stun?" He shook his head. "A bit of a headache . . . the usual."

"Here." She reached into another cabinet, came up with a spray hypo. Such was the level of his paranoia at this point that it was all Picard could do to hold himself still and let her administer it. He remembered what else had come out of one of her spray hypos, and poor Stewart, lying sweating and delirious in his sickbay, while this woman's counterpart looked at him and said, "What kind of doctor . . ."

"There," she said. "It's Aerosal." As usual, the headache began clearing itself away instantly.

"Thank you, Doctor," he said, getting up.

Crusher looked at him sideways, with a small smile. "My, aren't we formal today. I'll see you later."

That begged the question of where, but he let it be. He would have to go back to the bridge now, he supposed: there was really no excuse for him to go back to his quarters immediately. He was changed, he was "put right," as Beverly had put it. He desperately wanted to get back to that mission report; and now, considering what he had in his tunic, there was other business as well. . . .

But for the moment, it would be well if he was seen around and about. "Come on, Mr. Barclay," he said at the door to sickbay, "let's see what's going on around here."

They started off down the hall . . . and all his good intentions were abruptly derailed by the sound of the scream from down the corridor. He knew that scream: he had been within three feet of it, not long ago. And this time it was much worse.

"Come on," he said, and headed down the hall. Barclay followed, looking like a man who expects to see something he'll appreciate.

Around the curve of the corridor from the turbolift was

the source of the sound. It was a bay opening off the corridor, not too far away from sickbay. At first Picard wondered why it wasn't closed off if this kind of sound came out of it on a regular basis. But then he realized why. Others were *meant* to hear that sound. It was intended as a deterrent. He wondered if it was.

The bay had a raised platform in the middle of it, with a cylindrical force field shimmering around the perimeter. In the middle of it, suspended like a puppet on invisible strings, hung Wesley Crusher, his body twisting, racked with pain; and he screamed and screamed again. Not too far from him, at a console controlling the installation, stood Troi, with a couple of her own security people behind her. She turned as Picard stopped in the bay's doorway, and the smile with which she favored him was almost sunny.

"Captain," she said. "You're looking much better." She turned back to Wesley, admiring, with smiling detachment, the way he curled like a poked bug, and shrieked, and curled again.

"These do work so much better than the old ones," she said. "Those were blunt instruments at best, the old agonizers. Just general field effect on the nerves—no subtlety about it, no specificity. When they learned to tune the effect, though, when they learned to match it specifically to the requirements of the specific nervous system—so much better. No waste motion, no waste energy." She leaned against the console, smiling through the cries of desperate pain, the bark and wheeze of indrawn breath. "Each agonizer calibrated to the pain center in its wearer's brain, and matched to his nervous system, to the places where he hurts worst. One man might be better enervated in the hands than the trunk: then it's the man's hands that catch fire, not just the all-over pain that we had to settle for in the old days. And it does so much less damage than the old ones used to do . . . progress is wonderful."

She turned back to the console while Picard kept his face

from showing anything whatsoever. "And there are other refinements," she said. "Moment-to-moment evaluation of which nerves have overfired and need to rest before they become sensitive again. The shift of the load to those which have regenerated. All much more satisfactory."

"I thought I gave orders," Picard said very quietly, "that he was to be confined to quarters pending my decision on what further action was to be taken."

Troi waved a hand. "You know my authority supersedes yours in matters pertaining to security. You can't just let someone attempt to assassinate the captain of a starship and then walk away." *Oh, can't you?* Picard thought, furious, but kept his peace. "An eye for an eye, a tooth for a tooth: that's the rule, isn't it? He tried for the whole carcass. So?" She shrugged. "He gets what he's brought down on himself. How can you possibly object? . . . Or maybe you're just feeling that much better after Dr. Crusher's . . . ministrations." She gave him a half-lidded look that added a whole new set of meanings to the word.

"Counselor," Picard said. "Even in matters of security, unless there are most pressing reasons to be overridden, I expect to have my orders obeyed."

"Not in this case," Troi said, looking at him almost merrily. "You hate him! You always have. You hate him almost as much as his mother does. It hardly takes a Betazed to see that. She hates him because he reminds her of what she had that you took from her. And *you* hate him because you know that he reminds her of what you took. But you couldn't throw away good officer material, and his father still had some friends in Starfleet. This was a good way to throw them off the scent, or at best to appease them. So you bided your time and waited. You knew that eventually he would make this attempt. In fact, I think you encouraged it, so that you would then have the right to get rid of him without prejudice: who expects any failed assassin to be given mercy?"

She turned away, eyeing the console. "Some people,

today, were thinking that you had genuinely made a stupid mistake. But I don't believe that. I know you too well. I think you were careless on purpose. A good enough excuse: a tense mission, one of those quiet periods when the tension builds and people make mistakes . . . even captains. Even you." She looked at him. "So finally he makes his move, and you react, creating the perfect reason to get rid of him at last. Oh, no, I know what you want."

"Counselor," Picard said warningly. *I know what you want,* the voice said inside his head.

And it was her voice *and* his, at the same time—the same way that the Borg voice ringing through him had been the Borg's and his at the same time, that being what made it so intolerable—the feeling of a thought he was having himself that he *wasn't* actually having himself.

And hard on the heels of the thought came the deep, hard stab right to the center of him, the feeling inside of fingers picking up his thoughts and letting them trickle through hands, like pebbles, jewels, sand—flowing away, picked up again by the handful, flowing through those hands for the amusement of the one who picked them up and scrutinized them . . . idly, with amusement, hateful amusement. One thought in particular stopped her while he fought for control, struggling to throw her out. The fingers of the questing mind fixed on it, picked it up, held it up in the fierce light of her mind to examine it.

You don't *want him dead,* said the voice in his mind, incredulous. The rage was building in him at the horror of this violation. Externally he could barely move a muscle for shock; internally, he shook himself like a man coming up out of dirtied water and shouted at her, *"NO!"*

She actually flinched back from him, only slightly; then that smile came back. "Well, the things we do find. What kind of perverse desire—" She shook her head. "Unless it's something to do with the mother. Did she beg you for his life?" Again that stab, but this time it came up against the armor of Picard's rage. He felt the blow skid sideways and miss. "No, I don't think so somehow, that's not Beverly's style . . . anyway, she hates him, too, after all, and wouldn't waste her time. Then again, who knows? I really must have a talk with her about you. But it's very strange in *you*. Why should you want to keep alive the son of the man you killed, when you have a chance to get rid of him? You would think his absence would be much better for . . . domestic tranquillity."

Picard stood rigid and hung on to his rage like the armor it was. "Take him out of there, Counselor."

She stared at him. *"Now,"* Picard said. "Are you refusing a direct order?"

"No," Troi said after a moment. "Not yet. But in your present mood, I daresay you'll soon give me grounds to. And then beware."

Picard waited while her people shut the Agony Booth down. Wesley collapsed on the floor in a heap, moaning, his whole body trembling still with the overstimulation of the nerves. "Mr. Barclay," Picard said. "Call a couple more of my people. Have them come here and return Mr. Crusher to his quarters. Then stand guard over him there. He is not to be moved by anyone else. If anyone tries— stop them by whatever means necessary."

"Yes, *sir,*" Barclay said, glaring at Troi's people. Apparently there was no love lost among the officers' various guards.

Picard waited until other members of his bodyguard arrived and took Crusher away. Troi, still smiling that disturbing smile, went pointedly off in the opposite direction, toward the bridge.

"Are you all right, Captain?" Barclay said. "I felt her bearing down on you."

"You felt that, too," Picard said, inclined to shudder at the memory.

"When she's in that mode, sir, there's no *not* feeling it,

even at a distance. You're just glad you're not on the receiving end of her *real* attention. Some have been. Some die of it."

"Point taken, Mr. Barclay. Come on." Picard headed for the 'lift. "I was in the middle of some work when Dr. Crusher arrived. I need to finish it. Then we'll go back to the bridge."

CHAPTER **10**

Once back in his quarters, Picard moved swiftly, not knowing how much time he would have before he was disturbed again. Hurriedly he sat down at the desk and slipped out of his tunic the small, closed container and the wafer he had removed from Beverly's cabinet. Then he started working at the desk terminal, calling up a voiceprint-classified program, and carefully specifying an authorization code for it.

Wesley, he thought. His mind was in such turmoil on the subject of the young man, both here and there, that he hardly knew what to think. But of this he was certain: when he saw his own universe's Wesley Crusher again, he would have a word or two of exoneration for him.

Carefully Picard opened the container, slipped the wafer into it, and shut it again. He put the whole container on the media-reading spot on his desk and brought up a link between it and his desk terminal.

Now let's see how much of this I remember, he thought, and started to work. His programming was understandably rusty: captains had computers and programmers to do this kind of work for them as a rule. But he still remembered the rudiments, enough to do quick-and-dirty coding in C50 and Logex and Arian and some of the similar programs designed for directing automated tools. Tools were all these were, after all.

He brought up a visual of the contents of the container, by way of the link built into the contact wafer. There they were—a host of little six-armed creatures with crabby claws. They were one of a surgeon's most useful tools: tiny hands and manipulators that could stitch together a single nerve fibril as easily and dexterously as a sailor butt-splices a rope. They could cut and join and suture: they could weave muscle and nerve and even bone fiber together as if it were stiff cloth. An average microsurgery replacement of, say, a severed limb, or a patch of diseased brain tissue, might use a hundred, maybe even two hundred of these, depending on the size of the operative site and the amount of work to be done. There were—Picard laid a grid down over the view, using the computer, and then counted— there were about two hundred of them here. Would it be enough? He didn't know, but it had to be tried.

Some time back, after his ship had started selectively falling apart—after the string of bizarre malfunctions and systems failures—he had read, very carefully, young Ensign Crusher's science project paper on the care, feeding, education, and breeding of "nanites." Obviously here there was no time for the breeding. It would take at least a month to engender nanites who had the proper associational links and the number of neuronal connections in their joint neural network to become intelligent and self-aware. If he had such nanites at the moment, he could ask them politely if they would kindly give him a hand and then turn them loose. But the principle would still work for him now and was worthwhile. Until the damage was done, until it was too late, there was no way to detect the tiny microsurgeons loose in your optical network, or in your computer core, cheerfully chowing down on all the components in a starship's computer that made life worth living —that in fact made life possible to live at all.

Shields, life support, propulsion—and, Picard thought, most particularly, that large set of boxes down in engineering. They looked, if he was any judge of such things, to have their own set of backup computers. But there were ways around that. Chances were very good that they would be backed up to the central cores. Once the cores were out of commission—even one of them—not only would *his* chief engineer have an excuse to get at it, but those computers servicing the exclusion apparatus would be left to stand alone. And stand-alone equipment was always vulnerable. But meanwhile, why infect just one core? Geordi only needed one to work on, true, but the cores backed up to each other. He would infect them *all*.

Now—Picard got busy with his programming. These were still just machines: machines that did what you told them, though that doing might lack the charm of saying "please" to another sentient organism and having that organism say, "Why, certainly, don't mind if I do." But even without being intelligent, they were quite capable of "chewing up" and pulling apart bits of the toughest materials, one from another—even the molecules of magnetic storage medium in the cores—and reducing them, with dedication and energy, to finely divided fluff. Now he set about the specific instructions, as to what to chomp on and how and where. Communications first. Picard smiled grimly: he would teach them to value that, if nothing else. Then after that, the weapons systems. Life support—he thought about it, then decided not. "Though . . ." He changed his mind, added an instruction. Occasional random failures here and there would have a useful effect. Most of all, he instructed a party of about thirty of the microsurgery assistants to go find the area in the cores from which the agonizers and the Agony Booth were powered and programmed—if they could—and kill them.

After that, he sorted down through a list of priorities and instructed the nanites where to go to deal with each of them. As the captain of a starship, he had a fairly clear sense of in what particular associational network each grouping of information might be found. He didn't have the precise, brain-surgeon's knowledge that Geordi would have, the equivalent of the kind of knowledge that could pinpoint the spot in the brain that when triggered caused uncontrolled punning, or the memory of the scent of a garden decades gone. Picard's knowledge was more on the phrenological level, a sense of bumps and zones and likely spots, effective enough to go on with. Most specifically, he instructed his little assistants not in any way to damage the storage areas where the information about the "switchback" technique, the "inclusion" data, might be found, but to cut power to it as quickly as they might, once found—and its finding was an overriding priority for all of them. Some of them he instructed to do some work and then take themselves out of the immediate core area, holding themselves in reserve. Unless otherwise instructed, they would come out later and start the whole business again.

Picard checked his programming, twice, and three times, as he'd been taught. When he was sure that it would work, that no loops or loopholes had been left in, he activated the microsurgeons and swiftly resealed the container. Using the magnified view available from the reader, he could see them already climbing over and onto one another, trying to get out and do what the program told them, eager to be at it.

"Good luck," he said to them softly. "And if you people have time—feel free to be fruitful and multiply."

Picard slipped the container back into his tunic, then thought a moment and slipped it down a bit farther, into the waistband of his pants, where it would lie flat. If he had to suck in his gut a bit more than usual, that was fine; at least he could get at it quickly and unseen.

He got up, tried to pull his tunic down again, failed, said *"Merde!"* and checked himself briefly in the mirror and made for the door.

"Mr. Barclay," he said, looking out. "Let's go for a walk."

They went, and Picard tried to make it all look as innocent as possible. A captain, he reasoned, even here, should be seen about his ship. He found himself wondering whether the other Picard ever did this, and whether he was about to do something else that the people around him would find strange. It couldn't be helped if the other Picard never did this. At the very least, this action would serve to confuse people—and a little confusion, it seemed, could go a long way around here. But whatever result it had, it couldn't be helped: he had to get out there and sow his own little whirlwind.

Over and over, as they walked, looking into labs and research departments and armories and security post after security post, the question of what could possibly be done for this place came back to haunt him. He was not a man to believe that people were sent anywhere by any power to do anything whatever; but at the same time, the opportunity to make a difference for the good in whatever situation you found yourself was not one he had ever felt inclined to ignore. Though that urge had to be tamed and carefully watched, of course; it was one of the things the Prime Directive was for, a subset of the old medical-ethical rule *First do no harm.*

Now there's a thought, he wondered. *How would the Prime Directive be construed in this situation? Is there a tacit understanding that it's meant only for our relations with other species, not for our own? Or could one make a case that it's intended for enforcement only in our own universe? . . .* This wasn't just a can of worms: it was a barrelful. Picard smiled to himself wryly at the thought that they might come out of this danger with their skins intact, somehow, and get home, then have to go to court to prove why they should not be drummed out of the Service for interfering in the affairs of another Starfleet.

No, he was not going to spend any more time worrying about *that* prospect than he had to. He and Barclay took the 'lift down another deck and walked that one, then another and another. It was in the third 'lift they took, between decks thirty-eight and thirty-nine, that Picard took advantage of poor bored Barclay's turning away from him for a moment and turned away himself, "studying" the paneling inside the 'lift, and with his hands concealed, reached into his waistband, pulled free the little flat canister, opened it, shook its contents (except for the wafer) out on the floor, and then swiftly put everything back in place again.

They got out at deck thirty-eight, and Picard smiled and examined everything he saw with great interest, until even Barclay, so assiduous for his safety, was beginning to twitch with boredom. Behind him, Picard knew that the nanites would be escaping from the 'lift via the sheathing of its optical and power conduits and heading out onto deck thirty-eight at surprising speed. The rest of them would go down other conduits from there and get into the other computer core on the other side of the main hull, and not long after that, down into the core in the engineering hull. Tiny they might be, but they could move fast and would be unseen; and no one would associate them with *him*—which was much to be desired. And once they got into the cores . . . *I wonder how they'll like the FTL field,* he thought, and smiled. *It should help matters along nicely.*

Picard did a few more decks, here and there, finally making a point to go up to ten and see what Ten-Forward looked like. It didn't look like anything: it was an arms storage area. *How appropriate,* he thought, and made for the 'lift again. "The bridge, I suppose, Mr. Barclay," he said. "Everything down here looks as prepared for the next phase as it's going to get."

Barclay heaved a sigh that he didn't try to conceal, and they got into the 'lift and rode up there. When the doors opened and all the crewmen rose and saluted, Picard stalked in and tried to look as if he were in a bad humor—not difficult when his eye fell on Wesley Crusher's post, now filled by another crewman, and the thought of those screams came back to him again. He returned the salute, after a moment, but not before he saw this *Enterprise*'s Riker get up out of that center seat and offer it to him. *The man is trouble,* he thought. *If I'm lucky, I won't have to deal with it. Troi is bad enough.* She at least wasn't here: off in her quarters, perhaps, considering what she had found in his mind, or else off having that "talk" with Beverly. He felt like shuddering at either prospect.

"Status, Number One?" Picard said.

Riker grinned. "All normal, Captain. Preparing for phase two in about two hours."

"Very well. I'll be in my ready room for a while," he said, and went through its doors. "Mr. Barclay, a moment with you if you would."

Barclay followed him in. Picard sat down behind his desk, looking around at the place; it, too, was indistinguishable from his own ready room. "Tell me something," he said. "Are you happy with the audio security in here?"

"My people sweep it twice a day," Barclay said. "It's been adequate so far."

"Is it adequate *now?*"

Barclay's eyes flicked back toward the doors, and Riker. "I'll have it checked quietly, if you like, sir. But I think so."

"Very well, that will be all. Please post yourself outside and make sure that anyone who comes in here gives me ample warning."

"As usual, sir," Barclay said, and went out. Picard waited for a few moments when the door had shut, thinking, then bent over his badge again and said to it softly, "Mr. La Forge. Nanites loose. They'll ignore your department. One hour to an hour and a half—then we need to do that substitution. Two acknowledgments if you're all right, and if you have a way. One if not, on either count. Out."

Buzz, the badge said under his fingertips, *buzz.* Then nothing.

He breathed out then in relief, smiled slightly, and turned back to his desk terminal. "Display mission parameters," he said to it.

"Retinal scan required." He leaned in over the computer again, making sure to give it the same eye as last time—he wasn't sure that the Borg might not have done something to the other. "Scan successful," said the computer, and it began the display.

He read quickly. It was much as he had thought. The inclusion device had been installed in this *Enterprise,* and then she had been ordered to this area of space, where the device was coupled with her sensors so that she would be able to detect her counterpart. Once detected, the "target" was to be drawn into this space and a spy sent aboard to confirm information about her weapons array. *Confirm,* Picard thought, going cold; yes, the report made it clear that surveillance of Federation space, using a variation of the inclusion device keyed to subspace communications, had been going on for a long time—unencrypted communications intercepted and evaluated to determine what information could be found about fleet sizes and dispositions, the locations and armaments of starbases and Federation worlds, et cetera.

How long has this been going on? Picard wondered. *What do they know already? . . .* for the mission parameters made it plain what they intended to find out. If the *Enterprise's* shields remained down long enough, she was to be infiltrated and her command crew captured and beamed over to the attacking ship. They would be tortured until they gave up the secrets of whatever command codes were necessary for the removal of all pertinent classified information regarding Fleet ship strengths and dispositions—anything in the computer that would possibly be of use. Then those officers would be killed and replaced by their counterparts, who would sabotage the ship, supervise the "disposition" of the rest of the crew, and supervise the restaffing of the ship with their own people. A skeleton crew would take this universe's *Enterprise* back home, after the other one, Picard's *Enterprise,* had been returned to her home space . . . with his counterpart in command.

Picard's fist clenched on the desk. If fortune did not favor them, and his ship's shields were not down when the other *Enterprise* was ready, they would attack her and batter her until no shields were left, trying to do minimum damage. Then—board, storm, kill the inhabitants. Either way, she would be sent back to her home universe to follow her preassigned patrol schedule for a while. They knew what it was, knew that her patrol would be keeping her out of the more populated spaces, where discovery would be more likely. They would spend perhaps a month or so routinely receiving the communications and data uploads from Starfleet that could be expected, routinely requesting information on this and that.

And then, after a month or two . . . the invasion. A massive breakthrough on many fronts, hundreds of vessels bursting out to take the Federation on four sides, the Klingons and Romulans each on three. The latter species were to be wiped out, special attention being paid to their homeworlds—Picard thought of those great silent bulks down in the storage areas and went grim. The Federation fleets were to be swiftly divided and destroyed. The entire operation might be expected to take as long as a year, but might take as little as four months if early gains were promptly consolidated.

And afterward, when the Federation worlds were left defenseless . . . The mission specs said nothing specific, but Picard could guess very well what would happen. "Neutralizations," "prejudicial terraforming," other horrors. The explored tenth of the Galaxy would swiftly become a desert . . . to be repopulated and ruled by the Empire.

Picard stared at the screen, then cleared it. What troubled him most was the matter-of-fact nature of the whole business. It had been carefully thought out and was no madman's plan: the Starfleet here plainly had a good idea of the disposition of forces already and was simply making sure it had its numbers correct before moving. Their own forces were presently being redistributed to congruent areas in their own Galaxy so as to be ready, in a month's time, for the breakthrough. Everything was in order, and quietly the wolves were gathering around the fold, waiting for the dark.

The door chimed. Picard cleared the screen again, then reached out to one side and picked up the book there: the *Anabasis*. It gave him a brief shock when he saw the spine, but he opened it and leaned back in the seat. "Come," he said.

The door opened; Riker came in, with Barclay behind him. Riker turned to look at Barclay, frowning, but Barclay stood his ground.

"No, Mr. Barclay, it's all right," Picard said. "Wait outside."

Barclay looked a warning at him, but saluted and went out; the door shut.

"Well, Number One?" Picard said. "Anything on Kowalski yet?"

"No, sir."

"I think someone must have taken a phaser to him," Picard said, trying to sound casual. "Probably a waste of time. Still, the counselor will handle it."

"Yes, sir. Captain, you wanted a briefing."

"Let's have it then," he said, putting the book aside and assuming a look of attention, which at the moment was entirely genuine. "Sit down."

Riker did, looking at Picard with that odd smile again. "The ship is in good order, and the next phase will be ready in about two hours, as the counselor told you. Data analysis is just about complete, and the last threat work is being done in the computer. But I have other concerns."

"Speak up, Number One."

"Wesley Crusher."

"He's hardly of much importance."

"On the contrary, Captain. This matter is already being talked about all over the ship. The crew are seeing what they think is a split in policy among the upper echelons of command—one so severe that you actually counter-manded the counselor in a public place on a matter of security." Riker tried to look grave, though Picard noticed that he didn't seem entirely able to make that smile go away. "This is a very destabilizing kind of situation. Discipline aboard a starship is a delicate thing at best."

When it's enforced by the equivalent of the rack and the thumbscrew, I should think so, Picard thought.

"The counselor brought it on herself," Picard said, doing his best to sound stern. "If she is going to go behind my back to violate *my* orders, she may expect to be called on it."

Riker was silent for a moment, then said, "It's a delicate kind of situation, at any rate." *Aha,* Picard thought, *you're unwilling to come right out and say you think she was right. You still want my support—for the moment anyway.*

"There is a solution," Riker said, "which would put the crew's mind to rest about . . . matters among their officers—

and resolve the difficulty between yourself and the counsel-
or very neatly."

"And that is?"

"Call a court-martial. Empanel a neutral board. They'll
bring down the expected verdict—then Crusher can be
executed according to the usual formula, and the counsel-
or's concerns will be addressed, and at the same time your
hands will be seen to be clean of the . . . situation." Riker
smiled slightly. "It has advantages for you in that—"

"I'm sure that the reason you're pointing out the advantages," Picard said softly, "is that they're actually more
advantageous for you than for me. The counselor has been
riding your case about it, has she?"

Riker flushed.

"Well. You are just going to have to cope, Number One. I
have my reasons for sparing Crusher's life at the moment."

Riker smiled, that smarmy smile again, the one of which
Picard was getting so very tired. "I'm sure you have, sir,"
Riker said in the most insinuating tone of voice imagin-
able.

Picard was heading toward a slow boil and wondering
whether showing it would be a good idea. "My business is
to manage this mission as ordered. Have I not been doing
so?"

"With the exception of Crusher's case, yes. But that's
just the problem. Encouraging the crew to believe that
there's a breakdown in discipline in the middle of a
mission of such import . . ."

Picard set his mouth in a tight, thin smile for a moment:
he had had a sudden idea. "Why such vehemence over an
ensign? But he *is* fairly bright, isn't he? Energetic. Doesn't
miss his chances. He'll make a fine officer, once he works in
a little. Worried about your job, Number One?"

Riker got redder than he had been. Not because Picard
had hit any kind of target, but because he suspected Picard
was playing with him. In Picard's own Riker, that pride

212

was tempered with humor; but in this man, humor seemed to exist only for the sake of innuendo, and teasing only provoked rage.

"Never mind that. Number One, I have my reasons. They are personal, but I guarantee they are not the ones you have in mind. If the ship's efficiency is in question, that is *your* problem, by definition. On the other hand"— Picard raised a warning finger—"should anything whatsoever happen to Mr. Crusher, even if it's just a hangnail, I personally will take it out of *your* hide. Consider yourself warned."

Riker started to get up. "I haven't dismissed you," Picard said sharply. "Sit down."

Riker sat.

"I understand perfectly well that you would like to be in charge of this operation. Your—allies—among the crew are not as tight-lipped as you might think they should be." *There,* he thought, *why should I be the only one around here feeling paranoid? And besides, it's true.* "If anything *does* start to go wrong, the responsibility is going to devolve on *you,* for not delivering to your captain, as your job description requires, a ship and crew in good working order. So you had better keep your own nose clean, Number One, before you start trying to wipe *mine* for me. And another thing. Don't be confused by the events of the day. The conditions keeping Mr. Crusher alive don't in the least apply to *you.* It doesn't take the counselor to see you thinking, not by a long shot."

And that was true enough: there was a thuggish, brutal look about this Riker's face that Picard couldn't believe he wasn't aware of, and all the while he had been talking about discipline among the crew, and the "upper echelons," his expression had been one of naked acquisitiveness, a greedy pleasure in the prospect that something might go wrong . . . and come out in the end to his advantage, and Picard's discomfiture. *What must it be like,* he thought, studying that sullen face, *to not be able to trust your second-in-command, to know that he wants your job and is plotting against your life—along with just about everybody else on the ship, it seems.*

"Dismissed," Picard said. Riker got up—

—and the red-alert sirens began whooping. "They've sighted it!" Riker said, and dashed out.

Picard broke out in an instantaneous sweat and followed him.

The bridge was silent at the sight of the image caught frozen in the middle of the viewscreen. Picard stood there in front of his seat, watching the graceful white shape, torn. He had rarely been gladder to see anything in his life—and at the same time he wanted to shout, *Get away, for heaven's sake get out of here!*

"Lock on," Riker said to O'Brien. "Don't lose it this time." He looked over his shoulder at Worf.

"Her shields are down," Worf said.

"Riker to security. Counselor Troi to the bridge. Security teams to the transporter rooms, on the double! Phase two is ready to begin."

They waited. Picard sat down because he was afraid if he stood up much longer, the trembling that he was fighting to control might start to show. Off to one side, Barclay was looking from him to Riker, his eyes thoughtful, but for the moment Picard ignored this. He sat there with his eyes fixed on the tiny white shape. *What's the matter with the evasive program—get lost, get out of here!*

The screen flickered, then went back to normal again.

"What was that?" Riker snapped at Worf.

"Uncertain," Worf said, sounding concerned. "Possibly tachyar artifact."

"From what? There aren't any pulsars around here, much less quasars."

"Sensor diagnostics show normal," Worf said. Behind

him, the doors opened and Counselor Troi strolled in: apparently she did not consider that any order ending in "on the double" was addressed to *her*.

"Shield status," Riker said.

"Ready to go up after transport," said Worf.

Trapped, Picard thought. There would be no way out once they went up. He wished things had worked better, wished the away team were gone with what they had come for. *If wishes were horses, we'd all ride,* he thought, and did his best to calm himself: Troi was here, after all.

"Such nervousness," said the soft voice beside him. She had sat down in her chair and was regarding him with considerable amusement. "Is it possible that you're really beginning to be afraid about something? A historic event—"

"Shut up, Counselor," he said pleasantly. Just the presence of her now made him angry, which was probably a very good thing.

The screen flickered again. "Engineering!" Riker snapped. "La Forge, what's going on down there?"

No answer. "Engineering!"

Nothing.

Communications first, Picard thought, and kept his face like stone to stop the smile from getting out.

"Run the diagnostics again," Riker said. Picard sat there watching him, and Riker turned toward him and stared, and the look in his eyes was pure murder. Picard moved never a muscle. *Does he think I'm responsible somehow?* he thought. *Does he think I managed this to make him look bad? As an excuse to get* him *killed?*

This may be getting more complicated than I thought. The small white form on the screen abruptly vanished.

Immediately afterward, the screen went dead.

Picard simply sat there and looked at Riker, letting him have the chance to cover himself. He didn't take the opportunity: just glared.

Picard stood up. "It would appear that we have some systems functions that need to be seen to. Number One, take care of it. Have the security teams return to posts until we're ready and the diagnostics come up clean. Phase two will have to be postponed accordingly."

"Yes, sir," Riker said, sullen.

"It's fairly late in my shift," Picard said, and hoped it was. At any rate, ship's night was approaching. "I have some more work to tidy up in the ready room, then I'm going to go and get some rest. Call me if I'm needed."

He went through the ready room doors and waited for them to close so that not even Barclay would get a look at the eventual private, utterly relieved grin.

CHAPTER 11

La Forge's quarters were spartan. He didn't spend much of his off-shift time there, preferring to spend his time among his machines, and his staff, both of which gave him more amusement by doing what he told them—or by his efforts at correcting them when they failed him—than anything he might do in private, and most of the things he did in company. The quarters were comfortable enough, as all the senior officers' quarters here were, good for sleeping, if nothing else, and comfortably furnished, but otherwise unornamented.

Which was why he was mildly surprised to come in, at the end of his shift, and see Counselor Troi waiting there for him—sitting on the edge of the bed and smiling at him slightly.

At first sight of her, he was afraid. That was the wisest reaction to the counselor, for someone who had been as long aboard this ship as La Forge had and knew the stories that made the rounds.

"Mr. La Forge," she said softly, looking up at him from under those dark brows.

"Counselor," he said, beginning to feel a little more comfortable—though not much. So far he hadn't felt the dreadful stab at his mind that all too many of the crewpeople had felt in their time aboard. She didn't always behave that way, it was true: her moods swung in some impenetrable Betazed fashion, turning her very occasionally kindly, but more often deadly, or simply curious. The last mood was most to be feared. At such times she strolled through minds the way she strolled through the hallways, leisurely, abstracted, picking up a thought here or an emotion there and looking it over to see whether it seemed threatening or merely amusing. If it amused her, you would drag yourself away, sweating and feeling as if you wanted a bath, counting yourself lucky that she hadn't seen the idea or feeling as a threat to the ship. When she perceived *those,* you wound up in the Agony Booth, while Troi let the pain break down the mind's barriers and spent hours, with a dreadful professional detachment, going through every thought in a brain, looking for the one weak spot that represented the tendency toward weakness or betrayal. Once it was found, there was no question of mercy anymore. People who might fail the *Enterprise,* or worse, were found in the act of failing her, never came out of the Booth—and the horror of their screams was much worse than the usual cries of pain. The counselor specialized in making sure the maximum punishment was extracted from the condemned before they were allowed to die. And to those who had had even light brushes with it, the thought of that calm, amused regard sitting in your mind, watching while you died—even that last privacy denied you—was the greatest terror of all.

So when La Forge looked at the counselor as if Death were sitting there on his bed, demure and calm, he felt that he could be pardoned for the reaction. It was wisest to be safe, after all. But the counselor seemed to have other things on her mind at the moment. There were stories about this, too, that made the rounds of the crew. There were times when Betazeds apparently became more than usually . . . interested in the sensual side of life, and the whispered scuttlebutt said that the counselor had ways of making the experience more than usually . . . interesting for the other person involved: a flip side, as it were, to the ability to brush aside the boundaries of someone's mind like a curtain. Pleasures redoubled and reflected almost beyond bearing for their intensity, that was what the rumors said . . . what rumors there were. The counselor's lovers tended to be tight-lipped, if only because she could become murderous if she felt a confidence might have been betrayed. La Forge had never dreamed that he might find himself in *this* situation. But now, looking at her, he smiled, determined to make the best of it. The counselor could make a powerful friend; even the captain had to give way to her under certain circumstances. Her patronage could mean early advancement, privileges . . . and the obvious pleasures.

"Come sit down," the counselor said, patting the bed beside her. La Forge came toward her slowly, his grin broadening, taking his time. He knew he looked good; he didn't mind making her aware of the fact . . . and feeling the fear die away, feeling the desire come up, was enjoyable, too. He sat and decided to dare to be a little aggressive about it—she was rumored to like that, from Riker at least.

"Well," he said, "this is a nice surprise," and he slid his arms around her, grinning still. Her great dark eyes widened a little; she smiled, too, slipping her arms around him, holding him quite tightly.

"Yes," she murmured, "it is, isn't it?" Behind his neck, something hissed—and that was all he heard.

Troi disentangled herself from the unconscious form of La Forge and let him down gently on the bed. She looked over to the side of the room, the spot out of sight by the closet, and Geordi came out and smiled grimly at the sight of "himself."

"Glad we were able to tap into comms enough to catch him going off shift," Geordi said. He put his hands under the man's armpits and pulled him off the bed, half-dragging him over to an open access panel in the wall. "Didn't take long to get the message, did he?"

"No question of *that,*" Troi said, standing up and rubbing her hands together. She caught herself at it, analyzed it as a sudden urge to get clean of trickery and of the mélange of emotions she had sensed in him—that dreadful fear, coupled with desire that lay so close to the surface—the two potentiating each other. A lot of these people seemed unusually labile: not necessarily less complex than the crewmen with whom Deanna was familiar, but it was as if the controls normally trained into Fleet personnel to make living together easier had never been trained into these people at all—or as if no one had ever seen the need. These people wore their emotions very near the surface, released them more readily than usual. It made them both easier than usual to manipulate, and more difficult to accurately predict. A pretty problem.

Geordi was busying himself with sealing up the access panel. "My last scan showed the nanites almost into the comms functions," he said, "and working in all three cores. Things are going to hot up pretty quick now. Better signal the captain. Where are you going to keep yourself?"

"Here will probably be safest, but if as I'm monitoring the situation I see an excuse or an opportunity to head for the captain's quarters, I'll do that instead." Troi did not mention her terror at the thought of walking out into those halls and having to "be" the woman who was the cause of so much fear . . . but she would do it if she had to.

From outside came the whooping of red-alert sirens.

"There they go," Geordi said with a grin. "We're in business."

Troi touched her badge. "Troi to Captain Picard. Objective acquired and stowed." She smiled slightly. "Next move."

The badge buzzed once under her fingertips. "He's ready," she said. "Get yourself set."

On the bridge, everything had begun to go energetically haywire. Picard was watching it with well-feigned annoyance, stalking around as one system after another began to flicker, falter, go down, then up and then down again, as if the ship were one giant traveling short circuit. He was hard put not to laugh out loud, and he understood better than ever the delight Geordi had started to show at the prospect of purposely failing out the computers; it was hilarious to watch the results, especially when they weren't *your* responsibility to fix.

"This is becoming extremely annoying," he said severely to Riker. "What the devil are they doing down in engineering?"

"It's difficult to tell, Captain, when we don't seem able to reach them on comms," Riker said, moving from one station to the other, getting redder and redder with fury.

"Well, do it the old-fashioned way," Picard said with exaggerated patience. "Send a runner down there. I want La Forge up here to tell me what the problem is, since none of *you* seem able to manage it. And then I want it fixed!"

The volume of the demand brought some heads around, and Picard was slightly relieved. *Good,* he thought, *I'm not that much of a shouter here, either, to judge by the reaction. Just as well, I couldn't stand it if I had to rant all the time.*

Riker gestured at one of the security men who was standing by the turbolift doors. "You, get down to engineering and bring Mr. La Forge up here."

"Some diagnostics are running, though patchily, Captain," Worf said quite calmly, seeming immune to Riker's performance. "There would appear to be some kind of trouble in the computer cores."

"Cores *plural?*" Picard said, sounding outraged. "Two of them? *All* of them?"

"All of them, Captain, to judge by these readings."

"What kind of trouble?"

"Uncertain as yet, sir. As I said, the diagnostics are themselves malfunctioning."

"How very delightful." Picard stalked up to Worf's station and looked over his shoulder at the readouts. "What else might go wrong if *all* the redundant systems are contaminated this way? This ship *lives* by those computers."

"Our mission could be seriously compromised," the counselor said, getting up from her seat and throwing an obscure glance in Riker's direction.

"I am very concerned about the mission, Counselor," Picard said, meaning it entirely, "but I am just as concerned at the moment about the thought that the computers control life support as well, and I don't care to breathe vacuum, or freeze to death."

The turbolift doors opened, and the security guard who had gone out now returned with a grim-looking La Forge. He saluted Picard, who returned the salute and said, "Mr. La Forge, you had better come up with some answers for us pretty quickly."

"Yes, sir," Geordi said, and went over to the engineering panel and started working at it. At least once it went down on him, so that he swore and smacked it. It came back up immediately, leaving Picard wondering about the malleability of machines in their perceived master's hands.

"Damn," Geordi said. "All three cores are compromised. Nonselective holes are developing in the associational networks. Looks like the subspace field is down, but that alone wouldn't cause these problems."

He moved to another panel, touched it; it flickered and went dark. "Captain," Geordi said, "we'd better unlock these cores while they're still answering to command. If they go down before we do that, we've got problems."

"Quite right. Counselor?" Picard said. "We'll need your security code."

"I should think you might do that yourself," the counselor said, raising her eyebrows at him, "since you know the code as well as I do."

"I bow to your primacy in this matter, as I should have bowed in that other. My apologies: I overreacted."

Picard stood there and tried not to sweat too visibly while starting to recite "The boy˙stood on the burning deck . . ." in his head, by way of cover. The counselor studied him for a long moment: there was that feeling of a veil brushing across the face of his mind. . . . Then she bowed her head to Picard with a slight smile—a queenly gesture, and a condescending one. "And they say chivalry is dead," she said with another odd glance over at Riker, a different one this time, that left Picard wondering again. "But perhaps the reports of its death were premature."

She walked over to the engineering console and said, "Computer. This is Lieutenant Commander Troi."

"Voice ID verified," said the computer in a voice that cracked and wavered unnervingly.

"Release computer core security controls in all three cores. Code fourteen nine twelve twelve A."

"Code correct. Core security controls released."

"Thanks, Counselor," Geordi said. "Oops—"

For the console went dark again, and around the bridge, various telltales and lights that never went dark now vanished. Only the main viewer remained functional, and the image on it was stitched with signal artifact, normally filtered out, now making a nuisance of itself. "I'd better get down there. Counselor, will you release me some security people as well, to act as runners? We're going to need them, with comms down. I'll pull three teams from engineering."

"Go on, Mr. La Forge," Picard said. "Time's wasting, and we have a mission that won't wait."

"Aye aye, sir," Geordi said, understanding perfectly, and made for the 'lift in a hurry, with the security guard behind him.

The bridge crew watched him go. After a moment, Picard said, "Well, it's late in my shift, and I can do little here until we're operational again. I'll be in my quarters getting some rest." He looked over at Riker. "Number One, please send a runner immediately when we start to get any results with the cores."

"Yes, sir."

Picard nodded and headed for the 'lift, his pulse racing. *And but the booming shots replied, and fast the flames rolled on.* He could feel the counselor looking at his back as the doors shut.

Geordi headed into engineering at high speed, which was probably just as well. Though he had seen the schematics of the place, stopping to gawk at the sheer wonderfulness of it would probably have been a bad move at the moment. He made his way down the great central hallway toward the matter/antimatter exchanger in a hurry, with the security man behind him, and shouted, "Okay, people, we've got trouble, let's have a meeting!"

There were curious looks directed down at him from some of the crewmen up in the galleries, but obediently enough they started heading for the lifters and ladders that would take them down to the bottom level. While waiting for them to gather, Geordi did a quick cruise around the main status table, wondering at the differences of it, and noticing particularly the indications of the third main power conduit, the one leading off to something big and power hungry down on the right-hand side. *Buddha on a bicycle,* he thought, *eight* hundred *terawatts; you could boil a small ocean over that if you had a pot big enough!*

Engineering crew began to gather around him. He recognized them all, though on his own ship many of them were people who were assigned to science. It said uncomfortable things about the state of theoretical research and labwork on this ship, but he didn't have time to be overly concerned with that right now. At least he knew these people's capability: they could do the job—*and they'll need to, the poor kids: I still remember the nuisance it took us to fix the nanites in* our *core.* He simply hoped he could depend on them, for there were the differences in personalities to cope with as well: any one of these people could be assumed to be gunning for his job. Not a pretty prospect at the moment—especially if any one of them should guess his real intentions. They would take themselves off to the counselor like a shot.

He finished his circuit of the table, looked up, and was not shocked, but was nonetheless disturbed, to see Eileen Hessan gazing thoughtfully at him from behind a few other people. *Are we friendly here?* he wondered. *Well, no harm in being cordial, anyway.*

"I need two big parties and one smaller one," he said. "Two for the main cores in the primary hull and the engineering hull, and one for the secondary one in the main hull. We don't have a lot of time to sit around doing diagnostics, so we're going to just pull the affected media and replace them with new chips from stores. Analysis can wait until we have something to analyze *with.* We're going to have to start doing a selective purge of the isolinear chips in each core. Fortunately"—he pointed to the schematics now showing on the status table—"different parts of each core seem to be affected, so that we should be able to selectively restore to clean media from the other cores. But it's going to take a lot of running around with chips because we don't dare do it by optical conduit—they look like they've been compromised, too—and anyway, the backup protocols need to have at least one core running FTL. None of them are, just now: all the subspace generators are down. At least we don't have to worry about frying our brains." There were some covertly amused looks among the engineering staff: apparently there were some of them who wouldn't particularly mind seeing others' brains fried. That they made no secret of the fact bothered Geordi, but he ignored it for the moment, while wondering in the back of his mind what their accident rates were like here.

"So, Hessan, Gaulgo, Nassainen, you three choose your teams. Hessan, yours will be under me, we'll take the core down here. Work fast, everybody—once we get one core completely restored, we can restore to all the others from it." *Not that it'll help,* Geordi thought with silent amusement, *because the nanites that the captain instructed to remain in reserve will come out and reinfect them within a few hours.*

He looked up. "Let's get *that* off-line first," he said, pointing to the display for the inclusion device.

There was some muttering. "After all the trouble it took to get it *on*-line?" Hessan said pointedly.

Geordi looked at her and shrugged. "Look, you want its computers to get infected by whatever's in the cores?"

There was even more muttering at the prospect of *that,* and Hessan shook her head, seeing the point. "Go on," Geordi said, "somebody physically separate its links to the cores: we can't take the chance." *Of injuring the thing before I have a chance to get a good look at it and its software!*

Two or three of the engineering staff went off to see about

it. "Come on, everybody," Geordi said, "let's get cracking. Otherwise the captain is going to be *real* annoyed with us when he gets up from his nap and finds his ship still busted."

Elsewhere, Barclay was walking with Picard back to his quarters. The lights were dim in the corridors; as they came to his door, the lights brightened briefly again, then once more dimmed down.

"Not going to be a quiet night, is it, sir," Barclay said, stopping by the door and hitting its switch. It didn't open.

"No," Picard said wearily, "I can see that."

Barclay hit the switch a couple of more times. "Damn machinery," he said softly. "I never did like anything much more complicated than a knife to begin with. This place has gotten too automated."

Picard shrugged. "The price of progress, I suppose. I'll see you later, Mr. Barclay."

"Not me, Captain. It'll be Ramirez: it's his shift. Even chiefs of security have to sleep sometimes."

"Of course." Picard smiled at him; he might not entirely trust the man, any more than he entirely trusted anyone else here, but so far Barclay had dealt straightforwardly with him. "Have a good rest."

"Thank you, sir."

Picard walked into his quarters. The door slid shut and he had to hit the internal control a couple of times before it would lock. The lights were dimmed, except for one over by the bed. *Here too,* he thought, resigned. *I shouldn't complain. It means that things are finally working.*

He stopped still, staring. Something in the bed moved slightly. It appeared to be a person, sleeping.

Picard stood there a moment, simply flabbergasted, understanding what the Littlest Bear must have felt like. He moved forward softly. The shape in the bed stirred, turned over, looked at him. The long, dark hair fell softly from around the face as she shook her head a bit and blinked.

It was Beverly Crusher. Picard was too astonished to speak for a moment.

Finally, he managed to say—and it almost came out in a croak—"What are you doing here?"

She propped herself up on one elbow, looked at him with some slight confusion. "Oh. Wesley. I suppose you might be concerned. . . . No. What happened a long time ago was one thing. But this . . ." She paused and then said rather roughly, "Don't think my son's stupidity is going to make me throw away everything I've got left."

He took a couple more steps forward, more uncertain of what to say than he had been in a long time. He had been shaken enough by Troi's accusation—no, they weren't accusations; for her they were simple statements of fact. "Beverly . . ." he said, then sat down in the chair by the bed, unable to look at her or anything else.

One Crusher dead, one Crusher as good as dead, Wesley had said.

She was looking at him curiously now. "You have been behaving very oddly today. Are you all right?"

He could give her no answer that would make any sense, so he merely shook his head.

She looked at him, then got up out of the bed and walked over to the replicator. "Brandy and soda," she said, "and Armagnac straight up." She waited while the drinks appeared, then came back, handing him the Armagnac and sitting down on the bed opposite him.

"Are the aftereffects of that stun still bothering you?"

"No, that's not it." He got up in great discomfort and walked away, wondering where else in the ship he could possibly go, his one place of safety suddenly betraying him again, as the books had earlier. "I don't think you should be here."

Beverly looked at him, her face briefly working back and forth between puzzlement and anger. "Where else should I be? You went through enough trouble to get me here." It was what he had been afraid of, and the last thing he wanted to hear. *It was not I who have done these things,* he said to himself desperately. *It was someone from a much different life, a different world.* But there were parts of his brain that didn't want to believe it, that were insisting that maybe he himself might do these things, might have done these things, if history in his own world had gone differently.

"Where am I supposed to go?" Beverly said, her voice showing the anger now. "I'm the captain's woman. Who aboard this ship is going to have anything to do with me? They know you too well. Anyone here who touches me is going to end up like Gonzales all over again."

"Gonzales?" he said, turning around.

She laughed bitterly. "Don't pretend you've forgotten— not after the public way you killed him. It's a little late to play the innocent with me. You wander around the ship, making friends with every pretty ensign who crosses your path—you don't expect *me* to say a word—and who would dare? But the one time I stray a bit . . ." She laughed again. "But it's the pattern, isn't it? After Jack, you had a reputation to maintain. Anyone who got between you and what you wanted was going to suffer."

He looked at her, expressionless, not daring to react. It must have looked like a stone face to her, for she turned away again, with one of those soft, bitter laughs. "So it ends here, is that it? With no explanations." She got up, pulling the blanket about her, and began to pace. "And you never even told me exactly why it was that you decided to take me away from Jack, one way or another."

Beverly looked at him now, seemingly expecting an answer. Finding none, she returned to her pacing. "He told me once that you would praise me to him, then wait to see if he agreed. He said he thought you were trying to find out if I would be amenable to a little something on the side. Not that I was. And then the baby came, and that stopped for a while, didn't it? Everything was fine for a few years . . . until that day you chose the landing party and sent them out."

She sat down quietly on the bed again. "I never did understand. Oh, I saw it—that grim look on your face when you went to get the body back. Some last touch of remorse?" She looked at him. It would have been an expression of challenge were it not so dull, so weary with old hopeless thought. "Some last moment of regret at having had to kill your old friend? But friendship was never that much for you. Your blood ran too cold: friendship was too fragile a thing for you to get your teeth into. Domination, though . . ."

Picard sat very still. "Beverly," he said, just wanting her to stop and not knowing how to make her. "This isn't the time."

"No, with your ship coming to pieces around you, I should think not." There was some slight humor about that observation. "Find it difficult to bear, don't you? You were always fonder of the ship, half the time, than of the people who rode in her. Cut her, and you bleed. Shields go down, and your composure falls off. Well it might, in this situation. If we fail at this mission, most of our lives won't be worth much—certainly no one in command is going to survive unless they try pretty hard. Riker will just live to prove that this is all your fault somehow, all these things going wrong."

"And doubtless Counselor Troi will help him," Picard said thoughtfully, glad of anything that would turn the conversation away from him and Beverly for the moment.

Beverly laughed. "She wouldn't miss the chance for anything. They may hate each other like poison, but she can't do without him, and he can't do without her. I've had

to doctor the marks sometimes after one of their more . . .
mixed . . . evenings together." She smiled, looking rueful.
"We haven't had many of those nights together lately
ourselves, have we? Found something new to keep your
attention. The other woman."

Beverly looked out the window into the starry night.
"It's been driving you wild ever since they dropped this
project in your lap. The idea of an *Enterprise* you don't
control—that you *could.*"

"Ships of that name tend to be jealous mistresses,"
Picard said softly. "But then, as you say, you know that."

"You'd like me to think that, anyway," she said, looking
at him for a moment from under the beginnings of a frown.
"Could I actually be looking too close to my own nose to
see the truth? Could it actually *be* another woman?"

He stood up and started to pace. "Do you suppose I
wouldn't tell you if it were?" he said roughly.

She laughed at him again. "Nice try! As if you ever tell
anyone *anything.* That old cold, calculating mind, turning
in circles on itself the same as always—even trying to
imitate intimacy when it serves its purpose. Just another
way to hurt me. The old pattern hasn't changed." She
leaned back against the bedstead. "You still like to put a
pin into me, every now and then, or a knife if you can, to
see how I react. The way you did after Jack. I was supposed
to have had the perspicacity to immediately drop him
when you expressed interest in me. I didn't. So you
punished me the simplest way. You took him away, killed
him practically under my nose. That was good for a few
years' pain."

Her voice was quite steady, but the tears were showing in
her eyes, ever so slightly. "Then you engineered that
business with the Lagos mission—pretty setup, that. I
could have been cashiered, despite the fact that I was
following your orders. But you defended me to Starfleet
and made it plain enough what the price was. I got to come

out of 'retirement' for your amusement, whether I liked it or not. The knife again. So what will it be this time? I wonder. Wesley, perhaps?" She smiled at him. "If you think so, you misjudged. You'll have to do a lot better than that to hurt me at this point."

"I would think," he said, choosing his words with some care, "that having been a"—he could barely bring himself to say it—"captain's woman for this long, you might have developed a thicker skin."

"That's the problem. I would have thought so, too. The trouble is, you keep doing unexpected things. Like that." She gestured with her chin at the canvas on the other side of the room, covered over again, for Picard hadn't been able to bear looking at it. "Every now and then you do something that seems to break the pattern, and I almost forgive you . . . almost let it go. That's a hell of a thing." She looked him straight in the eye for the first time in a while. "To actually forgive the man who killed your husband in cold blood. And then the pattern reasserts itself, and the knife goes in again, and I realize I've been manipulated again and curse myself for a fool . . . because you ride relationships the way you ride your vessels: to destruction."

She watched him watching her. Silence was the best defense, Troi had told him often enough. Now he simply stood and watched her. She watched back.

The silence got heavy. It had to be broken, he had no choice: "I think for the time being, you're going to have to sleep elsewhere. I don't want to hurt you."

She gave him such a look as a mother might give a child caught in a substandard lie. "That's all you've done since you saw me and decided you wanted me and took me. But that's mostly what you do to everyone—just to make sure you're still alive. You put the knife in and listen for the scream. Did you never think that someone might put the knife in you? Apparently not, to judge by this afternoon."

"Oh, I think about it."

"But you don't believe it. As far as you're concerned, everything you do is right. It's always been the way . . . it's probably why you're so successful in this fleet. People only fail here when their scruples get in the way. You haven't had a scruple for years."

She stood up with the blanket gathered gracefully around her. "I'll take to my own side of the quarters for the time being." She made for the door at the far side of Picard's quarters. "There's no injuring *your* dignity—you might as well try to injure a glacier. As for me, I still have mine, and I'll keep it intact."

She paused by the door. "But one thing." In the dark, her eyes were indistinct, but they were narrowed, and the cast of her face went suddenly ugly. "If it *is* simply another woman . . . she'd better not get sick. It will be a short illness."

Beverly went through the door and it shut behind her; and Picard heard the extra *cheep* of the lock on her side.

CHAPTER 12

Standing on the ladder, Geordi gave a soft grunt as the third of the access panels in the core shaft came away. "Coming up, Eileen," he said, touching the control on the floater he had attached to the panel. It levitated gently upward past him, and Eileen, up in the crawlway that met the access shaft, caught it and put it aside, taking the floater pad off it. Two other engineering staff came floating down past him, carrying pouches full of isolinear chips. Geordi smiled slightly. The situation had this advantage at least: he would hardly stand out, now, for the sake of what he himself was carrying. For the sake of his own peace of mind, he had carefully applied a small scratch to the upper left corner of each of the chips he had brought with him, the high-density ones.

Now he gazed into the space behind the open panel. Set into the matrix inside it, end-on, were row after row of isolinear chips—thousands of them in each core, hundreds of thousands in the whole ship. At least a third of them, thanks to the captain, would have to be changed. At best, they could keep this ship out of commission for at least four hours while they were being replaced—more if the crew slacked off. And then, of course, the captain's reserve nanosurgeons would come out of their hiding places and get to work again.

Geordi sighed and got busy doing what he was supposed to be doing, while considering the best way to do what he had really come for. One part of his mind was cautious. He glanced down toward the bottom of the core shaft, a good hundred and fifty feet below him, and considered that this would be a wonderful place to have an "accident," if any of his work crew weren't kindly disposed toward him. On the other hand, there was no point in borrowing trouble. So far they all seemed willing enough, especially when the prospect of their not cooperating with or obeying his orders meant it was equally likely that they would all be blown up—or else, when the Empire caught up with a ship that had failed its mission, removed from their posts more or less permanently.

He hooked one arm through the rung of the ladder and turned around, holding his engineering tricorder and reading the bank of chips that lay open to him at the moment. Nine of them were shot in a big patch almost directly in front of him, and another few down several feet farther in the matrix.

He let the tricorder drop to hang from its strap for a moment and reached out to pull one of the isolinears free. Silently, Eileen floated down on one of the floater pads nearest, with her legs hanging over the edge, and a light belt strapping her to the floater. "How many do you want?" she said.

"I can use about a dozen. Look at this." He put his thumb on the pressure point that would allow the nutef facing to slide off the front of the chip. It came away and was followed almost immediately by a little cloud of brown dust. Geordi coughed and waved his hand in front of his face, thinking, *Thorough little monsters: they don't leave much sticking together, do they? Small bytes.* He chuckled at the pun, then, covering, said, "Look at it."

"Now what the hell does that?" Hessan said.

Geordi shook his head. "Well, there are a few possibilities. Repeated low-level power outages can cause something like this—though usually the pieces that the storage medium falls into are bigger, more granular." He poked the finely divided fluff, almost like powdery iron filings, with one finger, looked at the finger, then dusted it off against his pants. "Also, I read a paper a couple of years back about how a run of chips had trouble with the FTL field—it accelerated their materials' aging unusually, and they just fell apart inside."

Hessan looked at the panel critically. "I guess that could explain why they seem to be going in patches. These have been maintained away from starbase, from replicated stock. But there was a lot of swapping around when we were around Alphacent for the new gadget's installation." She raised her eyebrows. "Well, we'll hear all about it, and how we should have fixed it, when we get home, I guess."

"Probably." Geordi started pulling out the chips he had already designated as bad and put them on the floater by Eileen. "Bring me down that dozen and I'll get started on these. See if you can tell if any other panels on this level have bad ones." He looked down into the core. "They seem to be pretty evenly scattered around."

She nodded and floated upward again. While she was gone, Geordi got back to his more covert scanning. Into the slot from which he had removed the bad chip, he slipped his good one, with the search parameters. Then, using his tricorder, he instructed the computer locator program that was still functioning—the captain having carefully spared it—as to the memory location and address of the chip he had just installed. "Read program Search One," he said.

"Done," said the computer.

"Run."

"Executing," it said.

He breathed out a long breath. "Store three times randomly in other locations," he said softly, watching the top of the shaft to see if Eileen was coming down.

"Done," said the computer.

"Set no-warn," he said, touching the display to silence it as Eileen came down on her floater again. *Confirm,* the computer flashed on his tricorder screen.

He pulled his own chip out, tucked it away safe, and touched the display to change it back to the scan-for-bad-chips routine.

"Here you go," Eileen said, coming down level with him, and handed him the replacement chips.

He started replacing them while she pulled out her own tricorder and scanned the lower panels. "This is a little unusual, isn't it?" she said, looking sideways at him.

"What? The computer falling apart? Damn straight it is."

"No . . . I mean, you coming down and working . . . getting your hands dirty like anybody else."

Geordi swallowed. "Welllll . . ." The excuse was near to hand. "Sometimes you have to do strange things to be alone with a pretty girl."

She briefly gave him a superior look, then burst out laughing. "Is there anyone around here you haven't tried that on?"

Apparently this was at least one area in which he and his counterpart were similar. "Working my way through the ship, I can only hope . . ."

"Working your way through upward or downward?" There was a slight twinkle in her eye.

"Which direction do *you* favor?" he said, sliding a couple more chips into place.

She looked at him for a moment, then said, "Mine."

Aha, Geordi thought. "Well, I don't know. I assumed you

were hanging around me so that you could get a promotion."

"Well," she said mildly, "you *do* only have three assistant chiefs now . . . and frankly, they're all total losses, but I'm sure that's why you chose them."

Geordi kept his face straight and swapped another chip. "After all," Eileen said, "there's no point in promoting someone who's *seriously* going to be a challenge to your job. You have to have assistants, after all, but"—she gave him a wicked smile—"there's no use in their being too good at the job, is there?"

"You've got a point there," Geordi said, thinking it was hardly the point *he* would have made. What kind of decent work could get done on a ship when you purposely chose your subordinates not for their talent but for their lack of it? It was no wonder the maintenance in here was so sloppy.

"Well," he said after a moment, mock-seriously, "I would have to give it due and proper consideration, I suppose. After due and proper evaluation of your work."

On her floater, she leaned quite close to him, until she was practically breathing in his ear. "I had hoped we could bypass the evaluation."

"Oh? And use what instead?"

"Bribery?" she said very softly, and breathed in his ear again, more purposefully this time.

Geordi swallowed and tried to get some control of himself. "Ensign, the sooner we get this done, the sooner we can discuss this in more detail."

She smiled slightly at him. "It's still a little strange to see you actually interested in working. I suppose I can cope. But some people aren't going to know what to make of it."

Geordi made a wry face at her. "Let's just say that at this point I'm fond of *not* being turned into so much radioactive dust by whatever's chasing us out there. Or having someone from"—he "ahemmed" slightly—"'higher up' get hold of me."

"Yes, the counselor has been on the prod the last day or so. Harry thinks she's nervous about something."

"The counselor? Nervous?" Geordi thought of that cool regard on the bridge and shook his head, doubting it very much indeed.

"Well, that's the scuttlebutt . . . and you know how she is when she gets nervous."

"Uh-huh," Geordi said, sounding concerned, as he suspected he was supposed to. "Well, I'm gonna try to stay out of *her* way. In the meantime, what about those other panels?"

"There are two more bad ones under you there, sort of nine o'clock and six o'clock under." She studied her tricorder. "Nineteen of the chips have this dry rot."

"All right. Well, go up and get some more, and we'll get on with it."

She ascended gracefully upward and out of sight. He looked down, touched his tricorder. *Run complete,* it said. *Hallelujah.* Geordi instructed it to start displaying file names and sensitive areas that it had found. Swiftly it did. There were hundreds of them, but he had half-expected that. "Total storage," he said softly.

Eighteen hundred fifty-six terabytes. Geordi frowned, calculating. He was carrying 1700-odd. He would have to lift a few chips from here to make the difference. "Start copy," he said softly. "Copy to capacity, then notify and hold for replacement of media."

Working. It would take a while, though not too long.

Eileen came down past him, handing him a box of chips.

"Look," he said, "I'm still getting some weird readings off this panel—I want to check the matrix. You go ahead and change those. I'll be down shortly."

"Right," she said, breathing in his ear again as she passed, and sank down into the shaft below him.

The panels Eileen was servicing were on the other side of the shaft, so he had the advantage of having her being both below and facing away from him. About fifteen minutes passed quietly, during which time he slipped chips into the one slot he was using, waited for them to fill, then slipped the full one out and a new empty one in, pretending to take readings in between, and fussing with other chips in the array. Finally he had come to the last of his high-density chips; he filled it and found there was still another eighty terabytes of data to go. He was tempted to just forget it, but there was no way to tell in what area the information lay that might prove to be the most vital, without which everything else would be useless. It had to be all or nothing.

He had just put the last of them in his belt pouch when Eileen came floating up past him, carrying a batch of old chips. "You should see the insides of these things," she said. "You could powder your nose with them. Want me to take those for you?"

"No, it's okay, I'll be up," Geordi said, desperately trying to sound casual. "I want to get off this thing and stretch my legs."

"You and me both," she said, floating up to the top of the access shaft.

Very quietly he took from his pocket one of the tiny transporter tags for the transfer to the shuttle and the *Enterprise,* smacked it onto the pile of chips, and dropped a spare chip; then, watching it fall, he whispered, "Energize."

A second later the chips vanished, the transporter whine coinciding neatly with the clatter of the chip hitting the bottom of the shaft. He sat there gritting his teeth, regardless, at how loud the whine was in so small and confined a space. But then it was over.

Eileen looked over the edge at him. "You okay?"

"Dropped one," Geordi said casually.

"Butterfingers," said Eileen, and tossed him a clean replacement. He slotted it in. "You coming?"

"Is that professional interest or something else?"

She chuckled. "Come find out."

Geordi grinned and went after her. He was tremendously relieved to be doing, finally, what he had come here to do. Meantime, there was no reason he shouldn't enjoy himself a little as well.

Aboard the other *Enterprise*, Riker's attention was turned uncomfortably outward. Using passive scans, they had been keeping an eye on their ship's dark counterpart, and for a long time there had been no change: it had been sailing along quietly enough on impulse, doing nothing unusual—until now. "Power fluctuations," Data had said, and Riker had peered into the darkness of the viewscreen, straining his eyes looking at the small, dark silver shape, already at the farthest extent of their sensor range.

"What's the problem seem to be?" Riker said.

Data shook his head. "I am getting indications of variations in the power supply to the impulse engines. A very peculiar power curve indeed: errors in fuel consumption and injection."

Riker considered that. "Such as might be caused by a fault in the computer systems?"

Data considered, too. "That is an excellent probability. Though one must not automatically assume it to be the case. One could conjecture, though, that the captain and Mr. La Forge have created an extremely effective distraction."

Riker nodded and started to turn toward Troi's chair and started to ask her whether she felt anything at all from the other ship—then caught himself and sighed. It was about the twentieth time that he had done that, and every time he did it, the pain of his concern for her stabbed him hard.

He turned his attention to something closer to hand, on

the viewscreen. Just outside the *Enterprise,* tethered to one of the exterior access ports, a tiny elongated shape floated in the darkness, seeming, as it had for the past hour, to be doing nothing. They had not communicated with Hwiii since he went out: he had asked to be left in silence so that he could concentrate. "Any idea what he's doing?" Riker said.

Data shook his head. "He was not able to describe it to me in much more detail than to say that he had to 'go out and listen.' I think the problem is possibly linguistic: even Delphine is somewhat symbolic about the way it handles the subjects of sensory input. At times there seem to be almost mystical contexts to what we would normally consider simple seeing or hearing. But when you have a species which is almost a living sensor array—to so much greater an extent than other species are, at least—there is bound to be some difference in perception—"

Data was interrupted by a sudden upscaling squeal. He looked at his instruments with concern.

"Enterprise!" said Hwiii's voice.

"Go ahead, Commander," Riker said, glancing at Data.

"Commander Riker, beam me aboard, quickly!"

The tone was more jubilant than afraid.

"Is there a problem?"

Delphine laughter chattered in their ears.

"Problem? Problem, no, just beam me inboard, hurry!"

"Transporter room!" Riker said. "Beam Commander Hwiii in on the double!"

"Aye, sir," O'Brien's voice said. *"Transporting now."*

"Now what's *his* problem?" Riker said.

"I do not know, Commander," Data said. "I was monitoring his life-signs as you requested, and nothing was amiss."

"Come on," Riker said, "let's see what the fuss is. Mr. Worf, with me."

* * *

In the transporter room they found Hwiii resting on the platform, with his helmet off—O'Brien had just pulled it off him—though he was still in his space suit. Riker looked at it and was tempted to laugh: it was well emblazoned with commemorative patches, from the Utopia Planitia Yards patch on down through reproductions of such antiques as the NASA and ESA patches, so that the suit looked more like a spacegoing billboard than anything else.

Hwiii was wriggling and talking to O'Brien a mile a minute, half in speech, half in song. Now, as Riker and Worf came in, Hwiii looked at them with delight.

"I heard it!" he sang, deafening and triumphant, like a trumpet pitched five octaves too high, sounding the charge. "I heard it, I heard it, the one pure note! It oscillates! It *does* oscillate! It moves, it moves, *eppur s! muove!!"*

"I thought you said he had not heard about opera," Worf said to Riker, puzzled.

"I didn't think he had," Riker said, though the dolphin's song reminded him suddenly of the innocent Marguerite's victorious cry to heaven at the end of *Faust*. "But never mind. Hwiii! What is it? If you've got good news, believe me, I wouldn't mind hearing some."

"I heard it," Hwiii said, almost gasping with the excitement as he struggled out of his suit. "Oh, for Sea's sake, are your arms broken, give me a hand with this thing, I'm in a hurry!"

Bemused, they leaned forward and helped O'Brien wrestle Hwiii out of his space suit.

"It was the other *Enterprise,*" he said, wriggling out and onto his waiting floater pad. "I heard her. Something happened aboard that ship: there was a big energy discharge, the shields went up and down."

Riker looked at him in surprise. "They did? How could you tell?"

"I felt it, I tell you, I felt it on my skin! I explained all this to you before. I went out to see what I could feel. Nothing,

nothing at all for a good while: this part of space is good for that at least, the hyperstrings are sparse. But then I felt the knot, and it was as fat a knot as you get from a small planet. A great energy source all tied close and tight. And there was a fluctuation in the power source serving it, and I felt the knot loosen, then tighten again, and the whole string twanged!" The trumpets sang again in Hwiii's voice. "It oscillated, I felt the oscillation, its direction, its amplitude, the length of the hyperstring, what's wrapped around it, where it's headed!"

Worf looked at Riker, who asked, "Are you sure it was not something aboard the *Enterprise* that you sensed?"

"Oh, don't be silly," Hwiii said, laughing as someone might laugh at a child making a ridiculous but adorable suggestion. "I could feel *her* quite clearly, the great fat whale that she is, and there's been no such power fluctuation, nor has she anything capable of generating as much as nine hundred terawatts for any one single function—has she?"

Riker shook his head. *Great fat whale?* "I wish. She certainly hasn't."

"But *that* does," Hwiii said, wriggling his tail into the generator for his fluid-field suit. "I can hear it from here, I can *feel* it, you don't need sensors anymore to find them: shut them down! Or rather, I'll link the passive sensors to my hyperstring-sensing equipment, and you can trail the other *Enterprise* where you like without fear of detection . . . until you're ready to let her detect you. Then there will be trouble." Hwiii dropped his jaw in a grin, and Riker suddenly, as if for the first time, became aware of the teeth in those jaws, small and needle-sharp, in great number.

"We will go hunting," Hwiii said. "I have a good idea of the nature of the weapon she used on us: I'll start work on the remedy. Mr. La Forge will get us the details, the equations: he'll know which ones we'll need, he can't mistake them. We will build the same apparatus that the other ship carries. And then we will go hunt us a shark."

Hwiii smiled meaningfully at Riker and at Worf, and Worf, caught in the spirit of the moment, grinned back, also showing teeth. "My people are gentle, by and large," Hwiii said, "but as was true on your Earth, sharks are our great enemies, and we hate them. They have more teeth than we have, swim faster, live longer. But even the great whites have no defense when we hit them amidships at thirty knots." Hwiii smiled, more sweetly, but wicked-eyed. "They rupture wonderfully. I know where *their* 'amidships' is, now. We'll start building the beak to hit them there. Come on!"

It had taken Picard a good while to prepare himself for the sleep he knew he needed. He had forced himself to it finally, done the various small exercises that he had learned over many years, setting the "mental alarm clock" to wake him after four hours. Then he lay down, in a bed that to his mind still felt slightly warm from the body of Beverly Crusher. It was almost certainly an illusion, but he couldn't get rid of the image.

And still sleep eluded him. After a while, he got up and went over to the desk, sat down, and brought up his terminal there.

His own computer was one of the installations that he had required the nanites to spare. He had had some questions to which he had not yet found answers. Some answers Picard had guessed and wanted corroboration for; about others, he had no idea.

"Scan for records on Spock, Commander, Starfleet," he had said.

"Spock, Commander," said the computer, and began reading out a service record that sounded like that of someone who had entered wholeheartedly enough into what the *Enterprise* of that time was doing: intimidation, plunder, destruction. A long time it went on, then something odd happened. After a given stardate, that Spock was transferred off the *Enterprise,* at his own request; but the record said the transfer was "prejudicial"—meaning that someone on the ship wanted to get rid of him. Picard could guess who. That universe's Kirk had come back, found the secret of his great weapon—an alien device called the Tantalus Field, useful for making people vanish abruptly —had been compromised; in fact, given to Spock. As well, to judge from his own Kirk's debriefing, that other Kirk's "captain's woman" had suffered something of a change of loyalties.

Picard sat there with his chin on his fist, considering the ramifications. He still remembered, quoted verbatim, Kirk's final conversation with that Spock, daring him to be the "one man with a vision" who could change the brutality of the Empire before its victims finally rose up and destroyed it. Spock, according to Kirk, had estimated it would take two hundred–odd years for that to happen, and Kirk had invoked "the illogic of waste" as his reason for Spock to try to stop the present-day slaughter and to try to change the Empire into something more benevolent. The Vulcan to whom Kirk had spoken had been profoundly skeptical about the possibilities and had said only, "I will consider it."

To judge by this record, he had done more than consider it. He became a power in Starfleet, and in other ways as well. For a short time, people who frustrated his drive toward increased personal power vanished abruptly. He began to move—covertly at first, Picard suspected, then overtly, as confirmed by the documentation—to try to change the Empire's methods of dealing with subject species, conquered worlds, arguing that, logically, power benefits from benevolent use. For a while there was an uncomfortable shift and wash of opinion around him at

Starfleet, like the tide just before ebb or flow. Spock pressed his advantage in Starfleet Command, rising to the Admiralty. There was a period of some months when he seemed to drop out of notice—the records merely stated that he had been posted to a desk job—something affiliated with his father, the Vulcan ambassador. And then . . .

Picard shook his head. It seemed as if he pushed something, someone, too hard. His living quarters at Starfleet were raided; evidence was found there, the records said barely, of treason. No detail was given on what might have been considered treasonable. *Was something planted on him?* Picard wondered. *Or did someone decide they had better use for the Tantalus Field than he had?* And there was the enmity of his old captain to be dealt with as well—an old unhealed sore of disaffection and rage that had been festering since Spock left the *Enterprise*. Indications were that Kirk, embittered by his former first officer's rise to power, may have been behind the charges, trumped-up or otherwise, that sent Spock to his death. He was court-martialed and executed some twelve years after another Kirk had dared him to be the one man with a vision.

The vision apparently died with him. His father, the ambassador, was assassinated shortly thereafter by another Vulcan eager for the job. Picard had his suspicions about that assassination as well.

Picard paused his search, rubbed his face with his hands, and sat in the darkened room, in the glow of the screen, considering. For one who knew how to read the records—for bureaucratese had changed little from his own universe to this one—there were signs that Spock had indeed "considered it" as he promised and had attempted using various means, mostly subtly, to shift the Empire away from the blind cruelty of its course. And though one man, standing in the right place with a lever long enough, can move a planet, Spock's lever was too short, the fulcrum was too close, or . . . Picard shook his head. Any one of a number of variables was out of joint. Whatever, he failed, managing only to push the inevitable collapse of the Empire further into its future. The Empire went on, not realizing what his own universe's Kirk and that universe's Spock had known or come to know: that an empire based only on conquest is, tactically if not ethically, top-heavy and will eventually collapse under its own weight.

Picard stopped for a little while then, sitting there, his chin on his hands again, and thought. He could understand Kirk's motives: they were no different from his own. *He saw waste, suffering, folly, and wanted to change them, to stop them; but he may not have understood enough of the huge inertia of the force against which he himself wanted to strain . . . wanted that other Spock to defy.* For two and a half centuries the Empire had known no motivation except survival by exploitation. Picard remembered something his own Beverly Crusher had said to him once, about human psychopathologies: "If you're going to take a behavior away, you'd better have something superior to put in its place. Otherwise in about ten minutes you get a relapse." Spock had tried to substitute a different behavior, but there was no way to convince a mostly human Empire that logic and forbearance, even the prickly kind of forbearance that a Vulcan would have recommended, were better than expansion. Expansion had worked for them for a long time. They saw no reason to stop. They would go on as they had started.

But at the same time . . . Picard shook his head. *What are these people doing in* this *situation,* he thought, *where we find them today? It's been hundreds of years since, in this universe, anyone explored anything for pleasure, for the delight of knowledge. That whole school of thought is discredited now. Why are they* here?

He stared at the screen for a long time. Then, in the

unchanging darkness, a thought occurred to him. If there had suddenly been some difficulty in expansion . . . "Necessity is a mother," he remembered Geordi misquoting to him once. Even the most hardened behaviors could be shifted when there was no choice.

To the computer he said, "Display map of the Empire as of one hundred standard years ago. No: concurrent with the year of Spock's death."

The screen cleared and showed him a great, irregular blob of space, superimposed over the graceful curves of the outflung arms of the Galaxy. Against the Galaxy as a whole, it was small, surely no more than 6 or 8 percent of the whole. But it was still a very, very large amount of space. Earth was only roughly at its center: the major axes of exploration, or exploitation in this case, followed along the thickest drifts of stars in the arm, and the blobby amoeba shape bore little or no relationship to the shape of the Federation as he understood it for the same period.

"Go forward ten years," Picard said. The blob increased its volume, protuberances jutting out irregularly over its whole surface. The space involved was about 10 percent bigger.

"Go forward ten years more." Another increase, this time slightly bigger, again reaching along the galactic arm, outward toward the sparser stars, two-thirds of the way out toward the rim.

"Continue in ten-year increments until the present."

The image on the screen became a nested set of glowing amorphous shapes. Each time, the percentage of expansion grew larger and larger. The last ten years' expansion was the largest of all, including in its area of growth an area equal to nearly the entire size of the Empire eighty years before.

But there was a problem. The Sagittarius Arm, the arm of the Galaxy in which Earth and, in his own universe, the

Federation and the Klingon and Romulan empires and all other known species lay, was not directly connected to the Galactic core by anything but gravity. As other arms of the Galaxy had done in the past, it had been "sprayed" off the main mass of the curving, churning greater arm, like a droplet flung away from the main stream of a fall of water. The arm would later meld back into the main stream of the Galactic whirlpool again, or bisect and the pieces meld with other adjoining arms, but this would take hundreds of thousands, perhaps millions of years.

For now, the Sag Arm was discrete. Its size was so great that, in terms of the life span of most sentient species, it could make little difference whether it was connected to anything or not. The two time scales involved were too disparate. For federations and empires concerned with expansion on a modest scale, the problem didn't really arise.

But this Empire's scale of expansion had nothing to do with modesty, and everything to do with their perception of their own survival, their viability. Each decade, the amount of space explored had grown and grown. Not exploration for knowledge or pleasure, for adventure even, but simply for survival and the pursuit of policies a hundred years old now and too ingrained for those who executed them to see any way out.

Now, Picard thought, for the first time with a touch of pity, *I understand the awful overengining of starships in this universe. When all you had to do, when all you knew how to do, was find new worlds to conquer, and conquer them, you needed speed and power more than anything else. And longevity.* Heaven only knew how long some of these ships' missions actually were. Some of the farthest-traveling ships, if he was any judge, might have been traveling for—he shook his head. *Thirty years? Forty?* He shook his head, wondering whether in such cases assassination of

officers above you might not actually be understandable.
Either because you were tired of looking at them and
dealing with their behavior for year after weary year, or
because you could see no other way of advancement.

He saw now the nature of the trap into which the Empire
had fallen. From what little he had read of its history, he
could understand quite well what had happened. They had
spread as widely as they could through the Galaxy and
conquered everything in sight. They had subjugated every
sentient species, destroyed all the ones that would not
submit or were too alien to negotiate with them or couldn't
understand at all what the Empire wanted. They had now
succeeded in exterminating, or dominating, almost all life
with which they had come in contact. And at the end of it
all, they had been stopped, not by any ethical or moral
force, uprearing in indignation . . . but by the simple,
quiet, patient dark, in which everything ended sooner or
later.

Beyond the edges of the now-separated Sag Arm, in all
directions, reached great starless deserts of empty space—
well, empty enough for Picard, though Hwiii might argue
the point. The emptiness reached out on both sides—
twelve or thirteen thousand light-years to the next arm in
either direction. Above the arm, and below it, was nothing
—unless you counted the Magellanic Clouds, a million
and a half light-years to the Galactic south. The arm itself
was cut off from its coreward "parent" branch by a gap
thousands of light-years wide. The Empire had been quar-
antined by the Galaxy itself. Picard looked at the map,
judging the time it would take to cross even the smallest of
those gaps, toward the core. *Even with their engines,* he
thought, *with their durability—even with ships running
smaller crews, such as this one—no ship from the Empire
can now possibly reach any new, inhabited world in less
than ten years. Possibly twenty . . . and at high-warp speeds.*

And even these *ships won't take that for long.* He shook his head. For these people, there are literally no more worlds to conquer.

He remembered Worf saying, "How can it be otherwise?" This was the final truth of the prophecy at which Kirk and Spock had each arrived independently: an empire based solely on expansion fueled by conquest will conquer until it dooms itself . . . and this one had.

They had nowhere else to go. They had looked out into the darkness and finally seen the whirlwind they would soon reap. They had spent more than a hundred years teaching all their people the ruthlessness that had to be channeled into conquest. When there was nothing left to exercise that ruthlessness upon, those people would turn upon each other. The Empire would tear itself apart, die at its own hands, mad.

But they were survivors. Picard knew—few better—the lengths to which desperation will drive any organism, and an organization sooner than a single man. He stood up and walked slowly over to those windows, ignoring again the sight of the disordered and empty bed. In the past decade, or two, the Empire must have been brought most forcefully to this decision as it came up against the walls of darkness and knew there was no piercing them . . . not with any technology they would yet have for hundreds of years. Transilience, a starship that is here one moment and *there,* five thousand light-years or more away, the next, was possible in theory, but hedged about with such formidable theoretical problems still that they would not achieve it before the Empire fell.

So, desperate, grasping at straws, they must have started looking down other paths, other tunnels in the maze. And someone, Picard thought, someone reading history, came across some few references to some other universe, into which some of their own people had accidentally fallen long ago, and from which they were sent back. He suspected that the debrief that those officers performed on returning to this universe, though spotty as to detail, would have been indicative enough of a fertile place to start work. A parallel universe, structurally the same as theirs, as technically advanced—but a weak, soft place by comparison, crippled by ethic, populated, in essence, by sheep, to judge from the behavior of the people in the starship they saw. It was an unexploited place, unconquered—for from what little their misplaced landing party had been able to tell, the people over there weren't the conquering type. All that was needed was to find a way to produce, on purpose, the effect that once happened as an accident, and without needing other identical personnel or equipment to be transferred in the other direction at the same time.

Picard shook his head, thinking of the vast amount of mind and money and time and talent that must have been spent on answering the questions, sorting out the theoretical problems, and finally the technical detail that resulted in those great hulking boxes downstairs in engineering. They had solved the problem. They had, by (he had to admit) splendid use of the information that had fallen into their hands, created a whole new world, a world of worlds to conquer . . .

. . . starting with *Enterprise.* The pity and the anguish that rose up in him now were a match for his anger at the attack on his own world, his own ship. *This place cannot be left this way,* he thought. *The innocents here deserve a life freed of this tyranny. But how? How?*

He was back up against the problem of inertia. "One man cannot change the future," Spock had apparently said to Kirk. "But one man can move the present," Kirk had replied. There, as so often in his career, he had been right. *Give me a place to stand,* that ancient scientist had said. But you needed a lever long enough, and the *right* place to stand. Spock, able as he was, had not been able to do it.

There was this, though—the time of Spock's prediction

was eighty years closer than it had been. The whole system was now inherently less stable, more prone to being disordered. *With less effort?* Picard wondered. *But not until I get a few more answers. Who is the lever? Where do I stand?*

He stared at the screen for a long time; then the door chimed. He blanked the screen and stood. "Come," Picard said.

The door opened. Outside in the corridor, the lights were dimmed, whether because of one of the transient power failures, or the presence of ship's night, he wasn't sure. Either way, from the dimness, a darker shape moved in, graceful. He caught the swing of the glittering fabric, the metal of the harness and the gleam of the knife, and, very soft, the faint gleam of the light above his bed catching in the dark eyes. It was Counselor Troi.

CHAPTER 13

"**C**aptain," the counselor said. Picard sketched her a small half-bow and began rummaging in his mind for poetry—though right now he suspected that she would see in his mind not much more than a great sense of melancholy and distress.

"You're having trouble sleeping," she said. "I could feel it right up on the bridge."

Her tone was gentle enough, but there was a broad streak of innuendo—if kindly sounding—right down the middle of it. He chose to ignore it for the moment and gestured her to a seat.

She ignored the gesture and sat comfortably on the end of the bed, leaning back on her straightened arms and looking at him. Those dark eyes dwelling on him were full of a speculative expression.

"A great feeling," she said, "of dislocation, of stress. They did warn us that this would happen. An occupational hazard of the situation when we know that there are other . . . selves, like ourselves, out there. Curiosity is hard to stifle."

"I would suppose so," Picard said, "otherwise you would hardly be here."

"Yes, well . . . It's my business, after all, to keep an eye on the officers. To make sure they're functioning at maximum efficiency. But there are a couple who have been having problems."

He glanced at her.

"Yes. You and Beverly have had a little . . . disagreement, shall I call it?" She smiled a little at his sudden uncomfortable look. "It would have been difficult to miss. Her dreams were full of it."

"Oh," Picard said, abruptly glad that he had not been able to get any sleep. Heaven only knew what might have come out then when the mind was unguarded.

"The distress, the fear—it would be difficult not to feel them, especially in a sleeping mind. You should be careful how you frighten her, Captain. A frightened doctor can lose you crew out of carelessness . . . or spite."

He walked away, feeling uneasy, knowing that the subject of Wesley Crusher was still between them. "Captain, perhaps it's time for the two of us to come to some kind of agreement."

"What kind of agreement, Counselor?"

"I'll be frank with you. You are in deep trouble. Your mission is in crisis. Our timetable is already thrown considerably out of shape. Starfleet Command is not going to take kindly to this situation if it's informed."

"And you would have to inform them, of course."

"Of course." Her smile was the smile of someone who had been waiting for a specific position of strength for a long time and now finally finds herself in it. "We've been working at cross-purposes for a long time, you and I. I know that pride of yours—very few know it better. The mere fact of having to *have* a security officer whose authority runs near to yours annoys you. It always has."

"There's no point in being annoyed about something which is, after all, Fleet policy," Picard said softly.

"Why, that's quite true. And I've never had any doubt that you've been quite aware of that."

"Never mind that, Counselor. Put aside the 'soft words' for the moment. I believe that regulations in this situation require you to notify Starfleet . . . do they not?"

"Well, normally, indeed they do. But communications can always be"—she shrugged slightly—"delayed."

"I would have thought that the present state of the ship's computers would have guaranteed that," Picard said a little sourly.

To his growing concern, she smiled at him. "Oh, there are ways around that. Many of my functions, for good and proper reasons, don't have anything to do with the main computer or go through it—lest in an accident situation like this"—did she put a little more twist on the word *accident* than should have been there?—"the contents should be compromised. Now, on the other hand . . . a certain amount of delay to prevent misunderstanding can be quite helpful—and the situation may well resolve itself at that point."

She looked at him almost coquettishly. Picard, finding himself actively hating the role he needed to play at this point, started to move slowly toward her, his hands behind his back, looking at her with an expression that suggested he might have some interest . . . an interest that was at the moment the furthest from his mind. "And what circumstances," he said, "would be required to engender this 'helpful delay'?"

He got quite close to her, looking down into those great dark eyes; they really were extraordinarily beautiful— *With the skin he made him mittens,* Picard thought carefully, *made them with the fur side inside, / made them with the skin side outside, / he, to get the warm side inside, / put the inside skin side outside.*

"Well," she said, "your little disagreement with the doctor . . . it's been coming for a while now, Wesley aside. Certainly it seemed as if the situation would become increasingly stable over the last few years, as events receded in time. But there was a factor that neither of you thought of. As Wesley's grown up, increasingly she's seen his father in him. During his childhood the likeness was minimal, but now it's getting stronger every day. She has that image, recalling the man she lost, in front of her eyes for a good part of every day. And she's been given a fair amount of leisure, maybe too much, to reflect just what she did lose." The counselor's eyes flicked up to his. "What you took from her.

"But I think that trend, too, is on the point of breaking now. Certainly you've unsettled it. She doesn't know how to read your sparing her son. She thinks maybe some spark of that old friendship with Jack Crusher is alive in you still—so all her thoughts are shaken and changed, and everything becomes unstable again, dangerously so."

She looked at him for a moment.

"Well, Counselor. Go on."

"I would think you would welcome an end to all this instability. It would be simple enough. Simply declare your liaison with her at an end and start another one that's more to your advantage."

She was quite close now. Though she had made no move to touch him and had her arms behind her back in a position matching his, the air of almost stifling intimacy between them was quite palpable. Picard kept the poetry going and said, "And you would be that liaison, of course."

"I don't think you would find it unpleasant. Ask Commander Riker—if you need to." She rolled her eyes and gave a little scornful laugh. "It's not in his nature to keep quiet about something he's enjoying."

"I wonder how you bear that, considering that you are generally of more . . . delicate sensibilities." This was straightforward flattery, but he let it come out, needing time to consider the ramifications of all this.

She raised her eyebrows. "It *is* flattery," she said, startling him a little, "but accepted for the moment."

A lucky guess? Picard thought. *Or is she genuinely hearing something?* "It's an interesting prospect," Picard said, meanwhile thinking loudly, *His counsellors are rogues, Perdie! / While men of honest mind are banned / to creak upon the Gallows Tree, / or squeal in prisons overmanned.* "I should warn you," he said, "that the doctor probably will not take kindly to such a turn of events. If you should find yourself suddenly needing medical care . . ."

The counselor smiled at him. "Should we agree on this, the only one needing medical care will be the doctor . . . and by the time it arrives, it will be a little too late. I have friends in sickbay as well."

She took a turn away from him for a moment. "It would work out very well; we could command the ship together. You, the brains; I, the eyes."

"And what would Commander Riker be?"

The counselor simply laughed. "We'll have to look lower for a part for him. . . . All he thinks about are power and his lusts, but men of that kind have things they're useful for."

"Of course. And there are other kinds of men . . . useful for other things, I take it?" He bent closer to her face.

"So I've heard." For a moment they breathed practically into each other's lips—then Picard straightened a little bit, daring to push the moment no further. There was always the chance that something of his jerry-rigged shielding would slip, should the body become more interested than it already was.

"Counselor, you've given me a great deal to think about."

"So what will you do?"

"I will consider your proposal"—he was tempted to say *proposition,* but restrained himself—"and get back to you with an answer in good time."

The first spark of anger showed in those eyes. "Surely, it would be more to your advantage"—she leaned on the word—"to come to a choice now, so that I can begin acting in a way that won't be prejudicial. Your time is very short. If you have an ally, it will be possible to make more of it."

He drew himself up quite straight. "Counselor, I will not be pushed or rushed. I will give you my answer in good time, in due course—and not before."

She frowned at him. "One more chance, Captain. Just one. Don't let your stubbornness push you into a mistake."

He stood silent and merely looked at her.

"I see. That pride of yours." She shook her head. "No matter. If you recover this situation by yourself, then we'll talk further. I'll have no need to contact Starfleet." Somehow he knew that this was a lie: if she hadn't already done it, she was going to do it quite soon. "If I must do it, I think you know very well the aftereffects will be unfortunate. Commander Riker has refused several offers of command of other craft, as you know, because he's been waiting for this one. He won't have thought to be authorized to take command of it so soon."

Picard considered how many meanings rode behind the word *authorized.* She would call Starfleet and get permission to have him assassinated. Would she let Riker do it, he found himself wondering with an almost clinical detachment, or would she insist on doing it herself? *Hell hath no fury . . .*

"I'll leave you to your thoughts," she said, turning, and added with some scorn, "such as they are. Third-rate poets."

"There is nothing third-rate about Villon," Picard said mildly.

She snorted. "I have some other matters to attend to."

She turned and went quickly out. The feeling of rage that trailed behind her in the air was like smoke. He was meant to feel it, he thought, meant to take alarm.

He was alarmed, but not in the way she thought.

In the shaft servicing the computer core, Geordi pulled out another chip, scanned it, found it compromised, and slipped one of his own storage chips into place. He touched the "run" command on his padd again and started loading in the last eighty terabytes of material. It always seemed to take longer when you were so close to the end of a job. He whistled softly, looked around him, then started pulling some of the other chips to genuinely replace them.

The padd flashed at him: that chip was full. Only four terabytes. He shook his head, took another from the belt pouch and slipped it into the spot the first one had occupied.

"Mr. La Forge?" Eileen's voice said from above. "Can you come have a look at this one?"

"What—got a problem?"

"Yes, I'm not sure what to make of this."

"Right," he said, perching his padd just inside the open panel he was working on. "God," he said, floating upward —he had changed to a floater half an hour ago—"I'm so stiff from sitting on this . . . thing," he finished as his head rose above the level of the top of the shaft, and he looked up at those boots, those legs, that skirt—and, looking down on him, her eyebrows raised slightly, the counselor, with two security people behind her, phasers drawn and pointed at him.

He swallowed. "Counselor Troi." The first thought to pass through his mind was that he should simply push himself back off the floater and take the fall, a hundred fifty feet down to the bottom of the core, before she could—

—and it was too late. He was frozen like a statue where he sat, unable to move, and she was inside his head. The pressure of it was like bricks laid on his brain, squeezing it down, squeezing his will down and out of the way, while from inside a knife sliced delicately through layer after layer of thought, looking for something in particular—and then it found it.

With terrible clarity, clarity greater than even he had experienced in the moment itself, he saw his hands pull out the little transporter tag, put it on the pile of chips, and beam them away. Then his sight was his own again, and he was looking at Troi, and Hessan standing beside her, with a quirk of nasty smile on her face. And he still couldn't move a muscle.

"Why, it's quite true," said the counselor with great interest. "You were quite correct to send for me, Hessan. You *did* see what you thought you saw. Not the same chips at all. Where did those go, I wonder?"

She looked at Geordi. "Two of you," she said to her security people. "Haul him up out of there. Take him down to the Agony Booth by my quarters: that one's still working. We'll have a nice long talk. Good. One thing first."

She pulled the knife out of her boot and took Geordi's bare arm, studying it for a moment. "Let's see. Yes, there it is. I don't want us being interrupted."

She cut. Geordi couldn't even cry out, and a moment later the counselor held up the bloodied intradermal implant, dropped it on the floor, and crushed it under her heel. "That's better. Now, Hessan, as for you—you've been waiting for a promotion, haven't you? Some little while now."

"Yes, Counselor," she said, still smiling. "I didn't think it was likely to come soon, though."

"Oh, no problem with that. You take over this operation. Granted, there are three assistant chiefs ahead of you, but they can't really do the job, can they?—we both know that." The two smiled at each other conspiratorially. "Get moving now," the counselor said, "and get this ship running again quickly. We have problems to deal with."

Hessan turned to the other engineering staff gathered around. "Never mind this swapping back and forth between cores; it's too time-consuming. Let's simply break out the emergency 'hard' six-hour backups out of stores and use those instead. Get me more crew: I want all the diseased chips pulled and destroyed within half an hour. Take as many people as it needs."

Geordi swallowed. They were going to do it the old-fashioned way, the simple way—the way he had hoped no one else would think of in the face of direct orders and a sufficiently elegant solution.

The counselor nodded, satisfied, as people went into action around her. "Fine," she said to Hessan. "Meanwhile, I'll take care of him." She turned, and her eyes rested on Geordi, and that smile broadened.

In great horror he found himself understanding how the fly feels when the spider looks at it. *Do spiders smile?* he wondered. If they did, they would look like *this*.

They dragged him away.

On the bridge of the other *Enterprise,* Riker leaned over Data's console. There was nothing else to do at the moment, nothing to see on the viewscreen since the other *Enterprise* had taken itself out of range. "How's the data analysis going?"

"I am still completing it," Data said. "The amount of information Mr. La Forge has sent us so far is considerable. I have, however, been able to extract and abstract for Commander Hwiii those parts of it which are most practically oriented. There is some information in the package we have received about the actual building of the apparatus that causes the inclusion of another object into this universe."

"Does it say anything about getting an object out of this universe, back where it belongs?"

"Indeed it does, a great deal. Under average circumstances there does not seem too much difficulty in pushing an originating object back where it came from. There appears to be some question whether in the theory, hyperstring structure from one universe may not actually *extend* into another. It would seem that some traces of string structure remain about a dislocated object and may be used as a shortcut to 'snap' that object back into its original location- and duration-space."

"Like a rubber band," Riker said.

"The simile would be fairly exact. The only difficulty would appear to be if an object remained too long in this universe. Not only would the universes themselves move out of phase, complicating matters"—Riker rolled his eyes: Data was understating again—"but the strength of the hyperstring attachment attenuates over time. The relationship is expressed by the equation lV/pL equals kO. Once the final string connections are broken or weakened past the point where the apparatus can successfully use them, other means must be found to locate the 'home' universe." Data stopped a moment, considering. "This is an entirely different theoretical area, on which it would appear the Empire has as yet done no work, since there is only one specific universe they are interested in: ours."

Riker shook his head. The thought of the *Enterprise* having to bounce from universe to universe in search of its home . . . But it had to be considered. "Mr. Data, what would your estimate be of the number of alternative universes we would have to explore to find our way home from here under such circumstances?"

Data blinked. "An accurate estimate would require at least moderately reliable projections of the number of universal or semi-universal faces on the surface of the hypothetical solid, the rotation of which through hyperspace creates or can have been said to 'create' the alternative universes, but—"

"You don't know," Riker said gently.

Data opened his mouth, then shut it again. "No," he said a bit mournfully.

"Then let's not even bother with it just now. How's Commander Hwiii doing?"

"He has already started building the basics of the inclusion/exclusion device from some of the matrix information in the last upload."

"How far along is he?"

"I would estimate he and the engineering team working with him have already completed about fifteen percent of the construction work that will be required."

"You did tell him to take as much crew as he needed . . ."

"Certainly, Commander. But at this stage of the construction, sheer numbers will not be of much help. Among other things, not all the theoretical or construction data on the inclusion device is yet in place here. Mr. La Forge's upload is still incomplete: he has advised us that another hundred and forty terabytes of material are still to come."

Riker whistled.

"Until the information is complete and we have the necessary data on the fine detail of the device, we will not be able to progress too much further." Data thought for a moment. "It is as if the commander were building a subspace radio set. He has the information needed to build the chassis, as it were—the matrix into which the specialty frequency and modulations boards would be plugged—but as to the boards themselves, he has as yet neither an idea of what they are or where they should be placed and how they should be powered."

"He's done the groundwork."

"That is correct. And until the download is complete, there is little more that can be done."

"If there was only some way to find out what's keeping that upload," Riker said softly.

"Scrambled communications with the away team are possible at this point."

Riker thought about that. He thought about it for a long moment and opened his mouth to say, "Riker to La Forge"—then changed his mind. "No, no reason to stand over his shoulder and hurry him. No one works best in a situation like that."

Riker made for the turbolift doors. "I'll go down to engineering and see how Hwiii is doing, see if he needs any help."

The doors shut. Worf watched Riker go with some amusement, then said to Data, "Apparently, since he cannot stand over Mr. La Forge's shoulder, he will now go and stand over Commander Hwiii's."

"An example of irony," Data said after a moment.

Worf grinned. "It is an example of Commander Riker," he said, and went back to monitoring the other ship.

He screamed again. Screaming was becoming like breathing now. He couldn't remember a time when he hadn't done it. His throat was so raw with the pain that the sound of the torment in the Agony Booth was a new torment in itself, every time he did it—and he couldn't stop.

The pain came in waves, like the ocean, and felt as relentless. There was no way to stop it or block it. It rolled through his body, trailing an anguish after it that was like a prolonged version of the time the coolant gas got loose in engineering: a cold that burned like fire, all over him. But this was not cold. He might as well have been half-immersed in lava, or live steam, for the way his body felt. Then the pain would reduce, just slightly, he suspected; but to his agonized nerves, the change seemed so great that the difference was more like that between a mild headache and a migraine. He found himself absurdly, pitifully grateful when it decreased even so slightly. He felt as if he would do anything to keep it from increasing again. And that fear was much with him in those moments of decreased pain: that after a little while, he *would* do anything, say anything.

"Who came with you?" the soft voice inquired. His vision had long since stopped working correctly. Whether the Agony Booth's field was interfering with the visor somehow, or the optic nerves themselves were rebelling, he had no idea. He had to blink and stare through the shimmer of the field before he could see her standing there, smiling at him, waiting. She had something else to use on him, he knew, besides the Booth, but she was in no hurry. He had barely enough strength even to shake his head and thought he had better conserve it. So he merely hung there, said nothing, did nothing. Though his body twitched—the poor overfired nerves firing one another in sympathy and frightened anticipation. Every time he tried to move, his body wouldn't move the way he wanted it to—and it hurt.

"You may as well tell me," the counselor said. "I am not going to stop until you *have* told me what I want to know. And that's just the Booth I'm talking about. Once you've finally told me, I'm going to go in the other way . . . and make sure." Geordi shuddered all over and cried out again with the pain of it; every nerve cringed and twitched at the motion.

"The sooner you tell me," she said reasonably, "the more useful you are to me. And the more useful you are to me, the more likely it is that I'll keep you alive after we finish this. Your counterpart—oh, yes, we found him, that didn't take long, after you told us where to look—your counterpart is a very talented man. Having two of him in the Empire would be better still. I daresay we could make your working for us very pleasant. But there's no hope of it

happening unless you're alive at the end of all this.
. . . And whether or not you're alive depends on whether
you annoy me or not."

He shuddered again. *Told them?* he thought, through the
confusion of the pain and fear. *I don't remember telling her
anything about* . . . But that was the horror of this situation. He *might* have told them. He might have. And if he
had—what else might he tell them? *Stop this now,* part of
him shouted. *Stop it now and* control *what you tell her! Give
her a little piece of information at a time.*

The shock of the pain caught him again. "Don't you
want to live?" she said softly while it rolled over him and
left him writhing.

He knew it was a lie. He knew there was no way that they
could leave him alive—that she would kill him, and enjoy
it, after she had extracted the information she wanted. But
the pain began to build again, washing away reason, and he
drew a long breath and screamed again and again, the body
trying desperately to get someone to stop this. Everything
hazed out, nothing was left but that pain, a world gone
white and dead with it. It would not stop.

"I hate having to rush things this way," she said an
eternity later when the pain lessened a little. "It's so
slapdash—not to do things in neat stages, but to have to
chop and change." He felt, then, the first fingers touching
his mind—almost casually. The effect was horrific, like
being touched on an open wound by someone slowly,
delicately drawing a finger over the ragged edge, the place
where the hypersensitive tissue was beginning to crust and
dry. He sobbed.

"I suppose I can just be resigned to it. Unless you change
your mind very quickly and start telling me what you
know. It's so *draining* to have to go through someone's
mind the hard way . . . but I will if I must. I may be tired of
it at the end, a little, but I'll be better in an hour or so. But

you'll be dead." She smiled more broadly. "Not without feeling what will feel to *you* like several years of this pain."

He moaned. *Oh, yes, I can prolong it,* she said from inside him again, and it was as if his own mind spoke to him, having turned traitor, punishing him for all the secret wrongs of a lifetime. *Time sense is one of the most easily altered of all the interior senses. I can't spend a long while with you myself—I've got a lot of other things to do—but the little while I spend with you will feel like* months *of this. I know where to touch the mind to make it happen. See?—*

—and something happened, so that the moment froze with the pain increased to a point so shocking that he was no longer even able to scream, but had to merely hang there and feel it, burning him up as if he were a stick in a fire. When time started running again, and his consciousness emerged enough to get behind his eyes and look at her . . .

"See?" she was saying. "How simple. See how long the time between one breath and the next can be?" She laughed. "What was it they used to say about relativity? A second with a pretty girl—a second on a hot stove." She smiled at him charmingly. "See, now you've got both. And you'll have both for a good long while. Now, tell me"—the pain increased once again, though time kept running—"who came with you?"

The field wrung another scream out of him, and the mind touched him, just *there,* and he cried, helpless, "Counselor!"

"No use begging me for mercy," she said softly. "I have very little of that to spare today."

He gulped, desperate, realizing how close he had come to doing real damage. *Tell her!* his mind screamed. *Start telling her, control it!*

Don't! shrieked another part. *Do anything, but don't tell her you've got to slow her down, do anything to slow her that you can, don't, don't!*

269

The pain whited him out again. Desperate, he clawed at the edges of his mind, trying to keep from falling back into that burning whirlpool.

"Who came with you?" said the voice. And the fingers came down and gently pried loose the hand that held him on the edge of the pain.

He fell, screaming, burnt alive—and the image of Picard came and went before he could do anything about it.

The pain from *that* was worst of all.

Not very far away, someone else heard the screams, and the tears rolled down her face, and there was nothing she could do. Anguish of that sort was eminently traceable. Deanna, waiting in Geordi's quarters, knew that they had caught him, knew where he had been when they caught him, knew that the other Troi was involved somehow. They were coming here and would be here very shortly to rescue the other La Forge.

In fact they were quite close: she could feel them approaching. Horrible indecision and fear descended on her. She could feel what Geordi was going through, though, even if only at a remove; the pain of it frayed at her nerves like an old acid burn on the skin. She had to get him out of there.

This is how to start, said part of her mind, and got her up and wiped her face hastily dry.

The door opened, and the security detail came in. She looked at them and pointed at the wall. "In there. I can feel his mind. He's asleep, but otherwise he's all right. Get him out."

"Counselor," one of them said in surprise. "We weren't expecting to see you down here so fast."

Her heart rose. It was plain enough that these people, at least, didn't know there was a double of their mistress aboard. *Logical enough,* the thought went through

Deanna's mind. *She wouldn't tell them any more than they absolutely needed to know.*

"At a time like this," she snapped at them, "what do you expect?" They cringed, and she found herself enjoying it and didn't even bother to feel guilty about it. "Get him out of there. I have other business to attend to." They ducked their heads to her and went about opening the compartment.

She headed straight out the door and into those halls, moving fast. People got out of her way as they saw her coming, and she was grateful for that. *At least communications aren't functioning here,* she thought. *Odds aren't very good that anyone would figure out there are two of us, until . . .* At least she *hoped* the odds weren't very good. *But how is one to tell at this point?*

She strode down the corridor into the turbolift and headed for Geordi's last location—that shaft where he had been working. She got there to find a crowd of engineering people just now descending into the shaft, Eileen Hessan among them. They looked at her in some surprise. "Did you forget something, Counselor?" one of them said.

"Yes," Troi said, and brushed through them as if they were so many chickens. "Here—give me that." She gestured one of them off the floater he was standing on, got on it herself, and keyed in the commands that would take it down the shaft. It floated down gently. There, half in, half out of the open panel, was Geordi's tricorder, and one chip, with the scratch he had shown her on the corner. She bundled the things under one arm and floated back up again.

"There," she said to the nervously waiting engineering staff. "Now do what you were doing and hurry. We don't have all day here."

"Yes, ma'am," some of them said, and people started descending into the shaft again.

Sweating, Troi walked out briskly, her head high, and made her way without stopping straight back to La Forge's quarters. There, clutching the tricorder and chip, she sat down, then laid them aside, folded her hands, and tried to center herself enough to at least get control over the stress. It was very hard.

That wasn't too bad, she thought, *but I'm going to have to do it again almost right away. First, though . . .*

When she was adequately centered, Deanna did what she had not yet dared to do—felt around her with her mind and reached directly toward that other mind that so closely matched her own in structure. She got quite close, in that directionless, distanceless way that minds have of drawing near or apart from one another. She waited for it to notice her.

It didn't. It was very busy on some matter of its own, lost in cool enjoyment that rose and fell in time with the screams in Geordi's mind. Deanna shuddered, but she could understand the rationale for the torture perfectly well. Even powerful telepaths preferred exterior circumstances to do as much of their work for them as possible. Why bother breaking a mind's barriers yourself, and wearing yourself out, when good old-fashioned pain could do the job as well?—leaving you to go over the remains unwearied. All loathsome—but it might serve her yet.

She leaned up closer yet against that mind and actually put some pressure on it. There was no one else, Deanna knew, that she could do this with; but this was *her* mind. She could influence it.

And it noticed nothing. . . . She leaned there a good few moments, but it was so busy with its own nasty delights that it never noticed her. Deanna wanted to shudder again—how could anyone luxuriate in someone's pain this way?—but she repressed the urge, afraid it would attract notice. Indeed she must keep her own reactions very much to herself for the next little while, and she choked the revulsion moving in her down to almost nothing. It was horrible to see this "her": it indicated all too clearly what, if things had gone wrong in the past—or did go wrong in the future—she could become. She didn't let it distract her, though.

She slipped softly closer in mind, until she could actually start hearing some thoughts. It was eerie, and bitterly frustrating, that the only time she should approach anything like a Betazed's proper abilities should be while *en rapport* with *this* creature. But she kept herself calm and listened and opened her mind to the thoughts and the images. *Who came with you?* she heard the counselor demand—felt Geordi try desperately to resist and saw her own image flicker across his mind. *Counselor.*

Her counterpart mistook his meaning, pressed him harder. Deanna swallowed; by so little had her position been protected.

Then the next image came up out of the haze of pain. Picard. Down the link, she could hear her counterpart thinking, *The captain!* Her mind suddenly was aflame with conjecture, instantly satisfied. She realized that the man to whom she had spoken, who had seemed so gentle and noncommittal, was not at all the man she thought she had been speaking to.

The counselor opened her eyes and turned away from the suffering, screaming man, toward her guards. "You and you, come with me. You," she said to the third, "stay here. Leave him on this setting for about ten minutes, then lower it again—not long enough to let him recover completely. And make sure you keep an eye on the refresh rate."

"Yes, Counselor."

"I'll be back in a few minutes . . . then I'll let you know what's to be done with him next." And off she went, her guards in tow.

Deanna felt her do it. Immediately she got up from the bed, careful to sever the link at her end, as indetectably as she knew how. Then she touched her communicator. There was no more time for care or secrecy: speed was going to be everything. "Captain, my counterpart knows. She's on her way to find your double. There's still time to salvage something from this, though. If you get there first."

The communicator under her fingertips buzzed. She read him the coordinates of the storage area quickly and said, "I'll let you know as soon as anything else happens. Out."

She went quickly out and headed down the hall toward the turbolift, making for deck fourteen, where Geordi was. *The timing on this is going to be very close,* she thought. But she kept the fear out of her face and strode down the corridor with that proud, fierce look she had seen on the other's face, thinking, in her mother's best tone of voice, *I am a daughter of the Fifth House. Who dares stand in my way?*

No one did. Again she watched the looks on their faces, the fear, the concern, and felt a little sweet-sharp prickle of excitement, enjoyment, at it. Respect she had in plenty, back home, but not like this.

Deanna smiled ruefully at herself. The price was too high to pay: the temptations inherent in the enjoyment of others' pain were too great. *What does it matter how much you enjoy this kind of thing, if you lose your soul, your humanity? And it's all too enjoyable.*

She got into the 'lift. "Deck fourteen," she said, and waited for the doors to open.

Coming out, she heard the sounds almost immediately: sobs, a man's voice weeping, that cheerful voice always full of such good humor. She set her face, set her tone of mind, and strolled down to the Booth, saying to the guard there, "Very well—that other matter's in hand. Lower the setting on that—I'm going to take him out for a visit. The captain wants to see him."

"Uh-oh," the guard said, and started working over the panel.

"Take it slowly," Deanna said, though everything inside her screamed, *Hurry!* She could feel what his nerves felt and was concerned that stopping this torment too abruptly might throw him into shock. "Good," she said as the field cut out fully, and he collapsed finally to the floor of the platform like a puppet with its strings cut.

She unholstered her phaser. "Give me a hand up with him. He'll get his legs back in a moment."

The guard helped him up roughly. Geordi half-leaned, half-slumped against Troi, and she dug the phaser meaningfully into his ribs. "The captain wants to see you, mister," she said, putting into the words all the ferocity she felt toward the people who had done this to him. "Let's go."

"Do you want some help with him, Counselor? He might—"

She turned cool eyes on the guard. "He'll do nothing . . . but I thank you for your concern, Harrison." She turned her back on him.

Together she and Geordi started down the hall, he lurching, she half-dragging him, trying not to make it show in her urgency. "Come on, Geordi," she whispered in his ear, "we've got work to finish!"

Under the twitching, squeezed-shut eyelids, there was a moment's convulsive movement of surprise, confirming the great wash of desperate joy and fear that went through him. The walking began to strengthen a little; the breathing became less labored. Deanna straightened, too, slowing her pace, conscious of the guard's eyes on her from behind. It did not befit a daughter of the Fifth House to hurry through the halls, even on a matter of life and death. She walked on down the hall, haughty as a queen, and people she passed looked at Geordi and tsked at each other and grinned small grins—their emotions saying plainly that they knew Geordi was doomed. She ignored them. She would get him back to his quarters and do what she could to get him back in shape, and after that . . .

Heaven only knew. Or maybe the captain.

CHAPTER 14

Picard took his phaser, checked the charge on it, and went out in a rush.

He had never liked being out of control in a situation. He liked it less now than ever before in his life. The truth was that his officers were to be trusted, that they knew what they were doing, and that, as usual, the amount of time that he who *commands* spends standing and waiting was always worthwhile. If he could keep himself from meddling in areas where he shouldn't be.

"Come on, Barclay," he said to the constant presence outside his door, and went off down the hall. Then he stopped. "I thought you were going to get some sleep."

Barclay shrugged as he came after him. "I couldn't. Captain, what is it? Do we need more people?"

"No. You and I will do just fine."

"Where are we going, sir?" Picard cheerfully enough quoted him the coordinates. Barclay wrinkled his brow. "Storage? What's down there?"

The 'lift arrived; Barclay checked it, and they stepped in. "Mr. Barclay," Picard said when they were under way, "what do you know about our present mission?"

"Not too much," Barclay said equably enough. "But then we're used to that." *An uninformed crew,* Picard thought; *tyranny's best defense.* "Something to do with . . . another *Enterprise,* another starship. From some other universe." He shook his head. "It sounded like a fairy tale when most of us heard it. But here we are, and everything seems dead serious."

"Well, what does another *Enterprise* suggest to you?"

"Another crew, I guess," Barclay said, and looked at him sideways then, alarmed. "The same crew?—but different. Another—" He looked at Picard and wouldn't say it.

"Another Barclay? Yes. But more to the point . . . another Captain Picard."

Barclay's eyes went briefly wide, and Picard could just this once as clearly read the thought behind them as if he were a full Betazed. The thought was, *Isn't one enough?* "Another Picard," said Jean-Luc. "We're going to go catch him."

Twain had been in his mind all evening since his meeting with the counselor. Now he was there again, but not in verse mode: he was thinking more of *The Prince and the Pauper.* Troi had been right. When he got out of this, her quick thought was going to be worth a great deal of commendation . . . assuming they made it home to a universe where such works were considered worthy to be commended.

They went hurriedly through the halls together. "Mr. Barclay, it's very likely that when we get where we're going, and while I'm busy having a talk with my . . . carbon copy"—he gave Barclay a droll look—"Counselor Troi will arrive. She's going to want to get her claws into him, too."

"I can see that, sir."

"It is vital that she be kept away from that little tête-à-tête as long as possible. I need to talk to that man, undisturbed. If you need to call extra people, do it."

"Calling is a problem, Captain . . . comms are still down."

"You're quite right, of course. Do it any way you can. Commandeer someone to act as a messenger . . . but get the help you need. Just keep her off my case."

"Yes, sir." They were quiet together in the 'lift for a few moments.

Finally Barclay said, "Captain . . ."

Picard nodded at him.

"About my promotion."

Picard had to laugh out loud. "You know how to strike when the iron's hot, don't you?"

"We have been rather busy the past day or so. And I think without me . . ."

"Yes. Without you . . ." Picard looked gravely at the man, and after a few moments Barclay looked away. Picard hoped it wasn't because he had frightened him in any way. "I will look into it. If your general service record until now accords with your behavior of the last few days . . ." He nodded.

Barclay, astonishingly, blushed and looked away. "Thank you, sir."

The 'lift stopped. They came out together on deck fifty-four, far down in the engineering hull, a quiet place, no need for anyone much to be down there. Without much trouble they found the room. Barclay had stopped someone they passed as they got out of the 'lift, sending a message along. For the time being, he posted himself by the door to the storage area.

Picard looked at him. "Will you be all right?"

Barclay looked back at him with the kindly look that bodyguards reserve for their slightly insane charges. "Captain, I'm supposed to be asking *you* that."

"You stay here," Picard said, thumping him gently on the biceps. "I know who's in there." He smiled grimly. "No one better. Don't interrupt us. We'll be fine. And remember—don't leave the spot. If the counselor should come . . ."

"She won't get past me, sir."

"Good man." Picard nodded to Barclay. He went in the door cautiously, and it shut behind him.

And the instant it shut, the foot came shooting out, caught the phaser in his hand, and knocked it halfway across the room.

He did the only thing he could under the circumstances. He grabbed the foot and yanked sideways, hard. There was a crash, and for confusion's sake, he threw himself on top of it, grappling. Found a throat, seized it, looked—

—and the shock, the shock went through him worse than he'd thought. To have yourself by the throat, to see your own enraged and anxious eyes fixed on yours . . . He almost let go. It was close. If he had, he would have been dead. The other's arm came up between his throttling hands, over, then under, the standard break-the-throttle— and that hand had a phaser in it.

Picard did as he had been taught—let go with the left hand to break the twist, seized with it again from underneath this time, leaving the arm that had tried to break the hold useless above it, except that there was a phaser in it. And the phaser came in hard and hit him in the side of the head.

Everything went hot and shot with bright lights, and he fell back—but not before seizing his knees around the waist of the shape he had knocked sprawling and taking it rolling with him. His own hands came up, interlaced, and clubbed the other in the head. *Two can play at this game,* he thought, his own head still spinning. He clubbed again, but it did little good, and in a moment the hands were at *his* throat.

The phaser went flying, dropped out of the fingers that lost their grip for a moment, then found it again, on Picard's throat this time. They rolled over and over on the floor, two or three times. The other kneed him hard in the groin: the breath went out of Picard. He was grateful, at least, as he rolled away in a different direction, that he hadn't been hit in the head again. It would have made him throw up, and he was quite sure that the other would kill him while he did—thus putting him out of his misery in an effective but permanent manner. As he rolled, he came upon one of the dropped phasers, gripped it, rolled to his knees gasping—and found that his counterpart, on his knees as well and clutching his bruised throat, was holding the other phaser on *him*.

And the only problem was that Picard wasn't sure whether he had the phaser with the safety off or the one with it on . . . and he didn't dare look.

" 'Ill met by starlight' indeed," said the other, glaring at him and coughing.

"You heard that?"

"Hearing is always the last thing to go."

"So Dr. Crusher says, yes. Well, the meeting was your idea. Don't blame me for the circumstances, or if you don't like the taste of it when it's happened. You don't suppose that we could just sit back and do nothing."

The other laughed at him harshly. "I suppose we shouldn't have, but then Fleet said that's *exactly* what you'd do. Who was to know that you would be anywhere near as resourceful as we are?"

Picard had to laugh at the self-assured sound of it. "We are. The more fool you for taking Fleet seriously. What desk jockey ever correctly evaluated a field situation?"

The other looked at him. Picard felt like shivering. It was so strange, as if you looked in the mirror and the mirror spoke—words you never dreamed of, or words you had dreamed and put away as nothing you could ever say. "I must tell you immediately," Picard said, "you'll never succeed at this."

"That I see you at all means that you have, much to our

surprise, made some move that was not purely defensive." The other shrugged. "Our own personal success doesn't matter in this. If we must try again at a later date, we will . . . and this time we'll be prepared."

"I very much doubt that," Picard said softly. "Your intelligence, your *hard* intelligence on us, may be better by far than ours on you—but it's the soft intelligence that will trip you. The knowing of personalities and unwritten laws . . . those you'll never master. A day with your crew has made it plain."

"So you say." His counterpart gazed at him thoughtfully. "Are you so sure? Bears may dance badly, but they do dance. We *will* manage it again. There will be other parts of your Federation not so carefully watched. Back doors . . . weak spots. There are always such. You have had other conspiracies of late that nearly brought Starfleet itself down. Those were alien creatures involved, things not even human. Still they almost fooled you when installed near the heart of things. You'll be easily enough fooled by us when we come back."

"But there's no hope of that 'us' including you. Not if I understand *your* Starfleet. You'll be lucky to get out of this with your life."

"Oh, I'll manage," said his counterpart, grinning evilly. Picard wanted to shudder at the thought that such an expression could live on his face. "I am still the most experienced captain they have. They had to come to me for advice when they began to put this plan together . . . and I didn't spend the past five years of my career maneuvering to make sure that the mission was assigned to my ship."

"To *you,* you mean."

"You do learn, eventually. Of course. Once we've succeeded at this, even if the success isn't total, the power I'll acquire—"

It was in the middle of that sentence that Picard realized

what the other was doing and leapt at him, simply leapt like a mad thing, regardless of phasers—though he kept his clutched in his hand. He caught his counterpart in the chest, and again they went rolling over. *They'll be here shortly,* he thought as he grabbed for the other's flailing hand—managed to grab it by the wrist and began pounding it against the floor. The other rolled the other way, and the worst of it began, a thick, tangled, confused fight, all arms and legs, not the clean, efficient combat that had been taught Picard in school, but something more like the halves of a mind fighting. Two men who were one man, terrified of each other, trying to remember their expertise, losing it in the basic horror of the moment: that each of them was face-to-face with something that was his diametrical opposite, but each similarly equipped, each as sharp of mind, and the minutes ticking away. It could only be a matter of time before . . .

The other Picard caught him hard in the solar plexus, rolled away, lurched to his knees. Wheezing, gasping for breath, Jean-Luc came to his own knees and then threw himself sideways as the phaser beam sizzled past him, then once again threw himself straight at the other. The beam went awry, but only just. It singed his left eyebrow off, and the force of it passing through the air by his ear left him half-deaf on that side, the ear ringing. Not that it mattered in the wake of the red streak of pain that left him wondering whether he had actually been grazed. A graze it would have had to be, for anything closer would have left him without that side of his head. For a moment he struggled again with the other, then clubbed the phaser out of his hand with his own, and looked down into that snarling face, teeth bared, more an animal's than a man's.

He gripped his own phaser, checked the setting, the charge. The other glared sheer hate at him, made a grab at the phaser.

He stunned him point-blank, then reeled back, feeling sick to his stomach from the blows and the backwash of the stun. Picard staggered to his feet, tried to pull down his uniform, failed *again,* said, *"Ah, j'm'en fous!"*

The sound of phaser fire came from outside. He whirled. The door opened.

And the counselor and two of her guards rushed in, with Worf behind them. They looked from him, to the form on the floor, to him again.

Picard had no time for their confused looks. "Barclay," he breathed. He brushed past them as if they were hardly there, out into the hall.

Nothing. No one there: only the faintest smell of scorched meat. Not a body, not even a hand to clasp as the poor faithful soul passed away.

He turned, walking slowly back into the room. Troi was staring at him. He felt the brush of a veil against the face of his mind—but the fury was growing in him second by second, fueled by the tears starting to burn in his eyes. For a moment he tried to control himself—*No. I will hide no more of my humanity,* he thought, *though they kill me for it.* The anger burned, he could almost see the veil catch, bloom into fire, drift away as cinders—and Troi, looking at him, actually backed away from him a step, two steps, like death seeing Death.

"Where is Mr. Barclay?" he said softly.

"He should have known better than to put up resistance when a security matter was in hand," Troi said.

He stepped toward her, backed her right into the wall, and took her one-handed under the chin, gripping hard. Her guards stared, fascinated and afraid, and did nothing. The counselor tried the stab of the mind again, but she was uncentered and unsure, and the blow missed. It stuck in the armor of his rage, the intensity of his emotion trapping it, and down the channel Troi had opened between them, Picard's rage poured, transfixing her—open-eyed, open-mouthed, anguished, like a woman being burned at the stake in her mind.

"That was my best man," Picard said, low, even-voiced. "A young officer barely past the threshold of his career. A loyal man. Who knows what he might have been in a year, or five? Except possibly *you* knew." He looked at Troi, narrow-eyed. "Always better to nip these things in the bud, isn't it?" He let go of her, looked away from her, disgusted by the sight of her—

—and found himself looking over at Mr. Worf. Worf's expression was a strange one: recognition of something he had seen before, and confusion and dawning—Picard swallowed. He realized that Worf *knew,* beyond question he knew.

Picard simply stood there and looked at Worf for a second. There was nothing else to be done.

Worf looked back and never said a word. Confused, but not about to waste the moment, Picard turned back to Troi. He gestured at the floor. "Take that out of here."

"The Booth?" Troi said weakly.

Picard's mouth set hard. How many others had this other self ordered it for in his time? A little justice, though it came late, would suit his own present mood. "Yes. Wring it dry. How are the repairs?"

Troi actually stammered. "They're, they're coming along, Captain. We should be spaceworthy again, Hessan says, within—"

"Half the time she said," Picard said bitterly, "whatever it was. See to it. Meantime—" He stepped much closer to Troi. "That was most unnecessary, Counselor." He gestured with his head at the door. "You will rue this day's work."

"Not so much as you will," she said rather desperately, "when Starfleet Command catches up with you. Quite shortly, I should say."

"Trust me, Counselor," Picard said, and his smile must

have been terrible, for she took another step back, "other things will catch up with *you,* first, and I will watch and enjoy every moment." He pointed at the floor again. "Now get that out of here."

Troi and her guards picked up the unconscious body of the other Picard and carried him out. "Mr. Worf," Picard said, "perhaps you would wait a moment."

When the doors had shut, they spent a long few moments studying each other. "You didn't betray me," Picard said. "I thank you for that. But how did you know?"

"Your manner. Your courtesy. The way you spoke to me earlier—taken together with the fact that you cared at all about a dead bodyguard. These have not been typical of 'your' past behavior." Worf smiled grimly. "Unlike others here, I can see the unlikely when it is under my nose; I would not have survived long without learning how to notice things."

Picard nodded. "Time is short. I must recover my people and go . . . but I will not forget your help."

"I will see you safely away. But one thing quickly, before we go." The abrupt sorrow in his eyes was terrible to see. "In your universe—what has happened to my people?"

Picard smiled somberly. "They are a mighty empire, and our allies. Oh, we were enemies once; there were times when we had territorial ambitions that clashed, and our fears of each other's strengths blinded us for a long time to the ways we might help each other. But the will to peace, and some happy accidents, brought us together at last. Now the Klingon Empire is prospering, and its people are a noble and honorable race. Nothing is more important to them."

Worf nodded. "So it was once with us. But not for a long time now." He turned toward the door. "I will accompany you, Captain. Where are you going?"

Picard touched his communicator: there was no more time for secrecy. "Counselor—where are you?"

"The core access room above the starboard primary-hull core," the answer came back. *"Hurry, Captain!"*

"Where's Mr. La Forge?"

"He's here, sir. He's lost his transponder, but otherwise he's all right."

"We're on our way. . . . Come on, Mr. Worf."

"We're on our way?" Geordi muttered, touching his tricorder into life again.

Troi, standing by the locked door with her phaser drawn, shook her head. "Don't ask me. . . . How is it?"

"Security barriers are still down," Geordi said, rubbing his aching head as he worked. "Not for long, though. Eileen has been a busy little bee. But I still know a few tricks she doesn't."

He worked over the tricorder. "She's restored the core on the other side, but I can reroute this control pathway to the core in the engineering hull." He grinned. "You can't be in two places at once."

"Oh, can't you," Troi said, looking at the door. "We both *are.*"

Geordi snorted, then winced at the residual pain the gesture cost him. "We are, maybe, but Eileen's not, and her crew down that way aren't in that much of a hurry, to judge by what I see here. Some kind of place," he muttered, "where people won't work unless someone is standing over them. Ah . . ."

Troi looked nervously at the door. The emotional "temperature" of the ship was rather higher than it had been for the past few hours, and one particular bloom of emotion caught her attention: a dreadful cold rage, and closely associated with it, in another mind, raging anger so tinged with embarrassment that she shied from the touch of it . . . and that was in the mind that seemed, structurally, so like hers. She didn't dare open the link that had been between them earlier, but she could guess what was going on—the other counselor had discovered that Geordi was missing, taken away by another Troi.

Then came a feeling of movement—toward them, mentally as well as physically. She could feel that other mind feeling about it for its own version of the link, a way to tell what *she* was doing and feeling. "Trouble," she said, starting to erect her mental protections as quickly as she could. "Hurry up!"

"I'm going as fast as I can, Counselor."

When they had started training her, as a child, in erecting the mental barriers that kept a Betazed's mind from being littered with other people's emotional baggage all the time, Deanna had made one of those laughable mistakes that your family then teases you about for years afterward. Hearing the term *mental block,* she had always envisioned her barriers as just that, blocks—brightly colored and piled up in a wall between her and whatever she wanted to shut out. Now she started piling them up in her mind as fast as she could, the ones with the letters and numbers on them, and the ones with painted pictures of animals, the paint a little chipped and fading, but the blocks absolutely dependable . . . once they were in place. Nervousness sometimes made her fumble them. Today, though, she slammed them in place in her mind with frantic speed and saw the wall grow, willing it to be invulnerable—for there was more than just her behind it. Geordi would be very vulnerable at the moment, she must not allow—

"Got it!" Geordi said softly, and slapped another isolinear chip down on the console's reading pad. "Resumed."

That core of embarrassed anger came hurrying closer and closer. Troi pulled out her phaser, adjusted it to full stun, and waited. "She's coming," she whispered to Geordi.

She saw him shudder all over, and moan with the pain of

the movement. Nonetheless, he pulled the chip off the reading pad on the console and substituted another. "One-third done, Counselor," he said, and that was all he said.

Troi bit her lip, put herself behind the door, and waited.

The sound of phaser fire came from right outside the door. Troi got an image from her counterpart of the sparks and smoke jumping from the door control. The door flew open.

It was, of course, one of her guards that plunged in first: no chance she would have gone in first herself, if only because it was below her dignity. Deanna stunned the man immediately.

From outside, that mind seized hers. Its power was terrible, magnified by some kind of training that Deanna couldn't believe—and, terribly, that she coveted. *I could have that kind of power,* she thought.

The wall of blocks trembled. Oh, *no,* Deanna said, furious that she could be tempted that way. But she was having none of it. She reached out to that other mind, grappled with it. Then came the shock of satisfaction as the *other's* alarm came down the link, now reestablished, between them. The other might have raw power, but Deanna had finesse. The other battered at her blocks and found them too well established: hit them, hit them again, bristling with rage and scorn.

But her counterpart had no blocks up at all—apparently thinking she had no need for them. And it was hilarious, in a way, for she refused to acknowledge Deanna as another version of herself—if she had, she could have treated Deanna's blocks as if they were her own and demolished them, as it were, from the inside.

Deanna, though, knew perfectly well they were more or less the same person—no matter how loathsome the concept was—and knew she could affect that other mind as if it were her own. She laughed soundlessly and left the other battering at her own protective walls, while she slipped out from behind one of them and came at the counselor's mind from underneath, stabbing it deep with a well-whetted knife of rage at what the counselor had done to Geordi.

There was a soundless shriek of pain and surprise at the violation. Deanna enjoyed the feeling, and while the other was frozen with reaction, simply stepped around from her hiding place by the doorway and out into the corridor. Alone, the counselor stood there, trying to move, unable to escape the iron grip Deanna had on her—and Deanna, very calmly, stepped up to her and clubbed her in the side of the head with her phaser.

The counselor went down like a felled tree. "You can have too much of the life of the mind," she said softly, and reached down to take the counselor under the armpits and drag her in out of sight.

Geordi was still busy with the tricorder. "How much longer?" Deanna said, starting to feel the reaction now to what she had just done, and the nervousness—for other minds were coming toward them, very close. One of them was plainly Picard's—all stern resolution and an odd pity. In company with it was another, a smothered blaze of excitement and surmise. Another, though, was Picard's counterpart's, that icy rage very much in evidence, and they were both getting closer all the time.

"Just a couple more minutes!" Geordi said.

Down the corridor, Deanna heard the turbolift door open.

She peered out most cautiously, hearing the hurrying footsteps, holding the phaser ready—

—and saw the captain and this universe's Worf coming toward them. All was well with both their minds, there was no sense of compulsion. Her face lit briefly with the smile she hadn't dared to let out.

"Captain!"

"Counselor," Picard said, then winced a little and smiled. "Perhaps I might call you Deanna for the moment —I've had enough of the counselor for one day."

"It would seem *she* has as well," Worf said as they stepped into the core access room and found the other Troi collapsed on the floor.

Picard raised an eyebrow at this and looked over at Geordi. "Mr. La Forge, how is it going?"

"Almost done, Captain. One more chip."

"I meant, how are *you?*"

Geordi smiled, then groaned again. "I feel like elephants have been holding a tap-dancing competition on my body, and the finals are being held in my head. But other than that . . ."

Picard nodded. Worf was looking around at them, the expressions of relief, the humor, and Deanna got a brief mental image of a hungry man standing outside a window full of food, looking in with longing. "Fellowship," Worf said. "Honor. This would be a universe worth fighting for."

"We think so," Picard said. "But it's not too late for yours. Mr. Worf, the first officer of an earlier *Enterprise* of this universe said that the Empire had only two hundred years or so to run. One hundred of those years are gone. It is closer to its fall than ever . . . and perhaps for reasons that not even your Spock suspected. The Empire is overextending itself, parsec by parsec, day by day. In another— oh, even fifty or sixty years—its forces will be spread so widely through the space it claims to 'control' that the control will be a myth. That will be the time for the peoples who have been suppressed to stand up and throw off the yoke. Inevitably, the time will come. If you and your people can be ready for it . . ."

Worf's eyes gleamed. "A long time we have dreamed that things might somehow become better. But they were only dreams: no one ever took them seriously or did anything about them. However, to know that the dream is a reality, somewhere, *anywhere . . ."*

"The dream is alive, Mr. Worf," Picard said. "Who knows—maybe in seventy or eighty years, if our Fleet allows, we might put our noses back in to see how you are getting on. Or, if news of this technique for travel between congruent universes gets around, perhaps the Klingons will." He laughed softly. "I suspect that would make an interesting visit. But this is all conjecture: your worlds' fates are in your own hands. Just know that we will always wish you well."

"Damn!" Geordi said. "Lockout! Security protocols are back up. The cores are restoring from backup."

"Did you get everything?"

"Ninety-eight percent, but if that last two percent was the bit we need . . . !"

From down the corridor came the sound of the turbolift doors opening, and then the sound of running footsteps.

"No more time," Picard said. "Get that chip, Mr. La Forge."

"Mr. Worf," Deanna said, lifting the phaser. He looked at her in brief shock, then nodded and smiled the ghost of a smile.

She stunned him, and he crumpled to the floor over Troi as the captain touched his badge. *"Enterprise,"* he said hurriedly, "emergency, three to beam back *now!"*

They clustered together, Troi with one arm around Geordi, to compensate for the lost transponder, she told herself—but he sagged against her with such alarming weariness that she might have spared herself the excuse. The doorway filled with figures holding phasers, one of them being the other Picard. As the transport effect took them, Deanna caught a last blast of blinding rage from him, saw the face twisted with it, screaming. The phaser beams stitched through them, and as the world dissolved, Deanna heard that other Picard shouting, "Bridge, trace this transport and destroy the source!"

And it all vanished like a bad dream—

—and dissolved into the interior of the shuttlecraft. They stared around them, relieved to be somewhere completely normal, but Picard was unnerved. That ship's phaser capacity would be back now; it would be easy enough to detect this craft and—

They started to dissolve again. It seemed to take an unconscionable time. But no sooner had the singing whine of the transporter completely washed all other sound away than a sheet of white fire went through the place. Picard watched with a degree of fascination as the walls of the shuttlecraft blew away to nothing around them, the white fire fading to black, then to stars, which faded as well.

Light grew around them again slowly, through the unchanging shimmer, and slowly the transporter room became visible. When the soft singing noise finally dwindled to nothing, Picard and the other members of the away team looked at each other almost in disbelief, and then out at Chief O'Brien, who was bracing himself against his console like a man who needed help in standing up.

He looked at them and said, "I'm glad I handled that one

myself, directly from here. If the pattern buffer in the transporter on the *Hawking* had been—"

Picard shook his head and came down from the platform. "If it had. . . . Never mind. . . . Thank you, Chief."

From all around them came the whooping of the red-alert sirens. Picard touched his communicator. "Picard to Number One."

"Captain," Riker's voice said, *"forgive me if I say I'm very glad to hear you!"*

"Let's save the rejoicing for the moment," Picard said. "What's the situation?"

"The other Enterprise *is in restart cycle,"* Riker said. *"Looks like they had to shut down the warp engines toward the end of their computer problems, but they didn't have time to get too cold: we only have a few minutes' grace."*

"I don't intend to linger, Number One. Pick a direction and go to warp five immediately. I've had enough of this neighborhood."

"Yes, sir," Riker said with relish. *"Mr. Redpath! Bearing one, two, five, mark eight, warp five, go!"*

Picard didn't hear the response, but he could instantly feel the subtle difference in the ship's "feel" as she went into warp. Troi was helping Geordi down off the pad; he was still weak and looked pallid. "Mr. La Forge," Picard said, "my apologies. You've suffered worse than anyone else in this operation. And worse yet, we still need you."

Geordi nodded. "It's all right, Captain. We've got the goods. At least I think we have."

"Get down to engineering and find out," Picard said. "Commander Riker! Have a full team prepared to meet Mr. La Forge in engineering."

"Commander Hwiii is ahead of you, Captain," said Riker, *"literally. He and a team of fifty are waiting. Tell Mr. La Forge that a platform to support the apparatus is built and waiting for him."*

"Acknowledged." Picard looked over at Troi as Geordi went out. Troi's face looked odd. Then odder still—and then she sneezed.

Picard laughed a great laugh . . . and it felt extremely good. "My feelings exactly, Counselor," he said, looking down at himself. "Let's get out of here and slip into something more comfortable."

Engineering was in havoc when Geordi got there. People were running in all directions, shouting at each other, waving instrumentation, pieces of equipment, padds; the sense of nervousness and excitement in the air was thick enough to taste, let alone cut. Still, as Geordi walked in, there were shouts of approval and cheers, and a few noisy and approving wolf whistles from female crew. When he stopped near the main status board, half to get his breath and half to cope with the reaction, applause broke out all through the section.

He grinned, weakly still, and made his way over toward where great thick cables had been laid down from the main power supply junction, leading off to one side. There, a side bay that had been full of diagnostic boards was suddenly crammed full of three large, square instrumentation pallets. About thirty people were working on them at the moment, wiring in an astonishing assortment of equipment, everything from running tricorders in series and parallel to what seemed a small ion-discharge apparatus. Coasting around one side of it, as if swimming through the air, came Hwiii, whistling hurriedly at someone, "I don't care how many of them you have to use, just get them hooked in, we don't have time!"

Geordi grinned. Hwiii laid eyes on him and "swam" over to him at speed, nudging him not too hard under one mostly bare rib, and laughing delphine laughter. "Welcome home! Thrice welcome! We're ready for you. Quick, where's the rest of it?"

Geordi handed him the chip. "It's this or nothing."

Together they hurried off to one of the status tables on the side that had been installed specifically for the inclusion apparatus and dropped the chip on its reading plate. "Load in," Geordi said.

They watched the screen together as the information scrolled up. "Perfect," Hwiii crowed. "This is it, this is the one that didn't get away!"

"Some of it did. They locked us out. We're just lucky one of the antiviral protocols didn't follow the path up and erase the chip."

Hwiii swung his tail. "Never mind. Look, that's just what we needed, their replicator settings and everything."

Geordi was aware of someone looking over his shoulder. He turned and saw Eileen and had to stifle his initial reaction. She was smiling at him: the smile was identical to that other Eileen's.

"Those the replicator stats?" she said. "Good, we can feed them into ours and have duplicates ready to plug in in a few minutes."

Their glances rested in one another's, then Eileen turned away. "Don't forget to run the protect cycle on them," Geordi called after her. "We don't want to find out too late that this stuff is booby-trapped!"

"Was I born yesterday?" Eileen called back, then smiled one of those wicked smiles at Geordi and hurried off, shouting, "Cliff, Donna, Maireid, come on, get these checked!"

Geordi breathed out. "It's the last two percent that's missing. It had better not be critical."

"No point in making yourself crazy over it just now," Hwiii said, reading. "Let's be busy understanding what we have."

Geordi glanced around. "Some pretty heavy-duty cabling you've run out there, Commander."

"Well, Commander, if the thing's going to pull eight

hundred terawatts when it's running, we had better make sure it's got enough power feed. Be a shame to stop in the middle of our transfer back home because we blew a fuse."

Geordi laughed, but the laugh was uneasy. "Eight hundred terawatts is an awful lot to take off this warp engine."

"I know. That's why your assistant chiefs and I have been adjusting the matter/antimatter 'burn' ratio right upwards. We've got engine efficiency up to a hundred and ten percent at the moment, and we're pushing for one fifteen, maybe one twenty."

Geordi whistled. "We're not going to be able to hold that for long."

"We won't have to. Just long enough to get home. Just enough time to snap the right string."

"True enough."

"But once there," Hwiii said, "we're going to have another problem."

Geordi looked at him.

"What makes you think we're going to be alone?" said the dolphin.

Geordi blinked, then nodded.

"Now, I'm not suggesting that we alter the equipment . . ."

Geordi burst out laughing. "We haven't even finished building it! And as for testing it . . ."

Hwiii gave him a sly look. "We'll do what we have to. But I was simply going to suggest that we may be able to use it in ways *they* won't think of. We may not have an engine the size of theirs, but we have a resource they haven't."

"A resident specialist in hyperstring theory," Geordi said, giving Hwiii the sly look back in kind. "The string vibrates both ways . . . eh, Hwiii?"

"We have the best engineer in Starfleet," Hwiii said, dropping his jaw, "and one with a nasty, inventive mind."

"The 'nasty' I'll leave to others. But between us, I suspect we can come up with something."

Hwiii glanced down at the console. "Look there—Mr. Data has finished the abstracting."

"Good. Come on. I want a look at those couplings— then we'll start getting the replicated boards in place and have a fast look at those abstracts."

"Very fast. Somehow I doubt those people are going to coast around out there just fanning their fins."

Hurriedly the two of them squeezed or swam into the equipment bay, past bits and pieces of open matrix-layout, like huge open-celled honeycombs, and chips and boards being slotted into other boards for fitting into the matrix. One piece of equipment, standing off to one side, Geordi didn't recognize: a bucket. He looked down into it . . . then laughed at the sight of the fresh, shiny mackerel and went after Hwiii.

It was about fifteen minutes before Picard saw his own bridge again. He stopped long enough for a shower, wanting to wash the dust of that other *Enterprise* off him, literally and figuratively. And when he swung into the bridge at last, it was such a relief to have eyes turned on him with welcoming looks; no salutes, but people who stood to greet him because they wanted to, not because he would kill them if they didn't.

"Status, Number One," he said, and made for his chair.

"Proceeding away from the other *Enterprise* at warp five," Riker said. "No sign of pursuit as yet."

"Good. I want to have a look at the log entries for the period of my absence."

"On your screen in the ready room, Captain."

Picard went in there and sat down in his chair with profound relief, touching the screen to bring up the log extracts. Riker had come quietly in behind him; the door shut.

Picard looked up and smiled briefly. "Nervous, Number One? You've got the right one, never fear."

Riker grinned briefly as well, but his eyes were somber. "You were very lucky, Captain," he said quietly.

Picard shrugged at him. "Now what was I supposed to have done? I did what was required of me. As you did; as we've both done a thousand times before and will keep doing. But when we get home"—he touched the screen again to page down—"Troi and La Forge are due for a couple of more commendations. They both comported themselves with great courage and *panache*. Mr. La Forge in particular suffered a great deal to obtain the information we're now processing."

"There's a problem with that, Captain." Picard looked at Riker sharply. "It's the 'when' in 'when we get home.' Do you know that that vessel has all our threat routines?"

"I had assumed it. You'll have been preparing counter-measures, I know."

"Yes, Captain. But there's always the off chance that we will not make it home. Or that we will and will be destroyed on our side of things. In that case, we have an overriding responsibility to make sure that this informa-tion gets back to Starfleet Command, one way or another."

"I agree, Number One. Though I very much hope these people will not be so foolish as to destroy us here. Since it would in the long run doom this whole area of space." Picard frowned. "Though I would not lay great odds, I grant you, on them caring much about the long run."

"Neither would I. There's also a question of power requirements for that device. As presently installing, we may not be able to successfully support it. Eight hundred terawatts is a *big* fraction of our power output . . . and it may not be possible to get the thing to work without draining power from every nonessential system in the ship, and some essential ones. We might find that we simply can't get out. In which case something else must."

Picard nodded. "Go on."

"Commander Hwiii tells me that he thinks the device can be used at much lower power to push something from our ship—a probe, for example—back home into our own universe. I think we should load all the information we have about what's happened, this device, and the threat these people pose, into a probe and have it ready to send ahead of us if we can't get home. Starfleet *has* to be warned."

It was a problem that Picard had been turning over in his mind; he was glad to hear that there was at least this much of a solution to it. "Very well, make it so. It will, of course, then be our duty—should it come to that—to fight enough of a holding action so that probe can get away. Destroying ourselves, if necessary, to guarantee its escape."

"And the other ship?"

Picard looked up at Riker thoughtfully. "I confess to curiosity, about what would happen if one Galaxy-class starship rammed another broadside."

"The other ship is closer to Dreadnought-class. Not a close comparison."

"Pedant," Picard said mildly, and went on reading his logs. "But it can't be allowed to follow the probe over . . . can it, Number One?"

Riker shook his head.

"Better have Mr. Data get started on the probe," Picard said. "And get a projection from Mr. La Forge on when he'll have the inclusion device ready for testing."

"Yes, sir." But Riker still stood there. Picard looked up again.

"Something else?"

A long pause. "What was he like?"

Picard sighed and stretched. "My counterpart was, by all accounts, a murderer many times over, probably an abuser of his partner, a man who sent his best friend to die: someone sly, treacherous, brutal, cold, calculating . . . the conscienceless butcher of a great number of worlds." He looked up at Riker. "Now shall I tell you about *your* counterpart?"

Riker swallowed. "I'll just go see Mr. Data," he said, and hurriedly took himself out.

Picard smiled a very, very small smile and went back to his reading.

"A vessel is showing on sensors," Data said, working over his panel for a moment, then looking up at the viewscreen. "Closing at warp seven."

The center of the screen showed a tiny, dark silver shape. Riker looked at it and breathed out.

"Captain," he said, "the other *Enterprise* is closing. Go to warp eight," he said to Ensign Redpath.

"Warp eight, aye," Redpath said. The captain came out of the ready room, looking at the screen. As he did, Troi came in from the turbolift, wearing her normal uniform with an expression of considerable relief, and sat down in her seat.

"So it begins," Picard said. "Mr. Redpath, have you been looking at the new evasive routines Commander Riker and the tactical team have prepared?"

"Yes, Captain. They're fairly straightforward."

Picard sat down in the center seat, hiding a smile. "I will hope not, Ensign. If they are, the other ship will have no problem duplicating them."

"Sorry, sir. I meant—"

"Thank you, Mr. Redpath. Just keep us well away from them for the time being. Picard to engineering!"

"La Forge here, Captain."

"Progress report." From the background came a brief explosion of angry Delphine chatter. *"We're having to do some retooling, sir. The inclusion resonator array is out of—"*

"How long, Mr. La Forge?" Picard said as gently as he could with the sight of that slowly growing shape on the viewscreen staring him in the face.

"Ten minutes, Captain."

"I'm sorry about this, Mr. La Forge, but it's going to have to be five. Does that estimate include testing the apparatus?"

This time the Delphine in the background was even more untranslatable.

"Do you eat *with that mouth?"* someone could be heard shouting in the background; and someone else's reply, *"Don't encourage him, he's on his third bucket."* There was a pause, and Picard opened his mouth to say something cutting, but suddenly a ragged cheer could be heard. *"It's up,"* Hwiii shouted, *"it's up!"*

"We've got power to the apparatus, Captain," Geordi shouted over the increasing thunder of the warpdrive as they accelerated. *"Pulling eight hundred terawatts. Total warpdrive output holding steady at fifteen thousand terawatts, one hundred fifteen percent."*

"How long will she hold it, Commander?" Picard said.

"Hard to say, Captain. The power is feeding to the inclusion apparatus, but it's not operating as yet. When we activate, there'll be a substantial drain, and warp speed is going to drop off."

"Accelerate to warp eight point five," Picard said, standing up and pulling his uniform tunic down, and it pulled *down,* and he smiled for sheer joy. "All spare power to the shields, Mr. Worf. Mr. Redpath, start first-level evasive. Nothing showy."

"Aye, sir." The starfield flowing past them as seen on the main viewer began to pitch and roll.

"Some strain to the structural field," Data said. "Power drains are becoming apparent shipwide."

"Engines running at one hundred seventeen percent," La

Forge's voice said. *"I give you about five minutes of this, Captain. We're running the inclusion device through test cycle now."*

"Do you have any idea what you're looking for?" Riker said.

"The files from the other ship are quite clear, Commander," Hwiii said. *"In fact, they appear to have been written almost for technical illiterates. Which is fortunate for us, since the instructions assume they can take nothing for granted. Test cycle looks for altered-hyperstring frequency baseline and variation and checks frequencies against residual strings still attached to the vessel. When they match, we can go."*

Picard sighed, watching that shape in the viewscreen following them through the corkscrewing course they were running. "The sooner the better, Commander." He glanced over at Troi. "How are you, Counselor?"

"Much better, Captain, thank you."

"Crew status?"

"They are *much* improved," she said, and sighed. Picard raised an eyebrow at her. Troi caught herself and said, "Concerned, Captain, but ready for the best . . . or the worst."

"They are closing, Captain," Data said. "Within two hundred thousand kilometers now."

"Something a little more flashy, Mr. Redpath," Picard said, sitting down again.

"Aye, Captain," Redpath said, and keyed in a sequence at his console.

The main viewer's vista abruptly became dangerous for those prone to motion sickness. "Go to tactical," Picard said. The screen shifted to a schematic showing the *Enterprise*'s course and that of the vessel chasing her. Slowly but surely, that other was running her down, as Picard had known it would when he had seen that engine room, the monstrous power of the thing. *It's not fair,* he thought quietly. *We're supposed to be on life's side in this argument. Why can't the universe break out some odds in our favor?*

"Bridge," La Forge's voice said urgently, *"test cycle failed, repeat, failed. Power fluctuations in our warpdrive seem to be too big for the apparatus."*

"You are going to need to correct that situation, Mr. La Forge," Picard said as calmly as he could. "Our pursuers are getting uncomfortably close. How long for another test cycle?"

"Fifty seconds for reset," Hwiii whistled from the background.

"Get on it."

They watched the viewscreen. Picard began to sweat watching the dot that represented the other *Enterprise* draw slowly closer.

There was a soft *cheep* from Worf's console. "The other vessel is hailing us, Captain," he said, surprised.

Riker looked at Picard in shock. Very slowly Picard sat down in his center seat again, arranging himself comfortably. "On-screen."

The viewscreen flickered and went bright with the view of that other bridge. It was like looking in a mirror again, except for the differences in uniform. There were the other Riker and the other Troi, and in the middle, sitting in exactly the same position as Jean-Luc, the other Picard.

"Enterprise," he said, "we advise you to surrender. You cannot outrun us, and you cannot outfight us."

Picard allowed himself the slightest smile. "Captain, I told you: you will not be allowed to dictate any aspect of this situation. There is nothing you could possibly say to me that could convince me you would spare a surrendered ship or crew . . . especially not *this* one. As for outrunning or outfighting you—even given your engines and armaments, we might have a surprise or so for you. We have resources you cannot begin to understand or anticipate."

"That is exactly the point," the other Picard said. "Why

throw yourself needlessly into a situation which will only result in unnecessary loss of life? From what we have discovered about you, we can surely come to some kind of compromise, some . . ."

Picard glanced over at Troi. She merely smiled and put her eyebrows up, a tell-me-another-one expression. To that other Picard, Jean-Luc said, "Your counselor has picked up a favorite theme from rummaging in my mind and the minds of my people, I feel sure, and has briefed you. Her job, of course . . . and she has a certain competence at it. Though if I were you, I would watch her closely, Captain. She made some interesting suggestions to me regarding the possible disposition of your command."

That other Troi sat cool and unresponsive. The other Picard shot just one icy glance at her, then turned away. "In addition," Jean-Luc said, "even if I believed the foolish fiction that you would spare us, *any* of us, you had better check with your chief engineer about the viability of keeping another ship of our mass in your universe. If we remain here, whether destroyed or not, your universe will suffer serious derangement over time, culminating in waves of subspatial and hyperspatial 'distress,' which will rip planets apart and cause their stars to go nova, along a spherical boundary centered on the area of original injection."

The other Riker turned his head. "They're bluffing."

That other Picard did not react in the slightest. *He knows,* Picard thought. "You don't care, of course," he said to his counterpart, "because it won't happen in your lifetime. And you hope to conceal the fact from your superiors, who I suspect consider this data as theoretical or statistical artifact, not to be taken seriously. Just one more difference between us: you would as soon destroy us here as anywhere else—though even now you hope yet to run us down, catch us, beat down our shields, and take home your prize. Well, you will have no prize. Sooner than allow our capture, I will destroy this ship myself. And your Empire will be doomed as a result . . . so think about *that*. Also, we will find a way to let them know what you have done: don't think to hide it. If a universe is about to be destroyed, in the long term or the short, I will see to it that your Empire knows at whose doorstep to lay the responsibility. Meanwhile . . . catch us if you can. We would spare you if we had the chance. We probably will not get it; so . . . do your best."

The other Picard did not rage or fume or anything else: he sat coolly and looked at his counterpart. "I don't understand you, Captain. I am offering you a chance to survive."

"There are more important things than survival," Picard said very softly. "And no, you do not understand us." He glanced up at the other Worf, standing behind that Picard again, stony-faced. "May we never so change that you do. Out."

The screen went blank. Picard sat there, still sweating. It was astonishing, the effort it took even to speak to the man. . . . Riker, though, looked over at him with slight amusement. "Is that other Troi after his job?"

Picard laughed once, sharply. "To put it mildly. . . . She may get it yet."

"The other *Enterprise* is now within one hundred fifty-five thousand kilometers, Captain," Data said, "and continues to close."

"Is that probe ready?" Picard said.

"Yes, sir."

"Prepare one with our theoretical data about the side effects of inclusion and program it to head for Earth. Add Mr. La Forge's little screen routine to its shields, if you can. The more trouble they have finding it, the better."

"Aye, Captain. It will take a short time."

"Take it. Mr. Redpath, go up a level on the evasive. I want them to have to work for it now."

"Yes, *sir,*" Redpath said with relish, and started to work at it.

Picard's quick glance at the way *Enterprise's* course now started behaving on the tactical screen made him hide another smile. "Engineering!"

"La Forge here, Captain. Halfway through the second test cycle. It's looking good."

"We'll wait, Mr. La Forge," Picard said.

They waited.

"One hundred thousand kilometers," Data said. "They have increased speed to warp nine."

"Match it," Picard said.

"Captain, we're getting some spikes down here! The test cycle may go out again."

Picard swallowed. "Do you absolutely need it?"

"If it's not going to work," Hwiii said, *"I should think you would prefer to know about it now, Captain, rather than when we try to jump with it and fail to get anywhere, with them snapping along right behind us."*

"I take your point, Commander," Picard said. "Please put your tail into it."

Hwiii could be heard to chuckle. Behind him, Geordi's voice said, *"Is that it? Did it go?"*

"Positive result—the curve topped out at fourteen."

"Test cycle is positive!" Geordi said.

"All right," Picard said. "Get ready to do it, gentlemen. How soon?"

"Three minutes for the exclusion cycle," Geordi said. *"Captain, we can't have any velocity changes during the cycle. If you want to accelerate, do it now. Also, firing has to be kept to a minimum—shields are going to cost us enough as it is. Any spike in the power curve will abort the whole thing."*

"Warp nine point five, Mr. Data," Picard said. "Mr. Worf, full power to the rear shields. Watch the nutation, they may try changing attitude and coming from above or below. Prepare a full spread of photon torpedoes. Reduce all unnecessary life support and other systems to minimal levels."

They sat and watched the other *Enterprise* creep up behind them, more and more quickly. "She has gone to warp nine point five, Captain," Data said. "Energy output levels indicate she can hold this speed for a matter of some hours. We would be forced to drop out of warp at the five-minute point."

"Noted," Picard said. "Hold her steady. Mr. Redpath, your maximum inventiveness now, within structural limits. Remember that the structural field is running low."

"Yes, Captain," Redpath said, looking intent, and started working over his panel again. Picard sat quiet, hearing faint groans from the fabric of his ship that he didn't in the least care for.

"They are making warp nine point six, Captain," Data said quietly. "Eighty thousand kilometers now."

"Mr. Redpath."

"Doing what I can, sir." Redpath was sweating.

Picard watched him, thinking that at the moment he could do little more.

"Hold it steady!" Geordi's voice came from down in engineering. *"One minute!"*

"Steady as she goes," Picard said, though the phrase was extremely relative, considering what the tactical display was showing. The ship was moaning more loudly around them. "Mr. Worf, ready on the photon torpedoes. Probably the only effect they'll have will be to keep the other *Enterprise* from running right up our tail, but that may be enough."

"If you can keep them at a little distance, Captain, we can gain some ground," Hwiii's voice said. *"If they can be kept from transiting at the same time that we do—and they cannot transit during shield impacts, they would experience the same kind of power spikes that were giving us trouble."*

"Consider it done, Commander. Mr. Worf—choose your spread for maximum disruption rather than a clean breakthrough. Try to flank their rear shields as they come in."

"They're changing attitude, Captain!" Ensign Redpath said, his hands flying over his console. "Coming in high and wide, corkscrewing."

"I see it," Worf said, and went at his controls. Picard gripped the arms of his chair and did his best to radiate calm as usual.

"Twenty seconds!" Geordi said. *"Nineteen, eighteen . . ."*

"They are firing photon torpedoes," Data said. "Full spread of twenty."

"Evade, Mr. Redpath," Picard said, "any way you can, we can't boost shields now."

The ship's fabric made an appalling noise, a groan scaling down through into subsonics. "Structural field holding," Data said. "But marginal."

". . . eleven, ten, nine . . ."

"Impacts on their shields," Worf said, examining his console. "Minimal effect, but some power fluctuations. Torpedoes incoming."

"Repeat our fire, Mr. Worf," Picard said. "Another fluctuation or so can't hurt. Take out some of their torpedoes if you can."

"Setting up another spread, Captain." A pause. "Torpedoes away."

". . . four, three, two . . ."

The ship rocked with the impact of torpedoes on its shields: lights flickered—

—and at practically the same moment there was another flicker, a bizarre darkening, as if the universe had closed its eyes to sneeze—

—and then the lights came back up again, and they all looked at each other, blinking a little.

From the engineering section came a high-pitched cry, too pure to be called a squeal, that twittered down into a long happy chatter of noise. *"Positive result!"* Geordi shouted. *"Positive transit!"*

"Congratulations, Mr. La Forge," Picard said. "Are we where we ought to be?"

"We're home," Hwiii cried. *"I would know this space anywhere, Captain, I could feel it in my sleep!"*

"And did, as I remember. I'll take your word for it. Status of pursuit."

"We will not be able to tell until they come out of transit themselves, Captain," Data said, studying his console. "Most likely they have a record of the hyperstring properties associated with our *Enterprise* and will be using them to locate us."

"Let's not wait around," Picard said. "A little more speed, Mr. Redpath. In a straight line, for the moment."

"We're at nine point four at the moment, Captain. Lost some residual in the passage."

"That's odd," Hwiii said from engineering. *"There's no reason we should have dropped velocity."*

"First law of thermodynamics, Hwiii," Geordi said. *"Not between universal boundaries! Both universes' thermodynamic constants are the same. They have to be, or they can't have such a high congruency constant."*

"Gentlemen," Picard said, somewhat amused. "If you can let it rest for a few minutes . . ."

"The other ship has transited," Data said, and all around the bridge, heads turned and hearts seized. "Heading one zero three mark four, distance two hundred ten thousand kilometers and closing again at warp nine point six."

Picard looked at Riker. "Get that probe ready. We're only going to be able to outdistance them for a little while."

Riker nodded and got up to see about it.

"Mr. La Forge, Commander Hwiii, well done," Picard

said. "We have you to thank for getting us home. Unfortunately we now have another problem."

There was a brief silence. *"They* did *follow us,"* Geordi said.

"They did. We will at least be able to warn Starfleet, however, and pass on to them the information you've mastered for us." All the same, Picard was heartsore. Destroying that ship here would bring down on their home universe the same fate that would have befallen the Empire's universe. *Not in my lifetime,* he thought bitterly, *but everyone will know at whose door the responsibility for the loss of millions of lives must be laid. Maybe it would have been better to do it there after all.*

But if we had, Starfleet would have no warning. "We cannot outrun them," Picard said. "We can close with them and see them destroyed. That's all. The crew had best be told."

"Captain," Geordi said, *"wait! There's still a possibility."*

"Is it one I can count on?" A silence ensued. "So," Picard said. "It can't be helped, gentlemen."

"Captain," Hwiii's voice said, *"for your peoples' sakes, for the Federation's sake, stretch it out! Hope is thin in the water, but it's not gone yet."*

"I will not let them take us," Picard said, "and I will not let them destroy us piecemeal. If we must all die, we will do it cleanly."

"Fair enough. But buy us some time!"

"All that I can, Commander." Picard looked at Worf. "Give me allcall."

Down in engineering, Geordi and Hwiii were bent over the main console arguing, while people ran around them in all directions. Everywhere else on the ship people might be standing still and listening to the amplified voice that spoke to them, but down here, no one had time.

"Attention, all crew. This is the captain. Our situation is as follows . . ."

"We can't," Geordi said.

"We can!" Hwiii said.

"We'll get blown to kingdom come!"

"It's going to happen anyway! Wouldn't you rather take the chance?"

"Listen, you crazy fish—"

"Who're you calling a fish, you deaf-skinned, round-headed mammal? It will work, it *will!* Think of the sharks! All those teeth, they're terrible, yes, but who tries to attack a shark by biting it? You ram it in the gut instead. Better yet, you get it to swim at you as hard as it can, and *then* you hit it, so vectors add and its velocity turns against it. Get it to cooperate in its own demise, turn its own force back on it."

"The velocity." Geordi stared at Hwiii. "And they're *excluded.* They're excluded from their home universe and included in this one, just as we were excluded from *this* one and included in *theirs.* We can reverse the procedure! We need a little more time, and a word with the software, and some more power."

Now it was Hwiii's turn to stare. "We haven't got any more power!"

"So what if we got them to give us some?"

"Oh, absolutely, let's just ask them for a donation!"

"Hwiii, you've got herring for brains. The shields are working perfectly well."

"They won't be if we let those people near them! Their phasers—"

"—are rated at three terawatts each! Look! We take the shields and do *this.*"

A brief silence, and then a long, high, thoughtful whistle. "You're right about my brains. But if we miscalculate, this is going to rip the ship's skin up like so much seaweed!"

"Not if you invert the skinfield! We barely need the structural field while we're on impulse."

" 'Barely'! Do you know how many tons—"

"One point five million. Would you like them to keep sticking together in their present form instead of being distributed around as free hydrogen radicals? Good! Invert the skinfield, go for flat nutation on the fields."

Hwiii sang an excited scale. "Then invert the field supply generators and run the power *backwards* down into the switchback outphase generator? Yes, of course, and then—"

"Then all we need is a stable mass of more than ten to the eightieth metric tons within three hundred thousand kilometers."

"But there's nothing like that within—" A pause. "Wait a minute."

"Will this do?" Eileen said from the other side of the console. They both looked up at her in shock; she was pointing to a display.

They hurried over to her. "How did you know to look for that?" Hwiii said.

"It's in the equations," Eileen said calmly. "All that mass-relations material. Half of the business of the inclusion apparatus seems to involve ways to get around the mass-anchoring problem. But when you have one handy . . ." She shrugged. "I started looking just after you two began arguing about the phasers."

Geordi and Hwiii looked down at the readout. "It's 2044 Hydri," Eileen said, "or it used to be. It's a brown dwarf now. That enough mass for you?"

"Wow," Geordi said. "More like ten to the ninetieth, that one. Horrific. I wouldn't want to get too close."

"Four or five hundred thousand kilometers will be close enough," Hwiii said. "Where is that thing?"

"About three hundred light-years in the direction of the Galactic south pole," Eileen said.

Geordi frowned a moment. "At nine point five—twelve minutes. Assuming the warp coils don't give out first."

"We can do some reinforcement," Hwiii said, heading

314

off toward the engine control panels. "It won't last long, but it won't need to."

"Hwiii," Geordi said, going back around to the panel they had first been looking at, "wait a moment! This last part of the initial equation—couldn't you flip it around *again?*"

Hwiii looked over at Geordi in surprise. "What?" He came back to look at the panel.

"Another inversion. More like a subversion, actually. If you take the hyperstring elements here and *force* a change in the elements—even ten percent out of phase would be enough."

Hwiii's eyes went wide. "Wouldn't *that* just put the shark amongst the mullet. You wouldn't be able to hold it for very long, either."

"You wouldn't have to. But once you dropped out of warp again, the string congruencies would be broken. They wouldn't be able to do *anything.*"

"I'll get on it," Hwiii said, and turned back to the warp engine control panels. "Tell me what you want done first, though."

"Better see about reinforcing the warp coils first— they're what we're going to need real quick now." Geordi hit his badge. "La Forge to Captain Picard!"

Picard sat in his seat, watching the other ship slowly gaining on them again, while Mr. Redpath continued his frantic evasive maneuvers. "Are you *sure* this will work, Mr. La Forge? This is not a chance we can afford to mishandle. Much more rides on it than just us."

"I understand that, Captain—and this is the best chance we've got of coming out of this alive, let alone getting rid of our present problem."

"You're quite sure."

"We'll bet our lives on it."

"You will indeed," Picard said, thinking. "Very well—I

have no superior options. What is the heading you require?"

"Two seventy-one mark three, 2044 Hydri. We need to get within about five hundred thousand kilometers. Four hundred thousand, max. That's a very massive dwarf and we can't afford to get close enough for the gravitational conditions to start affecting the warp engines. We won't be in warp toward the end of this, but we're going to need the power."

"We're going to be on *impulse* near a brown dwarf?" Riker said. "Is that safe?"

"It's not safe at all, Commander, but it's the only chance we have to stay alive."

Survival, Picard thought. *How strong the urge is.* He glanced at the viewscreen, then over at Redpath.

"Mr. Redpath, you're showing signs of fatigue. Pass helm control to Mr. Data for the moment."

"Yes, sir," Redpath said, sounding both nervous and profoundly relieved.

Picard stood up and pulled his tunic down and smiled and went to stand behind Data. "You are going to have to be our ace in the hole at the moment, Mr. Data. You are one advantage we have over our adversaries: they do not have *you.* Have you had time to internalize the new antithreat routines?"

"Yes, Captain. I acquired most of them while working on them with Commander Riker."

"Good. You're going to need them—whatever else those people may be, we cannot count on their being stupid. They can be caught off balance as easily as anyone else, but they learn fast. Set Mr. La Forge's course and engage."

"Yes, sir." The view on the screen changed, going darker: there were not many stars down this way.

Picard turned from it after a moment to find Troi looking at him, her face quiet. "You're still troubled," she said.

"If we come through this, I will be troubled for a long time, I think."

She nodded. "You won't be alone."

He smiled very slightly. "No advice, Counselor?"

Troi's expression was wry. "At this moment in time I find my advice badly contaminated by my reactions. Myself, I'm wishing I had hit her harder when I had the chance." She grimaced. "Not very self-actualized."

"No, but that place had a tendency to bring out the worst in one. . . . I suppose it would be foolish to come away from there without expecting some aftereffects."

"True, Captain. I'm merely concerned about how long they might last."

"Believe me, Counselor," Picard said, watching that other ship still slowly drawing closer to them, "so am I. And at the moment I'd prefer that they last quite a long time . . . rather than have them go away extremely suddenly."

Troi nodded.

"They continue to close, Captain," Data said. "They have increased to warp nine point six."

"Mr. La Forge, can we match the increase?"

"*You'd better not for the moment, Captain,*" came the answer. "*Commander Hwiii is working on the warp coils, and some of the shifts he's having to make are fairly delicate. Can it wait about two minutes?*"

Data looked at the screen. "At this rate, they will be within firing range in two minutes fourteen seconds."

"Do what you have to, Mr. La Forge," Picard said, beginning to sweat again as that image in the screen continued to grow and grow. "But let us know the minute we can increase speed. How long will the engines hold out at this rate?"

"*I make it another fifteen minutes or so, Captain. By that time we'll be where we need to be, and we can start decelerating for the drop out of warp.*"

Picard was not entirely wild about *that* idea, either. "Are our shields going to be able to handle their phaser output?"

"Not for long," Geordi said, sounding entirely too cheerful, *"but it won't be necessary."*

Picard nodded and looked over at Troi, then at Riker. "Is that probe ready?"

"Yes, Captain. Waiting your word."

"Launch it."

Data touched his console. "Probe away."

"Keep an eye on it. I want to make sure they don't spot it and destroy it. Mr. Worf," Picard said, "copy over the data that went out in the probe to an encrypted packet and send it by subspace to Starfleet immediately."

"Yes, Captain."

"The 'belt and suspenders' approach," Riker said.

Picard nodded. "In this case in particular, I'd sooner be safe than sorry."

"Captain," Worf said, "subspace is being jammed." He scowled at his console. "The pursuing vessel is the source of the jamming."

Now is this just their resourcefulness? he thought. *Or is this standard equipment for starships in a universe where treason is so commonplace?* The image of what the rest of that Fleet must be like rose up and started to horrify him again. He pushed it aside.

"The probe continues unmolested," Data said. "They have in fact passed it. Either they are unwilling to break off pursuit to deal with it, or they did not detect it."

"Probabilities?"

"Uncertain," Data said. "But it was very thoroughly screened. If they had detected it, I would think they would at least attempt to fire a photon torpedo at it en passant."

Picard nodded. "All right. We'll assume it got away—but Mr. Worf, keep trying subspace. Even if we can't get through, they may detect the effort and assume that we have no other way of getting the news to Starfleet."

"Aye, sir." They all sat and watched the ship get closer.

"What's the word, Mr. La Forge?" Picard said.

"We're pretty close to being ready, Captain. By the time we're in the neighborhood of 2044, I'll let you know. But there's no reason this shouldn't work."

"Very well." Picard glanced over at Riker. "If he's wrong about this, I'm tempted to demote him."

"You'd have to do it posthumously," Riker said.

"In both our cases," Picard said, and his mouth set grim.

"How are those warp coils doing?" Geordi called across to Hwiii.

"Nominal," Hwiii said. "I've increased the frequency offset by about twelve percent—it should be enough to hold things together for the moment."

"It had better," Geordi said. "Keep an eye on the balance. We'd look pretty silly if a nacelle fell off in the middle of this."

"About six minutes to destination," Eileen said over Geordi's shoulder. He looked up from his console and found to his distress that he still had some trouble looking at her.

"What's your problem?" she said. "You look like you have mental indigestion. Is it just stress, or is it something I said?"

"Not you," Geordi said hurriedly.

"Then who—" And she stared at him. "Oh, no. I was there, too."

"Not *you*," Geordi said, looking down, but finding no refuge there. The computer was still crunching the numbers needed for their close approach and field-anchoring to the brown dwarf. He looked up at her again. "Another you."

She swallowed. "What did I—what did she do?"

"She was nice to me," Geordi said after a moment. "But it was mostly because she wanted my job."

Eileen stared at him, then pursed her lips in indignation. "After we finish all this craziness, I am going to have a fight with you. What would I want *your* job for? Especially as it's so much fun watching you bust your butt doing it." She flounced off to the other side of the console and got busy over one of the screens there. And she looked up at him, making a "mad" face—but there was more kindness in that anger than in all the other Eileen's smiles.

Geordi found his grin coming back without having to be forced. "How's the balance?" he said to Hwiii.

"Holding nicely," said the dolphin from the panel where he was working. "I think we can leave these things to their own devices for the moment."

"Oh, no way, Hwiii—you have too much trust in machinery! Brewer, come here and keep an eye on those readings. If they vary more than point five percent in either direction, call me. Okay, Hwiii, let's get on with the main act."

"Destination in four minutes," Eileen said, looking down at the main status board. "Engines are beginning to show some variance in the warpfield."

Geordi and Hwiii looked at each other, shook their heads, and looked down at the main status board again. "Okay," Geordi said. "There's 2044. What's the gravitational field strength?"

"One point eight times ten to the eighty-fourth atts," said Eileen. "What we expected."

"All right," Geordi said. "Hwiii, do we have hyperstring interaction yet?"

"It's virtual. It will be real when we come out of warp. Virtual strengths are now at"—Hwiii checked one of the instruments that was reading from a piece of his own equipment now built into the inclusion device—"fourteen point six milliwaynes. Increasing with the inverse square of the distance as usual."

"We'll need more like twenty, won't we?"

Hwiii laughed softly. "I'd be happier with fifty, but twenty will do."

"You talking about fish or field strengths?" Geordi said. "Never mind. That's half the battle handled. Now we need the rest of it. La Forge to bridge!"

"Here, Mr. La Forge," said Picard, still sweating.

"We're just about ready, Captain," La Forge said. *"We're coming up fast on 2044, and its gravitational field is interacting with our equipment the way it should. Now what we need is some more power."*

"The engineer's lament," Riker said. "Usually that's your department."

"Not today, Commander. Captain, the ship has to drop out of warp as soon as she's within a million kilometers of the dwarf. The sudden deceleration is going to cause a lot of the energy in the warpfields to blueshift and go kinetic. It'll give us some of what we need, but not enough. We need them to fire on our shields and give us the rest . . . and then they're going to get the surprise of their lives."

"How much firing are you going to need?" Riker said.

"With their phasers, not much," Geordi said. *"That's the beauty of it. A couple of minutes will be enough. But you're going to have to let them get pretty close—that's the only undesirable facet of this routine."*

"I assure you, Mr. La Forge, it is not the only undesirable aspect. How close?"

"Two thousand kilometers. Five hundred would be better."

Picard made a face. "That's almost whites-of-their-eyes range, Mr. La Forge. Are you sure this is wise?"

"Captain, none of this is exactly ideal, but at that range you can self-destruct and be relatively sure of taking them with us!"

Picard nodded grimly. "You're right there."

"The other *Enterprise* continues to gain," Data said. "One hundred thousand kilometers now; 2044 Hydri is within a parsec and a half."

"Prepare for high-speed deceleration," Picard said. "Picard to all crew! We are about to undergo high-speed deceleration, and as usual in such circumstances the artificial gravity will be subject to fluctuations. Secure yourselves."

He waited a moment, while the red-alert sirens whooped again in warning, then went silent. "Position of our adversary, Mr. Data."

"Closing directly behind us at warp nine point seven, Captain."

Picard smiled just slightly at hearing that. "They may overshoot a little, then."

"It seems likely, Captain," Data said, working over his console. "Synchronizing with engineering subsystems now. Commander La Forge."

"We're as ready as we're gonna be, Data," Geordi's voice came back. *"Go for it!"*

"Captain?"

"As planned, Mr. Data. Execute!"

The warpfields shut down. *Enterprise* fell out into normal space, shedding the built-up energy not by gradual deceleration, but in the form of great blasts of radiation and visual light. Inside her, everything rocked and jumped. Picard hung on to the arms of his seat, knowing what the other *Enterprise* would be seeing, a ship suddenly turned into a core of disastrous-looking, searing light, slowing down, plunging toward a dead star.

It may buy us a moment's confusion, he thought. *They may think we've exploded already. Then they'll check the mass readings and see that they're wrong, come in for the kill.* "Status, Mr. La Forge!"

"Deceleration completing, Captain. Entering wide orbit around 2044."

"The other *Enterprise* has overshot by two point six

three light-years," Data said. "Coming around now and decelerating in the usual manner. Preparing to drop out of warp, if energy readings are correct."

"On-screen," Picard said. Now that the wild maneuvering was done, visuals were of some use again. Far under them turned the brown dwarf—not brown, but a sullen, glowing red with the heat remains of ancient gravitational collapse, not yet finished: an old, tired ember, soon to die out and go black.

"They have dropped out of warp, Captain. Center screen, magnified."

The dark silver shape was there again, coming about on impulse to meet them, coasting in closer and closer.

"Their shields are up," Worf said. "They are arming all phaser banks. The power—" He looked at his reading and looked up with an expression of unpleasant surprise. "The power is considerable."

"Yes, indeed," Picard said. "Raise our own shields, Mr. La Forge!"

"We're getting ready for them, Captain. Thirty more seconds to make fast the 'connection' between us and the dwarf."

"Make it so, Mr. La Forge!"

Slowly they orbited, "standing their ground," and the other ship came in closer and closer, holding its fire. Picard looked at the dark, cruel shape, lowering at him, and something in the back of his mind said, *The boy stood on the burning deck.*

He had to laugh, though just once, as that other ship came closer. Riker looked at him. "Captain?"

Picard shook his head. "Just that I had no idea my brain had retained so much dreadful doggerel as it has produced in the past day or so. No matter, one way or another, I won't have to bother with it again."

"They are firing," Worf said. They saw the phaser beams

lance out: the ship rocked as they hit the shields. The other *Enterprise* came in closer and closer and went by just off their port side, taunting, no more than a thousand kilometers away.

"Mr. La Forge," Picard said, very unnerved indeed, "was that close enough for you?"

"We need a couple of more passes, Captain."

"The line between power drain and shield overload is going to be extremely fine, Commander," Data said. "A few megajoules in either direction is going to mean the difference between a successful operation and an exploded ship."

"Tell me about it, Data! You just keep your eye on the red line. But try not to move until we give you the word! If this works, we won't need to move at all."

The ship lurched and rocked again as the phasers hit, this time from behind. "Loss of power to rear shields, fifteen percent," Worf said. "Some odd readings, however."

"That's us," Geordi said. *"Hang on, up there! We have to do some string manipulation just before the balloon goes up."*

"Pull whatever strings you have to, Mr. La Forge," Picard said, "but hurry up about it! We can't take much more of this phaser fire."

"Hwiii, poke that baby, we need more!"

There was a pause. *"Captain, you've got to let them shoot at us, we* need *the energy. As much of it as we can get."*

The other *Enterprise* came in again and made another pass. "All phasers firing, Captain," Worf said, as if Picard needed to be told. This time the ship shook as if a giant had picked it up and rattled it, and the lights went down, and only the emergency lighting came up. "Rear shields down," Worf said, "damage to decks forty-three and fifty. The other *Enterprise* is coming about again."

"Mr. La Forge!" Picard said.

"Just one more time, Captain!"

"It may be all you get," Picard said, watching on the screen as the great wicked-looking silver-dark shape bore down on them.

In engineering, Hwiii and Geordi were working together over the main status console. "That's it," Hwiii said. "The 'tether' is in place. One more shot!"

"Here she comes."

"On automatic," Hwiii said, touching the last control. "Check it?"

Geordi looked over his shoulder. "The power conduits are holding. Come on, you son of a—"

—and the other *Enterprise* fired, and the whole ship shook—

—not with the phaser impact, though: that was absorbed. Clutching the status board, they watched on the schematics as the dreadful flame of energy channeled down in a searing line from the shields into the inclusion apparatus. All around them the air seemed to vibrate and go thick with power as the gravitational and hyperstring forces they had harnessed to "tether" them to the bracing mass of the brown dwarf now reached back and seized on the target that Geordi and Hwiii had designated. The dwarf was the anchor of one side of a slingshot; the *Enterprise* was the other. *If we can just keep from snapping before it does,* Geordi thought desperately. The vibration got worse. The universe darkened, as if getting ready for a *really* big sneeze this time, and everything and everybody not fastened to something fell down.

On the bridge, Picard watched the other *Enterprise* fire at them point-blank. He fully expected to see what he had seen in the shuttlecraft, the bloom of fire, the walls blasting outward, fragmented, into darkness. But instead everything went thick and dim with a huge buzzing feel of power in the air, and everything shook—

—and that other ship abruptly went *away* from them, without moving. It did not so much get small, as simply become more distant—impossibly distant for something that had been moving on impulse. Yet it was not going into warp, either—the usual chromatic aberration was absent. It simply went farther and farther *away* . . . and then was gone entirely.

"Mr. Data," Picard said, looking at Riker and Troi; they looked as stunned as he felt. "Evaluation."

"The ship is gone, Captain," Data said. "It was not destroyed—but rather dislocated from our space without changing local location."

"Engineering!" Picard said. At first the unrestrained noise he heard frightened him. Then he realized it wasn't screaming, or rather, not screams of pain, but of joy: cheering, hoots and howls of applause.

"La Forge here," Geordi's voice almost sang. *"Ow! Cut it out, Hwiii, I'm still sore there!"*

"Report, Mr. La Forge," Picard said, unable to suppress the smile now.

"They're gone, Captain," Geordi said. *"Right back where they came from! And it was their own hyperstring residue that let us do it, the same way that we used our own to bring us back home again. But we're not done yet."* He still sounded surprisingly urgent through the triumph. *"Hwiii is busy doing another permutation on the string structure hereabouts—meaning ours. As soon as he's ready, we—"*

"Now!" Hwiii whistled from the background. *"We need to head out of here at about warp nine, Captain, so that our inherent hyperstring association changes enough that they can't follow us back again."*

"Warp nine, *now,* if you please, Mr. Redpath," Picard said.

The ship leapt forward; Picard looked with great satisfaction at the viewscreen in front of him, flowing with stars again. "For how long, Mr. La Forge?"

"An hour or so will make it impossible for them to latch on to us again without a major retool of their own readings, Captain . . . which they won't be able to get because we will be a long *way thataway, on a course they can't predict."*

"Very good, Mr. La Forge. Mr. Redpath," Picard said to the helm officer, "amuse yourself. Make sure 'they' couldn't *possibly* predict our course."

"Yes, sir!"

Picard stood up and pulled his tunic down and smiled. "I am going down to my quarters. You and I, of course," Picard said to Troi, "will need to do debriefs for Starfleet, and for the . . . edification, if that's the word . . . of our fellow officers. I want Mr. La Forge to stop in sickbay, however, before he bothers with his—he's had a bad enough day."

"I'll take care of it, Captain," Troi said.

"Very good. Meanwhile, I would appreciate a department heads' meeting this evening, though when things have quieted down a little and we've all had some rest. Anything else?"

He looked around the bridge. People looked back at him with expressions of satisfaction, and Riker said, "Welcome home, Captain."

Picard nodded and went out.

Down in his quarters, when the door shut behind him, he simply stood there for a moment and looked around him. Off to one side, covered, the easel stood. He went to it, tossed back the cover. The wood in the Luberon looked back at him, the shafts of downstriking sunlight, the tiny scrap of fluttering light. Odd, though, how much more prominent the shadows in that landscape seemed, the dark places under the trees.

He turned away and walked over to the bookshelf. Everything in place, everything looking as it should—

though that had been deceptive, not so long ago. He reached out for the Shakespeare again, weighed it in his hand, flipped it open.

It fell open where it always did. He looked down the column. There he found Portia where she should be, mercy all in place, and the gentle rain from heaven, and further down, Nerissa's joke about the ring, the teasing wives, and the love at the end.

He closed the book and looked over at the painting again. The little scrap of light fluttered there among the trees, against the shadow. It needed the darkness to make that tiny bit of life look so bright: it would not have shown, otherwise.

Picard smiled to himself, all alone there in the dimness, and went quietly to the desk to start his debriefing.

CHAPTER 16

In his ready room, Picard sat going over his notes to see if he had missed anything. Surprising how little time it had seemed to take to tell everything that had happened to him—at least, everything that was anyone's business. All the same, he wanted to make sure he had forgotten nothing that might later prove of importance.

The door chime went; he looked up. "Come."

The door opened, and Mr. Barclay came in, looking faintly nervous. "Captain, you sent for me?"

"Yes, Mr. Barclay. Sit down."

Barclay sat, his face showing a little less nervousness now.

"I've been looking over your record," Picard said, sitting back in his chair. "Your work in the sciences and with the computer departments has been commended by your supervisors, including Commander Riker on several occasions. I note much extra, nonscheduled time put in."

Barclay twitched a little. "I can't just sit around doing nothing, Captain. It makes me crazy."

"Yes. I know it does." Picard studied the screen for a moment longer, then said, "Your next career review isn't

329

scheduled for another year or so, but I see no reason not to add a special commendation to your file." He smiled slightly. "It's my pleasure to do that effective immediately."

Barclay blinked, then grinned widely. "Thank you, Captain!"

"You're more than welcome . . . and as I say, it's my pleasure. You're dismissed."

Barclay stood, still grinning, nodded to Picard in acknowledgment, and went out.

Picard sat there for a moment, smiling, too, though the smile had an edge of sadness on it. *The promise might have been kept at a remove,* he thought, *but that's better than not keeping it at all. Symmetry.*

He went back to looking over his notes.

The department heads' meeting got under way as usual. The department heads had already read Picard's and Troi's initial debriefing memos. Geordi's was still forthcoming since Dr. Crusher had been infuriated at "the state of his nervous system" when she had finally gotten him into sickbay and had forbidden him any further work or duty of any kind for at least three days. She had permitted him to attend the department heads' meeting, "but more out of his need for closure than anything else," she had said angrily to all of them once they were around the table, "so don't push him!"

As it turned out, Geordi was amused but unconcerned by the concern. He wanted to talk about what he and Hwiii had done: "There are a lot of other possibilities inherent in the inclusion apparatus, and the changes we rang on its basic equations. But the most important one—at least, the one Starfleet is going to consider most important—is the 'subversive' use of the device to toss back ships originating in another space."

"The technique of sourcing the hyperstring structure in a

large mass, with another smaller mass as the control, is the key," Hwiii said from beside Geordi. *"Any* large mass can be used for this technique—stars, planets, any large astronomical body. If we were concerned about an invasion fleet from this universe—we need not be. Any planet can now mount its own defenses against vessels originating from another universe: you simply supply the power necessary for their own, attenuated connection with their own universe to 'snap them back.'"

"The Imperials made a tactical mistake," Geordi said, "by not carrying their theoretical research through to its logical conclusion. If they had, this development would have become obvious to them—and maybe they would never have bothered with this at all or would have gone down some other theoretical avenue, one less likely to be turned against them. In any case, now we know about them; we know their state-of-the-art equipment, too. And any starship or planet can be equipped to throw them back where they come from as quickly as they emerge, should they try it again."

"Subspace radio distances being what they are," Picard said, "it will be a little while before we hear back from Starfleet about this episode. I am minded to keep us in this general area of space for a little while, until we hear from them and know that defenses are being prepared—just in case. It would be a shame to have come so successfully out of this encounter only to fail in our trust now, through carelessness."

Around the table, people nodded. "I have a feeling, though," Dr. Crusher said, "that Starfleet will not be releasing information about this incident for general consumption. Psychologically . . . it's a bit of a time bomb."

"You're right," Picard said. "And I think for the moment that we had better instruct our own crewpeople to restrain themselves as regards this incident when it comes to communications home and so forth, since this information is more than likely to be classified under need-to-know strictures. Among other things, I suspect Starfleet would not be wild about the Romulans getting their hands on the technique."

"Indeed," Data said, "since it can logically be adapted, though with fairly extensive modifications, to go looking for other alternative universes, as posited in other hyperstring work which Commander Hwiii has done. Imagine, for example, a universe in which neither the Federation nor the Klingon empires exist, and the Romulans have become dominant. Think what the Romulans in our own universe might bring home from a visit to such a place."

They thought about that, and concerned glances were exchanged around the table. "Not our problem at the moment," Picard said, "fortunately. We'll leave that to Starfleet. Full reports from all your departments will need to go in to them tomorrow. I'll expect them by eighteen hundred hours. Is there anything else?"

"One thing," Dr. Crusher said. "The stress levels around here the past couple of days have been unusually high. Intervention is required."

Hwiii turned an interested eye on her. "In what form?" Picard said.

She pushed a padd over to him. "This should be posted on all the private terminals."

He looked at the screen. It said:

CMDR. W. RIKER AND LT. WORF
INVITE YOU TO A NIGHT AT THE OPERA

COME AS YOU ARE

TWENTY HUNDRED HOURS
BLACK TIE OPTIONAL

MAIN HOLODECK TWO

Picard pushed it back toward her. "Medicine takes strange forms sometimes," he said. "Make it so."

When one stepped in the door of the holodeck, the noise of shouting, laughter, and the orchestra tuning up was considerable. A great gilded hallway hung with glittering chandeliers stretched off in either direction, with red velvet–backed doors set in the far wall, the entrances to the boxes. Picard walked down to box twelve; a liveried footman in a powdered wig, standing outside it, bowed to him and opened the door.

The dimness inside the box made it hard to tell clearly what was going on, but the bigger chandeliers of the house beyond the boxes were dimming. Picard made his way carefully among the occupied seats. The audience, borrowed from some other time and place, were having scattered fistfights already, and the performance hadn't even begun.

Picard sat down on a velvet-cushioned Louis Quinze chair and looked around. Off to his left, Worf and Riker were sitting.

"I could not get the tie done," Worf said, frowning, to Riker. "This business of ceremonial ligature is very strange."

"Here, let me help," Riker said, and sat there for a few moments reworking it. "What have you got here, the Gordian knot? It's going to take phasers to get this thing loose."

"I could not stop tying it. It just seemed to want to keep on going."

The noise from down in the orchestra was increasing, both the musicians' and the crowd's. "Is this a private riot," Picard said over his shoulder, "or can anyone join in?"

"Paris Opera," Worf said to him as the overture began, "June 1896. Apparently there was another resurgence of anti-Masonic feeling."

"Oh, dear," Picard said. "Poor Mozart."

The overture finished. The opera began, with Geordi running across the stage in his uniform from the other ship, synching with the voice of the tenor singing Tamino, the hero of the opera, something along the lines of "It's after me, it's after me!" He was promptly pursued across the stage by the required Monster, a creature that looked suspiciously like numerous of the staff from engineering operating a hastily cobbled together Chinese "street dragon" made of used blankets from sickbay and a painted waste container for the head. "Tamino" swooned convincingly at the sight of this apparition and fell over. The Three Ladies appeared in the form of Lieutenants Hessan, Renner, and Egli, stunned the Monster with phasers, and began "singing" charmingly about the beautiful daughter of the Queen of the Night, and how Tamino really ought to get together with her.

The boxes continued to fill up. Picard glanced around him and saw mostly bridge crew, but Lieutenant Barclay was here, too, being feted by his coworkers in the computer department, and Dr. Crusher was sitting off to one side, laughing herself weak at both the audience and the crew. Shortly Commander Hwiii came floating in, carrying a tray in his manipulators, and paused by Picard, smiling. Picard smelled caviar and chuckled.

"Commander," Hwiii said, looking down, "is that the lady you were mentioning to me? 'Asti Spumante, the Queen of the Night'?"

"Close," Riker said. "Astrafiammante. My, doesn't she look good?"

In fact, it was Troi, her hair built up into an astonishing structure diademed with replicated diamonds the size of robin's eggs, and the Queen's flowing ebony robes glittered like night itself. In the spotlights, Troi dazzled. She began to sing, or rather to appear to, and the annoyed Queen's furious and melodious complaint about her "kidnapped" daughter stretched itself out on the air like harpstrings of fire. The audience fought on.

"Ah, sweet Concord," Picard said softly.

"It's not," Hwiii said, handing Picard a champagne flute. "The grape is a gewürztraminer. A very nice *sehr trocken,* actually."

Picard took the glass and smiled. "I didn't know you drank wine."

"I do," Hwiii said genially, "when Mr. Worf hasn't stolen my straw."

"I would not have thought that the counselor would have opted for the part of the Queen," Data said. "She is, after all, more or less the villainess of the piece."

"Better watch out, Commander," Geordi, up briefly from the "stage" for a snort of champagne, said to Riker. "She may be getting a taste for that kind of thing." He grinned. "You should have seen her over there. *Grr!"* The sound was approving. Riker gave him an amused sidelong look and went on watching Troi.

The madness continued for a long while, people dodging in and out of the performance, by plan and improvisationally, but staying true to the score if not to the costuming or characterization. And the voices rang out sweetly over everything, reinforcing the triumph of structure and love over chaos and hate. A noble theme, Picard thought, and one he was glad to hear more of, after the past day or so. There had been times, in that dark place, when he had had his doubts.

The farrago went on very late. Picard actually didn't realize how tired he was until he abruptly found himself looking at Riker and Worf down on that stage, both still in black tie and in the middle of a glittering, chorusing nineteenth-century company, "singing" frantically—

something about "their hats." *I nodded off,* he thought. *And in the middle of* Die Fledermaus. *Not a good sign.*

Looking around the almost-empty box, he saw the glitter of eyes resting on him from a distance through the dimness. Slightly unnerved, he got up and went out of the back of the box, out into the bright hallway, and toward the holodeck door. It opened for him, and Picard went through and just stood there a moment in plain corridor light, dimmed, but exactly as it should be.

"I was wondering when you were going to call it a night," Beverly's voice said from behind him.

He nodded, crooked his arm to her. It seemed only right, she standing there as she was in astonishing nineteenth-century splendor, jewels at her throat, all in a rustle of blue silk. They walked down the hall toward the turbolift.

"I was thinking of that other Worf," he said; he had been for a good while before he dropped off. "All alone on that ship . . . probably the only decent one there. Or what we would call decent. Though—I don't know—others seemed to have their moments, too."

" 'The gods,' " Beverly said, " 'have two jars: from one they take good, from the other evil, and so make men: some have more of one than of the other: of such are human kind.' "

"I didn't know you'd read that translation," Picard said.

Beverly nodded. They went on in silence for a little way, down to the 'lift doors. It stopped for them.

"But I think of him," Picard said as the doors shut. "Deck twelve. I think of him there and wonder. Will what happened really make a difference to him? Can it? We were there such a short time. Hard enough to make a difference even in this universe, even over many years." He shook his head. "Can a word or two spoken *really* change the world?"

The 'lift stopped. "I don't know," Beverly said, looking

affectionately at him. *"Engage* seems to do a pretty good job."

She kissed him on the cheek, raised her eyebrows at him, and went out.

Jean-Luc Picard looked after her, and the turbolift doors shut on his smile.